BEASTLY KINGDOM

Also by L. Penelope

Earthsinger Chronicles

Song of Blood & Stone

Breath of Dust & Dawn

Whispers of Shadow & Flame

Hush of Storm & Sorrow

Cry of Metal & Bone

Echoes of Ash & Tears

Requiem of Silence

The Eternal Flame Series

Angelborn

Angelfall

Other Romance

The Cupid Guild Complete Collection

Writing As Leslye Penelope

The Monsters We Defy

BOOK TWO OF THE Blass Wars

BEASTLY KINGDOM

L. PENELOPE

HEARTSPELL

Heartspell Media, LLC

ISBN: 978-1-944744-28-1 (eBook)

ISBN: 978-1-944744-29-8 (trade paperback 1)

ISNB: 978-1-944744-30-4 (trade paperback 2)

Cover design: James T. Egan of Bookfly Design

The Story So Far

In *Savage City*, Talia Dubroca is transported from her deathbed in our world to Aurum, a post-apocalyptic city that is an alternate world's version of San Francisco. Here, two clans of shifters reign. The Nimali, who change into animals that match the form of the daimon spirits they harness. And Fai, who also link with daimons, but keep their human forms and merely take on animal abilities. Talia is saved from an attack by the monstrous Revokers and healed of their poisonous venom by Ryin Arinson, a Fai healer and prisoner of war.

Talia is mistaken for the missing princess of the Nimali, Celena. Prince Shad, Celena's stepbrother, advises her to continue the ruse, as outsiders do not survive among the Nimali. Talia is opposed to the plan until she meets King Lyall, who believes she is his daughter and has lost her memory. Faced with the loving father she's never had and the adoration of the people, she agrees to the charade until Shad can find a way to send her home.

Lyall assigns Ryin to shadow Talia in case she requires healing. She is horrified to discover that the Fai prisoners are essentially slaves and vows to use her position as princess to improve things. However, she struggles with the unfamiliar rules of Nimali society and is convinced that Lady Dominga, the princess's best friend, is suspicious of her.

Forced together, Ryin and Talia fall for one another. They learn that Revokers are being experimented on and their venom synthesized into a poison, which Lyall plans to use to eradicate the Fai.

Ryin discovers the keys to Fai freedom, their stolen souls, are being kept in the vault that Talia has access to. Together, they free the Fai drudges who face the Nimali army in order to escape. Von, a Fai rebel, captures Talia, wanting to use the "princess" as leverage to aid their retreat, but Dominga reveals the truth: that Talia is just a pretender.

When Shad defies Lyall, the king shifts into his dragon form and burns the man badly. Then the Revokers escape from the lab and attack. Nimali and Fai fight together to defeat them, and Talia undergoes the ceremony to gain a dragon daimon before shifting for the first time. Ryin is apparently killed, but revived by his phoenix daimon.

King Lyall dies in the battle after rushing to protect Talia because she reminds him of his daughter. Before leaving, Ryin heals Prince Shad's injuries, trusting that he will be a more just king and deal more fairly with the Fai. Ryin and Talia head off for the Fai lands, unsure of her reception as a dragon shifter.

ONE

Shad

THE FIRST TIME I DIED, it was at the hands of my stepfather. I'd learned early to never underestimate him—it was probably around the same time I witnessed him kill my father in front of half of the Nimali in the city. Still, when he killed *me*, it was arguably my fault. I had not expected the suddenness of his shift, and my response was fatally sluggish. One moment, he was human, and the next he was the red dragon, and even as my daimon came to the forefront, changing my body into a matching form that could withstand his fire, I was consumed.

I don't remember pain. Merely the sense of hovering in a liminal space between life and death, each breath an eternity. And then the delicate balance teetered, toppling me over the edge into oblivion. I awoke warm and calm, nestled in a serene space alongside the comforting presence of my daimon. Death was unexpected. I had not been ready. But at the same time, part of me had been relieved.

I was finally free.

Free of the duty I'd never wanted. The expectations. The pain. Even free of my dragon, the daimon I hadn't hoped or asked for. I thought that back in the Origin, in the place where all life began, I would find peace.

But it was not to be.

I'm reminded of my death as strong fingers wrap around my neck from behind. I hadn't seen them coming, but I should have been more vigilant—there are many hiding places here, plenty of chunks of upturned concrete on what used to be a basketball court in the center of the city of Aurum. A flash of glowing blue eyes is all I get before my airway is constricted. When I woke up weeks ago, alive after all, I vowed never to be caught off-guard again, but as it turns out, that was a lie. I can't even depend on myself.

Beside me, Harshal lets out an enraged roar, but the hand on my neck tightens and a low voice warns, "No shifting, or I crush his neck."

A woman's voice. The throaty purr would be enticing under other circumstances.

"I told you this was a bad idea," Harsh says through gritted teeth.

"Yes, this is the perfect time to say I told you so," I eke out.

The woman squeezes tighter, her grip punishing enough, aided by daimon strength, that if I don't do something about it, I'll pass out soon. I've been practicing shifting faster ever since that day I died and came back. And I could. Before this Fai woman's grasp could crush my airways, the blue dragon could emerge. But it would destroy Harsh as well as her under its massive weight—just standing this close to me while I shift is deadly—and I don't want to start off the first peace talks between the Nimali and the Fai by killing one of them. That would definitely set a bad precedent. Of course, it's clear this Fai, at least, doesn't feel the same about killing me.

"What are you doing here, beast?" she asks, warm breath puffing against my cheek.

"Xipporah?" a voice calls from not far away. I can't turn to see, but that must be my attacker's name because she swings her head so fast, her thick locs whip me in the face.

"Xi, what are you doing?" a man asks urgently, closer. His voice is familiar.

"The question is what are *they* doing skulking around here?"

"Let him go." Seconds tick by slowly while she decides. The man tries again. "You heard what Citlali said at the meeting. Let. Him. Go."

Finally, she does, and I can breathe deeply again. I step back to where Harsh stands seething and get my first good look at the two Fai before me. The woman, Xipporah, is tall and brown-skinned and incongruously lovely for someone so bloodthirsty. Round, doe eyes, set wide in a heart-shaped face that should be delicate, but she's sturdy and well-muscled. A soldier. The locs that hit me fall nearly to her waist and are tied back in a queue. Her daimon is at the forefront, making her eyes glow blue with power. That plus the still lit torch on the ground—the one Harsh dropped when I was attacked—reveal her expression, still twisted into a scowl. But the man next to her looks apologetic. Him, I know.

"Thank you, Ryin," I say with a small bow. "I suppose now I owe you twice."

He bows in return. "Your Majesty."

Xipporah does a double take and narrows her eyes at me. "You're the king?"

I rub my bruised neck. "In the flesh."

"And why does he owe you?" she asks Ryin.

"Well, I certainly didn't save his life a few weeks ago to have you kill him now," he replies evenly.

"Why would you save one of them?" she sneers. "Don't they all deserve to die for what they've done to us?"

Harsh's hand curls into a fist, but I reach out to halt any action or reaction he wants to take. My friend's general stoicism masks a temper I don't want unleashed here tonight.

Ryin raises an eyebrow in response to her question. "All of them?"

Xipporah rolls her eyes and crosses her arms. She finally recalls her daimon so the blue glow recedes from her face. Her eyes are dark brown and look at me accusingly.

Her skepticism is cutting, but not unwarranted. If I were in her position, how would I feel? The plight of the Fai was never my primary concern while I served as prince under King Lyall. Survival was always top of mind. And then trying to figure out a way to wrest control away from him, to stop the destructive slide his policies and personality were causing for my people.

I take a half step forward. "I'm willing to issue a formal apology for the actions of my predecessor," I say. "But I know that's not enough."

Ryin speaks up. "The new king of the Nimali honors his covenant. That is why I saved his life. Plus, Talia trusts him, which is enough for me. We have seen the alternative. King Shad has agreed to the peace meeting, which is more than the old king ever would. The only way that our two clans can cease this endless conflict is if we have people of honor to deal with." His voice is even and reasonable, but Xipporah is obviously not mollified.

"The peace meeting is *tomorrow*. What cause does he have to be here the night before if not to plant traps or some kind of sabotage?"

"What are *you* doing here the night before...Xipporah, was it?" I ask.

The look she shoots me is fearsome, and had I not been through some of the hardships I have, it would give me more than a ripple of unease. I wonder what type of daimon she hosts. A ferocious beast, no doubt.

"We are simply here assessing the security," Harsh says. "So we know what to expect for tomorrow." His implacable mask is firmly back in place.

"As are we," Ryin says. "And I apologize for my cousin's

actions. Peace is important to many Fai." Xipporah looks away.

"Not all of them, I see." I try to catch her eye, but she's stubbornly not facing me. "My advisors told me not to come to the meeting tomorrow. They are very opposed to it."

She turns to me now, surprised.

"Trust is lacking on both sides, is it not?" I continue. "But if we want peace, then we must at least be open to the *idea* of trusting one another."

Her shoulders relax slightly, but her posture is still stiff.

"How about this?" I offer. "We both do our security checks together. That way we can keep an eye on each other."

Her expression hasn't shifted, but she shrugs. "We're leaving a guard here overnight to make sure no sabotage is done."

"We had much the same thought." I turn to Harsh, who sniffs, not liking where any of this is going. He's probably still upset this woman got the drop on us, creeping up so stealthily.

Xipporah's nostrils flare, and she finally relaxes her stance. "You are truly interested in peace?" she asks.

I place my hand on my heart. "I am. Nothing but mutual destruction will come of a continued war between our people."

Her cousin nudges her. Xipporah looks at him with annoyance, those delicate features still appealing even while scowling. She huffs out a breath. "Then I apologize for attacking you."

"I appreciate that," I reply, with as much graciousness as I can muster. "I take it your bloodlust has been satisfied?"

"It won't be satisfied until my people are safe from you all permanently. No matter what that takes." Then she turns on her heel and stalks off.

"Things are tense here," Ryin says. "Not everyone is in favor of these talks."

"I understand. I've been harangued by my own advisors

for even thinking of coming. But the invitation from your Water Priestess couldn't be ignored."

The letter, folded and placed in an envelope—all real paper—with my name written across it neatly, had fluttered down from the sky at the edge of the Nimali section of the city, right onto the head of one of the soldiers patrolling there. It caused quite a stir, as well as a security alert, but after several experts in poisons and explosives had deemed it safe, the invitation was delivered to me. The note was not long.

KING SHADRACH,

The death of the old king will not be mourned by a single Fai. Nor is your rise to be celebrated. However, I have it from a trusted source that you represent a change in agenda and manner from your predecessor. One that may bode well for our two clans.

If that is true, and you are willing to negotiate with us and discuss an end to the hostilities which have raged for so long, then I suggest a meeting. A summit in neutral territory in the Independent Zone on the first day of the Wood Month, where I may present a unique proposal for peace. Send your answer by eagle to the location rendered on the map below.

With sincerity,
Citlali Lolasdaughter,
Priestess of Water and First Crown of the Fai Court

TO MY KNOWLEDGE, it's the first time one of the four leaders of the Fai has ever contacted a Nimali ruler. I was intrigued and curious and hopeful. It was obvious that the priestess had done her homework on me…enough to know that my most trusted soldier, Harsh, is an eagle shifter. After the deliberations and the cajoling by my king's Council—all still holdovers from the previous regime—I had Harsh fly out to this crumbling park, a location about halfway between Nimali and Fai territory, a piece of the original letter in his beak with my response scrawled on the back.

That was a week ago. Now, Ryin looks across the broken tableau spread around us, lit by moonlight and our guttering torch still on the ground.

"Our Water Priestess has been very secretive about exactly what she hopes to accomplish at the meeting tomorrow," he says. "She has some plan for peace that she will unveil to all of us. But not all Fai are advocates of this summit. Many fought her on it. The Crowns had to open the idea up to a forum to gain consensus from our people before even approaching you. Citlali convinced a majority—barely—to trust her. Much depends on what happens tomorrow."

I'm grateful he took the time to explain the situation. "It is much the same on my side as well." I waver on whether to admit the next part, but this man saved my life when he didn't have to, and he did it so that his people could deal with a just king. He deserves to know.

"My rule is being contested."

He raises a brow.

"I did not beat Lyall in combat. Many view it as the other way around, that he bested me when he…" I cannot bring myself to say when he killed me. Ryin was there; he knows.

"But you are the only dragon, and none alive among the Nimali can defeat you," he says.

"That is true. But there are many ways to topple a king. Even one who is a dragon."

His brow furrows, but he has nothing to add. These are Nimali problems, not really any of his concern. Harsh is silent beside me, no doubt disapproving of me sharing so much. But I'm willing to take the first step in proving I am trustworthy. Besides, if I give them some information, perhaps they won't go digging to find the truth of the rest of the struggles I'm facing back home. If they knew everything, they might be less likely to meet at all.

Ryin begins to turn away but pauses. "Why did you come *yourself*? Tonight?"

The breeze picks up, and the rusted-out remains of a chain still attached to a swing set across the park creaks. "I don't like surprises," I answer. "I wanted to have an idea of what to expect tomorrow. To see it with my own eyes."

He nods as if that makes sense, though I can tell he doesn't understand. But I've shared enough for one night. He doesn't need to know that the people I trust can be counted on one hand—and still have fingers left.

"How is Talia?" I ask as he turns again.

"She is..." He chooses his words carefully. "...adjusting. But she is well. Her faith in you has swayed some here. And I have staked my reputation to convince others, based on her trust. Do not let that go to waste, Your Majesty."

I touch my fist to my heart and give a brief bow to show him I understand the magnitude of what he's saying. He was a prisoner of the Nimali for years, and his willingness to stand for me in any way is inspiring. It shines a tiny flame of hope into the darkness.

Ryin fades back into the shadows clinging to the desic-cated park. This place is just a shell of whatever it once was, just like everything else in this city. Soon enough, he has disap-peared into a field of waist-high grass.

"Should I follow him?" Harsh asks, voice pitched low. "Watch for mischief?"

There are plenty of hiding places perfect for an ambush, as we so recently found out. And many on their side who would still like to take out the enemy king. But I think we're done here for now.

"No. Let's head back. Assign someone to guard overnight if you think it's best, but I don't believe there's anything more for us to do here now."

He shifts into his eagle immediately and takes flight as if eager to be away from these bleak surroundings. I stay a few moments longer, watching the shadows, feeling unseen eyes upon me. It's much like being in the Citadel: always watched, never trusted. The whispers of how I'm unfit to be king grow louder with each passing day, and I know there are those plotting against me, the way I once plotted to overthrow Lyall. Except instead of ousting a tyrant and ushering in a new age for the Nimali, they would rather see the brutality and inequality of the previous regime continue. I stand in their way, and so does the very existence of the Fai. If I am not willing to wipe out our enemy completely as Lyall was then, it is said, I am too weak to hold the crown.

I have always believed that if peace could be achieved, a peace that included some way for both our clans to get what we want and need, as impossible as that sounds, then the people's minds would be changed. I still believe it. And tomorrow could be the first step to making it a reality.

The sense of an unseen watcher still haunts me. Is it Xipporah, still suspicious and angry, or some unnamed Fai who sees this as their opportunity for vengeance against the Nimali? I give them their opportunity for a few moments more. My dragon can eliminate just about any obstacle that comes, but sometimes I wish that my stepfather had finished the job.

I believe I am the king they need, if not the one they want, but I do not know if I have what it takes to make the changes I dream of. Peace with the Fai would be a miracle, and one that could portend brighter days for the future. If I can make it happen.

When no further attacks come, I allow the shift to take me with a flash of light and the scent of sulfur. The blue dragon takes over, transforming my body and sharpening my senses. This dragon that makes me formidable is also responsible for the worst things that have ever happened to me. Things that I'm reminded of every time I shift.

I flap my wings, making the tall grass of the nearby field fold nearly in half from the force of it. If there was anyone hiding in it, waiting to cause mischief, they're gone now. My heavy body rises into the air, where I glide, circling the old park once and not seeing anything out of place. Then, I head back east, toward home. We will see what comes in the morning, and if I can manage to survive another day as king of the Nimali.

TWO

Xipporah

MY PALM TINGLES where it touched the beast's neck, as if his very skin were radioactive. The thick column of a Nimali's throat was within my grasp. So why did I hesitate to crush it?

Of course, I hadn't realized he was the king when I sprang upon the two men who were making no effort to hide their so-called surveillance. Nimali in their human form are clumsy and crude. Who would have guessed the tall, broad-shouldered man with almond-colored skin and closely cropped black hair was the king, out so late at night as part of his own advance team?

Now, if it had been Lyall, the one responsible for so many terrors wrought against my people, the one who my sister still has nightmares about each night, then I would not have delayed in sending him back to the Origin. Then again, he never would have been caught unawares.

My steps grow heavier as I pace the perimeter of what was once probably a lush and beautiful park. Now, much of it is a wild and tangled forest, overgrown and unmaintained with many places for an enemy to hide. I'm on alert, waiting for a betrayal by the Nimali regardless of what their new king said.

Is he as barbarous as his stepfather was? Ryin doesn't

believe so, and he made quite the gamble by saving his life, but I'm not so sure. He's certainly not as menacing as Lyall—tonight, he'd been woolgathering when he should have been watchful. And would a brash, tyrannical warrior have smelled of cinnamon? Such an odd detail to remember, but as I held him in my grip, the scent filled my nostrils. Warm and comforting and disconcerting. It confused me. Maybe that's why I didn't choke him when I had the opportunity.

Footsteps sound behind me. With my daimon still buzzing inside, I scent my cousin. I release the spirit, losing the heightened senses, the additional strength, grace, and speed of the tiger who shares my body.

"Are you all right?" Ryin asks when he catches up.

"I'm fine." The words emerge through a jaw so tight I can barely get them through my strangled throat.

He comes to stand beside me. "You held back—I'm grateful, killing our only hope of a reasonable leader among the Nimali would have been a problem."

I breathe deeply then turn to face him. The moonlight glances off his features. His face is also precious to me, and being able to see it is a gift. He was in the Citadel longer than my sister, and the fact that they're all home now, my family and so many others, is something I thank the bliss for every day.

"I still think 'reasonable' is a stretch," I say. "There's no reason the king should have been out here himself."

"He does things differently than Lyall, thank the tors. There probably aren't many people he can trust."

"The Nimali are so depraved they all stab each other in the back. Talia really trusts him?"

He rocks back on his heels. "He saved her life. Protected her. So, yes." And Talia is precious to Ryin; that is obvious to anyone with eyes.

"Well, we'll all see tomorrow if I made a mistake in not

killing him." My lips quirk, and he snorts. "But I'd better get back home. Noomi still isn't sleeping well."

Ryin looks worried. "Her nightmares haven't slowed down?"

"I think they've gotten worse."

"If she ever needs anything…" he begins.

"I know. And thank you. I'll see you in the morning."

He raises a hand in goodbye, then his eyes flash blue as his daimon joins him. In moments, he's rising into the air, a wingless bird taking flight across the city. I call my daimon as well; running the few miles home will burn away some of this energy so it won't prowl around inside me searching for prey.

What's left of the buildings in the Independent Zone flash by as I race along the streets, dodging intersections clogged with rusted-out vehicles and avoiding the choking weeds and other plant life that have taken back as much as they could of the urban jungle.

Soon enough, the Greenlands come into focus ahead. Here, the wilderness has reclaimed the remains of the city completely, with a lot of help from the Fai. Five city blocks, razed of every structure that once stood there, separates the edge of the Independent Zone from our territory. Low grass lies where concrete and asphalt once did, and then the line of mature trees begins. No Nimali or mundane human dare tread beyond the line of demarcation.

Once I'm beneath the tree cover, the moonlight disappears, hidden by the thick foliage overhead. But soon enough, glimmers of light wink on around me, illuminating the byways of the Fai lands. Unlike the paved avenues of the city behind me, Greenlands pathways are more subtle, narrower—they wind their way around wide tree trunks and branch off in many directions only to reconnect later.

A series of twists and turns lead me to the dwelling that my grandmother built and where my parents and sister all now live. And though it's my childhood home, it still feels foreign to me. After Noomi was captured, I moved out into the barracks of the Defense Division, a place that, while not as warm or comfortable, offered the distinct benefit of having only my superior officers there to chastise me, and the promise of occasional praise when I did something well.

Our home is considered a ground-level aerie, but here, that just means it's only twelve feet off the ground, accessible by a natural staircase of branches that wraps around the thick eucalyptus tree serving as its spine. I race up the steps, allowing my daimon to fall away before entering, just in case Mother is still awake. She hates shifting in the house.

Fortunately, the main room is empty. I creep across it with practiced feet, not that there are any boards to squeak and give away my presence—it's just habit from childhood. Grandmother Emeli and her incredibly rare yeti daimon grew our house right from the tree, coaxing the wide, flat branch that forms the entire floor under my feet into existence. Our entire home lives, still a part of the tree, just manipulated using a Land daimon's power into the shape my grandmother desired, the same as with the walls and ceiling.

I climb the smooth branches of the steps in silence to the room I share with my sister, and only once I'm behind the door—a person-sized knot rendered in the wood with a thick, sound-proof mat drawn across it—do I relax.

Just as I suspected, Noomi is tossing and turning in her bed, sweat slicking her nightgown, soft moans rising from her. I swiftly change into my night clothes and climb in next to her, wrapping my arms around her and burying my nose in her hair.

I missed her so much when she was gone. The day she was taken will always be imprinted on me. She'd gone with a group of worshippers to assess the state of a temple in a formerly disputed territory in the north of the city. A small contingent of guards had accompanied them—since there had been no Nimali sighted in the area in nearly a year, the powers that be hadn't thought a larger detachment was required.

I'd been on duty in the northern Greenlands; when the alarm was raised, I raced to the location faster than I'd ever run in my life. But she and the others were already gone. And the beasts hadn't even gotten more than a few buckets full of the liquid bliss they'd been sent to steal from the temple.

That day was the beginning of an unflagging horror I was never able to escape. The guilt over not being there for my sister was corrosive and ate away everything except the single-minded focus to do whatever it took to get her back. I trained ruthlessly, rose through the ranks, spent two years on nothing else, all so I could be in a position to be on the front lines whenever the attack against the Citadel finally came.

My superiors in the Defense Division compared me to my grandfather Markus, one of the greatest Fai warriors to ever live. He led a legendary assault against the Nimali that to this day is immortalized in song. The fact that I was able to be there the day the Fai were freed from the Citadel makes me feel closer to him, like those years of sacrifice weren't in vain. But Noomi did not come home unscathed.

In my arms, she stirs. "Xi?" she says, blearily.

"I'm here. Were they bad tonight?"

She doesn't respond, just holds the arm I have wrapped around her tighter and falls back into a tormented sleep, running from dragons I can never slay.

———

"How did it go last night?" Noomi asks in the morning as she dresses, putting on a loose white gown that makes her look like the old stories of angels.

"The new king was there himself, scoping out the territory. He claimed he wasn't there to set any traps, but…" I shrug. "You know how they lie."

Noomi's eyes narrow. "You spoke to him?"

I fiddle with the buckle of the dark green armored jacket of my uniform. "I may or may not have tried to kill him. Ryin stopped me," I add hastily when I see her jaw drop from the corner of my eye.

"Talia trusts Shad, you know," she says matter-of-factly, echoing Ryin's earlier words.

"Well, Talia has her own problems. There aren't many besides you and Ryin willing to put much stock in her word. She's practically a Nimali, anyway."

"She is not!" The old fire I'm used to from her, a spark that I've only gotten mere glimpses of in the past weeks, is back in her eyes. I mostly just said it to goad her into a reaction. My sister is fiercely protective of Talia, the odd young woman who looks identical to the missing Nimali princess and also now shifts into a dragon.

Noomi crosses her arms. "My daimon trusts Talia, and so do I. She's a good person. The fact that she shifts… Well, she didn't exactly know what she was doing when she underwent the trials and joined her daimon." Noomi always wants to see the best in people, while I prefer to take a more realistic view. Talia shifts like a Nimali, even though technically she isn't one.

We're both dressed but stand in the middle of the room with nothing left to do but head downstairs. Noomi looks to the door with apprehension, knowing what we're going to find on the other side. When she gazes back at me, it's apologetic. "You know, you don't have to stay here anymore. I appreciate it, but I don't want you to have to——"

"It's fine. I'm used to it."

"It's *not* fine." She shakes her head for emphasis. "But Mother doesn't listen to anything I say, and Makani——" She flaps her hands uselessly.

I wrap an arm around her, pulling her close. "I've battled worse foes than our parents. Though I admit, if I had a choice between them and a Revoker, not sure who would come out on top."

"At least you *could* fight a Revoker," she says, wistful. Then she straightens and nudges me with her shoulder. "I love you, Xi-Xi."

"Love you, too, Nooms."

We head out of the quiet cocoon of safety that has always been our bedroom and right into the thick of it. Noomi goes down the steps first; she's not even to the main floor before our mother is there, exclaiming and wrapping her in her arms like she didn't see her yesterday. Every morning is the same performance, the theatrics and the tears, the heady fluctuation of emotions that make my sister uncomfortable but that my mother refuses to rein in.

"Oh, my precious girl. Every day I see you is better than the last. Come, let's work on getting some meat back on those bones." She continues fussing as they head into the kitchen. Me, she ignores. As usual. But being beneath her notice is actually my preference.

I usually don't stick around—it's easier for me to grab a meal at the barracks, but Noomi stops me. "You're on duty for the meeting this morning? Can you stay for breakfast?"

It's the fear in her voice that does it. She knows what she's asking is big and will open me up to scrutiny I'd rather avoid, but though she defended the Nimali king just minutes ago, the idea of me attending a gathering with them, even in the role of guard, frightens her. I can see it like paint covering her skin.

I move into the small kitchen and sit on the stool growing out of the floor. I don't miss my mother's pursed lips, but she doesn't gainsay her favorite child.

Makani bustles in, dressed in his Crown regalia—a full-length shimmering white robe with all the adornments of his station as the Air Priest: sparkling belt, amulet, epaulets. His feathered headdress is constructed to look like wings situated behind each ear, though he sets that on a side table before sitting down to eat.

Makani is the only father I have ever known—our real father was killed before Noomi was born, and Mother remarried quickly afterward. When I was eight and Noomi was six, our stepfather was chosen as the Air Priest and Fourth Crown of the Fai Court. Little about our lives changed. The position does not give power or prestige to the family of the Crown. Our leaders live among us simply, just like every other dweller of the Greenlands—very different to the way the Nimali treat their king and royal family. And while he is not as dismissive or critical of me as Mother is, he and I are not close.

He nods a greeting to me before settling at the table and availing himself of the tree nut citrus mash my mother prepared, one of Noomi's favorites that she's actually starting to dislike after eating so much since her return.

The conversation is strained and awkward. Mother is determined not to include me and Noomi is equally determined to point every question in my direction. I'm happy her spark is firing again even if it's partially because of this miserable situation.

It should have been you. Why was she taken and not you? Mother screamed at me the day Noomi was captured, and there were few days since when she hadn't spewed those words at me with venom. *You wanted to be a soldier like your grandfather—he would never have let my baby girl be taken.*

I shake off her voice in my head and answer Noomi calmly, ignoring my mother in kind. Though it's been served often, the mash is good. I'm spooning another serving onto my plate when Mother says, "I'd thought this portion would last until dinner. I'll have to figure out something else to make for this evening." The comment sinks like an anvil in the quiet room. It's never been a secret that Noomi's more delicate features and smaller figure are more in line with what Mother deems acceptable.

"Xi is a warrior!" Noomi exclaims with pride. "She needs her strength. Especially if she's going to protect the Crowns today from those beasts." Her voice breaks on the last word and my chest cracks open. Those sparks of flame that had been flickering go out completely.

For a moment, I think she's caught in her head again, stuck back in the tower with the rules and the threat of trammeling over her head every day. She says that nothing spectacular or truly violent happened to her. She wasn't beaten or assaulted, neither were just about any of the other former drudges. But some light within her has been diminished. Living under that kind of stress day after day changed something within her fundamentally. I just hope it won't be permanent.

Makani shoots an alarmed glance my way; he doesn't do well with displays of emotion, odd since he chose to marry my mother. But Noomi visibly pulls herself together and pastes on a tremulous smile.

My mother shoots me a vicious glare. I shovel mash into my mouth. When I'm done, I stand. Put my plate in the sink. Squeeze my sister's shoulder and head to my duty station.

Maybe I will move out again, after all.

THREE

Shad

I FEINT LEFT to dodge the punch aimed for my jaw and jab with my right hand, connecting with Callum's ribs. The pain of the contact shoots through my fist, but it's invigorating. I relish it. He winces, darting away beyond the reach of another blow. We circle one another, dripping with sweat, breaths heaving, but both delighted. His grin leaves little doubt as to how euphoric these sparring sessions leave him feeling. I allow a smile to split my face as well. Then we're back to it.

I move forward, protecting my left side from Callum's powerful blows and trying to connect another punch. I admit: I hold back a little with my friend. He's only been fighting in human form for a few years, whereas I grew up doing so. Cardinals see no reason to hone their bodies, instead preferring to wait until they leash a daimon and have no need to work hard in order to be formidable. If they leash a predator, that is.

But unlike the aristocrats, Umbers have no expectation that the daimon trials will connect us with a beast of prey. Some will, like me, just as some Cardinals will leash lesser animals and experience a humbling reduction in rank, but those things are not *planned* for. For a Cardinal to admit the possibility that they will reach adulthood and have to accept the lot of a lower caste is deemed bad luck. And while Umbers and Azures both hope for advancement, we prepare ourselves for lives without a change in circumstances. So we train. Shifting into a rabbit or a pigeon or an eel is of little use when someone attacks you. And though all the training in the world won't help a weak human body take on a wolf or lion, we do it anyway, taking control of our lives where we can. Strengthening ourselves as much as possible.

I met Harsh, Callum, and Zanna in the Atrament Corps —the Nimali army—and eventually introduced them to my training regimen. We spar regularly now, not because our human bodies truly need to be strong, but because they also have learned the value in working hard for something. Even though growing up as Cardinals, they've had so much given to them for so long.

This morning, only Callum is here to fight, the others being on assignment. Our session ends when he leaves an opening too large for me to ignore, failing to block his left side from my high kick. I don't use my full strength but give enough effort to take him down. He lies flat on the thick mat beneath us, wheezing. I stand over him and offer a hand to help him up.

"I almost had you, though," he says with a breathy chuckle as he takes my hand and rises.

"Eh," I respond, grabbing my towel to wipe off. "I can't say you're not improving."

"You just don't want to admit that I got close."

"Close only counts in fire strikes."

He shakes his head; when he turns to grab his own towel, I wince. Lyall used to tell me that. *Close only counts in fire strikes, my boy.* I hate to repeat anything that monster taught me, useful though some of it is.

The empty building where we hold our sparring sessions has no bliss powering it; light filters down through unrepaired holes in the roof. It's only a block from the Citadel, but not all the buildings in our territory have been reclaimed, and we gather here so as not to answer any inconvenient questions. A glance above shows the day has started overcast. The rainy season is past us, thankfully, with its near-constant deluges and flash floods, but that doesn't mean a powerful storm won't pop up at random. Something tells me today is going to be a tempestuous one, and the wind already beginning to whip up, screeching through the various holes in this building, gives credence to that.

"I need to get back to get ready for the summit," I say.

Callum nods, solemn. "Did you decide whether or not to fly in?"

Arriving in my dragon form could be seen as an aggressive move, and I'd spoken with both Harsh and Callum about the best way to make my entrance.

"I'm still uncertain. I will definitely fly across the city, but I'm thinking it may be best to shift a block or two from the meeting place and walk in as a human. They all know I'm a dragon; there's no need to rub it in their faces."

The long-ago decision by some far-flung ancestor of the Fai to keep their own body when they join with their daimon instead of transforming like we do has always mystified me. Then again, considering all the woe my dragon has brought me, maybe not changing forms would have been a blessing.

"Not flaunting your strength doesn't make you weak," Callum says evenly, raking his fingers through his blond hair. If Harsh were here, he'd say something like, "It's not flaunting to display your power." He's not wrong, but I'm not certain he's right, either.

I move over to where I'd slung my shirt to find my communicator lighting up in a peculiar flashing pattern, unlike a regular ping. I huff out a breath.

"What is it?" Callum asks. I hold up the unit, and he

swears under his breath. "I can't keep all the codes straight for the life of me. What's that one say?"

"Someone is trying to override the access to my apartment and sneak in. Perhaps they think I'm still in bed."

He snorts. "Or they know you're gone and are trying to plant listening devices again."

"Yeah. I'll do another sweep when I get back." I open the comm, shutting off the patterned pulses of light. "Ping Harsh."

In a moment, his face extrudes from the device. "Your Majesty?"

"There's a level-three situation at my quarters."

"On it, sir," he says before disconnecting.

"There won't be anyone there for him to find by the time he gets there," Callum says.

"True, but you never know when they'll get sloppy."

We wait at the exterior door to ensure no one is passing outside on the street. I know there are those watching my every move, but I don't have time this morning for questions about why the king is spending time in an abandoned building.

The path to the Citadel is empty, but once we enter the lobby, the normal contingent of guards is on duty. Callum melts away, off to the main elevator bank, while I go to the royal elevators, which head all the way to the top floors. I reach the forty-second floor, swathed in darkness with only small points of light along the ground to see by. This is one of the energy conservation mechanisms we've had to adopt, though as I step out of the elevator, the light doesn't increase the way it does on other levels. The other apartment on this floor has been empty for years, and I don't mind the darkness.

I can barely make out Harsh standing in front of my door, arms crossed. "Didn't find any evidence of tampering, but in this light my daimon isn't helpful."

"I didn't think you would," I say.

"They must have left just before I got here. We could leave recording devices—"

I cut him off. "Don't want to waste the bliss. Besides, there are too many ways around it."

He looks around, frustration evident. "If you'd let me bring in one of the bloodhound shifters…"

I just shake my head. My reasons for not involving anyone else haven't changed. Not even now that I'm king.

"They'll keep coming, you know," he says. "And today will not help matters."

I clasp his shoulder. "I'm hoping it will. Maybe not today, but if peace is the eventual outcome, then that will help everyone."

He sighs and heads back toward the elevators, having other things to attend to. "See you down there at 800."

"Copy that."

I listen to the silence left in his wake. Harsh's eagle eyes work best at a distance, and Callum could sniff out an intruder, but over the past weeks, those trying to access my apartment or office or throne room have masked their natural scents with purifiers or heavy perfumes. With no sound or evidence of anyone in the hallway, I press my hand against the indentation in the wall, and the door slides open.

The shadowy figure is upon me before I know it, hidden in the darkness of my apartment. Leashing my daimon is not exactly possibly within the tight confines of the interior of this building, not unless I want to destroy several floors.

I can't believe this is the second time in less than a full day when a woman has caught me unawares. However, at least this one doesn't want to kill me. Not at the moment, at any rate. And she actually has permission to be here.

I activate the lights as she removes the hood of her black cloak, then doffs it completely to reveal the blood-red gown underneath. I cross to a shelf that holds several dampeners I've collected over the past months and activate it. Dominga is an expert at moving about undetected, a skill I could stand some improvement on, but even with regular checks for bugs in my home, the tower has many ears and eyes.

"Is all of this drama really necessary?" I ask once I can speak freely.

"Thank you, Dominga. You're holding up your end of the bargain, Dominga," she says mockingly. "I'm so grateful you alerted me that someone was trying to break into my rooms. I don't deserve you, Dominga."

"Was there really someone trying to break in here, or were you just flexing some muscle?"

Her eyes narrow. She is small and fine-boned, with bird-like features; if she were Fai, I wouldn't be surprised if she harbored some sort of carrion-eater within. Her delicate beauty masks a skeleton of iron.

"My information is always impeccable," she snaps. "And as I was already in here—I heard them trying to gain entry. Besides, I do not need to flex or preen. I am not the one shirking the terms of our deal."

"What are you talking about?"

"The check-ins," she replies impatiently.

"There is nothing to check in about. Zanna has been gone for just over a week. She checked in daily until the communicator went out of range, which you already know. When she comes back into range and makes a report, I will alert you immediately."

"Even no update is an update. I want to be informed when you know something and when you know nothing."

I throw up my hands and fall back wearily onto the sofa. "This is ridiculous."

Dominga walks around my suite, observing the sparse furnishings and tapping her finger on her lips. "Why haven't you moved downstairs yet?"

"Why should I? These rooms are fine for me." I'm already ready for this little visit to be over.

"These are not the king's rooms. And people know it. How do you expect them to take you seriously if you flout every standard? It's little wonder they're planning a coup."

I sink back into the cushions of the couch reclaimed from my childhood home. It's brown and patched over with synthetic fabric—not at all fashionable for the Nimali—but it's mine and it's comfortable. Dominga eyes it with obvious distaste, her lip actually curling.

"King Lyall's apartments reek of evil," I say.

She snorts. "Then exorcise them. Have them cleaned, painted, redecorated. But if you want them to treat you like a king, you must act like one. Like what they expect a king to be."

"I want to innovate."

She rolls her eyes, letting out a disgusted sigh. "Why a dragon daimon chose you is the enigma of the millennium. Remember, our bargain only exists if you *remain* king. If one of your enemies defeats you, then you are of no use to me *or* to Celena when she returns. And to remain king, you must bar the doors from the angry villagers. Or better yet, make the villagers happy." She spreads her arms like this should be self-evident.

I rub my forehead. "You and I only have a deal because I'm not willing to do things the way Lyall did. I know that Princess Celena's return and our marriage would make my rule more legitimate, and even if it didn't, if she's out there and can be found, then we should do so. She doesn't deserve to be abandoned in the wilderness…if she's still alive."

"She's still alive. She had a plan." Dominga has never wavered on this, though she has steadfastly refused to tell me what this plan was. "Your soldier will find her—if she's as good as you claim she is."

"Zanna is the best tracker in Aurum. She would have found the princess earlier if you'd told us what you knew before."

Dominga clenches her teeth. Her ferocity reminds me a little of the woman last night, Xipporah. The one who tried to kill me. And if Dominga ever decides she wants me dead, she'd be every bit as capable as the Fai warrior woman. The information she's shared with me so far about those plotting against me—including her own father, Sir Barrett—has been incredibly useful. She's entrenched in the aristocracy in a way I never could be and has access to many of the hidden eyes and ears keeping track of me.

For her father, she plays the dutiful daughter. But, as she told me, if Sir Barrett manages to oust me and take power for himself, and Celena returns, the man would have her killed in a heartbeat rather than relinquish rule. It was when I realized Dominga was more loyal to her best friend than her own kin that I knew she was someone I could trust—at least as long as our goals are aligned. I have a hard time understanding how Celena could inspire that kind of fidelity, but then the two of us were never close.

We were betrothed almost as soon as King Lyall adopted me. He knew it was the only way to keep an Umber turned Cardinal, even one with a dragon daimon, on the throne. And of course, if the princess had ever leashed a dragon, my throat would probably have been cut in my sleep.

Celena and I never talked of marrying. We didn't talk much at all, so I wasn't clear if it was something she wanted. But she was the dutiful daughter, raised to rule, expecting her daimon trials would result in an appropriate animal spirit. It was a confidence borne without reason, and Celena's failed attempt—and loss of her shadow soul—flew in the face of Lyall's faith. So Celena had ventured outside the wall, searching for an untouched pocket of bliss in which to try again to leash a dragon. A wild and foolish decision and one that I hope hasn't gotten her killed.

I wipe a hand down my face. "I'm due at the meeting site

soon. I promise to give you weekly updates, even when the update is 'no news.' Will that suffice?"

She purses her lips, then gives a curt nod. In moments, she's donned her black cloak again. "Do you really think that anything will come from this summit with the Fai savages?"

My brows lift. An actual question, not a command or a demand. "I think they are motivated. I think they know we can destroy them and every tree in the Greenlands with our new weapon."

"But the chances of them giving up access to their precious bliss are still close to zero. And if they know we have that kind of leverage over them, what could they possibly hold over us, other than bliss, to make any sort of lasting truce possible?"

It's a good question. One than me, Harsh, and Callum have discussed since the invitation arrived. "I will find out shortly, and then we'll all know."

She glowers, shooting daggers from her eyes at me. "Beware of where you step, King Shadrach. It's easier to walk around a pile of excrement than scrape it off your boots."

And with that pithy reminder, she disappears into the darkness on the other side of the door.

FOUR

Shad

IF I'D HOPED LEAVING for the meeting would be a painless affair, as soon as I step onto the long, grassy plaza in front of the Citadel, those hopes are dashed. The entire Council waits for me, each determined to have their say, along with a cadre of advisors who don't want to miss any drama.

As I approach, Harsh's expression is baked into his usual stone mask, while Callum wears his traditional, disarming smile. It's as much a mask as Harsh's, and I once made the mistake of underestimating him, the privileged son of a council member that he is, but only once.

Lined up to face me are Callum's father, Sir Denby, who also uses charm to keep opponents off-guard. Next to him, Lady Linh is an icicle, her long, straight black hair glimmering in the morning light like a sheet of dark glass. Dame Ayisha and Lord Godrik, the oldest council members, have their white heads together as they whisper, gazes tracking me like prey. Lord Edwin stands apart, pale skin bruised under dark eyes, his clothing somewhat disheveled as if he'd hastily thrown them on this morning. A late night, I suspect. And Lady Raina—the youngest, only a decade my senior— appears amused. The thick, dark coils of her hair are a halo of froth around her head today, unbound by the heavy braids she often puts them in. They all stand like sentinels awaiting me.

The last member of the Council, Sir Barrett, is accompanied by his daughter, Lady Dominga. Both are straight-backed, regal, and wear matching expressions of disdain. Dominga's sentiment from this morning reverberates in my head. Why *did* the dragon daimon choose me and upend my life? Even when I returned to the Origin for those brief eternities when Lyall's fire killed me, my daimon revealed nothing of itself to me. As mysterious as ever.

Though I don't want to be like Lyall in any way, I know that this display of opposition in front of me is not anything he ever dealt with. Is Dominga right? *If you want them to treat you like a king, you must act like one. Like what they expect a king to be.* If I don't want to deal with a petulant tantrum every time I make a decision they don't agree with, then I should probably listen to her. I square my shoulders and stride forward, taking a page from Lyall's playbook.

"What is the meaning of this?" I roar. Overhead, birds take flight. Satisfaction wells within at the faces before me, gone ashen and wan. I do not relish brutality, and I refuse to believe it's the only way to rule, but for the moment, for these people, it is effective.

Sir Barrett is the one who shakes off his alarm the fastest and steps up. "Your Majesty. We must object to you heading to a meeting with our great enemy with so little retinue. The Council is here to accompany you, since you have insisted on this course of action." His bald pate glints in the early light.

The plan was for just Harsh and Callum to accompany me, along with the king's guard—with Zanna out on her mission, the number of people I trust in this city has shrunk considerably.

But now I take them all in, the schemers and plotters. Men and women jockeying for position, for more power and influence. I choose to smile, trying Callum's method of attack. "To be presented with the entire Council would certainly overwhelm the Fai. But since we are to be met by four of them, let us have four as well. Dame Ayisha, Sir Denby, and Lady Raina, you shall accompany me."

I had considered inviting them earlier, so the choices are easily made. Sir Barrett and Lady Linh are co-conspirators, according to both my sources and Dominga's information. There is no need to have them looking over my shoulder. Besides, it will annoy them the most to be left out.

Sir Denby is the only one I consider an ally, and not just because he is the father of one of my closest friends. I have witnessed true kindness from him, a genuine desire to oppose Lyall's edicts. As far as I can tell, Dame Ayisha is neutral. She was a fearsome warrior in her day and wields power like a blunt instrument, but, again, without cruelty. I hope to win her to my side.

Lord Godrik and Lord Edwin are easily molded and will doubtless throw in with whoever has the best chance of winning. Lady Raina is the true outlier. Even Dominga cannot get a read on her motivations or desires. She is deeply intelligent, extremely cunning, and plays everything very close to her chest. That is why I wish to keep her near: to see if I can gain her loyalty, either that or monitor her treachery.

As I could have predicted, those I did not name are irate at being left behind. They raise their voices, talking over one another, pleading their case. It is a show of my weakness that they dare to do so. They never would have with Lyall.

I could behave as he did and cow them with threats—and then back them up with brutal action—but I am determined to be a different kind of king. Dominga's disgust is clear. She crosses her arms and barely holds herself back from rolling her eyes.

Instead of raising my voice again, I move a few steps away and begin my shift, trusting that everyone has enough sense of self-preservation to get out of my way. It seems like a more effective method of indicating I am done talking about this issue. I'll trust them to figure out how they'll get to the meeting place.

The city rushes by, a sight I don't even pay attention to anymore. When I first leashed my daimon and took to the sky, I found it all fascinating, this once-vibrant metropolis left a desiccated husk by the Sorrows. I used to wonder what it had been like in its heyday, what these buildings were used for, what composed the people's lives.

The Sorrows occurred long before I was born, but much of my childhood was spent investigating the unclaimed areas close to Nimali territory. It was me, Sylph, and Lynara, "the trio," as my father used to call us. We grew up in the same commune—Sylph, the mischievous one, Lynara, the smart one, and me, the dreamer. Pretending to be Fai, we'd scavenge "treasures" from crumbling buildings and wonder about life outside of Aurum. We once made a pact to leave together once we all went through the trials. Back then, we thought Revokers were just bedtime stories, not monsters to fear, and that anything would be better than living under the brutal thumb of the king and the Cardinals.

Now I'm the only one left and my actions are taken in their memory, so their fates don't befall anyone else.

I cross the city faster than I even want to, headed southwest, with Harsh's eagle at my side along with the other flying members of the king's guard. Dame Ayisha's crow and Lady Raina's hawk aren't far behind. Approaching the tangled mass of greenery surrounded by crumbling brick and concrete structures, I make a split-second decision. Next to the flattened area where the meeting will take place is a white building, mostly caved in but with the original facade of the entry still intact.

I noticed it yesterday, a former school or church with a domed tower ornately decorated in scrollwork and sculptures.

In the daylight, I can now see the dome itself was once tiled, but only a few remain clinging to the surface—brown and green and blue. Instead of landing several streets away to hide my shift, I settle my bulk onto the portion of the roof next to the dome.

Gargoyles rest on each of its four sides, staring sightlessly across the city. I could imagine myself as one of them, up here, slowly turning the stone. Across the crumbling street, the Fai have gathered. They have set up a large stone table in the center of the basketball court. A line of soldiers stands behind it dressed in green, their uniforms similar but distressingly unique and, I suspect, customized to the individual. All hold the glowing blue eyes of their daimons. I spot Xipporah immediately. She stands at the end, her thick hair loose and falling nearly to her waist.

Ryin is there, too. Part of me is surprised they use their healers for soldiers, but I know almost nothing of the ways of the Fai. On the whole, we are even in numbers. Bringing the entire Council would have been a mistake, a show of force that would belie the goodwill I hope we can establish here today.

They all notice me sitting here watching them. I hope that it's a show of strength but not aggression, a happy medium that we can build on. It takes those traveling by land several more minutes to arrive. In that time, rain begins to fall. It glides off my scales unfelt. The hide of the dragon allows me little sensation—a benefit during battle, but otherwise, it's like being wrapped in a shell, separated from the outside world.

I jump from the roof when I hear the paws of lion, wolf, jaguar, and coyote racing toward us—the king's guard—and shift before I've reached the ground. Once they arrive, they follow my lead, taking their human forms. Before Callum shifts from his lion, a little scorpion crawls from his back. In a flash of blue light and pop of sulfur, the scorpion becomes Sir

Denby. The other councilors shift as well and we approach the Fai, presenting a united front.

The rain is soft, but the sky is growing angrier. None of my people flinch or bat an eye at the weather, determined to tough it out if the Fai are. It's only water, after all.

Instead of chairs, boulders have been placed at intervals around the table, which is a perfect circle. I stand behind a boulder and the councilors fan out around me, but the Fai half of the table is empty.

Then the tangled foliage behind the line of soldiers is disturbed and an old woman steps through. Her robe is a pale blue, embellished with beads of various sizes. She is laden with sparkling necklaces, bracelets, rings, several belts, and large earrings of complex design. These are not the pre-Sorrows jewels that fill our vault, scavenged and reclaimed decades ago by Nimali fortune seekers. I haven't seen their like before. I don't recognize the stone or the metal; they are shot through with color and wink in the light.

The woman herself has weathered brown skin with long gray-white hair, some of it braided and adorned with beads and more trinkets. She tinkles gently when she walks, and I get the sense her clear gray eyes have seen much. She likely remembers the Sorrows and even the days before.

Behind her, the other three Crowns approach. An elderly, pale-skinned man in a yellow tunic and robe; and two middle-aged men, one dark-skinned wearing green and the other in white, whose race I can't identify. He could be a mix of things, like I am.

The woman speaks first. "Be welcome, King Shadrach of the Nimali. Please, join us at the table."

We all manage to sit at the same time, and the old woman makes a hand movement, which sets the Fai guards into motion. My people tense when the line of guards moves into a half-circle formation. Then, even more strange, they all hold hands. I sense shock from my half of the table, but suddenly, the rain stops. Or rather, it stops falling on us.

I see its evidence beyond the table, but those of us seated and the guards behind both of us are now dry. The woman smiles. "I thought it would make for a more pleasant chat if we were a little more comfortable."

I nod in acknowledgment, not trusting myself to say anything else. Keeping their forms gives Fai abilities we Nimali don't have, but it's obvious there is much we don't know about them.

Introductions are made. The woman, Citlali, is the Water Priestess. As the oldest, she seems to have some authority among the four of them. I present my "trusted advisors" with a perfectly straight face.

I hold myself back from glancing toward Xipporah, though my eyes want to stray in her direction. Ryin, however, is within my line of sight, and the kindness he showed me grounds me. There *are* honorable Fai; I only hope that the Crowns can be counted among them.

"I was gratified to receive your invitation," I begin. "And I hope that our two people can move forward in peace." There is more that I have prepared to say, a brief speech about putting the past behind us, but Citlali's eyes flash with humor. She places her hands palm down on the table; the other Crowns turn to her with expectation.

"I know that not all Nimali share your sentiments, Your Majesty. Not all the Fai do, either." She glances at her companions. The Fire Priest narrows his eyes, and the Air Priest scowls. "That is why I have not shared my vision with them, either. It is best we all hear of it together.

"You are aware, King Shadrach, of some of the powers Fai daimons bestow upon us." She motions above to the invisible magical umbrella, keeping us dry. "Fire daimons give us healing power. Hosts of Air daimons can fly, Land daimons can grow a plant in any condition, Water daimons purify."

I nod. The Fai who were captive in the Citadel often did work that matched with their daimons.

"There is, of course, more to it than that," she continues. "Secrets we do not share with outsiders; suffice it to say our spirit familiars grant us other gifts. Water Fai, for example, are gifted with future-seeing."

Of the Fai gathered, all but Citlali eye us coldly. *Future-seeing?* Now the tension is on our side: surprise and affront, judging by the shifting postures of the Council. But we were never deserving of their secrets.

"Over my lifetime, I have seen many things," Citlali says. "These futures can always be changed, but not always by me." Her eyes go vacant and distant. "I saw the human wars, the natural disasters, and all that followed. Nothing that I could alter. It was my grandmother who saw the prosperity our people could achieve by settling here in Aurum, in a place with so many powerful bliss matrices. But she also foresaw the turmoil it would bring, for we are not the only ones who need to live near the bliss." Her gaze sharpens, landing back on me. I feel it like a knife blade through my flesh.

"Two nights before I sent the invitation, I had a vision. I saw the Greenlands destroyed. Trees dead from poison, the earth charred, the bliss...gone." She flutters her fingers in the air. "I also saw a crater where the Citadel used to be."

Dame Ayisha sucks in her breath, and Lady Raina's fists tighten on the table. Sir Denby is frowning, and I...I do not doubt her words. There is truth in her eerie, pale eyes. How I feel about this possibility is another matter. Horror, yes, but also something I'm not quite ready to admit. Something akin to relief. I squash it down mercilessly, shamed by the notion.

Citlali continues. "I saw the Nimali section of the city as a smoking, charred wasteland. Both our clans turned victims in a war that has been chasing us for generations."

I swallow and scan the faces of her compatriots. They are

all aghast. She really did not share this with them before. And it is clear they all believe her as well.

"I do not want what I witnessed to come true," she continues. "I do not want my people, or even yours, destroyed. Though perhaps you deserve it. And so, I am here to propose a solution. We cannot solve all our disputes in one day, but I would ask for a series of peace talks. So that we may negotiate how we may be of service to one another and maintain each of our people's well-being."

The Water Priestess turns and glances at Xipporah, whose eyes widen at the sudden scrutiny, before turning back. "But how can either of us trust anything the other says, you might ask."

"That would be my first question," I say with grim humor.

Citlali smiles. "To that I answer, we do as was done in days of old. To keep the other side honest, we each send a hostage."

The Fire Priest, an elderly, white-haired man seated to her left, begins coughing in a sputtering fit. Outrage paints the faces of not only the other Crowns but my Council as well.

"A beloved child," Citlali says, raising her voice, "offered in matrimony to the other clan. Two marriages. To bond us by blood where we cannot be by faith alone. That way, each of us loses something precious if we destroy the other side."

There is quiet for a long moment, and then the shouting begins.

FIVE

Xipporah

IT TAKES everything I have to remain at attention, amplifying the power of the others with my daimon to keep the rain shield up, and not allow my face to betray my horror at Citlali's words. Chaos can't even begin to describe the outcry raised at the table. Both the Crowns and the Nimali Council begin yelling, talking over one another to voice their opposition.

"This is preposterous!" Fire Priest Abner cries.

"How dare you suggest such a thing without consulting us!" Land Priest Eamonn is irate.

The white-haired woman next to King Shadrach flails her arms, while the golden-haired man points and shouts. And the youngish, brown-skinned woman stands like she's ready to leave.

The only two who remain quiet are Water Priestess Citlali and the Nimali king himself. She is an unmovable rock amidst the storm, and he is thoughtful, considering, while madness rages around him. He leans forward and speaks to Citlali, words impossible for me to hear amid all the noise. But she makes them out and responds, and soon they are conversing.

The others notice and begin to calm, sitting down again, not wanting to miss what's being said.

As the First Crown, the eldest, Citlali serves as the spokesperson for the four of them, but she has rarely ever used the authority in this way: keeping secrets from her own people to make a suggestion like this. Marry one of the beasts? It's almost beyond comprehension. It was wise of her not to alert the others as to her real purpose here. She knew what the reaction would be.

Now that the others are silent, I can make out Shad's voice. "…actions of my predecessor. But the Fai do not have the means to take down the entire Citadel."

"Do we not?" Citlali says mysteriously.

My heart seizes. On our own, we have not developed the sorts of advanced technologies the Nimali insist upon, trying to make their world match the one from before the Sorrows. However, we have highly skilled minds among us who have figured out certain ways to turn their technology against them. Von comes to mind, my former commander who disappeared the day the Fai trapped in the Citadel regained our freedom. He did not arrive in the Greenlands with the rest of us, and his whereabouts are unknown. The last I saw of him was on the Nimali plaza, just before the Revokers attacked.

Before then, during the few short days when he and I were held as drudges, Von was working on some way to override the Citadel's biometric systems in order to access restricted areas. Though I am not privy to the upper-level plans at play, I imagine there are those who have been studying ways to take down the entire Nimali fortress in the way Citlali has seen in her vision. And now there are no Fai trapped inside, those plans can be advanced.

Of course, Citlali does not reveal anything like that. But the king can make his own inferences. And apparently does. He sits back and purses his lips. For some reason, the action reminds me of the scent of cinnamon, which I now associate with him.

"What makes you think that our daimons would ever consent to these matches?" he asks, mystified.

"That is what the engysis is for," she replies.

The king appears surprised. "But that hasn't been done in at least a century."

"Our covenants demand it when the marriages are arranged such as these," Citlali says. "The minimum period of engysis courtship is thirty days, though in the old days it was up to a year. However, one month will be sufficient time for us to hold our negotiations for peace. And if the daimons refuse the pairing, more time will not help, and it is my sincere hope we will have come to an agreement by then."

King Shadrach taps his fingers on the table, mulling her words. "Have you a proposition for who is to marry whom?"

"Our best chance of an alliance will start at the top, with you. We betroth one of our beloveds to you and you send someone precious to wed one of ours."

My thoughts scatter as he responds. "You have no king or queen. And as you know, I am already betrothed to Princess Celena."

Citlali tilts her head. "The true Princess Celena has not been seen or heard from in some weeks. It is said she went beyond the wall. A place none have survived for such a time period. How long will you hold out false hope for her return? Especially while mutually assured destruction weighs on our heads?" Her voice is kind as she speaks of the assumed death of the man's stepsister.

"And though the Crowns are not kings or queens, our influence is equivalent. It is true, none of us are of marriageable age or condition." She motions to Fire Priest Abner, who is almost as old as she is. And Land Priest Eamonn and Makani already have a husband and wife, respectively. "However, I believe a child of one of the

Crowns will be of sufficient rank to wed a king. And a child of one of your advisors could fill the need?" The question hangs in the air.

"A council member is different to a monarch," the king says, but his tone indicates he is considering.

"Among the Crowns there are two daughters and two sons of marrying age," Citlali continues, and my guts twist. "One of these men or women would be betrothed to you and go to live in the Citadel, while your tribute would come to live among us during the month of engysis."

King Shad's expression turns a bit sheepish. He may even be blushing.

My breathing speeds as her words sink in. Eamonn's two sons are both a few years older than me. Citlali has no children, and Abner's daughters are already married. Though his back is to me, my stepfather straightens.

"Assuming your preference lies with women, Your Majesty," Makani says, "my beloved daughter would be an ideal match."

I actually gape at him.

"Yes, I do prefer women," the king says.

"Well then, she is demure and deferential and already familiar with the Nimali territory."

Horror coats my skin. Demure and deferential? He means Noomi. He wants to marry off Noomi to this beast and send her back into her nightmare. My fists clench, and my daimon takes note, stirring from its slumber ready to rise and fight.

Citlali nods her agreement. "Just so. Once all parties are in agreement, the two couples will enter the engysis, so that their daimons may acclimate to one another and approve the match."

The king eyes the Crowns warily. "And your children, they will be amenable to such marriages? I will not wed a bride coerced or forced."

I take my first breath since understanding what Citlali has

planned. Perhaps Ryin was right and there is some honor in this beast.

Citlali clasps her hands. "None will be forced. Our children understand that peace must be fought for and that violence is not the only way to battle. I am confident they will agree to this duty out of love for their people."

I fear my body will turn to stone if I stand here much longer. I can't feel my legs anymore, and there is a strong possibility that I will pass out. My sister, my sweet and dutiful sister, whose savage dreams of the Citadel have not even begun to abate yet. They would send her back into her literal nightmare and call it duty.

With anguish, I stare at the king. His gaze rests on me for the first time. Honorable or not, I should have snapped his neck when I had the chance. Now Noomi is the one who will pay the price.

RAIN SOAKS me to the skin as I run. Between the dark skies and the thick tree trunks, which blur as I pass them, I rely on familiarity more than sight to guide me. With my daimon speed, I'm practically gliding over the earth, but if I don't keep moving, I will fall apart, I'm sure of it. I don't stop to think—but images of the meeting fill my mind, unbidden.

The proceedings concluded with the king requesting time to consider and confer with his advisors. Once I was dismissed from duty, I escaped immediately, not wanting anyone, especially Makani, to witness my inevitable breakdown.

I emerge at the edge of the Northwestern district. Thankfully, no one is around. It is only midday and most will be about their service duties. The Cedarknoll bliss shrine should be empty. Maybe there I can find some clarity about the situation.

An enormous boulder indicates the entrance, and stone

steps lead underground. With the weak daylight from the cloud-filled sky, the blue glow of the bliss pool lights my way. I emerge in a small space, mostly taken up by the pool of liquid bliss. It's bordered by a night garden, leaving only a narrow walkway surrounding it. Little alcoves hide in shadow around the perimeter to hold offerings from Air, Water, and Fire daimons.

The purity of the liquid entrances me, and I kneel in a sparse patch of greenery at the edge of the pool. The strain of the day—the fear and anger—melt away. In the presence of spirit, there is peace. The bliss is still, waiting, but I sense its anticipation. Then I plunge my hands into the earth and call my daimon.

While Fai with other types of daimons bring ritual items into the temples, those of us with Land daimons make the earth our altar. I strain to find a seed deep in the ground and urge it to grow. The seeds were embedded here long before Fai ever came to this land, and for our prayer, we cultivate them. Soon, a shoot sprouts up. My power funnels energy into it, accelerating its life process until it's a flowering plant—one of the little blue and white striped flowers we call prayer blossoms.

The intense, painful emotions roiling within me, the desperation and shame and anger and sorrow, all leach away until I'm only conscious of myself, my daimon, and the plant I'm growing.

When it's done, I lean forward and press my forehead to the ground, breathing in the rich aroma of soil. My chest heaves, not from the effort of growing the flower, but from releasing the storm inside me. The bliss pool is in motion now, responding to my offering with one of its own. The small reservoir churns with an invisible current. It brightens, offering me the harmony I usually lack inside.

The Nimali believe we Fai worship the bliss, but that is not precisely true. It is not a deity. We do not bow down to it and serve it, but we do honor it. The spirit energy, which comes in many forms, is a direct link between our world and the Origin. It is a conduit not only for our daimons but for ourselves, as we live in the Origin before we are born and return after we die.

Why do they scoff at our desire not to enslave the bliss—a sentient entity—and to want it to always flow free? To respect the energy that feeds us and our daimons instead of forcing it to fuel technology and slowly kill it. Even before the Sorrows, shifters from all over the world flocked here to Aurum because of all of its powerful bliss matrices. So many of them across the globe were destroyed during the wars and disasters that this became a kind of sanctuary for Fai and Nimali alike. That they would strip their lands of this precious resource, then war with us because we will share none of ours, is madness. And because of this, because of their rampant wastefulness and disrespect, our people have died. Had their souls stolen. Were enslaved for long years, traumatized, and controlled.

And now they want my sister to go back to the very people who did this?

But even as these thoughts arise, the spiritual energy of the bliss seeps into me. Comforts me. Lends me its power. It helps me not to remove or forget my emotions, but to manage them. Funnel them into something useful, not just use them as an escape valve that could boomerang back to harm me.

Movement in the darkness across the pool causes me to sit up sharply.

"Who's there?" My daimon comes to the forefront, ready to fight. But the figure who emerges from a nearby alcove is no threat. Talia steps into the light, looking chagrined.

"I'm so sorry. I didn't mean to spy, but I didn't want to disturb you. Then I got a leg cramp." She grimaces.

"You were here the whole time?" It is a testament to my distraction when I came in that I didn't sense her.

She nods, looking miserable. "It's soothing here. And I'm not exactly welcome in most places."

"It's all right. I should have been more vigilant. You have committed no great offense." Ryin's chosen one has had a difficult time of it here.

She slowly walks toward me. Her hair is in neat rows of braids that hug her scalp. The cream and gold dress she wears is familiar to me.

"Is that Noomi's dress?"

"She lent me some of her clothes since I came here with nothing." Talia plucks at the skirt. The hem hits her mid-calf, whereas it's full length on my sister. The fabric is a blend of natural fibers cultivated by Land Fai textile workers, thick and soft. "She's been great, really welcoming. I owe her much more than a few dresses." That certainly sounds like my sister.

I motion for her to sit. "You are new and an oddity. People aren't quite sure what to do with you. But they will come around, eventually. Ryin's voice can hold sway if he wants it to. And he's motivated."

"They're not wrong to be wary of me, or even afraid. I turn into a dragon and you guys have had a pretty bad time of it with dragons. Or at least, one of them. I don't *think* I'm a Nimali, but if it walks like a duck." She shrugs.

That Talia, an outsider to our world, joined with a daimon at all is remarkable. But that she joined a dragon daimon, and one that changes form as the Nimali do… Her daimon and Ryin's are parallels, soulsmates, so why her dragon chose to physically shift is a mystery to all. If the Crowns can't figure it out, I certainly won't be able to. But her words lead me in another direction.

"I'm actually glad you're here." Her brows shoot up at this. "When you were in the Citadel, I know Ryin said their new king offered you aid."

"Shad? Yes. He saved my life." She smiles.

"And you believe he will be a good ruler?"

She settles, looking at me seriously. "I believe he wants to change things. He wasn't a fan of Lyall and how he ran things, and behind the scenes, Shad had been working against him for a while."

I hug my knees close to my chest. "It made little impact."

"I don't know. You were there. You saw what happened on the plaza when Shad went against Lyall openly. He reminded the Nimali about their covenants before Lyall took him down."

I shudder as the memory replays. Shadrach, the prince then, refused to murder innocent and powerless Fai. And then the red dragon transformed in the blink of an eye and burned him before the prince could complete his shift and defend himself. Dishonorable combat. But Ryin had saved the man's life.

Talia leans forward. "Shad truly wants peace. Did the talks today not go well?"

I sigh. "Citlali offered a marriage exchange. To stop us from completely wiping each other out while we negotiate for a lasting agreement."

She smiles tentatively. "That's a good thing, isn't it?"

"They want Noomi to marry King Shadrach."

The smile wavers. "He won't harm her, if that's what you're thinking."

"No. That would defeat the purpose. But there are still many there who did *not* oppose King Lyall's rule or his policies. Noomi was there for so long. She's barely begun to recover. To even *think* of sending her back is madness."

Talia looks shaken and nods her agreement. "Why her?"

"Because she will go. Because she is dutiful and honorable and will sacrifice herself for the rest of us."

"And you wouldn't?"

My eyes widen. I must look fierce because she holds her hands up. "I just meant…I'm guessing they needed the daughter of someone powerful, and the Air Priest is your father."

"Stepfather."

"Stepfather. Why Noomi and not you? You're the warrior. Aren't you just as dutiful?"

My heart races and the old ache pulses deep inside. Makani is not my mother. He is kinder and more patient than she ever was, but he has spent close to twenty years hearing her tear me down. Did it truly never occur to him to offer me?

"I'm sorry," Talia begins, "I didn't—"

"No, it's all right. You're…you're not wrong. It should be me."

Once the idea takes root, it will not let go. It has to be me. I would do anything to save my sister. The question now is: What will it take for us to switch places?

SIX

Shad

"ABSOLUTELY NOT." The reply is just as emphatic as I knew it would be, but the vehemence of the statement is still a little surprising. "Are you insane?" Dominga hisses. I'm half afraid she's going to shift and unleash her venom on me.

I hold up my hands. "It's not as bad as you think."

"I cannot wait to hear why." Sarcasm drips from her lips.

"There is absolutely no chance our daimons will suit. It's never happened. Fai and Nimali? It's absurd. Their priestess just wants to buy time. Engysis is a contract, a *spirit* contract, so we have at least thirty days of forced peace while we try to come to some accord. At the end of that time, the Fai woman will return to her home, our tribute will come back here, and if Celena has been found, our plans can proceed as well."

Dominga's jaw clenches. "And this plan of yours, it has no room for the unexpected?"

"Unexpected? Like our daimons suiting?" I almost burst with laughter. "According to their Crown, they're saddling me with some mousy, quiet, little lamb of a woman."

"A sheep shifter?" Doming raises a brow.

"I don't know what kind of shifter she is—you know the

Fai are touchy about revealing their daimons. But my dragon will not see hers as its equal. Trust me, that is the least of our worries."

"Well, you *should* be worried about marrying another when you are supposed to be marrying the princess and rightful queen."

I spread my arms wide. "If Celena were here, then I would, but if we don't want the Citadel reduced to a smoking crater, I will do what I must and negotiate with the Fai." I'm shouting by the end of the sentence, and Dominga is seething.

"You actually believe that Fai witch? You think they can manage to take down the Citadel?"

"All of her people believed her, that much was clear. And it stands to reason that their covenant gives them additional gifts, since they do not change forms. It is not hard to imagine future-seeing being one of them since we already know they can heal and purify."

She is quiet for a moment, contemplating. "Well, if you're able to convince them to part with some of their bliss…"

I shake my head. "I will certainly do my best, but I don't have much hope."

"Then this peace is merely a pause, and at the end of thirty days, what will have changed? You know, the engineers are on their way to tell you that the bliss reservoir in sector three is at a catastrophic low. They are going to suggest rolling brownouts in the Umber and Azure regions of the territory."

I stare at her in shock. "How do you know these things?"

She just shrugs.

"And why not reduce bliss usage everywhere? The Citadel uses more bliss than the Umbers and Azures combined."

"Do you want to tell the aristocrats that they will have to make do with hours per day without power? Use candlelight and warm their food over fires like some Fai savage?" Her lip curls in disgust.

"What will they do when it all runs out?" I ask. "And how is sector three running dry? It was at fifty percent capacity last week. Is there some kind of equipment failure?"

"The engineers will not say it, but I suspect sabotage."

That makes my blood run cold. "What have you heard?"

She shakes her head. "Nothing. Not even my father would waste bliss by damaging the storage equipment, but there is a chance others might to make their point. It makes little sense otherwise."

I keep my thoughts to myself, but not for the first time, I wonder if the Fai are on to something and the bliss *is* sentient. Maybe it is working against us, protesting the way we mine it and use it to fuel our technology—our lights and heat and data and security systems. Our entire way of life is completely dependent upon bliss, and our reservoirs are the lowest they've ever been. It wasn't until Lyall's death that I discovered exactly how low, how much of a tightrope we are treading between living in the Stone Age again.

That is the true reason why Lyall was so willing to decimate the Fai and the entire Greenlands: to get at what we know are rich stores of the precious energy source stored in their temples and beneath their land.

I rub my forehead. "Brownouts among the Umbers and Azures will not be enough, Dominga. You know this."

"You're right, it's only the beginning."

"Even Celena could not help us out of this kind of crisis. We need more bliss. Which the Fai can provide...if they're willing."

She turns away in a huff, but her lack of retort means she knows I'm right. The only question is, will thirty days be enough time to convince the Fai to do what they have sworn they never would—allow us to use some of their sacred bliss?

"Fine. Have your engysis," she says with a sniff. "Take your Fai betrothed. But when Celena returns—and she *is* coming back—I intend to make sure she becomes queen. With or without you." Then she's gone in a swirl of black fabric as the notes of a funeral dirge play in my mind.

My daimon pulses through me with relief at her absence. Dominga's daimon makes mine antsy for some reason—probably the same reason the woman herself makes me recoil. To have her as an enemy, on top of all my other enemies, would not be wise.

One month is not a long time at all. Will I be able to convince the Fai to help us before my daimon rejects whatever docile creature they send to be my betrothed? Glowing blue eyes flash before me, and the feel of a hand tightens around my neck. For a moment, at the meeting today, I hoped that it would be her. But that's ridiculous, impossible. Dangerous, even, because my daimon comes awake at the idea, releasing a subtle thread of anticipation. Xipporah. I swallow down the unwelcome regret. Whatever animal she hosts within her is definitely not a mouse. And being tied to her for a month would be trouble.

XIPPORAH

"ABSOLUTELY NOT." Noomi crosses her arms and glowers at me.

Makani wasn't lying when he called my sister dutiful. Devoted and determined are also descriptors that come to mind. Delicate, certainly, but docile? Not even at her lowest. She is one of the most stubborn people I have ever met. If she had a mind to, she could have been a warrior. Even with a dolphin daimon, I think she would have excelled. But Mother'd had an apoplexy at the mere thought of her precious baby girl training with our Defense Division, and Noomi didn't press the matter.

"It's a good plan, Noomi. You don't want to go back. I don't want you to go back. I take your place. What's the problem?"

"If there's no problem, then why not just tell Makani?"

I sigh and roll my eyes. "He would have suggested me in the first place if he thought I was the best choice. He's got blinders on."

"Or maybe he knows you nearly killed the king for simply doing advanced reconnaissance? Imagine living in the same building with him, in close quarters?" She crosses her arms in challenge.

"It doesn't have to be that close," I grumble.

"Engysis requires a good faith effort to allow your daimons to connect. Are you seriously telling me you would make the effort? You'd risk your covenant."

"If it would keep you out of the Citadel again, I'd do anything. Marry a dragon, marry a harem of dragons! Besides, the whole thing is absurd. There is no way my daimon would accept a Nimali dragon husband."

She raises a brow. "Are you so certain? Your daimon is fierce and…" She averts her eyes, not wanting to hurt my feelings.

"You can go ahead and say it. It is fierce and bloodthirsty. Not so different from a Nimali." I sigh and sit on my bed, holding my head in my hands.

"That's not what I was going to say at all," she says, sitting beside me. "But you do have trouble with your temper sometimes. And you hate them."

"Don't you?"

"It's not the same. Sometimes I wonder whether what you went through, staying behind and not knowing what was happening inside the Citadel, was worse."

I go to protest, but she raises a hand to stop me. "I know the nightmares are bad and you think I'm fragile, but I'm not. And you're too volatile."

It hurts my heart to hear, and she's not wrong, but I can rise to the challenge. "Noomi, I can control myself *and* my daimon. Killing the king now would only doom us all. You heard what Citlali said. I wouldn't risk the lives of everyone in the Greenlands just for revenge."

She squares her shoulders, determination in bold relief across her face. "I can handle myself. It's only one month. I was there for years. Another month will *not* kill me." She sounds sure and strong, but her eyes... They tell another story. As do her nightmares. I am certain that my sister *could* survive the Citadel again, but in what condition would she return to us? Worry over her has consumed me these past weeks, and that will not stop. Leaving would mean she'd be facing her nights alone, but at least she'd be home, in her own bed.

I leave her upstairs packing, obstinately resolved to go through with this, but I pause at the top of the steps. My mother's screaming, which filled our home for at least the past half a day, has finally stopped. Now her words to my stepfather are too low to hear but are spat with the venom of a thousand vipers. Her steps echo as she stomps out of the house. I'm honestly surprised she allowed Makani to stay after what I know she views as a betrayal. Perhaps his being the Air Priest helped.

I find him in the kitchen, seated at the table with his hands folded. His head hangs low, and he seems tired.

"Your mother has gone to the temple to pray," he says.

"For your disembowelment and dismemberment?"

His lips quirk. "Doubtless."

I lean against the entryway. "Not to be repetitive, because I'm sure she asked you, but why Noomi? Why not me?"

His brow creases, and I hold my breath. I can tell he's trying to be diplomatic, choosing his words carefully. "Xipporah, you have a great many talents and skills, but I am uncertain that your…*temperament* is conducive to living among the enemy and negotiating with them, even for a month."

"Negotiating?"

"The Crowns met. We've decided that the negotiations for peace should occur between the two betrothed couples. The king's new fiancée will be the Fai representative and ambassador. You are a soldier."

"And Noomi is a scholar. That makes her more qualified?"

"It makes her more patient and less fierce. And though she was the one captured, her desire for vengeance has yet to come to the forefront."

I blow out a breath. "Why does everyone think I will murder their king?"

He raises a brow, and I wonder how much he knows of what happened last night. Ryin wouldn't have said anything, but the Air Priest does tend to keep watchers flying around.

I purse my lips. "Well, he's still alive, isn't he?"

Makani's eyes crinkle with kindness and pity, but I look away. "She can handle it," he says. "She's strong."

I don't answer. Her strength is not the issue and should not have to be tested again.

He stands, sighing. "Your mother will come back eventually and want to fix a goodbye breakfast for your sister tomorrow. The endive stalks are practically bare. It would be nice to have something fresh, don't you think?"

The change of topic is jarring. It's not a command or an order, but a dismissal nonetheless. I knew it would be useless talking to him and that I was unlikely to change his mind.

"Fine," I say and storm out. Tending our family garden will give me some time to think—to figure out a way to defy both my stepfather and my sister, in order to protect her.

The garden surrounds the tree below the house, and many of the vines and plants grow right up the side of the massive trunk. Mother's been picking the endive, making Noomi's favorite meals so much that their naked stems stand out sadly. I shake my head and call my daimon, then lay my hands in the earth. The beast inside me unfurls from its rest and gets to work. Pulses of life energy roll up the stems of the plants and force growth. Buds sprout and mature before my eyes. In minutes, the ravaged crop is full and ready for picking. There will be plenty of fresh greens for breakfast.

Tucked into the corner between two tree roots is another emaciated, spindly plant—one I don't recognize at first. I tilt my head, staring, until my daimon senses its essence. Lavomile. A powerful hybrid of lavender and chamomile used as a sleep aid. I wasn't aware we had any growing here.

I place a hand at its root and nurse it back to health and strength as well, until its purple and white flowers are practically bursting. The scent is subtle, an odd mix of the two components, the leaves of which become tasteless when brewed into a tea. While very effective for sleep, too much could put a person into a coma, so its growth is usually monitored by the Land Priest and his acolytes. When Noomi first returned, I obtained a powdered blend to help her get through the nights, but it gives her a headache upon waking, so she doesn't use it anymore.

I stand, but my daimon jerks within, urging me not to leave yet, which is unusual. It's happy enough to tend plants but usually only makes its preferences known when bloodshed is involved. However, it definitely doesn't want me walking off just now.

I turn back to the lavomile. I haven't spent much time studying greenery cultivation with the Land Priest, my soldiering duties having taken over the past few years. Does my daimon want me to pull the plant so that someone doesn't accidentally come upon it? Non-Land Fai may not recognize it, though it's not really harmful unless consumed in large quantities.

I crouch again, staring at the narrow, sharp-looking leaves, and the reason for my daimon's hesitance becomes clear. What a clever and devious little tiger.

"Noomi, I hope you'll forgive me," I whisper.

SEVEN

Shad

An ENGYSIS CEREMONY has not taken place in many years among the Nimali, so I had to visit the library to get information on what I should expect. In the past, they were celebrations with entire communities coming together to dedicate themselves to the success of the arranged union. Elaborate decorations and music and feasting would take place. But I highly doubt a ceremony has ever occurred on a broken recreation area in the middle of a crumbling city.

Once I'd waded through the opposition of my councilors, my advisors, and of course, Harsh, I'd sent back a note with my agreement. Two days later, we're here at the same disintegrating park, only the round table and stools have been cleared away. The gravel and chunks of missing concrete littering the ground have been removed, and the resulting holes in the basketball court's surface filled in with dirt. The Fai have attempted to make this place presentable. It seems wasted, but it's at least something.

Callum stands next to me, both of us arrayed in our crimson dress uniforms.

"I wish you weren't doing this," I say to him, under my breath.

"Well, marrying a man wouldn't be my first choice," he says just as quietly. "But I'll do what's necessary for peace."

Of the eligible children of the council members, Callum was the only one who consented to this pairing. And the Fai Crowns thought it best to have their tributes spread out amongst two families, so the sons of the Land Priest were the only ones available for Callum to be betrothed to.

"Besides," he continues, "I was destined for a political marriage. Might as well get it over with." His lips curl in a wry smile, but I don't feel any better. He will stay with the Fai in the Greenlands as a fiancé/hostage, bringing my trusted companions in Nimali territory down by one more. The loss will be felt acutely.

Movement behind us makes me turn. I brought the same members of the Council as before; they stand in a line behind us. Callum's father looks more severe than usual, his expression reminding me he is a decorated warrior, capable in his scorpion form of inflicting a great deal of damage on unsuspecting enemies.

Dame Ayisha and Lady Raina appear grim as well. While Ayisha was the lone councilor who supported my decision to agree to this, today is no celebration. It's fitting that we're in a bleak and uninviting setting for this sham of a service. Across the court, the overgrown greenery rustles.

"They're coming," Callum says.

We both reach for the dark, mesh fabric around our necks and pull it over our heads. In times of old, when engysis was a contract between parents to form alliances, overcome disputes, or find peace in times of war, the identities of the two parties actually being promised to each other were less important than the connections of the daimons. People can learn to live with one another, but daimons are a little more complicated. They can be neutral on sight, form an immediate connection, or reject one another instantly. The veiling was to prevent one from refusing the other before the contract was sealed and the minimum thirty-day time period of acclimation engaged.

Since the morning sun is bright, my vision isn't too impeded by the veil. The overgrown weeds and high grasses part to reveal two pairs of Fai guards followed by the four Crowns. They line up before us as additional civilian Fai follow, including a veiled man and woman. The woman, my intended, wears a gauzy flowing forest green gown, which hides her figure. Swathes of fabric embroidered with vines and leaves and studded with crystal beads in patterns I can't discern cover her from neck to feet. Even her hands are obscured by the long, lacy sleeves of the gown.

The man intended for Callum wears a yellow tunic similarly embellished with embroidered flames. He is tallish and slim with long-fingered dark hands clasped before him.

Once again, the Water Priestess takes the lead with no preamble. "The king's ceremony shall be first. Who represents those to be betrothed?" she calls out.

The Air Priest steps up next to my proposed bride. "I will stand for my stepdaughter."

Sir Denby has agreed to represent me since I have no living blood kin. "I will stand for King Shadrach," he says.

"Then join their hands," Citlali intones.

I extend my arm, stepping toward the woman, whose name I still do not even know. She lifts her hand, but the sleeve covers her fingers, giving me no glimpse. Taking a deep breath, I slide my hand inside the sleeve and our palms meet. Warm skin greets me in a surprisingly forceful grip, which gentles after a moment.

I cannot remember when I last held someone's hand, but the touch is remarkably intimate—at least it seems so to me. The sensation is jagged, a disruption to the calm I've been striving to cultivate. It's not unpleasant, not at all, but when a pulse of intense longing rushes through me, I struggle to push it aside.

Swallowing down my reaction, I try to repair my equilibrium. It would not do for my body to get any ideas about this situation. In a traditional engysis, physical intimacy is permitted, though not required, but this is not a normal situation. This woman, whoever she is, will need to live in the Citadel and spend time with me to meet the requirements of the spirit contract, but that is all. I would never consider a physical relationship with a Fai who is there, if not under duress, at least through no desire of her own. Or mine. Even if a different sort of desire is what I'm feeling as tingles ripple up my arm from where our hands are connected.

I straighten my shoulders as both the Air Priest and Sir Denby work together to tie my and my bride's wrists together with a white ribbon. If there was once more to the ceremony than this, it has been lost to time. Even the library had no further information. After the knots are tied, one by each of our representatives, the contract has been made. She and I stand to the side while Callum and his groom go through the same ritual.

Because of the way our hands are bound, we must stand facing one another, but though I squint and strain, I can manage no glimpse of her features. I want to ask her name, but everyone is silent as Sir Denby and the Land Priest wrap their sons' arms together with ribbon.

Once they're done, Citlali speaks again. "Ordinarily, the unveiling occurs once the betrothed are in their home, but as the contract is complete, let us not stand on tradition. Lift each other's veils and begin this period of discovery."

The curiosity as to whom I've been bound has been boiling over like a teakettle. With my free hand, I reach for her veil as she reaches for mine.

When she pulls mine off, I blink at the sudden brightness and allow my eyes to focus.

"It's you." My gasp is loud in the quiet morning. Louder still are the sounds of shock from the rest of the Fai. One glance at the perplexed and then quickly furious Air Priest and I know this wasn't what he expected, either.

"Xipporah," her name falls from my lips almost reverently. The shock is couched by a strong sense of relief. One I don't want to process.

Water Priestess Citlali stares at Xipporah with an inscrutable expression. She doesn't appear shocked, though at her age, I'm sure there isn't much she hasn't seen. The rest of the Fai quickly regain their composure, though the Air Priest continues to seethe.

A few steps away, Callum is introducing himself to the lean, dark-skinned man he's been tied to. The man blinks owlishly at my friend, who has a cool mask of politeness in place. If this is awkward for me, it will be infinitely more awkward for them. Not for the first time, I wish another option was available to us.

I turn back to Xipporah. "Guess we don't need to introduce ourselves," I say, hoping to lighten the weighty atmosphere.

She narrows her eyes and tightens her grip on my wrist by a fraction. "No. Though I suppose I should apologize again for our first meeting."

"Hmm. And you are aware that neither of us can cause harm to the other during the engysis?"

Her eyebrow raises. "I am aware that I cannot directly cause you harm."

Her wording and the challenge in her tone are somehow invigorating, though they cause the scowl on the Air Priest's face to deepen.

"You were not who I expected," I say.

She glances at her stepfather and the other Fai, many of whom are glaring daggers at her. "Story of my life."

I'm curious as to the background here, but my daimon becoming alert within me stops my tongue. The dragon has noticed her and whatever daimon she holds. I freeze, gauging its emotions as best I can. Curiosity. Nothing more than that, thank the bliss.

It's not picking up on what the sensation of her hand in mine is doing to my breathing and my temperature. Or it's just ignoring it. I take another deep breath and wrangle my body under control.

"How long do we need to keep this on?" she asks, holding up our joined arms.

"In the old days, a day, I think. But——" The ripping of a ribbon sounds as Callum and his partner step away from one another.

"Looks like Lex isn't too happy. He's not interested in men, you know," Xipporah confides.

"Neither is Callum. But it's not like these are real betrothals."

"Oh, really?" she says sarcastically. "Just when I was planning on promising you my heart forever." Her eyes flash blue with her daimon, and she slices our ribbon with the blunt edges of her short fingernails. I shake my head at the Fai magic as her daimon retreats, leaving her eyes a bold, dark brown.

The Air Priest appears at her elbow. "Xipporah, a word?"

Her expression blanks, but she nods, her acquiescence still seeming fairly obstinate. I really want to know what happened to the meek little lamb I was supposed to be tied to, but her stepfather is pulling her away and, in her absence, my daimon sends out a pang of longing.

I stiffen and turn away.

Thirty days is all we need. One month for us to be in each other's company, make an agreement that will save both our clans, and then go our separate ways. I just hope my daimon understands that.

EIGHT

Xipporah

MAKANI'S FACE gives nothing away, but he was never one to show his anger where others could see. Most of his feelings are kept locked up tight, something that I think actually comforts my mother. Maybe because hers are on display one-hundred percent of the time.

He leads me to the edge of the fractured pavement, nearly to the street corner. Shifter ears are powerful, but no one at the ceremony has their daimon called, so we should be able to speak privately. Steps away, waist-high overgrown weeds have taken over what was once an asphalt-covered street. I turn to him, shoulders back and head high, ready to face his wrath. He crosses his arms and taps a hand against his biceps, dark gaze boring holes into me.

"I will not apologize for protecting my sister," I say, wanting to get this over with. "But I'm sorry if my actions will cause you any problems with the Crowns."

"The Crowns I can handle, though it makes me look bad that my family defies me so openly." He's worse than angry; he's disappointed with me. I struggle to keep my chin lifted. "But it is done, and we can't go back now."

"I can hold my temper," I tell him. "I vow to you I will."

His eyes narrow, but the discipline I earned in Defense Division training that allowed me to rise through the ranks, to work for freedom for our brothers and sisters locked in the Citadel, to go undercover and help to achieve it—I do have the ability to control myself. I just wish others could see it.

"I believe you," he says finally. "I suppose I have no other choice." He's quiet for a time, looking off at what's left of the building across from us with its majestic dome still clinging to the caving roof. Then he closes his eyes.

When his voice sounds in my head, using the gift of his owl daimon, only years of training stop me from jumping out of my skin. *Since you have blustered into this situation, upending my other plans, I will make use of the opportunity.*

My heart still beating wildly, I stare at his eyelids, which barely hide the blue sheen beneath them as he continues. *While you are with them, you will have two missions. The first, you already know: Negotiate with the beasts as best you can. Between you and Lex, Citlali is expecting a workable proposal for a lasting peace plan.*

But you think I'll fail. My mental voice holds a challenge.

It doesn't matter, because your actual mission is the same as it was the last time you were in the Citadel. You will watch for weaknesses and find a way to take down the Nimali from within.

His words cause a chill to ripple through me. I rear back. *But Citlali's vision—*

You well know that a Water daimon's visions of the future can change. Citlali is pinning her hopes on this exchange, but time has shown us that the Nimali are not worth the breath they use to speak. Their word, their promises, mean nothing. They are dishonorable through and through. Your sister's own experiences have shown you that, as have your many skirmishes with them over the years. Besides, we have cause to believe the program King Lyall began for our genocide is still in place. They still plan to use the poison synthesized from Revoker venom to destroy the Greenlands.

I need to sit down and struggle against the weakness that

has overtaken my legs. *Why would their king agree to this betrothal if they're planning to destroy us, anyway?*

Makani shrugs. *They are treacherous and not to be trusted. Besides, our reports show King Shad faces substantial opposition and may not be in power for long. This ploy of Citlali's is noble but doomed. However, it gives us the best option for getting another Fai spy into their territory—you.*

My jaw is literally hanging open; I close it purposefully.

You are a soldier, Xipporah. You will be alone, embedded among the enemy, and without the support you're used to. But I know you are resourceful. The Genus Fidelis may have been officially disbanded when our people were freed from the Citadel, but it's an ancient military order that is called upon when needed, in times when Fai lives are at risk. Once a member, always a member.

When my silence continues, he places a hand on my shoulder, voice still reverberating inside my head. *Your grandfather restarted the GenFi in his time, and his victory over the Nimali made him a hero who will be sung about for generations. He infiltrated the enemy and brought about a destruction so severe, they did not attack us for years afterward. Not until Lyall took the throne. You are a part of Markus's legacy. I would give anything to have his blood flowing through my veins. Use your birthright and his example to strengthen you in the days to come. Because rest assured, if we don't destroy them, they will destroy us.*

I swallow as his words penetrate. The legacy of my grandfather has always hung over my head, a paragon of Fai courage and ingenuity I've longed to live up to. Makani is giving me the opportunity to do just that. The question is, am I up for the challenge?

I wouldn't even know how to begin to take down the Nimali. How can one person even do such a thing? I ask.

There are plans that were set in motion before, Makani replies. *Von was working to gain access to the control rooms that power their buildings.* I nod, recollecting. *Reports from other GenFi members aiding him indicate he was close to success.*

My muscles tense with wariness. I suspect Von was far

more than close to success; I'm fairly certain he actually gained access to restricted areas in the Citadel, but I've already given my opinions on that to my superiors and I have no proof. Whatever Von did likely killed him, and could have killed just as many Fai as Nimali. To level that kind of accusation on a fellow Fai is not something I'm prepared to do now, though.

Makani continues. *Get access to the facilities that power the building. Determine if the Revoker poison and the distribution mechanism they created are still in existence. If so, we will find a way to release it on them instead.*

I blink in shock, my hands going cold. *You actually want to poison them?*

They had no qualms destroying us. Besides, it will be a moot point if they've destroyed all their supplies, as they've promised. Otherwise, the king can't be trusted, and the only way to guarantee our survival is to turn the tables on them. You were willing to live with the enemy for your sister; her life is still at risk if the Nimali have this weapon.

His words sink in like a toxin seeping into the soil. Though Ryin and Talia trust King Shad, that doesn't mean he deserves it. He likely has only shown them one side of his true personality.

Do the other Crowns know of this plan? I ask.

Land Priest Eamonn agrees with me that this is the only way.

And the others? I cannot believe all the Crowns would go along with this.

Don't worry about the others, Makani says. *I will handle them. The safety of the Fai is their principal duty, and this will ensure that. You have the chance to save us all. Eradicating this poison will save the Greenlands. Your name will ring as loud as your grandfather Markus's through the treetops.*

I shiver at that. Makani has never paid much attention to me—at least that's what I thought. He's never really stood up for me against my mother's tirades, but apparently, he's far more perceptive that I ever imagined. He's seen deep inside the hidden parts of my soul, excavating the thing I want most: to be a great warrior and protect my people. I defied him to save my sister. The question is, what am I willing to do for the entire clan?

You have thirty days, Xipporah. Do what you must for this farce of a betrothal, but remember your true mission. The entirety of the Fai are depending upon you.

His voice echoes through me, sealing the words inside my heart. *I understand.*

When he turns back to join the others, I peer over at my fiancé. The king stands with his people, commanding and tall. If he were not Nimali, perhaps I would think him handsome. His face isn't hideous—his features are broad with evidence of African and Asian ancestry. He's strong and well-muscled; even if he weren't the king, I'd guess Nimali women would think him a catch. Plus, he smells delicious. But what plans is he cooking up behind our backs? How many lies has he told?

As if he can feel me watching, his eyes meet mine. Though we're far away, I make out the question in his gaze. He's wondering if I'm all right. In another context, from another man, the action would be touching. But I can't soften my heart to him, no matter what Talia believes. No matter Ryin's actions. I need to stay on my guard because the beasts are sneaky, and he is now their leader.

"How could you?" a voice cries from behind me. I spin around to find my sister glaring at me. Damn.

"Nooms—"

"Don't 'Nooms' me!" she shouts, vibrating with rage. "I told you I could handle this, but you insist on treating me like an invalid or a child!"

I step closer, but she backs away, wobbling a little. Guilt tightens my chest. The effects of the lavomile are evident in the cloudiness of her eyes and her unsteady stance. The fact that she made it halfway across the city alone in this condition only underscores her fury.

I hold up my hands. "I know you're angry."

Her nostrils flare. "*Angry?* I'm incandescent. You *drugged* me! I only awoke because Mother doused me with water. You're back in her good graces now, by the way. She's ecstatic that you took my place."

The relief that washes through me is surprising. I'd given up long ago on being in Mother's favor. "So you would prefer I'd have let you go through with this and then leave me alone to face Mother's wrath? I've already spent two years hearing about how the wrong daughter was taken, how it should have been me captured."

Her face softens somewhat and I push on. "I want to believe that I did this just for you, so you wouldn't have to face that place again, but part of me did it for me, too. And the thing is, Mother is right."

Noomi's brow descends. I stop her before she can speak. "It should have been me, not because you're weak or incapable or anything like that." I move forward and grab her hands. "You're the best of us, Noomi. You represent the best of the Fai traits—you are kind and generous and openhearted. I have a tiger inside me that is only truly satisfied when I'm on the hunt. I couldn't sit by and let you walk into this situation again. I had to do something."

My sister's eyes well with tears; she squeezes my hands. "I'm still mad at you, you know," she says, sniffing.

"I know. But you won't send me off into the jaws of the dragon without a hug, will you?"

She relents and holds me in a tighter embrace than someone her size should be capable of. Then she pulls away and marches across to the king of the Nimali with me on her heels. He turns and regards her with his brows raised.

"You take care of my sister. If she comes to any harm while in your territory, you will not only have the Fai army to deal with—you will have me."

Surprise is stamped on his face, but then he gives her a

bow. Complete with a hand on his heart, like some kind of chivalric gentleman. "I give you my word. Her life will be treated more precious than my own."

Noomi narrows her eyes, not looking the least bit intimidating, but a small part of me is grateful to the king for pretending she is. Then she nods and shoots me a glare. "I need to go back home and to bed. For some reason, I have a pounding headache."

She's stomping off again, disappearing as quickly as she arrived, and I feel like I just survived a whirlwind. I watch her leave, tears welling in my eyes. It's only a month, then I'll see her again.

"Are you ready?" my new fiancé asks.

"How are we getting there? I don't fly," I add, surly.

He looks like he's going to question me about my daimon, but then doesn't. And I'm not of a mind to give him any information he doesn't strictly need.

"We brought the vehicles today, in the event that was the case."

At that moment, three large, boxy automobiles drive up over the crumbling street, right over the high weeds clogging the pavement.

I haven't ridden in one of these before. Nimali vehicles run on bliss and are extremely wasteful, just like all their other tech. But they're already here and will drive back anyway, and while I could call my daimon and run across the city at high speed, I'm actually exhausted. The stress of a poor night's sleep in anticipation of today has taken its toll. Worry for my sister, my people, and my land are all heavy. I could push through, but it's wiser to save my strength. I will need it for this mission.

"Fine."

He leads the way and opens the door for me, even going so far as to lend me a hand into the car like some old-fashioned knight. When our hands touch, something in my brain shorts out. It happened before, during the ceremony. The feel of his skin against mine is actually…nice.

I shake off the feeling and pull away, having to repeat inside my head over and over again that he can't be trusted. My hand and skin and nose have to all get in line because though his manners are impeccable and his calloused hand is unaccountably appealing and his scent makes me think of crisp fall nights under the stars, my mission is to prevent him from harming my people by the worst means possible.

NINE

Xipporah

MY RESOLVE TO do my duty hardens when I look over at those gathered to watch us drive away and spot Lex's cousin, Hendrik. The middle-aged man stares vacantly into space, there but not there. He'd been a capable soldier, captured as a prisoner of war five years ago in one of the many conflicts with the Nimali. His memory soul had been stolen, then he'd been trammeled for some infraction or another. The barbaric practice is akin to the destruction of a soul. It left Hendrik with the inability to make no new memories.

His sister holds onto the crook of his arm and whispers in his ear, causing his hollow expression to shift for a moment. She leads him away, among the first to leave. For the rest of his days, Hendrik will need someone at his side to help him navigate life. He will awake each morning and have no recollection of anything that happened since he was trammeled and every few minutes will forget it all again. It was one of the cruelest punishments the Nimali devised and one that we do not yet know how to undo.

The man responsible for this torture is dead, but there are many in the Citadel who aided him. The prince I've just been betrothed to inherited this legacy of shame. Without Lyall to blame, responsibility must fall to Shad.

He is agitated on the seat beside me, leg jumping rapidly, fingers tapping on his knee. We are alone in the back seat, and the action is irritating. I have to stop myself from reaching over to push his knee down. Instead, I turn to the window, watching the scenery as we pass.

We bump over uneven streets, though some effort has been made recently to clear the path of the vegetation that has overtaken most of the city's roadways. Charred husks of plants indicate that Shad himself might have burned the path. Though that wouldn't make any sense. Surely he would have had some servant or underling do such a menial job. I don't know what other Nimali can breathe fire, but maybe they used a more mundane means of delivering the flames.

We're silent as we roll along in the center of a caravan, three vehicles strong, the others carrying guards and councilors. It's so wasteful, but I suppose they all wanted to travel together. And though I have no wish to ask about Shad's hopes and dreams or really to get to know him, the engysis contract may require it. It demands a good faith effort for our daimons to get to know one another, else we risk our covenants.

I take a deep breath and force myself to face him. But I can't do it—I'll ask him about himself sometime later. "What types of activities do you expect I will do once in Nimali territory?"

He appears surprised. "I'm sure you can do whatever you like. What are your interests?"

Training. Sparring. Exercising. But somehow, I doubt I'd be allowed to engage in anything resembling combat preparation. And I will need to do something that gives me an excuse to explore the Citadel, and the territory in general, to search for the poison. Before the Fai escaped, Ryin and Talia discovered a secret laboratory where Revokers were being experimented upon. Is that lab still operational, or would they have moved it to an even more hidden place? Assuming it still exists at all. I'm deciding how to respond to Shad when the vehicle rocks violently to the side.

I grip the bar on the door. Metal crunches, and someone screams. It may even be me. My daimon comes to the forefront, much more able to withstand trauma, and the vehicle sways before coming to an uneasy stop. At one point, it seems like it may tip over, but manages to stay on its wheels.

I rip open the door and find myself surrounded by animals. There's a wolf, a coyote, and a jaguar. Screeching birds circle overhead. I crouch into a fighting stance, the ingrained response from years of training and experience in battle. But unlike every other time, none of these creatures attack me.

For long breaths, we're all together waiting. My daimon-enhanced nose picks up a foul, bitter scent. Smoke rises from in front of the auto I just emerged from. There's a giant crater in the road just ahead of it.

The car that had been ahead of us screeches away around a corner; I'm not even sure who was inside, but it leaves the last two vehicles in the caravan behind.

Heavy footsteps sound and Shad steps up beside me, still in human form. He's looking around wildly; I'm processing the vast amount of information all my senses are collecting, filtering through the various sounds and scents, trying to understand what is happening.

Beyond the rasping breaths of the shifted animals around me and the settling engine of the vehicle, a low whistle begins. I've never heard the sound before, but it's out of place and growing louder. The birds overhead kick up a riotous fuss, and the wrongness of the whistling sound as it grows closer makes me scream, "Take cover!"

I race into the nearest building—a burned-out husk that once was a shop of some kind. I leap behind the precarious safety of a crumbling wall just as the vehicle I was standing next to explodes in a mélange of smoke and fire.

The ground shakes. Brick and cement crack and groan. The beasts howl and roar, and another flash of light streaks in front of my closed lids.

Gasping for breath, I peek around what's left of the wall and onto the street beyond. All I see are blue scales. The massive dragon covers the entire view out the front of the building.

A violent wind blasts as he flaps his wings, then he's up in a graceful leap, gliding into the air. I stare, awe mixed with fear. I've never faced a dragon in battle. It is likely I wouldn't be here to tell the tale if I had. But Shad is fearsome. The beating of his wings puts out the fire raging in what's left of the vehicle.

A roar, louder than any other I've ever experienced, sounds, shaking the walls and ground and my bones, knocking loose chunks of brick and plaster. Cowering and hiding are not my style, so I take a deep breath before running back into the street, encountering a growling coyote and giving it a wide berth. It wasn't growling at me, but even so, old habits die hard and if I'm not here to battle it, I should keep my distance.

The acrid smoke, alongside the scent of burning metal and rubber, obscure just about everything else. My tiger's nose isn't as good as many of the canines, but I still sniff out as much information as I can, and there's something in the mix so potent and noxious, it must be part of whatever caused the explosion. If the Nimali hadn't been the targets of the attack, I'd assume this was some new weapon of theirs, though they've used nothing like this before.

I walk a wide perimeter around what's left of the vehicle, trying to pick up any other scents. On the other side of the street, unwashed flesh and misery hits my nose. Straining to listen, I identify the sound of heartbeats in the building—several of them. Our attackers?

Silently, I pick my way through the entrance of what was once an office, climbing over empty desks and shelves that have been toppled over and jumping easily over rubble from portions of the caved-in ceiling. The heartbeats and breathing grow louder, and when I duck under a partially collapsed doorway, the heartbeats get faster. A chunk of concrete blocks my path, but with the daimon's strength, I toss it to the side easily.

Cowering in a corner is a group of half a dozen mundane humans. Dressed in rags, they're too thin, as though food is scarce for them. They smell rank and shake with fear—these are definitely not our attackers.

Few humans survived the Sorrows. The ones who did and stayed in Aurum live in the Independent Zone between the Fai and Nimali territories, eking out an existence as best they can. Sometimes they cause mischief for our scavenging teams, but they've never been a threat to us, weak and disorganized and downtrodden as they are.

I leave them without speaking and head back to the street where the giant shadow of the dragon passes overhead. It's several minutes before he sets down again with another earth trembling thud of his bulk. Shad shifts back to human, brushes off the sleeves of his jacket, and approaches me.

"Do you know what that was?" I ask.

He shakes his head. "Some kind of weapon I'm not familiar with." He sounds sincere. My daimon cannot detect any increase in breathing or heart rate that would indicate a lie.

"I've never seen anything like it, either," I add.

Wings sound overhead, and I step back, alarmed, as a giant golden eagle, bigger than I've ever seen, settles on the ground before us. He shifts in a fluid motion into the lean, dark-brown-skinned man with his shoulder-length hair pulled back in a ponytail. The one who was with Shad the night before the summit.

"Harsh, what do you know?" Shad asks.

"There were two figures in black retreating from a rooftop two streets over, carrying some kind of launcher. But the interior of the structure is a maze with many passages to nearby buildings. I couldn't track them."

"They were human?"

"They smelled of garbage, so that's the working theory."

We're all silent for a moment. For humans to attack the Nimali—it's unprecedented. Shad looks troubled and, moreover, weary. He wipes a hand down his face and takes a deep breath, like the weight of the world is on his shoulders. The expression causes a fissure in me I need to patch quickly. There's no point in feeling sorry for him because of the various enemies his people have acquired.

He's turning toward the four-legged soldiers gathering again in the center of the street when a cry of pain reaches my ears from another nearby building. I cock my head to the side, listening.

Harsh notices, though. "What is it?"

"Someone is hurt. Over there." I point to the shop I'd originally taken cover in. The entire front was already destroyed; the interior barely clings to its foundation. Even as we watch, another piece of the ceiling comes down.

Shad is back at my side, peering across at the space. "Can you tell how many people are inside?"

I tilt my head, sniffing and listening. Three heartbeats. One sluggish and slowing. "Three people, one young, and one possibly dying."

His expression hardens, becoming more focused and fiercer. "I'm going in."

I grab his arm to hold him back. "That building is about to come down."

He shakes me off. "So I'd better hurry. Harsh, find some

medical supplies." Then he's moving, crossing the street and disappearing into the darkness. Harsh looks as exasperated as I feel.

"Is he always this ridiculous?" I ask.

"When he believes innocents are in danger, he is."

That gives me pause. I'm bound to this man for the next month, and though my mission is to reveal and stop his treachery—or that of his people—I need him whole and hale in order for that to happen. What does the king of the Nimali care about mundane humans stuck in this pulverized pile of bricks? Starvation and disease take out most of them—neither shifter clan has ever concerned itself with them at all. But he went in with no protection, and I doubt his dragon will be of much use. I can't let a building fall on him, so I follow.

Once I'm properly inside, I have to stop myself from gagging. This space is even worse than the last structure. It smells fouler, and there's even more debris to get past in order to find the occupants. Low light comes from holes in the ceiling; a disturbing creaking sound indicates the walls are barely holding on. Shad struggles with a chunk of plaster blocking his way; I lift it easily and he nods in thanks before continuing.

In the back of the interior, we find an old man, a woman, and a small child. They are grimy and dust-covered, clones of the wretches I encountered across the street. Unfortunately, the old man is bleeding from his head, and a large section of ceiling has fallen on one of his legs. I close my eyes; death would be a mercy for these pathetic souls.

I move forward to lift the wood and plaster off him, but Shad stops me. "He may bleed out if you move it. We need a tourniquet first."

In the Greenlands, there are always Fire Fai around to deal with wounds and injuries, so I have little knowledge of mundane healing. But the prince seems confident. He looks around for something before finally taking off his own belt and wrapping it around the old man's thigh, pulling it tight.

The man shies away from him, and the woman stares at my glowing eyes in fear.

"We are not here to harm you," I say. The child, perhaps three, stares up at me with large green eyes. It's covered from head to toe in filth. I turn away from the intense stare to watch what Shad is doing.

"All right, let's move this now," he says, and I lift the wall. The man groans and passes out. It's just as well. What's revealed of his leg is a mess.

Footsteps sound in the outer room. I stand, suspicious. To my intense surprise, Ryin's face greets me. "We had scouts following you who saw the explosion. I led a detachment here to investigate."

"Everyone in the caravan was all right, I think," I say, grateful to him for being here.

"Yes," Shad confirms. "We had no casualties. But this human was injured; the blast destabilized the nearby structures even further."

None of the humans have said a word. The mother clutches her child tightly to her chest, but the little one keeps squirming around to get a look at us.

Ryin's brow is creased with worry. "This place is coming down at any moment." He approaches and kneels before the man, who is still unconscious. "I can heal him. Is that all right?" he asks the woman.

She just stares, dumbfounded, either too scared to speak or too stupid. Ryin looks to Shad, who nods. "Please. They don't deserve to be collateral damage."

I do a double take as Ryin's eyes begin to glow with his daimon and he gets to work fixing the damage. Outside, the low voices of Fai soldiers murmuring brings comfort. While Nimali speech is clipped and sharp, the tones of our clan are more melodic and slower, more evidence of our intrinsic differences.

In a few moments, the leg looks less like an animal that's

been picked over by carrion and more like a proper appendage. Then the building shudders.

An ominous crack sounds, and the shaking intensifies. I dive to cover the woman and child, hoping to carry them to safety, but it's too late. The ceiling groans, the walls twitch, and then the whole thing is falling down on our heads.

It's like being inside an explosion. Hard chunks pummel my back as destruction rains down. Dust clogs my throat and nostrils, and both the mother and child scream. It's too loud in my sensitive ears, but only my daimon can protect me from this devastation. The spirit makes me stronger and more able to withstand damage, but I'm not invincible—the constant barrage opens up wounds all over.

Just when I think it can't get any worse, the ground drops out from under us. We plummet in a free fall. My hold on the mother and child tightens, and I twist to take the brunt of the fall, only it takes much longer than I expect.

The Fai have a network of tunnels that run across the city, which we use for scavenging. As the fall continues unbroken, I wonder if we're heading into one of them. I'm not familiar with this sector, though, so while I don't think we have a presence here, I can't be sure. Finally, the ground meets my back in a crushing blow. The wind is knocked out of me because even though the humans I hold don't weigh much, they land right on top of me.

I can't move for long moments and don't even try. Eventually, the woman shifts, rolling off me. The child wiggles free, appearing perfectly fine, and I groan, body on fire.

A round, dirt-streaked face appears in my field of view. "Are you all right?" the woman whispers.

I'm not entirely sure. I don't think anything is broken, but nothing feels quite *un*broken, either. However, I'm able to sit up and mercifully find Ryin groggily righting himself just a few feet away. The old man moans and rolls to his side, and Ryin is there to heal him again from the trauma of the fall.

We're in a tunnel of some kind, with light coming only from the hole above our heads. Way up there, I can see the sky. The woman begins speaking to her child in another language, something lilting and musical. She pats the little one down, assessing, and appears to find nothing amiss.

The blue glow of Ryin's eyes moves closer, and then he's healing me, binding up the various nicks, cuts, and contusions. Soon, I feel as good as new.

"Where is Shad?" he asks, and I freeze. We both look around wildly. It's the old man who points at a pile of debris a few feet away.

Ryin and I race over. I tug a small vehicle's worth of building materials off Shad's motionless form. He's in rough shape, but before I can even see what's wrong, Ryin is healing him.

Soon, Shad's eyes blink open, their dark depths shooting straight to me. He sits up suddenly, gasping for breath.

"Take it easy," I tell him. The healing will likely leave him tired in a few minutes. The immediate burst of energy wanes quickly.

"Where are we?" he asks.

"In some kind of tunnel. I don't think this is one of ours," I say.

"No," Ryin agrees. "These haven't been maintained as well. I'm going to head back up there and get help."

He bounces on his toes a few times and then lifts into the air, flying under the power of the phoenix within him.

"Do you want to go with him?" I ask Shad.

"That opening is too small. I could go, but it would bring the rest of the building down on you. We'll just have to——"

His next words are stolen as he grunts and topples forward to reveal a masked figure behind him. A growl rips its way from my throat and I crouch, ready to pounce, when an icy sensation spreads over my neck and shoulders. Too late, I hear what the shifting and crunching of the debris still falling overhead had masked. Someone has come up behind us, hidden in the dark.

My daimon shrinks inside me, the below freezing temperature of whatever's on my skin making it go dormant. As the hood is placed over my head and my hands tied behind me, I scream and thrash, but can't break free.

TEN

Shad

ONE THOUSAND TINY dragons roar inside my skull. My skin is chilled, and the scent of stone and earth fills my nostrils. I come to consciousness painfully and work to steady my breathing before moving. What happened?

"Are you awake?" a low, feminine voice asks from behind me. Xipporah.

"Unfortunately." I reach for my head to quiet the rumbling chorus within only to discover my wrists are bound. My feet as well. I chance opening my eyes, and darkness greets me. Soft, golden light radiates from somewhere in the vicinity, but it's barely enough to see by. However, I twist until I can make out Xipporah, sitting hunched over.

"Where are we?"

"Some underground cooler they found." Her voice is pure animosity.

"Who?"

"Isn't that the question of the hour?"

My eyes adjust quickly. She's positioned oddly, arms tied behind her at the wrists, and the ceiling here is so low that even seated, Xipporah must keep her head ducked. I shouldn't even try to sit up.

"A group wearing masks took us just after Ryin left to get help. They knew to use cold to mute our daimons. They blind-folded me, and we walked here. I think we're about a half mile from where we started."

"Did they drag me the entire way?" I say, testing my bonds while trying to stretch out the kinks and get rid of the aches and pains wracking me.

"I heard them say something about a pallet. They must have put you on it after they knocked you out. Apparently, you're even heavier than you look." She sniffs.

"Did they say what they want?"

She shakes her head. "Not yet. Just threw us in here and left."

"There's water, though." She nods toward a misshapen bowl a few feet away. "I haven't tried it. Though if they'd wanted to poison us, they probably wouldn't have gone through the trouble of bringing us wherever we are. Not exactly sure how we got in here—I don't see any doors."

The floor and two of the walls are dirt. The other two walls appear to be rough-hewn rock, but that doesn't explain where the light is coming from. Shadows abound, dancing with a tremulous flicker; anything could hide in them.

"It's not quite freezing down here," I say. My daimon is alert, the chilly temperature not enough to keep it suppressed.

"You could probably shift if you wanted to, but I'm not sure there's enough room. And they put this thing on me." She shrugs, bringing my attention to the short, shawl-like garment draped across her shoulders and tied around her neck. It's thick and oddly shaped, but old—some sort of pre-Sorrows contraption. "This thing is freezing."

"I can probably get it off of you if you lean down and—" I grunt, rolling to my side and trying to sit up, but I need to bend my body almost in half because of the tiny amount of vertical space.

"We would prefer if you didn't," a new voice says. I twist

in that direction to find a masked figure poking their head around what I now see is a break in the stone. The low light and distance made it seem like an uninterrupted wall, but it's a cleverly disguised opening.

Dark fabric obscures all but the newcomer's eyes, peering out of a light-complexioned face.

"Who are you?" Xipporah asks.

"I'm called Zero." The figure steps fully into the opening, where the ceiling is significantly higher, revealing a lithe man, on the shorter side, dressed all in black.

"I take it you know who I am?" I ask.

The fellow sketches a bow. "King Shad. I admit, I'm honored to be in your presence."

"Wish I could say the same."

He chuckles, leaning against the wall casually, crossing his ankles.

"All right, Zero," I say evenly. "What will it take for me and my companion here to leave this place?"

"You're free to go whenever you want."

I hold up my bound wrists, which belie that statement.

He straightens, the insouciance from a moment ago gone in an instant. "I apologize for the theatrics, but we needed to get your attention without you dragoning out on us, or you"—he turns to Xipporah—"doing whatever it is you do." He holds his hands up. "We just want to talk."

"Then knocking us out and tying us up may not have been the best way to communicate that," Xipporah says through gritted teeth.

Zero places a hand on his chest. "Personally, I agree, but I lost the vote, and the decision was out of my hands."

"You're not the leader of your group?" I ask.

"There are no leaders. We're a collective. I'm just the spokesperson, as it were."

Xipporah snorts in disbelief. "Care to remove the bonds so we can have our chat?"

Zero blinks at her, then turns to me. "We try to stay abreast of the goings-on in the city and got word of the attack against you just before it began."

"You expect us to believe you weren't the ones who attacked us?" Xipporah spits.

"Assuming the attacker wanted one or both of you dead, then yes. After all, you're still very much alive."

"Yes, unless the attack was a way to stop the caravan, draw us out, and then capture us," she says, leaning forward.

He shrugs. "You'll believe what you want, of course. Fai are stubborn that way." He shifts his attention back to me. "As I was saying, my...*faction*, I suppose you could say, of those who live in the Free Zone, is peaceful."

I give up on trying to sit up and lie back down on my side, though, of course, it's not very regal. Then again, neither was sitting bent in half. "So, there are multiple factions of humans?" I ask, reading between the lines.

"Of course."

"And you know who bombed the caravan, what kind of tech they were using? There haven't been any functioning incendiary devices like that since just after the Sorrows."

Zero crosses his arms, leaning back once again. "What we are proposing is an exchange of information for supplies. You have food, clothing, other things we need. We have information, and a network of observant parties across the Free Zone who are always gathering more."

"Spies, you mean," Xipporah says, still suspicious.

He spreads his arms apart. "Call them what you must."

"And you believe this information is worth bartering with?" I hate having to look up at him from this position, but I wonder if that was by design.

"It's valuable to you, isn't it? To know who your enemies are?" He looks pointedly at Xipporah, and the already cool temperature seems to drop a few degrees.

"Wouldn't that get you in trouble with these attackers?"

I ask.

"They're no friends of ours. I suppose you imagine that we in the Free Zone are just as aligned as your clans are, but there are constant battles between various groups for territory and supplies. Always have been. Gangs emerge for a while, cause trouble, then disperse again regularly."

"And does your gang have a name?"

"The Silent Hands." He raises his hands and waves them around. Xipporah snorts in disdain, but his action tickles a memory within me. Something just out of reach.

"We also want to negotiate with you so you don't come back and raze this sector to the ground. There are families living here. Children. Schools." He is serious once again.

The three miserable mundane humans I was trying to help before the collapse come to mind. It would stand to reason that they would have some version of a society, just like we do.

"Is all of this underground?" Xipporah asks, with less venom in her tone than before.

"I'm not able to tell you any more than that. Not until we have an agreement in place. Just know that *we* have no beef with either the manimals or the spooky glow-eyes."

This time I snort. "All right. Message received. I will consider your offer. And you can prove your goodwill by releasing us." I hold up my hands.

"If I have your word you won't attack me. You will need me to get out of here, after all. The tunnels are a maze."

I look at Xipporah, raising my brows. She rolls her eyes. "Fine," she says. "I won't attack you and deliver the retribution you deserve for the way you captured us. Not right now, at least."

Zero barks out a laugh. "Not today at all. Retribution is always best served tomorrow."

"Fine, tomorrow." Xipporah grins viciously, and Zero laughs some more. Then he whips out a pocketknife and flips it in his hands.

He frog walks over because of the low ceiling and cuts through the string tying the cold shawl on Xipporah, then through her ropes. She leashes her daimon immediately, her glowing eyes lighting up the space. Displaying either trust or foolhardiness, he turns his back on her to release me.

"The Silent Hands seek an alliance with the Nimali," she says as he saws through my ropes. "What about the Fai?"

"We aim to be neutral. If we had information we thought you'd value, we would find a way to contact you as well. Honestly, we don't care if you beasts destroy each other. It would leave more for the rest of us. We just don't want you destroying us in the process. Too many of your battles wipe out infrastructure of ours, which takes quite a lot of time, effort, and resources to rebuild."

Guilt sweeps through me—he's right. The Nimali don't consider the fate of the mundane humans, and I'm fairly certain the Fai don't, either. How much collateral damage have we caused them, those who have no technology, no magic, no power of any kind? It's something I'll need to contemplate moving forward.

"How many of you are there?" I ask.

"Silent Hands or humans in general?"

"Your faction."

His eyes crinkle with what must be a grin. "Not allies yet," he says, wagging a finger. "Now come on, I'll show you the way out."

We follow him in silence, crawling to the entrance, where we're finally able to stand up. Though at my height, the ceiling brushes my head, so I still have to hunch. The tunnels he leads us through are narrow and short and often half-blocked with old debris. He's quite nimble and hops over obstacles. Xipporah does as well with the aid of her daimon, which I'm beginning to suspect is some kind of large cat. I'm not nearly as light on my feet and struggle, getting the feeling that I'm slowing them down.

He was right about the fact that these tunnels are labyrinthine; however, I suspect he's purposefully leading us in a circuitous route to disorient us. Finally, we enter a wide-open space where multiple tunnels converge. This looks more like it was built by humans and had some purpose before the Sorrows.

"A subway junction," Xipporah announces, though there are no longer any rails beneath our feet. The metal has long since been scavenged, leaving the old concrete pockmarked with holes.

"The third tunnel from the left will connect you to the Fai throughways," Zero points out. "You should be able to make your way wherever you need to go from there."

I turn to Xipporah, who appears confident.

"Well, thank you for the hospitality, Zero," I say drily. His eyes crinkle with mirth. Here, where the light is brighter, I see they're an unusual hazel blend. Once again, something tickles my memory, stronger but still dancing away from my grasp.

"Anytime," he replies with a bow.

"How about never?" Xipporah mutters.

"How will I contact you?" I ask before he turns away.

He fishes a small pouch from his pocket and tosses it to me. "Throw this onto a fire at one of your territory checkpoints. It will make the flames burn green. We'll send a messenger to your soldiers."

I nod. Then with a whirl of energy and movement, he's gone again, leaving us in this cavernous space.

"You're sure you know how to get back?"

Xipporah points at a bit of graffiti scrawled on the wall. "That marking is one of ours. I can read the signs. We're in the south of the city, but it should just be a few hours' walk back to your territory."

Needing to trust her, and hoping that the engysis contract is enough to do so, I follow. She keeps her daimon called, and as we enter the tunnel she indicated, it's the only light source.

"Will you be leading a mission to find them and punish them?" she asks.

Surprise makes me almost trip. "Who, the Silent Hands? Why would I do that?"

She stops suddenly to face me. "Because they kidnapped the Nimali king."

"So they could talk."

She spreads her arms. "There are a thousand ways that they could have talked to you."

"Are there? Really? Do you think they could have just walked up to the Citadel and knocked on the door? I understand why they did what they did."

Her expression is incredulous. "So you're not going to retaliate?" She looks like I've said the sky is green and made of cheese.

"What good would that do?"

Her eyes narrow. "You're not really this naïve or stupid, are you? I thought it was my superior skill that let me get the best of you, King Shadrach, but now I'm wondering seriously about your intellect."

She turns around and continues walking.

"It's just Shad."

"What?"

"Call me Shad. Please. No one but the old king called me Shadrach, not even my mother." The chill that my own name sends down my spine is ridiculous, but it's still there, mostly from the venomous way Lyall always said it.

"Whatever," is her only response.

"There's nothing wrong with a bit of mercy," I say as we walk on in the blue-tinged darkness.

"Since when has a Nimali known the meaning of the word mercy?"

I let the silence cover us for a while before I answer.

"Since me."

ELEVEN

Xipporah

"WHAT'S WRONG, are you in pain?" Shad asks.

"No, why?"

"Your shoulders are in line with your ears, and your entire body has tensed up."

I'm feeling defensive, not sure I like that he's noticed these things about me. The exhaustion from earlier has doubled, maybe tripled. Once we emerged from the tunnels, I released my daimon; the strain of having it called for so long, as well as the emotional upheavals and physical exertions of the day, have left me bone weary.

Also, we've nearly arrived at the edge of Nimali territory.

I take a deep breath and will my shoulders to relax. Fill my lungs over and over again to slow my rapidly beating heart. "I'm fine." Though that may be more believable if I hadn't spoken through clenched teeth. "I just had no desire to ever see that place again." I nod in the direction of the spire rising in the distance. While the place doesn't haunt my nightmares like it does for my sister, it still makes my skin crawl. Living there for a month… everything tenses again, and I work to hide the signs of stress.

A good soldier doesn't let the enemy see her weaknesses.

Shad flattens his lips, looking thoughtful. I do a double take. The motion is very close to a pout and his lips are… I give myself a mental shake and then a mental slap. This is not a real betrothal. It won't be a real marriage, and Shad's lips will never be any of my business.

"No one will harm you there," he says. "I know you are perfectly capable of taking care of yourself, but you're also under my protection. That means something to my people."

Actual physical danger from the Nimali is not the highest of my concerns—at least not danger to me directly. The Greenlands, however… Makani's words echo in my head.

"Are you so sure you know what your people do behind your back?"

He whips his head to face me. "What do you mean?"

"Simply that the Nimali are treacherous by nature. Do you really think your rule goes unopposed? That you can know what's in the hearts of all of your subjects?"

The haunted look in his eye makes me feel almost bad for testing him like this; however, I suspect an inconvenient strain of naïveté exists within this kindhearted man. That thought almost makes me trip over my own feet. The word *kindhearted* has no business being associated with a Nimali. Fortunately, Shad doesn't notice my near stumble, caught up as he is in his own thoughts.

Too soon we're at the Nimali checkpoint marking their border. It's at the edge of a line of demarcation between buildings damaged or destroyed in the Sorrows and those that have been reclaimed by the beasts.

Two guards stand at a movable barrier blocking the street. However, I sense others watching me from nearby buildings, nondescript stucco structures with no visible damage. The Fai have mapped out each of these stations. Back home, someone in the Defense Division knows how many troops are stationed here, what their rotation schedule is, and probably what they all eat for lunch.

When the guards catch sight of their king, they salute, four fingers pressed to their chins. The stiff postures and the inscrutable expressions are so abhorrent to me that it takes extreme effort for me not to twist my face in disgust. Which of these soldiers captured my people, killed us in battle? Attacked us to steal our precious resources? Now, I must live among them for what Citlali hopes will be peace and Makani is expecting to be destruction. I manage to remain impassive, just barely, as we're ushered past the barrier, and suddenly, there are a dozen beasts circling us, both shifted and unshifted.

Most assume their human forms and shout greetings to Shad, along with declarations of gratitude that he's safe and unharmed. They circle him like he's a celebrity, and at one point, I'm certain I'm about to be pushed several streets away, just so they can reach him for what appear to be very undignified pats on the back and handshaking. If the initial salutes of the soldiers were repulsive to me, this familiarity isn't much better. His subordinates certainly feel comfortable around him.

Though no one comes out and asks any pointed questions about where he's been, Shad repeats the same talking points: We were caught in the collapse of the building and had to hunt our way through the underground tunnels until we found a way out. No, we don't know who attacked our caravan yet, but we will soon.

I don't see how gainsaying him would help me at all, so I stay quiet. I'm practically invisible, anyway.

A vehicle arrives from down the street, and I almost fall to my knees in gratitude when it becomes clear it's for us. I'm nearly dead on my feet, and though the bliss-powered machine is shameful, I will just have to make several offerings the next time I'm at the temple to make up for it, since not having to walk the rest of the way feels like a dream come true.

All too soon, we're pulling up to the round drive in front

of the cement stone pillars in the entryway of the Citadel, the Nimali stronghold and center of power. Only when we come to a stop do I notice the seven people in nearly identical shades of the darkest red imaginable waiting for us at the entrance. They stand in a semicircle with expressions etched from stone.

Shad alights the vehicle first, and they all bow as one. The creepiness of the action makes my skin crawl. When he comes around to open my door and give me an arm out that I certainly don't need, some of the granite making up their faces cracks with surprise. That almost makes me smile. I suppose they think he should treat his new Fai fiancée as an enemy combatant? Keep me in chains and force me to eat off the floor?

Three of them I recognize from the ceremony—was it only this morning? This must be his Council. The faces arrayed are hardened as if for battle. Cold as the blasting winds that blow during the Month of Sacrifice.

The bald, dark-skinned man is the first to speak up. "We are gratified to see you back safely, Your Majesty. We were informed of the attack and feared the worst."

For the first time all day, and in the days since I first officially met the man I'm engaged to, he is nothing but ice. "Sir Barrett, I must say I am glad to be back." Shad's tone is clipped, his expression pinched. Pained, even. "And we will discover the parties responsible for the bombing. They will face the full wrath of the Nimali."

When Shad tries to get past this human barricade, Sir Barrett speaks up again. "I must ask, Your Majesty, if I may. When you were trapped underground in the building collapse, why did you not shift and use your great daimon strength to free yourself and your…er, prospective bride?"

Already a head or more taller than everyone present, Shad straightens even further. "I am certainly grateful that the burden of a dragon daimon did not pass to you, Sir Barrett," he says with a sudden, cutting smile. "I imagine it wouldn't occur to you that shifting in a small, underground space with other people nearby would cause even more destruction and not less. That I would have crushed everyone around me, including my new fiancée, and I'm not certain the Fai would take kindly to that."

The odious council member's attention now turns to me, the aforementioned fiancée, with a look that wouldn't be out of place if I had somehow managed to cover myself in raw excrement.

"I see," he says coolly. "So we have this unusual situation to thank for today's disappearance."

"No, you have the Sorrows to thank," I retort, quite tired of Nimali political jockeying or whatever is going on here. This earns me additional scrutiny from the rest of the Council watching this little exchange in silence. I notch my chin up and stare them down, unrepentant.

"I'm sure you all had things well in hand during my brief absence," Shad says magnanimously. "Though perhaps it was not as brief as some of you would like."

Several councilors make sounds of protest and denial. But Sir Barrett doesn't move a muscle.

"Now, if you will be so kind, we have had quite the day and would like to retire and freshen up."

"We have been informed that there will be no celebration tonight of the betrothal," Sir Barrett says when Shad tries to move past him. "That is unprecedented."

"As is the Nimali king becoming engaged to a Fai. It is too early for a celebration, as we are still in the period of engysis." His tone is even, but I see strain around his eyes. "As I've said before, the frequency and extravagance of our *celebrations* is something I am looking to curtail."

"But the people expect certain rituals," a dark-haired man says.

"And they need to be informed of their king's plans for marriage," an elderly man adds.

"They will be," Shad pronounces through clenched teeth. "Tonight, in fact. I have planned to announce my betrothal to all Nimali via vid recording."

And with that, he pushes his way past the group. I follow at his heels, internally gleeful to be away from them. Vultures and leeches all of them, I can tell, even if their daimons are less reviled animals. They are exactly the sort of beasts we've always known them to be. The kind who wouldn't blink at destroying my homeland and all of my people.

More soldiers salute in the small lobby of the building. Shad acknowledges them but marches past to the elevator bank. We are alone for the ride up into the heights of this towering structure, taller than any tree in the Greenlands.

"Your Council is full of teddy bears, I see."

"More like a fox, hawk, scorpion, lion, shark, crow, and moose," he says with a sigh, leaning back against the wall.

"Moose?" I match his pose, thinking back to a battle I had two years back with a moose daimon—a mean bugger. I refrain from asking if this councilor was a soldier. Most of them are too old to have battled recently, even if some are former military. "They preferred your predecessor, I take it?"

He wipes a hand down his face, looking as weary as I feel. "My predecessor scared them out of their minds and threatened their families and loved ones constantly. But they are used to that. My leadership style chafes."

"Because you are not threatening to eat their babies?" I guess.

That earns a small smile from him. Then the doors open and we're in a dimly lit corridor. Shad steps out first, and blue lights flicker to life overhead, revealing a waiting figure. My daimon is upon me before I can consciously call it—the product of years of training—but Shad actually relaxes when he sees who it is: the golden eagle shifter, Harsh.

"I've called back all the search parties," he says in a monotone. "And sent word to the Fai that Lady Xipporah has been located and is healthy."

Lady? The Nimali are so obsessed with titles. I nearly tell him not to call me that, but what's the point? It's only thirty days.

"Thank you, Harsh. We have much to discuss. First, let me get her settled."

This floor has only two doors that I can see. Shad stops before the one nearest the elevator. "These will be your chambers during your stay. I'm right over there." He points down the hall. "Give me your palm."

I hold up my hand; he takes my wrist gently with thick fingers, presses it against an indentation in the wall, then makes a series of gestures on the panel. Their biometric security system scans me with a soft blue glow, and the door snicks open. "You have access now via your handprint."

I shiver before he lets me go. "Cold?" he asks.

"No. Just thinking how much bliss has been wasted just so you all don't have to use doorknobs."

His lips purse again, catching my attention. "I understand the Fai feel differently about the bliss—"

"Differently?" I thank the tors for the distraction. "Sure, if wanting to preserve the link between the spirit world and the material one, and not destroy it completely is *different*. I'll take that."

"Regardless, at the moment, this is the only way to access your rooms from this hallway. There is another entrance, the one which servants use, via the stairwells in the back."

"I'm familiar, if you'll recall."

His expression grows pinched. "Someone will have been assigned to your suite, and a guard will be posted outside your door at all times. Just let them know if you need anything. I can record the announcement alone tonight if you're too tired."

That suggestion stinks of weakness; I throw my shoulders back. "No need. I'm up for whatever you Nimali have to throw at me."

Behind Shad, Harsh stiffens, his brow furrowing. Shad peers at me, thoughtfully. "All right. I will meet you here in two hours, then."

He bows at me with an efficient, military-style motion, and then he and his guard are hustling down the hall and disappearing into his suite. The elevator dings behind me, revealing two soldiers who take positions on either side of my door. They acknowledge me with a short nod, but that's all—otherwise, it's like I don't exist.

Their presence may make my mission a little more difficult, but I doubt it's an impediment I can't get around. As I enter the suite of rooms I'll be calling home for the next four weeks, I repeat my mission in my head: Find the poison, turn it against the enemy before they can use it on us.

I have thirty days. After that, I will be able to return home in peace and never think about this place or any of these people again.

TWELVE

Shad

———————

ONCE HARSH and I are in my suite, he starts to speak, but I grab one of the dampeners from my shelf. "Not here," I tell him.

When his brows raise, I motion up toward the ceiling. He understands and leads the way through the servant's room, empty since I gave them the day off, and out to the stairwell.

The throne room is six flights up, on the uppermost floor of this pyramid-shaped tower. It's empty, as it should be, and Harsh heads straight for the controls of the retractable wall that allows flying daimons easy access.

"Akeem?" he guesses. I nod in response. Then, with a burst of light, the golden eagle explodes from him. With a few flaps of his wings, he disappears into the night.

Lyall had this place adjusted to fit his specifications, but my dragon is bigger than his, so it's a tight fit. Shifting inside of any building is usually impossible for me, but with the fortified floors and adjustable space, it's workable in here so long as I'm alone.

I don't have enough room to move my wings, though, so I must take the leap of faith. Jumping off the edge of the building and plummeting for a moment before stretching out my wings and catching the air is an unpleasant sensation, as I haven't taken off from here often enough for it to have become comfortable. But I manage and fly a circle around the Citadel's spire before heading for my destination.

The library is just across the plaza, less than one hundred yards away, but I don't want my visit to be common knowledge. Anyone on air patrol might catch a glimpse of me, but far more would see me if I walked through the Citadel lobby and out the front door. As much as I'd like to believe there's no need for this subterfuge, someone tried to kill me today. And there are others in the tower who want to take my position.

Aside from the Citadel, the library building was the one we altered the most after the Sorrows. We needed a fortified base of operations—a fortress to house our royals, our aristocrats, and our military forces—but we also needed a place to store our knowledge. I don't know what the humans used the large, modern, and oddly shaped metallic silver building for, but it was perfect for our archive.

I circle the library's roof until a large portion retracts, then I descend into its depths. The interior is dark and massive and completely empty at first glance. But the data stored here is precious to us and represents the work of countless scholars over generations, both before and after the Sorrows. Lifetimes of knowledge have been collected, the data stored in the liquid bliss tanks lying just beneath the flooring of the main level.

And the librarian himself, Akeem, the one with the most detailed knowledge of every nook and cranny of the archive, stands waiting for me. In his elephant form, he is just over nine feet tall and has the distinction of being the only Nimali who can speak while shifted—a product of a rather unusual covenant with his daimon. Harsh waits next to him, grim and impatient.

I shift back to human form so we can speak, but I engage the dampener first.

"Your Majesty," Akeem intones, voice deep and rumbly and remarkably clear considering elephant physiology.

"Akeem. Sorry to drop in unannounced, but I don't have much time. There's urgent research I need for you to do." His dark eyes flash with deep intelligence as he listens.

I run down everything that happened today: the attack, the cave-in, Zero with his warning about the multiple factions at play in the Independent Zone. Xipporah's push for revenge. When I'm done, Harsh is still processing. He stares straight ahead for long moments. I've seen this enough to know not to disturb him. Akeem's expression is harder to parse, but he stays quiet, thoughtful.

"Are you going to tell the Council?" Harsh finally asks.

"Not until I decide what to do. Akeem, I need any information we have about mundane human technological capabilities. We had spies monitoring the Independent Zone until Lyall pulled them back a year or so ago. See if there was any indication the humans were advanced enough to be able to create this kind of device."

He hums in a deep rumble. "What makes you think it was advanced? Many simple materials can be combined to create rudimentary bombs."

"You're right, but this one was so precisely aimed, it didn't feel rudimentary to me."

Harsh speaks up. "While you were missing, I sent out the canines. The accelerant used today was not something humans could have whipped up in some underground tunnel laboratory. It was sophisticated. More than I'd ever think mundane humans could do on their own."

Chills race through me. "So you think it was ours?"

"Didn't say that. But it's highly unlikely that a group who can barely find enough water to survive on much less wash themselves has come up with an advanced explosive device. Could be the Fai." He shrugs.

"You think they'd risk killing the daughter of their own

Crown? Xipporah was in the car with me—she could easily have been a casualty."

"They are savage, vicious creatures. I wouldn't put anything past them, including murdering one of their own just to get to you."

"And where would that leave them?" I ask, exasperated. "They believed their water priestess that mutually assured destruction is upon us. No Nimali king who would replace me would be willing to deal with them. You think they'd rather take their chances with Barrett or Linh or bliss knows who else if I'm gone?"

Harsh is unflinching. "They don't know our inner workings. They only know they hate us. I highly doubt they'd be thinking that far in the future. Perhaps one of these factions is actually working with the Fai. What did Xipporah say when you were captured? Was there any sign of familiarity?"

I think back, but it's a blur. What comes through clearly is the recollection of anger pouring off her in waves. "Xipporah was a simmering pot of rage. I truly don't believe she was in on this, and I don't believe that weapon belonged to the Fai."

He crosses his arms. "You want to see the best in everyone, but most of us are never at our best."

"Are you including yourself?"

He snorts in response.

"So the Fai are either brutal savages or sophisticated tacticians. Which one is it?"

"Your good judgment is the only thing holding back chaos at our gates, Shad," he says quietly. My shoulders sag. He doesn't need to tell me this, but keeps going anyway. "There are many of us depending on you to succeed. We need a better clan than the one we were born into. Only you can give us this."

This weight has been on my shoulders since I was eighteen years old and my world changed forever. "Well, I'll only survive to change things if I have allies, and those are becoming fewer and further between. Many of those who supported my plans against Lyall have been suspiciously quiet now that I'm king."

"They're waiting to see how the Council shakes out. You agreeing to marry a Fai won't help things," he says.

"It won't get that far—you know that's absurd. But I think it may be worth it to see what these Silent Hands fellows have to say."

"You can't be serious."

"Why not?"

My friend's mask breaks, with true anger showing through. "I can't believe I have to say this, but I agree with the Fai woman. What we should do is assign some troops to scour the tunnels and find the bastards who took you. Hold them accountable for daring to kidnap our king."

"And what of the information they provided? What of the factions at play?"

"Who's to say they were telling the truth? If a human group *did* build the bomb, these Silent Hands are the most likely suspects."

"Not necessarily. Plus, trying to enact vengeance is too much like what Lyall would do for my taste."

"He wasn't always wrong."

When I gaze at him in shock, he holds his hands up. "All I'm saying is a broken clock is right twice a day."

I look at him questioningly.

"My grandpa used to say that. Something about the way they told time pre-Sorrows. The point is, Lyall's way was not always the wrong one."

Take down your enemies with no mercy, that his philosophy. But I'm not certain the Silent Hands are my enemy. And if I go hard against a potential friend, one with valuable intel, is that good leadership?

Akeem finally breaks his silence. "King Shad, whether you model yourself on Lyall, or Lyon before him, or walk in the entirely opposite direction, you must be decisive. Choose a course of action and stick to it, then reevaluate once you have some data. Information is power."

That's just it, I'm not certain what the right path is. Leadership is difficult, that much is certain, and I was not meant for it. Like everyone else, I question why the dragon chose me just about every day. But it did and like Harsh said, it's only me holding back the chaos.

My old friends' faces come to mind, Lynara and Sylph. The sound of their laughter. The freedom we felt when we made our plans to escape. Those memories ground me. They help me to withstand reliving what happened after. The heart-wrenching pain of the holes they left in my life when they were gone. The tattoos on my back keep them close to my skin —a feather for Lynara because she hoped to leash a bird daimon and fly away one day, and a shooting star for Sylph. Because he always teased me for being a dreamer.

I've stayed here because I dreamed the Nimali could be better. I've stayed to make my father's sacrifice mean something. To honor my mother's loss. To improve things for everyone back home, everyone that Lyall harmed.

I take a deep breath. "So you both think I should find the Silent Hands?"

Harsh nods emphatically, and Akeem swings his trunk. "I am not qualified to advise you, Your Majesty," the librarian says, "but gaining information on your allies is just as vital as doing so for your enemies."

"We should at least look into them before agreeing to anything," Harsh adds. "See if we can verify what they've told you."

I release all the breath in my lungs. "I'm not eager to send our troops into the tunnels. We don't know our way around down there like the Fai and humans evidently do."

"We don't have to use soldiers." Harsh looks at me significantly.

While we were planning the coup, the idea to use Umbers as spies had come up several times. While their daimons are often considered useless in a Nimali culture that values battle readiness, snakes, rats, moles and the like are perfect for certain kinds of assignments. I had personally recruited people loyal to me and begun training them, but that work fell off once Lyall died and my time became scarcer.

"Do you think they're ready?" I ask.

"Now is the time to find out."

"Fine. Ask for volunteers to search the tunnels. I don't know what they'll find, and I don't have much guidance to give them—the place is a maze—but see if they can locate the person they call Zero or any evidence of the Silent Hands. And then we'll see. They aren't to engage anyone, just observe and report."

Harsh salutes. "I'll get it done."

"And I will search our records on the humans," Akeem adds. "Just keep in mind, any information we have will be over a year old."

"Well, if the humans did create the weapon, it would have taken them some time. I don't imagine it could happen in a few days, especially since in the decades since the Sorrows, we haven't seen them use anything of this magnitude."

The librarian nods.

"There's something else. If these Silent Hands really are on the up and up, we need to consider their demands," Harsh says. "Food and supplies—I'm not certain we have any to spare. How many people are in his faction?"

"He wouldn't say until we agreed to the alliance."

"Well, another bliss reservoir has taken a hit. I got a report this afternoon that sector six is running thirty percent lower than this time last week."

My gut clenches. "You can't be serious. This has to be sabotage."

He looks grim. "The rolling brownouts will need to

continue indefinitely. And the cold months are coming. They won't be pleasant to endure without heat, but we'll need to divert everything we have to the food labs and produce houses."

I start to pace in tight circles. "Well, the Umbers will not have to face it alone. Brownouts will have to be implemented for Azures and Cardinals as well—regardless of their protests. There's just no way around it."

"If the sabotage extends to the food facilities, and we don't have enough bliss to power them, then I don't know how we'll make it until next year. We're three to four months away from a massive famine."

Harsh's words echo in my skull. I wish the library had a place to sit down. My head swims for a moment, but thankfully, I stay steady on my feet. "How is this happening so quickly and with no evidence of treachery?"

"I do not know, but we have guards watching all the power stations."

"Guards at each station and produce house, at the wall, the borders, plus the extra protection demanded by the Council." I tick each one off on my fingers. "Our forces are stretched too thin."

"Yes, they are," Harsh agrees.

About as thin as I feel.

How did Lyall keep all of this running? And is the fact that it's falling apart so quickly under my rule more proof that I'm ill-suited to be king?

The past weeks have been like juggling a handful of live grenades, and each day another gets thrown into the mix. One misstep and it all goes up in flames.

Taking everyone I care about with it.

THIRTEEN

Xipporah

THE SUITE I've been assigned is spacious, as large as our entire aerie back home. There are a variety of salvaged furniture pieces, all in good repair, scattered around the space. Everything is clean, but I can tell no one has lived here in some time. An emptiness clings to the corners, a soullessness even more pronounced than in other places in this building.

The door nestled in the wall behind the dining area opens and a pale woman with a halo of frizzy, black curls rushes out. She's not old, probably only in her late twenties, but she has a rundown quality to her that reminds me of the human woman in the Independent Zone.

She curtsies, then looks up at me with wide, green eyes. "Lady Xipporah, I apologize for not greeting you directly. I'm Aggi. I'll be taking care of whatever you need while you're here."

"Hello, Aggi. Who did you piss off to get assigned to the Fai?" I say, trying to make light of what must be an awkward situation.

But she doesn't smile. Her eyes only grow wider, if possible. "Oh no, my lady, it's an honor to serve King Shad's betrothed."

Poor Aggi seems one scare away from full apoplexy, so I simply nod. "Well, I appreciate it." I turn to take in the surroundings and spot a hallway off to the side that must lead to the bedroom. There is probably time for a short nap before this evening's announcement. My stomach rumbles, alerting me to the fact that I haven't eaten in longer than I can remember.

"Oh, let me get you something to eat!" Aggi says, appalled.

A pained cry rises from the servant's room behind her. I tilt my head. "What's that?" It sounds like someone in distress.

Aggi holds up her hands in a panic. "Oh, no, it's nothing. Nothing for you to worry about, my lady. I'll handle it."

"Mooooommy." A child's yell.

Her face turns an uncomfortable-looking shade of purple. "Please wait here," she says, then races through the door.

I push through behind her into the narrow area meant both for staging meals sent up from the kitchens and for servants to catch a few winks of rest during overnight shifts. Noomi was stuck in a place like this for years serving the Nimali princess. Aggi hovers over the cot, which bears a small boy rolling around in pain. His skin is warm brown, but when his eyes flash open, they match the mossy green of his mother's.

"It's all right baby, I'm here. You're okay," Aggi coos, patting his unruly coiled hair.

"It hurts, Mommy," the boy mewls.

"Shh, now. Just relax. That's it. Have some medicine." She pulls a small vial from her pocket and uncorks it to pour a few drops down the boy's throat. I call my daimon forward and sniff, using its enhanced senses to identify the liquid. An herbal blend hits my nose including ginger, chamomile, and valerian. There's also a few notes I can't identify.

The boy quiets almost immediately after drinking, the tension in his body melting away.

"Your son is ill?" I ask quietly.

Her back is to me; she pauses before answering. "Yes. There's something going around. He's too sick for school, and I have no one to watch him, so I had to bring him with me. I know it's not right to have him here while I work, but...I had no other option." Her anguish is palpable, and when she turns to face me, tears fill her eyes.

"It's perfectly fine. You cannot abandon your child. I understand."

She stares, incredulous, like she doesn't believe me. I'm not quite sure what she expected. "Th-thank you, my lady."

I release my daimon, knowing it's likely to frighten her more, and I do feel a pang of sorrow for this woman. "Why aren't you allowed to bring your child to work, especially when they're sick?"

She shudders. "Cardinals are very particular about how their servants behave. They were used to the drudges..." She trails off and looks down, but I understand.

Once the Fai prisoners of war escaped, who was left to do all of that work? The cooking and cleaning, the laundry, serving, and maintenance tasks. It must have been tasked to the lowest caste of the Nimali to pick up the slack. And the upper classes had been used to meek slaves threatened with unimaginable harm if they stepped out of line. Umbers were still Nimali, but their whole culture is so vile, it must be easy for them to treat their own like trash.

This is no business of mine, but the sick child, now sleeping calmly, tugs at my heart. Both he and this woman are innocents. They do not deserve my ire.

I clear my throat. "I was a Fai drudge." She looks up sharply. "Only for a very few days there at the end, but I'm certainly no Cardinal. Where I come from, mothers have a whole community to rely on when they need help with their young ones. But even with assistance, no one would bat an eyelash if a parent had to bring a sick child with them to their duty stations rather than leave them alone."

The boy stirs in his sleep and sticks his thumb in his mouth.

"What's his name?"

"Kit. He's four."

"And his father?"

She grips her hands together, squeezing tight. "Revokers killed him last year while he was on patrol."

I drop my head. "May he be at peace in the Origin."

Nimali waste extends far beyond the bliss—they treat their own lives as expendable. The Fai don't venture into No Man's Land the way the beasts do, though we must maintain our section of the wall to keep the monsters out. But until the Revokers being kept in this building for experimentation escaped and we fought them off while fleeing ourselves, I hadn't even seen a live Revoker before. They are invoked during bedtime stories as a way to keep children in line. *Mind your parents or a Revoker will get you.*

Speaking of her husband has seemed to drain Aggi even further. I wonder what type of creature rests within her. Here the lower castes have animals that are considered weak. Among the Fai, even rabbit and gopher shifters, humming-birds and goldfish, have value and intrinsic purpose. Their talents are needed. Though they may not be as useful in battle as predators, they are not esteemed any less. Here, things are very different. Yet another reason I am eager for this month to be up so I can return to my home.

"Your child must always be your priority, Aggi. Anyone who tells you different is a villain, never forget."

She wipes her tears and stands. "Thank you, my lady. I'll go and fetch something for you from the kitchens." She curtsies again and then rushes out the back door to the stairwell.

I look down at her child, sweat dotting his forehead from what is likely a fever. Sucking his thumb innocently and dreaming. This boy is the future of the Nimali. What will he grow into, I wonder. Will he be taught to hate my people, or could he learn something different? Could his generation be something entirely new?

AFTER EATING a meal of nearly tasteless vegetable mash, I do feel a bit restored. I've whisked the exhaustion into the corners of my body but am still hoping for that nap when a chime sounds at the door.

"I'll get that, my lady," Aggi says and takes off at a dead sprint for the front door. I follow behind her at a more sedate pace. The last thing I want is visitors. I also have no desire to record this announcement later, but I refuse to shy away from it. Hopefully Shad isn't as long-winded as some of the Crowns. Land Priest Eamonn is famous for rambling verbose soliloquies at holidays and celebration days.

A pang of homesickness vibrates through me like the ringing of a bell. I wouldn't even mind listening to Eamonn drone on and on if it meant I was home again. Straightening my shoulders, I lock the longing up tight—it has no place here now.

A commotion rises at the door as nearly half a dozen people sweep into the suite, led by a waspish man of middle years wearing red. All the others are in blue.

"My lady," the Cardinal man says with a bow. Unlike when Aggi says it, there's a hint of condescension in his tone. "I am Daggett Eltonson, the Citadel's majordomo. If you require anything to make you more comfortable during your stay with us, please do not hesitate to contact me." He bows again and apparently is waiting for some kind of response from me, so I thank him.

His chest puffs up at that, which makes me wary. Then he waves a hand at the people clustered in the doorway, burdened with large wheeled cases and a rack of clothing. "These are the royal stylists. They are here to dress you for the announcement this evening. We have been anxiously awaiting your arrival. We don't have much time left to—" He looks me up and down, assessing. "Make you look queenly."

My brows raise. I'm quite certain I don't want to look queenly. Not at all.

The rolling rack is filled with blood-red finery in fabrics I don't recognize. In the Greenlands, we wear natural fibers grown and woven by the textile workers. If I hadn't chosen the Defense Division, I may have been a fabric worker. But the bliss only knows how the Nimali materials are created. Some of it looks hard like armor, some is soft and flowing. There are gauzy pieces, lacy creations, a thick quilted material that looks quite warm, and everything in between. I spot some scraps on hangers that look too small to be considered actual clothing. My previous short stay in the Citadel acquainted me with the sorts of fashion the Cardinals deem acceptable, far more revealing than I am comfortable with.

"I don't want anything fancy. Can't I wear what warriors wear?"

The majordomo glances at the sharp-faced woman with the blunt haircut and the others with her, a pair of twin sisters and a thin young man, who all gape in shock.

Daggett's mouth opens and closes like a fish, then he pivots toward the door. "I will leave you in Filomena's capable hands. She will answer any fashion questions." Then he's gone in a whirl of disdain.

Filomena turns out to be the woman with the vicious black bob. Her expression of dismay reminds me of Mother's. "My lady, are you certain you do not want to wear something befitting your station? Something that will not embarrass His Majesty when he is seen next to you by everyone in the clan?"

Her words are impertinent, just shy of rude, but I take her meaning. Exactly how amenable do I need to be here? My daimon is alert within me, paying attention to this exchange. The moment I break the engysis contract, I will also break my covenant. Will my daimon give me a warning? Will I feel its displeasure before it breaks with me to return to the Origin, leaving me nothing more than a mundane human? Spirit contracts are not to be trifled with.

I take a deep breath and steady my shoulders. Engysis only requires that I stay near Shad for thirty days and make a good faith attempt to see if we can be mates. It should not dictate how I dress. But uncertainty makes me indecisive.

"All right, but I don't want anything fussy. I need something I can move in. Full ranges of motion." I swing my arms in circles and kick my legs to demonstrate.

The stylists recoil in alarm, but Filomena recovers quickly. "Very well."

She goes to the rack and slides hangers around, conferring with the young man who I take it is in charge of wardrobe.

"My lady," one of the twins says, "might we begin your hair and makeup?"

"No." I stare them down. They share a fearful glance but step back.

"All right," Filomena announces. "How about this?"

I look at what they've picked out. *Only thirty days*, I remind myself.

AFTER AN HOUR of being pushed and prodded into this ridiculous outfit, my fuse is short. Technically, the garment meets my requirements. I can move in it rather easily and fight if I need to. It is composed of padded leggings and a top that allows full motion of my arms—but calling it a shirt is pushing it. The thing is more modest than what most Nimali wear in that it covers my clavicle, but it's molded to my body like paint. Some sort of structure inside supports my breasts, helpful I suppose, or at least as helpful as the bindings I usually wear, only a lot more decorative. The fabric is abrasive against my skin. It is also gaudy and needlessly ornamented and I hate it. However, it fits, after a lot of nipping and tucking and hemming of the unnatural fabric.

Filomena frowned when she pronounced me as passable, but I take it I won't embarrass Shad completely, so hopefully that fulfills the covenant. A tiny voice inside me whispers, *What about Makani's mission? How does that fit into your covenant?*

The thing is, you don't always know what your daimon will think about an action until you've taken it. Some daimons are more flexible in their interpretations than others. Still, it is a rare Fai who breaks their bond and has their daimon abandon them, and I'm determined not to be one. After all, if I do find the poison, that means the Fai are in danger, and it's within my daimon pact to protect and defend when others are trying to kill me.

I still need a plan on how to proceed in the mission, but my thoughts scatter when Shad appears at the appointed time looking even more handsome than this morning, if possible. He's in an identical formal uniform to the one he wore in the ceremony, one that seems to be cast from a mold of his muscles, highlighting each of them. I'm frazzled and exhausted and that is the only reason I can't tear my gaze away from the rippling display of strength before me. When he extends his arm in that chivalric way I'm coming to expect, I shake myself, grit my teeth, and take it.

"Where are we going?" I ask, trying to distract myself from the feel of his arm under my hands.

"We'll do the recording in the Great Hall. It shouldn't take long. You look lovely, by the way."

I mumble a thanks. The elevator ride down is quiet; we emerge on the sixth floor and are swept through a pair of large doors into an enormous space. Not being familiar with Nimali technology, I imagined we'd be confronted with some sort of recording device manned by a crewperson or two. However, at least one hundred people have gathered, including the entire Council, and dozens more Cardinals arrayed in their finery.

Shad's jaw clenches and limbs tense. This certainly looks like the type of celebration he indicated he did not want. I wonder if he'll respond to this blatant act of disobedience, but he stays quiet.

A raised platform has been set up on one side of the room; on it sits a large cube, almost knee-height. A man in blue stands behind another glowing cube several feet away, and this one is propped up on a stand so it's at eye level.

As we approach, Shad explains what's going to happen. "We'll stand in front of the recorder, which will capture our image and sounds. The whole thing will be broadcast to the comms of the entire clan simultaneously, so it will be like they are here with us as well."

I appreciate his taking the time to make it clear, knowing I'd have no idea what is happening. As we pass by the Council, he shoots a glare in their direction, which causes more than one person to flinch away. Sir Barrett, however, just scowls, not looking ashamed at all.

At least the entire place is not filled with screaming, shouting people. After the day I've had, that would likely tip me over the edge into raving lunacy.

"Why are they so set on this being a celebration?" I whisper as we step toward the stage.

"It is how things have always been done, that's all. Change is difficult to take."

"But isn't tradition important?"

He glances down at me soberly. "Some traditions need to die a quick and merciful death."

I blink, shaken by his response. A small group of Azures steal the king's attention while I process. One thing is certain: King Shad is not what I expected.

The Azures wave devices around Shad's face to check the light and ask him to speak so they can test the audio volume. Me, they ignore. Being around this many Nimali makes my skin crawl, but I stand with my head held high until we get the signal that they're ready to record.

Shad's speech is blissfully short. He relays simply and clearly everything that has happened, from receiving Citlali's invitation, to her unusual plan for peace.

His voice resonates as he wraps up. "I urge you all to welcome Lady Xipporah as an ambassador here to secure a better future for both her clan and ours. Too many have been lost, too many families grieve loved ones sacrificed to this conflict between the clans. We have survived dark times and there will doubtless be rough roads ahead, but we are Nimali, and we are strong. We have what we need to face all challenges. And I intend to see us through whatever comes with the leadership you deserve."

Those gathered give polite applause at the speech, not the riotous clamor that would accompany a Fai gathering, even of this size. I wonder if his words were not what they expected or wanted.

We remain standing on the platform until the woman behind the recording device gives a hand signal. "We're clear. Thank you, Your Majesty." Her voice rises over the lingering clapping.

"I appreciate your efforts on this. Your service is valued," Shad says.

The woman beams, and she and the crew begin breaking down the equipment. The night is finally over, and I'm eager to get back to my echoing and soulless apartment to finally get some sleep. But first, we must pass the gauntlet of the Council.

"Interesting speech," an icy dark-haired woman announces.

"Lady Linh," Shad says, nodding in her direction. "I believe that's high praise coming from you."

The king is personable tonight, letting this and other comments I consider rude roll off him without a reaction. Perhaps a reaction is what they're looking for, and if so, he's wise to not give it to them. Personally, I'm not sure why he doesn't shift into a dragon and burn them all for their impertinence, but he chooses to take it all in stride.

This jockeying for power or influence or whatever is happening is not something I'm familiar with. The Fai Crowns are chosen by the people, with each daimon grouping —Air, Water, Land, and Fire—selecting the strongest among them in a series of objective tests. The Crowns serve until they lose a challenge, resign, or die. It's simple.

The sideways compliments, obvious brown-nosing, and calculated disobedience are strange to me. More evidence of the cutthroat society the beasts have cultivated for so long. Still, Shad seems like he's playing an entirely different game to everyone else here.

When we finally break away and I'm in my suite, getting ready for bed, it occurs to me to wonder whether I want him to win or not.

FOURTEEN

Shad

AFTER A NIGHT of fitful sleep beset by dreams I can't remember, I'm eager for the sparring session scheduled with Harsh this morning. The hallway outside my suite is nearly pitch black, but the bliss lighting overhead wakens in response to my movement. I nod to the soldiers stationed outside Xipporah's door—they do most of their guard duty in near darkness, which is not ideal. However, both can shift quickly into a wolverine and anaconda, respectively, and don't need light to sense a predator.

I'm nearly to the elevator when Xipporah's door slides open. She stands there in a flowy red nightgown that looks decidedly out of place on her.

"Where are you going this early?" she asks.

I'm dressed in my workout gear, a sleeveless black shirt and loose pants. I can't think of a lie, so I go with the truth. "I'm sparring with Harsh. I will be back in a few hours to escort you to breakfast."

She shakes off my suggestion. "No, I'd rather spar with you all. Give me two minutes." Then she races back into the suite, leaving me with my mouth open. She wants to train?

I haven't even decided how I feel about her joining us when she's back in less than two minutes in the outfit from the night before. She tugs at the material around her neck.

"You realize that's a formal outfit?" I ask.

"It's what I have available at the moment. But I can move in it."

I shrug and lead the way to the elevator. "How did you know I was out here?"

"I had my daimon called. I can hear everything."

Why would she have her daimon leashed at such an early hour? Maybe it's just due to waking in a strange place. "I understand it is impolite to ask a Fai about their daimon."

Her eyes cut hard at me as she ties her long hair into a queue down her back. "It's a tiger. And yes, it's quite rude. That sort of personal information is usually given voluntarily."

The tiger makes sense—I'd thought she was a cat. I don't feel bad for asking, but after that, the rest of the ride downstairs is in silence.

Harsh waits in the lobby. His annoyance that my fiancée is joining us doesn't bleed through his mask. I can only tell because I know him.

"She wishes to train," I explain. A grunt is his only reply.

Outside, the air is crisp, the pre-dawn sky just beginning to brighten. The short walk to the building we use for training is quiet. When we arrive, Xipporah looks around, eyeing the hole in the ceiling.

"Why didn't you fix this place up?"

"Resources are at a premium. Only buildings that are necessary have been reclaimed. Starting with the ones that sustained the least amount of damage in the Sorrows. This one was too badly done."

She seems suspicious and sniffs at the water-damaged walls before evidently deciding this place meets her standards.

Then she begins executing a series of stretches that are foreign to me: twisting, lithe movements that bring attention to the strength of her body and its flexibility. I tear my gaze away, and Harsh and I begin our own stretches, which are not nearly as enticing.

Every now and then, he'll look over at her with curiosity. I, on the other hand, have to force myself not to watch. A growing dread creeps over me at my body's reaction to her. I *cannot* be attracted to my fiancée.

"Is this place big enough for you to shift?" she asks, shaking me out of my thoughts.

"We train as human; those are the rules." Harsh's answer is clipped. "Will that work for you?"

Xipporah grins. "Works just fine."

Do the Fai train their soldiers without the benefit of their daimons? It's one of many things I don't know about their culture.

"Why don't you two go first," I say, pointing at them. Xipporah shrugs. Harsh glowers.

I don't know what I was expecting, but one thing is clear: The Fai definitely train without their daimons. Xipporah is good: fast on her feet, strong, and trained to make up for being less physically strong than a man. Her movements are lightning fast. I would be convinced her daimon was at the forefront if I couldn't see her eyes, their dark-brown depths shining even as her forehead glistens with sweat. She gets Harsh into a hold he can't get out of, and I call time.

Afterward, she helps him up, grinning. "Not bad. Didn't realize the beasts didn't always rely on their animals."

At the derogatory term, Harsh's eyes narrow, so I speak up before he goes off. "Most of us don't, but I've always seen the value. Probably for the same reason your own people do?"

She shakes out her limbs. "We keep our bodies when we shift, so they have to stay strong. Daimons increase our strength, but they need a solid foundation. And if we relied on them entirely, we'd be at a disadvantage."

This echoes my thoughts, and I nod. "Exactly. And if we're in a cold environment and can't call them, we still want to be formidable. I've been saying that for years."

Her lips curve. "They should listen to you. So are you next?"

"I'll take it easy on you since you're not as fresh as I am."

She laughs. "Don't bother. I can take you."

I raise a brow, eager to find out.

When we fight, it's like a dance. I pull my punches because I truly don't want to hurt her; however, even though she's fought once this morning, she's still fast and capable. She gets me in a hold; I twist out. Her disappointment is evident, but it fuels her determination. She comes back stronger. Punching harder, forcing me to hold back less and less.

Facing her is actually a challenge. I could still beat her easily, but I fall into the flow of the movements, practicing my dodges and strikes, batting away her punches and occasionally having some land.

It's fun, the way it used to be when I was a child sparring against Sylph while Lynara looked on. He was a small and scrappy opponent, movements lightning fast. I couldn't rely on my bulk and strength alone then, either.

Finally, I sense Xipporah tiring and decide to put an end to the match. I flip her over and pin her down, most of my body covering hers.

"Do you yield?"

In another context, this position would be intimate. Our breaths mingle as we both pant from exertion. Her breasts push against my chest; I'm nestled in the vee of her legs with heat pouring from both of us. She struggles for a few tension-riddled moments but is wholly unable to move me off her. I need her to give up before my body reacts to this level of proximity in a way she would probably consider ruder than asking about her daimon.

"Fine, I yield," she says, finally, teeth gritted. It costs her something to admit defeat.

I roll off her and clamber to my feet, then reach out to help her up, but she doesn't take my hand. She jumps up, giving no evidence that the closeness of our bodies elicited any reaction whatsoever.

"Good match. You're an excellent fighter," I say.

With the sweat glistening on her skin in the morning light, she looks like a goddess. I blink and turn away.

"Thanks," she says. "You're far better than I would have imagined."

I freeze, then choose to let that one slide off me.

"I'm going to report for duty," Harsh announces. "You have a council meeting at 800."

I sigh and nod as he leaves, then go to pick up my shirt and towel. When I bend over, I notice Xipporah checking me out. That puts a smile on my face, which I cover by mopping my head of sweat. When I lower the towel, she's scowling. She hasn't brought one, so I toss her mine.

"Gross," she says but proceeds to use it. "Do you all do this every morning?"

"Just about. It's a good way to start the day."

"I don't disagree."

We stare at each other, and I wonder if finding points of agreement will always be this easy. I know it won't—that's a pie in the sky idea unworthy of a king, but something about this moment of camaraderie takes the edge of strain off.

"I'd better get back," I say with remorse. "These sparring sessions aren't common knowledge."

Her head tilts at that. "All right. I'm sure I don't have anyone to tell, anyway."

I shrug and lead the way out. The guards in the lobby

greet me with a salute; they're the only people we encounter on our way to the elevator.

Back on our floor, I stop at her door. "Thank you. I enjoyed that more than I expected to."

She huffs out a laugh. "Thought I'd be terrible?"

I shrug, unwilling to deny it. She shakes her head, not taking offense. "Well, you surprised me, too."

We share a look that lasts too long. She's the one who turns away first, and I wonder what she sees when she looks at me.

"Shad," she says when I move away. "I'm not sure what I'm supposed to do here. Would it be possible for me to get out and see some of the territory? It may help my work as an ambassador."

I hide my surprise, but a tremor of excitement ripples across my skin. If she could see the Nimali as I do, then she could take that knowledge back to her people. Maybe it would help bring context to some of our actions. And I want to show her. Help her see that not all of us are the boorish aristocrats who look down their nose at others. I want to show her my home.

"That is an excellent idea. After my meeting, I will show you around."

She jerks back. "Yourself?"

"Yes."

"I'm sure you have better things to do. I can just walk around myself or…"

"No, I'll do it. Better you get an unbiased view."

She frowns, but finally nods. "I appreciate it." Though she agrees, her forehead is still creased as though something about this troubles her. No doubt her expectations of my duties as king don't include personal tours, but the opportunity is too great.

"I will see you soon," I say and move down the hall to prepare for what is no doubt going to be a hellish meeting.

But more than once, I'm distracted by the memory of our sparring. The feel of her body is imprinted on mine, a lingering sensation that I'd do well to push away, but I only draw it closer.

Do not be attracted to your fiancée, I remind myself, knowing that I won't listen and it's already too late.

FIFTEEN

Xipporah

_____

THREE HOURS LATER, Shad shows up at my door looking harried. If his hair weren't cut brutally short, I'm sure it would be sticking straight up, because even as I answer the door, he's running his hand across his scalp.

"Everything go okay?" I ask.

He huffs through his nostrils, visibly calming himself. "As well as can be expected. Do you still want the tour?"

"Yes, if you have time. Though I understand if you don't," I hasten to add. A pair of guards flanks my door, but they should be easy to get around. I've set a goal to access the mechanical room that Von and the other GenFi had begun to sabotage. However, that's best done after dark, when the hallways are quieter. Getting eyes on the territory as a whole with Shad at my side will be helpful as well. And I certainly won't make any headway on my mission if I spend all day locked in this suite entertaining a sick child.

Since the Citadel is short staffed, Aggi has a variety of responsibilities including laundry and cleaning elsewhere, so I sat with Kit this morning telling him the stories I used to regale Noomi with when she was younger. All while awaiting Shad's arrival and thinking of how I'm going to verify whether the Nimali destroyed their cache of Revoker poison.

Shad is king, he will know. But his actions are not of someone secretly planning to decimate his enemy. I actually believe he really wants peace. So that means either his capacity for lying is greater than I give him credit for, or he doesn't know everything happening in his domain.

"I would like to show you around," he says. "There are parts of the territory I haven't visited in too long. It will be good to show my face again. Remind the people that I'm here for them." His sincerity surprises me, like so much else about him has. "Though, there is likely much of the Citadel you haven't seen. Would you rather start here?"

I shudder. "Being cooped up indoors isn't normal for me. I'd much rather get outside, if you don't mind."

He chuckles, and soon we're on the grassy plaza in front of the Citadel, half a dozen guards in tow. "Do we really need this much security? We're not leaving your territory, right?" I ask, as two more guards in their black uniforms flank us.

Shad's mouth turns down. He approaches a grizzled, barrel-chested man and has a conversation too low for me to hear; it doesn't seem appropriate to call my daimon just to eavesdrop. Moments later, the soldier collects most of the guards and heads back into the building, leaving us with only two.

"Thanks," I say.

His grin is wry. "My, ah, predecessor, preferred a show of strength whenever he left the Citadel. But you're right, I don't expect to be attacked within our borders."

We walk along the pathway around the lawn, with Shad pointing out the buildings as we pass: offices, factories, library, storage, school, apartments.

The side street we turn down bustles with activity. It's a strange sight, this re-creation of a pre-Sorrows world. Here, there are small shops and even a few restaurants. Places where craftsmen sell their wares with Azures and Cardinals shopping. I spot a few Umbers here and there, but they're usually marching purposefully, focused, and often carrying something heavy, not lingering and chatting like the others.

Aggi's general air of weariness comes to mind. The Fai are far more egalitarian; we work trades in line with our daimon's abilities and our own interests, share in the communal food stores, and live without class divisions. Of course, it's not perfect. There is greed and theft and laziness, cruelty and sorrow, but we do not have second-class citizens entrenched in our society.

The people we pass bow and curtsy to Shad, who greets everyone warmly. I've really only seen him interact with the vile Council, who don't seem to deserve warmth, so witnessing the genuine excitement "regular folk" have when meeting him is like night and day.

"Why is that place guarded?" I point down a side street where two soldiers stand on either side of the entryway to a nondescript building.

Shad glances at the place disinterestedly. "There's been an uptick in theft of certain resources. Guards have been posted as a deterrent."

A young man approaches and bows, stealing his attention, but I make a note of our location. Anything being guarded must be precious, and whatever's in there is something I want to know more about.

We don't stop anywhere for long; I sense he has a specific destination in mind. I'm keeping mental notes of the businesses we pass and the path we take, creating a map in my head of the territory that I hope will be useful later. I also spot several more buildings with guards stationed outside—this mission will definitely not be easy.

We turn down a street quite a bit dingier than what we've seen so far. The buildings show visible signs of repair, and unlike elsewhere, no attempt was made to either match the original materials or paint over them to achieve a cohesive appearance. Just like everywhere else, all the windows have been filled in, but here it's been done in a hodgepodge with mosaics of cement and stone or bricks or whatever else they could find. How does air flow through these buildings with no windows? How do they breathe?

I am used to waking with the sunlight on my skin, the breeze bringing fresh air in from the ocean. What miserable lives these beasts lead.

Shad stops in front of a building and stares up at it, his thoughts far away. It's a nondescript structure, a six-story box whose exterior resembles a patchwork quilt.

"What is this place?" I ask after we've been standing here a while.

"This is the commune where I grew up." His voice is low. No emotion bleeds through, but I can practically see him straining to hold it inside of him. "Forty other families lived here as well. I haven't been inside it in quite a while." He blinks rapidly and turns away.

An older woman is crossing the street toward us, dragging two enormous bags. Her gray hair looks like it was shaved recently and is growing out, and her skin is unusually pale.

"Mother Akiko!" Shad rushes over to relieve her of her burdens.

"Oh, Shad—I mean, King Shad, you shouldn't do that. The king can't carry an old woman's laundry."

"The king can do whatever he wants," he replies, a sparkle in his eyes. Then he turns to me. "Lady Xipporah, this is Akiko Naomisdaughter."

The woman has very bright eyes, for all that they're nearly black, and a friendly disposition. I execute a low curtsy and, as I suspected, she giggles over it. Now free of her bags, she gives me a curtsy as well, though hers is shallow and I can tell it pains her.

128 • L. PENELOPE

"Very nice to meet you," she says. "I'm so happy you found a nice girl, Shad. Your mother would be proud."

Shad's skin is too dark to see a blush, though by the way he ducks his head, I can tell he's embarrassed. "Mother Akiko, you know this is a political arrangement. We're just trying to come to a peace agreement."

"Oh yes, we heard your speech. But still, she's a fine woman and you should not let her slip through your fingers. The spirits do everything for a reason." She taps her chest, and I guess she's indicating her daimon within. I wonder what it is, but a lifetime of Fai manners doesn't permit me to ask.

"I'll just help her take these inside," Shad says.

"Of course," I respond, grabbing a bag from his hand. You'd think I tore his clothes off and ran away, the way his eyebrows climb to his hairline.

"I can carry them," he says, affronted.

"So can I." I turn to Mother Akiko. "I'm also quite strong, you know."

She smiles, revealing a few missing teeth, and my heart pangs. "You look like you can handle yourself, dearie, but there's nothing wrong with letting a man lift the heavy things."

Then she taps her nose and teeters off toward the building's entrance. Shad grumbles but doesn't try to take the bag from me, which *is* fairly heavy. He gives a hand signal to the two guards who've trailed us across the city, and they take up positions beside the front door.

The interior of the building is pitch black, and to my surprise, Akiko lights a candle with a match. The burning wick tickles my nose. I didn't realize the Nimali had candles.

"Have the brownouts hit you here already?" Shad asks, dismayed.

"Brownouts? We haven't had bliss power in three days."

Shad stops short. "What?"

She looks over her shoulder from the first step of the staircase. "I heard we might get one day a week of power some-time soon, but I'm not holding my breath."

If they are turning off power to portions of their people, that must mean they are trying to conserve the bliss. They've got to be growing desperate. The information is useful for negotiating, but the Fai would never give up bliss for the beasts to waste, so does that mean they'll become desperate enough to destroy us for it? My stomach hollows as I follow Shad up the narrow steps.

SIXTEEN

Xipporah
___

THE DARKNESS in here is oppressive and the flickering candlelight ominous. An array of scents hit my nose, layering on my discomfort. I smell food—unfamiliar, but more palatable than the mush served in the Citadel—and also bodies. Nothing foul, just the scent of many people living close together.

We climb to the fourth floor, where Akiko opens a heavy door and light streams in. The room we enter is large and seems to take up most of this floor. Support beams divide a space cluttered with furniture. Mattresses dot the ground almost at random. Chairs and couches, tables and chests of drawers, all well patched and repaired, are crushed together. Cloth dividers have been hung to section off the space, but they're all gathered to the side and tied off, likely to let light in from the open windows along one wall of the building. Neat holes have been cut into the material which had sealed them shut.

Shad stops short just in front of me. "You all have opened the windows," he says, dismayed.

Akiko nods. "Had to. Not enough candles to last us, plus it was a fire hazard."

"But it's not safe."

She pats his arm. "Life isn't safe, child. Not here in the Burrows. Besides, there hasn't been a poison air storm in nearly seven years. It's a risk we have to take." Then she turns and raises her voice. "Look who I found outside!"

I hadn't noticed any people before, but nearly a dozen pop up at her words, having been hidden by all the clutter. Several elderly people rise slowly, along with a handful of younger women—two of whom are visibly pregnant. The rest are young children, not yet school age. But everyone knows Shad. The chaos that ensues when they get sight of the king is enough to make it feel like a hurricane.

Children run up screaming his name. He sets down the bag of laundry and instantly two little ones leap into his arms. I place my bag down as well and back up to the wall to get out of the way of his small admirers.

One of the pregnant women, a flame-haired beauty who's about to pop at any moment, lumbers over. She bends to pick up the discarded laundry bag and I rush to help her.

"No need. I've got it." She's impressively strong and has no trouble carrying the weighty bag across the room. I pick up the other one to save her a second trip.

"Thank you," she says softly, kneeling to open the bag and begin sorting clothes.

"Does he come often?" I ask, motioning back to Shad in the entry.

"He used to come more. But we haven't seen him since the coronation. He's busy running the clan." Pride laces her voice. For someone who grew up here—I can't in good conscience call this squalor, as everything is clean, if not orderly—to become the king is an achievement, indeed.

In all of my battles with Nimali over the years, I'd never considered how they lived. That they have children and elderly to care for is obvious, but we trained endlessly not to see them as people but an enemy to be defeated. I find it difficult to see these gentle souls as opponents.

I cross back over to Shad and peer at a collection of gray, opaque cubes stacked against one of the support beams. Each cube is the size of my head and the pile is three deep, reaching nearly to the ceiling. They have something to do with bliss, but none glow. All have the feel of emptiness about them.

A sharp *bang* sounds, and I call my daimon without thought, crouching and ready for action.

"Uh oh!" a chorus of children's voices sound. A curly-haired boy looks sheepish at a chair toppled over onto the ground.

"That's all right, Bennie. Just pick it up," Shad says, still covered in children. One is on his shoulders and two cling to his legs.

I rise, feeling foolish, release my daimon, and step back, knocking into the pile of bliss cubes. One topples to the ground at my feet; I pick it up and replace it on the stack.

Akiko wanders over, grinning her gap-toothed smile. "This place is not what you expected, eh?" she says.

My ears start to heat with embarrassment. "What makes you say that?"

"You have an expressive face."

I blank my expression, hoping I haven't caused offense. "Nimali live very differently to the Fai," I say, hoping it's diplomatic enough.

Akiko's laugh uses her whole body. She presses her palms into her belly to stop shaking, but it's a long moment before she gets herself together. "Certainly, child. Certainly. But are we truly that different to you?"

My jaw works as I try to find an answer. It's much more difficult than I would have thought. I'm hesitant to say yes or no. At this moment, I'm truly not certain. Thankfully, Akiko's attention is drawn elsewhere, to a growing brightness behind us. She tilts her head, and I follow her gaze to the stack of strange cubes—one on the top of the pile is glowing.

"Mina, these cells were all tested, weren't they?" the old woman calls out.

The redhead who took the laundry from me strides over, gazing at the glowing cube with a frown. "Yes, they were all empty."

"I think that's the one that fell," I say. "Maybe it shook a little extra energy from it."

Akiko and Mina nod. "Maybe we should drop them all to see if we can squeeze more life out of them," Mina offers with a grin. The two confer about the bliss cubes, and I take my leave of them. Living in darkness is not ideal, but perpetuating the enslavement of the bliss rubs me wrong as well.

Shad has finally freed himself from the young ones and meets me in the center of the room, sheepish. "Sorry about that," he says, his lips twisting in a hesitant smile. "It's been too long since my last visit."

I shrug, not wanting to admit that I've enjoyed seeing this side of him and of the Nimali in general.

"Before we head back, would you like to see my favorite spot?"

My brows rise. "Why not?" I say, trying to tamp down the eagerness that rose with his question.

He says his goodbyes and is greeted by waves of disappointment, but he promises to visit again soon. Then, we're back in the stairwell in pitch darkness.

"Do we need a candle?" he asks.

"Shame to waste one," I respond and call my daimon for a little light. We climb the steps until we reach the door to the roof. The day is overcast, air crisp, but after the close stillness inside, it feels like a miracle.

The roof is flat, with scattered puddles from yesterday's rain. Fully half of it is covered with raised planting beds full of the scraggliest vegetation I've ever seen. I walk straight over, scowling and indignant on behalf of the plant life.

"What's happened here?" I demand.

Shad glances at the garden, which holds several varieties of greens, as well as tomatoes, cucumbers, onions, and peas. "What do you mean?"

"These look awful. Who tends this garden?"

"Everything looks normal to me. There's a duty roster; everyone takes a turn up here."

"This looks normal?" I point to the limp, thin leaves. The spindly stalks and hard, bitter-looking tomatoes ready for harvesting. Shaking my head, I call my daimon and dip my hands into the soil. I'm barely acting with conscious thought; the idea of this sad garden just can't be borne.

When I'm done, it looks the way it should, with healthy, fat stalks, juicy fruit, and vibrant green leaves.

Shad's jaw hangs open. "W-we found plants in the closets after the Fai left. We didn't understand..." He shakes his head.

I lift a shoulder. "Land daimons are attuned to the earth. They enjoy growing things." I release my daimon, who practically purrs with satisfaction inside me. It's almost as content as it is after a fight.

"Well, thank you," Shad says. "I know the rationing will hit them hard. This will mean a lot."

My cheeks heat. Then I hear what he said. "Rationing?"

He sighs, expression grim. "A conversation for another time. Come on, this isn't what I'd meant to show you."

Brownouts and food rationing indicate desperate times, indeed. I have no time to waste in executing my mission because Makani's theory is sounding more and more realistic.

Shad leads me to the edge of the roof and makes a short jump down to the roof of the building next door. We cross in this way along the tops of buildings until we get to an old church from before the Sorrows. It's made of stone with a lower section at the back and a tall spire at the front. There were once two spires, but the other was a casualty of the destruction.

I wonder how stable it is; huge cracks are visible in the stone and many chunks are missing. "Where are we going?" I ask.

"Up there." He points to the spire, confirming my fears. I freeze and he shakes his head. "Not all the way to the top of the steeple, to the base."

"And it won't crumble beneath us?"

"I've been up there a thousand times. It will be fine."

I purse my lips and nod. If it's really unstable, my daimon will help me get away quickly, but I still think this "favorite place" of his is very foolish.

We step carefully across the sloped portions of the roof, then approach the base of the spire. Indentions in the stone are in a pattern that looks like handholds. I call my daimon for stability on the climb, but Shad makes the trip unaided with obvious years of practice.

The stone part of the tower ends in a grayish material, and then the steeple rises up overhead. We settle onto the ledge and it's like we're on top of the world.

Back home in my grandfather's aerie up in the north, there are views like this, where you can see the Greenlands spread out before you and the ocean beyond. Here, the view is of the city—the reclaimed Nimali section, as well as the remnants of the once-vibrant urban landscape beyond. Crumbled buildings, half-destroyed towers, rusted-out vehicles clogging the streets, vegetation taking back the creations of men. But from this height, somehow, it's beautiful.

In the distance, the remains of the bridge that once connected the peninsula we call Aurum to the eastern mainland hangs, the gap in its span like a missing tooth.

"This is breathtaking," I whisper.

Shad wraps an arm around his knee, dangling his other foot in the air. "My friends and I would come up here and remind ourselves that the world is vast. Much bigger than this territory, than our clan. Than Aurum itself."

His expression is so wistful, I can't tear my gaze away. "Did you ever want to leave? Aurum?"

"Every day," he breathes.

I consider the land before me again, this time viewing it through his eyes. The once-neat grid of streets and city blocks could be confining. A prison to a small child living on a single floor with a dozen families pressed together.

"I've never wanted anything other than life in the Greenlands," I say. But what I don't admit is that I wanted a different life than the one I was given.

"Maybe if I'd been born to Cardinal or even Azure parents, it would have been different. I can't complain. I had a good childhood. There was lots of love and joy, and my parents loved each other very much. But we struggled. I always wanted more."

I feel like I'm seeing a side of him not many do. It scares me.

"So does being the king satisfy that?" I ask.

He chuckles without humor. "I never wanted to be king. I leashed a dragon daimon at my trials and my life—" He breaks off sharply and takes a deep breath. "My life changed. This is what it is now. But at least I have the opportunity to make things better for them." He motions behind us, and I assume he means the people he grew up with. "That's my goal now."

My daimon hums within me, pleased with this openness. I don't know what possesses me to reach for his arm, to grab his hand, but his obvious melancholy calls to me. I squeeze his hand, and he squeezes back. Is this a man who would commit genocide for an energy source?

We sit here long enough for the sun to begin its descent in the sky. Long enough that his eyes seem to glow amber in the sharpening light. Still hand in hand for some reason.

Looking at him like this, I can no longer deny that he's beautiful. From his slightly canted eyes to his full lips. He wets them and something clenches between my thighs. I'm hit with a wave of madness, a pull of attraction so strong that I find myself leaning in, drawn by the sunlight, the moment, the feel of his skin against my hand. What would those lips taste like?

Images from this morning surge over me like waves. His body against mine, pressing into me until I yielded. He's caught in this as well, leaning forward, eyes locked on my mouth.

The desire tows me forward like a magnet until a gust of wind blows. Nearby a bird caws, and the thought that it might be a Nimali soldier watching us makes me rear back.

I pull my hand from his and jump to my feet, balancing precariously on the ledge. Shad holds up a hand as I wobble, but I call my daimon and leap down the ten feet to the sloped roof below. Then, I climb down the stone face of the building and stand on the street to wait for Shad to descend.

That was too much; too close. The engysis is a thirty-day strategy for peace, that is all. Feelings for him could doom me forever. This is not, cannot be a real betrothal, and my daimon cannot get any ideas that I want to stay trapped in Nimali territory for the rest of my life, wedded to a dragon.

I shiver uncontrollably and nearly devolve into a panic attack. This hasn't happened since my first months of training, when the mere thought of an upcoming battle would paralyze me with fear. I practice the deep breathing exercises I learned then to combat it. By the time Shad arrives, I've gotten myself together.

We walk back to where we left the guards in silence. But really, what is there to say?

SEVENTEEN

Shad

HARSH CALLS my name and I jerk, still worrying the scrap of fabric between my fingers. The drab gray walls of the conference room come back into focus. From the expression on his face—something akin to wanting to murder me—I'm pretty sure this wasn't the first time he said my name.

"What was that?" I ask, putting away the little handkerchief Mother Akiko gave me at the commune.

"Where is your head?" he asks.

Back on that roof with Xipporah. Staring at her mouth and wondering how it would feel against mine. How it would be to tug one plump lip between my teeth and taste her.

And that is something that cannot ever happen. I focus back on my friend and the report he's been trying to give me.

"If you're done woolgathering," he grits out testily, "the new reports have come in from the produce houses."

"And?"

"It's bad. We've lost so many crops that we'll need to start food rationing at the end of the week."

I run a hand down my face and shift on the uncomfortable chair. "Sabotage?"

"We still have no proof, and the extra guards we've set

have witnessed nothing, either. We're spread too thin, I suspect. And so many Umbers have been called into service for the Cardinals, there aren't as many to work the shifts at the produce houses and keep watch."

"So, the problem is not just that someone might be intentionally destroying our food supply and our energy stores, but we don't even have enough workers to manage the various plants and factories, either?"

He nods. "The Fai drudges were holding up much of our society, and too many Azures were promoted to Cardinal under Lyall's watch. He used promotion as a carrot and demotion as a stick, but people were scared enough of him that fewer and fewer got demoted. As such, we have an imbalance of power. Too many aristocrats who all believe they deserve special treatment and not enough people to give them that treatment."

When I was young, becoming a Cardinal had been the dream. It meant a life of relative ease and comfort. But the reality is, if everyone believes they're too good to work for a living, then very little will get done.

"Well, the Umbers are in darkness for a week at a time already," I say. "We can't cut their food drastically as well or they'll have nothing left. We'll have to make the rations across the board."

Harsh shakes his head. "You know that people will fight you on this."

"And by people, you mean the Council, right?"

He shrugs. "And everyone wearing any color from blush pink to royal burgundy."

"It's just a chance I'll have to take. We can't put this all on the Umbers. Even if we did, it would trickle up the line eventually."

A ding sounds at the entrance to the conference room where Harsh and I have holed up. I press the button in the table that opens the door to reveal one of my guards, Abdul.

"There's a Blake Tristanson and a Tawana Camilles-daughter here for you, Your Majesty."

"Please, send them in."

Blake is dark-haired and heavy set with piercing brown eyes, which remind me a little of his rat daimon's. Growing up, he lived across the street in a slightly smaller commune to ours, but we were always on good terms. The woman who enters with him is short and muscular with deep brown skin. Her smooth face and closely cropped hair make her age indeterminate, and her no-nonsense attitude bleeds through.

They both step in and bow. Blake says, "I don't believe you've met my other half, Your Majesty. This is Tawana."

I greet her with a nod. "I didn't realize you'd gotten married."

He shakes his head. "Oh, no, we're not married."

"We are parallels, Your Majesty," Tawana adds. "Our daimons are bonded, but we're not romantic partners."

"Ah, I see." Parallels are extremely rare and have nothing to do with romantic attachment, but are a souls-deep bond. Daimons plan to find hosts near one another and live their human experiences together.

"Calling me his other half is his attempt at humor." Neither of them seems particularly jovial, but then again, they're both Umbers facing power outages and rations. Joviality might be expecting too much.

"I take it you all have a report?" I ask.

"Yes," Blake answers with a terse nod.

"If it's bad news, I don't want to hear it."

Harsh rolls his eyes, but neither Blake nor Tawana cracks a smile. "Go ahead," I tell them.

"The team is making progress. We've begun mapping the tunnel system and have located the strongholds of several human factions. None call themselves the Silent Hands, but we're getting a good feel for the relationships down there. Things are complex. Lots of alliances and betrayals."

"I'm sure," I say. "And no one on your team has been spotted or compromised?"

He shakes his shaggy head, and Tawana speaks up. "They're used to rats and snakes and the like down there. We're easily able to avoid their traps and no one can sneak up on us."

"All right, just be careful. And anyone who feels uncomfortable should retreat. You all are doing great work."

Blake's expression shifts very subtly, but there's pride there. "Thank you, Your Majesty. We enjoy doing it."

They turn to leave, but a question bubbles to mind and I call out to them. "Can I ask you all something?"

Both turn and wait.

"Being parallels…what is it like, considering…" I wave a hand between them, indicating their lack of a romantic relationship.

Tawana looks up at Blake, whose eyes go soft in thought. She responds first. "It's like feeling complete for the first time. Like half of you, a half you never knew you were missing, is restored."

"I always felt whole, before," Blake says, looking down at her, his somber expression cracking for a moment. "But having a parallel is a new level of wholeness. My daimon was restless. Now, it's at peace."

I wonder if either of them is also in a romantic partnership but feel I've already delved into their personal lives a bit too far. When I nod and thank them, they take their leave. I rub my chin, turning over their words for a bit.

Finally, I turn to Harsh. "At least their mission seems like it's going well."

"So far," he agrees. "And having the maps will be helpful in the future."

"It was a good idea. All right," I say with a sigh. "What else is on the agenda?"

Before he can speak, the door chimes again. Abdul. Only this time, he looks stricken, eyes wide and brown skin graying.

I stand, alarmed. "What is it?"

"We got an urgent message from the wall. It cut out before it was finished, but Captain Neelia was calling for assistance. She sounded…" He swallows, more ruffled than I've ever seen him. "*Panicked.*"

The idea of the unflappable, veteran soldier coming close to panic has my chest contracting.

"I'll go," Harsh says, already moving toward the door.

"I'm coming, too."

"You have three more meetings today."

"I'm coming. Whatever could make Neelia sound anything other than completely in control needs my eyes on it. I've seen that woman battle two Revokers single-handedly and barely break a sweat."

Harsh just grunts. The woman is a legend.

The elevator opens and Sir Denby comes out. "Oh, excuse me, Your Majesty. Are you going somewhere? We have a meeting scheduled."

"I'm sorry, Sir Denby, I have an urgent situation." I brush past him into the elevator car and press the Lobby button impatiently. Harsh and my other guards file in after me.

"Have you heard from Callum?" Denby asks.

"Not yet, but I'm expecting a message today. I'll keep you abreast." I call this out as the doors close.

On the plaza, we all shift. Harsh, me, and the others with Air daimons take flight while the rest of the guard follows on foot. I cross the dead parts of the Independent Zone, my mind focused on the wall. In minutes, the barrier we constructed long ago between Aurum and No Man's Land is upon me. I circle one of the watch stations and find a small group of soldiers on the ground on the south side of the wall.

The land there is foggy and empty, a wasteland devoid of life other than Revokers. Unlike in Aurum, No Man's Land doesn't contain any evidence of pre-Sorrows society. We regularly patrol the ten square miles next to the wall, and there are no buildings, no streets, no rusted-out cars stuck where their last occupants left them…or died in them. There's nothing at all but gravelly dirt and monsters.

I land a safe distance from the gathered soldiers and shift. Soon enough, Harsh is at my side with my Air guard. I spot Neelia and we approach. She is a stiff-backed, gray-haired woman who has been soldiering longer than I've been alive. My respect for her is immense, and I heavily relied upon her expertise after my trials when I first began to lead our forces.

She has pulled herself together, if in fact she was ever panicked to begin with, and wastes no time with bowing or greetings, something I actually appreciate. She merely leads me to the section of the wall that seems of so much interest to her soldiers. They all move away to let me through.

"Your Majesty, at the shift change today, during our normal inspection, my people found this." She points to the wall, which has stood for nearly fifty years. It was first built during the Sorrows, amidst the chaos and destruction when the Revokers emerged as the vast majority of humans died. Over the years, it's been fortified and strengthened, widened, and had additional layers added until it reached the current dimensions of eight-feet thick and twenty-feet high. We keep our section in good repair, and the one thing we can depend on the Fai to do as well is maintain the portion in their territory. No one wants Revokers breaking through.

But today, a section has been gouged out. I lean in to inspect it. "What could have caused this damage?" I ask.

"And who?" Harsh murmurs.

"Revokers have certainly never tried to come *through* the wall before," Neelia adds.

"I'm not sure it's possible for them to do," I say. "They can't dig. At least we know they can't dig underneath the wall. They can't fly or dig or cross water—those are the rules that have kept us safe for half a century. Could this have been done by some other kind of animal?"

Neelia puts her hands on her hips, gazing at the damage. "We've never seen any evidence of animal life out here in the years since the Sorrows."

"Maybe something new has emerged or migrated to the area?" I study the gouging, looking for evidence of some kind of tool involved.

"Captain!" a voice calls out from thirty feet away. A young soldier approaches holding an object wrapped in cloth.

"What is it, Hans?" Neelia barks.

"I believe it's a claw, Captain."

My heart seizes. I approach him and pluck the thing from his grasp, mindful that if this belongs to a Revoker, it could be coated in their deadly poison. The sharp, curved talon certainly looks like the broken-off claw of a Revoker. And at its tip, a bit of gray dust, the same color as the wall.

I hold it up so everyone can see. The soldiers around me are silent as we consider what this means. How this changes everything we know about the security of our city.

"Who knows about this?" I ask Neelia.

"Only the people here."

"Double the wall inspections, but I don't want news of this to spread. The last thing we need is a clan-wide panic."

She salutes, and while I believe her people are loyal and obedient, there are just too many present for this to stay a secret for long. But if the Revokers are really trying to dig through the wall, my problems have just increased exponentially.

EIGHTEEN

Xipporah

FRUSTRATION WELLS inside me like an inflating balloon, but the pressure has nowhere to go. I refuse to take it out on Kit, who is attempting to teach me the rules of a game involving tiny pebbles and stones. I can't make heads or tails of it, and at four, his command of language isn't up to the task of explaining. He babbles on incoherently, but happily. However, he has to stop every few minutes for a coughing fit.

Aggi warned me that he would be pleasant for a short time after awaking from his nap, before the pain in his chest and limbs grew again and it was time for his medicine. Then he'd turn cranky, but so far, I'm the only one feeling crabby. It must be the exhaustion.

Last night, I'd stayed awake until the Citadel grew quiet, only those on night duty still awake. I'd snuck out the back and down to the sixteenth floor, and even with my daimon, descending two dozen flights of stairs was taxing. In the laundry facility, I'd stolen a black uniform that fit reasonably well, then headed to the pre-Sorrows machine room. The blueprints for the machinery were still laid out on a rickety table, just where the GenFi had left them before we escaped. Scrawled on the crumbling paper were instructions for how to add a bit of blood directly to the central control system and gain access to the locked doors of the entire Citadel.

I'd read the directions twice, struggling to understand the arcane Nimali tech, but still I managed to prick my finger and go through the steps of the process. I tested it on the secure room that Ryin and Talia had stumbled into—the one where the Nimali had been experimenting on the Revokers. Thankfully, it worked. I could now roam the building freely.

The lab was empty, thank the bliss, and I experienced the full-body weakness of relief. This was evidence that the Nimali really had ended the program to synthesize the poison. Of course, it wasn't proof they'd actually destroyed the toxin already created, but it was something. By the time I crawled to my bed, close to dawn, I was feeling better than I had since I decided to come here.

After breakfast, I'd intended to go back to sleep, but when I caught Aggi crying in the servant's room, I caved and offered to watch Kit for her. At first, she was unsure, but finally, she accepted. Then she proceeded to give Kit detailed instructions on staying quiet, not going anywhere, and not pestering me too much.

The child hushes suddenly, looking green around the gills, and I wish I was a Fire Fai and had the ability to heal him. He coughs raucously then rubs his belly.

"Don't feel well."

"I know, little man. Why don't you lie down again?"

He nods and climbs onto the cot before curling into a ball. My heart goes out to him.

The door chime rings, so I stand, brushing off my leggings. "I'm just going to see who that is." Kit doesn't respond.

I move to the front and open the door to reveal Shad, dressed today in black. He looks like a soldier and smells like dessert. My gaze gets snagged on his shoulders, which almost fill up the entire doorway.

I blink when I realize he's repeating himself and focus in on what he's saying without making it obvious I'm staring at his lips.

"Xipporah, is everything all right?"

I finally move aside to let him in. "Of course, why?"

"You were staring at me." The corners of his mouth bend upward in an attempt to conceal a smile.

I straighten, clearing my mind. "Sorry. I wasn't expecting you."

He squints at me. "Your hair is…" He trails off awkwardly and waves a finger in the general area of my head.

I pat my hair to discover that it's still in the "style" Kit attempted before he grew bored and moved onto the pebble game. Something like half a dozen little braided buns rest on the front half of my head; I work to quickly pull them out.

Shad is still trying not to laugh. "Here," he says, taking me by the shoulders and turning me toward the wall, where a mirror hangs.

It's still strange for me to use a mirror. We don't have them in the Greenlands, but they're everywhere in the Citadel from what I can tell. Vanity isn't valued among the Fai, and the materials for creating mirrors are too precious to be wasted. Also, since no one lives alone, any repairs needed to someone's appearance are assisted. Still, I do find it helpful to be able to do things myself.

Just as I pull the last bun down, Kit starts coughing again. This time, it sounds like he's hacking up a lung.

"Is that Aggi?" Shad asks, concerned.

"No, no. Don't worry about it. Just wait here." I'm still not sure if Aggi will get in trouble for Kit's presence, so I don't mention it. Instead, I run back to check on him.

"You okay there, little man?"

Still coughing, Kit holds up the cup of water he'd been drinking. I think it must have just gone down the wrong pipe. Then, Shad is there, bursting in as if he'd thought something was on fire. He stops short, almost comically, looking down at the child on the cot.

Kit's eyes get big and round as he stares up and up at Shad. He scampers down and executes an impressive bow for a four-year-old. Of course, the effect is lost when he coughs midway through it.

I pat the boy gently on the back. "I was watching him while Aggi does her chores. He's been sick and she doesn't have anywhere for him to go. I don't want her to get in trouble." My voice is defensive.

Shad's frown deepens. "Why would she get in trouble?"

"Because she brought her son to work?"

He crosses his arms. "Was she supposed to leave him alone?"

Confusion settles over me. "But…"

He sighs and squats down to the boy's level. "How are you feeling? You breathing okay now?"

Kit nods, eyes still bugging.

"Drink slower next time."

Just then, Aggi appears at the back door, arms full of a big bag of what I assume is laundry. The space we're in is already very small, so Shad's bulk leaves not much available room. Aggi bumps into him.

"Oh, excuse me," she says before doing a double take, the color draining from her face. Shad nods at her in greeting and she bows as best she can considering the burden in her arms. "Your Majesty, I'm so, so sorry! I didn't…I would never…"

Shad holds up a hand. "It's all right. No harm done. I am intruding in your domain, after all. Please forgive me."

The woman seems so flustered, she isn't sure what to say. Her mouth opens and closes for a few moments.

"I will get out of your hair. I just need to borrow Lady Xipporah for a while."

Aggi nods mutely, and I wave at Kit before following the

king out. I suppose I should have known that he would not punish her the way I suspect others in the aristocracy would.

"What did you need me for?" I ask.

His expression is very sober, and for a moment, I worry. "Would you be willing to repeat what you did at the commune yesterday, the thing with the plants?" He waves his hand in the air, indicating my magic usage.

I tilt my head to the side. "Where?"

"Most of our agriculture is grown indoors in produce houses under bliss light. We have far more indoor territory than outdoor and they're protected from the elements, the cold and weather, and the vagaries of nature."

"Well if they're so well-protected, what do you need me for?"

He sighs, then pulls out a small cube from his pocket and presses it. It begins to glow blue—bliss-powered. I eye it warily.

"This is a dampener. It's so we can't be overheard. What I have to say is sensitive. But it's information that could be useful to the Fai for negotiating. I would rather certain of my advisors not know I'm sharing it with you."

My ears perk up.

"There have been problems at some of the produce houses. Their capacity has been reduced significantly. Artificially. The plants are dying, and we're not sure why."

"How bad is it?"

"If we continue losing our crops at this rate, we will be on the brink of starvation by Second Yule. And that's with aggressive rationing."

That's only four months from now. I take a step back. "It's that bad?"

He nods, gravely.

"Why are you telling me this?"

"Because my only goal is to serve and protect my people. Some may not deserve it, but many others are innocent of any crimes against the Fai. You could use this information against us, I'm sure. But I can't have my people starving. Your presence here indicates the good faith of the Fai; I hope that counts for something."

Makani's words replay in my mind. *Find a way to take down the Nimali from within. If we don't destroy them, they will destroy us.*

It looks like they're already being taken down, no intervention from us needed. Is letting them starve so different to poisoning them with their own weapon? But as I look at Shad and consider the man I've seen so far, the idea that he is planning to poison the Greenlands seems less and less possible. It doesn't fit at all with the evidence.

Still, Makani seemed certain, and it's only been a few days. The Nimali are known to be treacherous and clever. Everything I've experienced so far could be part of a very strategic lie.

There are innocent Nimali—the mother and child in the next room are evidence of that. But I cannot so easily forget the cruelty of these people, either. The years of captivity so many endured.

I blow out a breath. "I don't think I can help you. If the Nimali are starving, it's through the folly of your own arrogance, believing you can harness the power of bliss and keep it bent to your will."

His head drops. "The food shortages will hit the Umbers first and worst. Cardinals will horde food as they do wealth, keeping the best for themselves until the last possible moments."

I cross my arms and turn away. "This is not my fight. Ask Citlali when you negotiate—she could send dozens of Land Fai with the ability to strengthen your crops."

"You're right, I just thought…"

I spin around, angry. "You thought what? Since I volunteered to come here to spare my sister, that I would feel sorry for you? Do you know why I'm here? Noomi was held for two years. Since she's been back, she wakes up screaming almost every night.

"You stole our souls, Shad. Your people cannibalized our lives. Robbed memories and futures and possibilities. War is one thing, but you raided our temples, took civilians to punish us and force us to bend. Our Water Priestess offered this deal as a gift. Not even knowing how close to destruction you all have already brought yourselves." I chuckle. "You may be trying to undo the policies of a tyrant, but we're still living with the pain of Nimali actions every day. Actions *you* helped carry out. And now you want more?"

My chest heaves and my eyes feel wild. I had no intention of unloading all of that on him, but the frustration reached a boiling point. Shad stays calm through my tirade, his only movement the rising and falling of his breath.

"We are not all Lyall," he says. "The damage he did to you, he did to us as well. Maybe not the exact same, but comparable. Trust me when I say that. His victims span both clans."

He comes closer and lowers his voice regardless of the dampener in his hand. "When that child in there is writhing in pain and his mother passes out because she gave him her last bite of food, I want to know that I did everything I could for them. You're right. This isn't your problem, it's ours. But you have an ability we don't have, one that could help. That's all I'm asking for. Any pride I have is not more important than that."

He turns silently and walks out the door, leaving me with my righteous anger and my shame.

NINETEEN

Xipporah

I AWAKE WITH A START, and it takes several moments before I know where I am. When it all comes back to me, I groan. On top of the realization that I'm not home in my own bed, my night was wracked with dreams I have no recollection of, but that left me unsettled. Grasping at the flashes of images quickly fading from my mind, I rub my eyes.

A flicker of something green from the dream tickles my memory. Another glimpse of the rich color of earth, tinged with an odd light. However, when I try to bring the pictures into greater clarity, they slip away into mist.

Reluctantly, I get my morning started wondering what the day will hold. Sparring with Shad and Harsh would be a good distraction, but after our argument yesterday, I'm not certain I should intrude on them. And facing another day of Major-domo Daggett's curated activities is decidedly unappealing.

Yesterday, he'd arrived with a troop of assistants to "aid in my acculturation to life as the queen"—a phrase uttered with the maximum amount of scorn. He knows as well as I do that I will never be queen. But I suffered through a tour of the building's entertainment facilities: an arcade on the nineteenth level where children and young adults gather for games and imaginary play; the Common Hall on the same floor that appeared to be where Cardinal women get together for tea and gossip; a small library on the fourteenth level mostly full of Azure scholars; and the sixth level's Great Hall, which, when not being used for gatherings and speeches, is filled with people of all castes and ages walking, jogging, and riding bicycles and other self-powered contraptions.

Throughout the tour, my every step had been monitored by several pairs of eyes, all no doubt reporting back to Daggett. I'd had no ability to go beyond the prescribed route and even attempt to get a glimpse of what might be hiding on any of the floors I was on.

So last night, I snuck out again, going floor by floor and searching for something, anything that would indicate there was an active poison program still happening, or anything else afoot that would potentially harm the Fai. I found nothing.

Today, I dress in one of the stiff red outfits that have appeared in my closet, thankful for my own comfortable boots, made of a sturdy but soft weave of textiles. Out in the dining area, Aggi greets me with a warm smile.

"Good morning, my lady. I hope you had a restful evening."

Guilt pangs within me at her kindness. Certainly it's her job, but she is also genuine. "It was fine. How is Kit doing today?"

"Not much better but no worse. I guess that's something to be grateful for. More children are getting sick, so whatever this is, it's still spreading." She sets my breakfast before me and removes the lid covering the tray.

"Do you have physicians or healers monitoring them?"

"An Umber child would have to nearly lose a limb before one of the healers would make time to see them. We have our own remedies, though." Her smile is small. "I'm sure he'll be on the mend soon. He's generally a hearty boy." Then she bustles off, back to the servant's room, where Kit's voice chirps happily.

The reminder of Umbers' low status in Nimali society gives me a chill. The food before me is as unappetizing as ever, but for the first time, I truly consider where it came from. How it's grown. How many people it feeds. Who gets priority access to it. I gaze sightlessly, unable to take a single bite. What is the bigger betrayal, helping to save my enemy from starvation or potentially poisoning them? Kit's laughter rises from the next room, followed by a coughing fit. But what if there isn't any poison? If Makani is wrong and Shad did what he said he would and destroyed the toxin along with the delivery device Lyall planned to use?

I replace the cover on the tray and set my elbows on the table, head in my hands, considering my mission. If I actually acquiesce to Shad's request, I might get the access and freedom to move around more and investigate. And maybe the earnest and unseasoned king will let something of his plans slip. Being in this suite or participating in one of the majordomo's approved activities will certainly not get me any closer to discovering a Nimali secret plan. But being in one of their produce houses...

I massage my scalp for long minutes, thinking through various strategies. Then I stand and move to the front door and ask the two guards stationed there to contact the king.

THE PRODUCE HOUSE Shad takes me to is underground. Of course. No wonder the food tastes so horrendous. We're inside a building just across the plaza from the Citadel. A few Azure scientists and engineers mill around on the main level, but the rest of the workers are Umbers. They tend the raised beds, plant and weed and harvest. Crops here are at all stages of the life cycle—without the "vagaries of nature" as Shad put it, there's no need to observe normal periods of sowing and reaping, which means they should have constant access to the yields. Everything is done under a suffusion of bliss light, with concentrated beams shining down on the plant beds to mimic the power of the sun.

Back home at the shrines, the pools of bliss are peaceful and beautiful. Here, the trapped bliss used for Nimali energy production is dimmer, sadder, more confined. Unable to be in its natural, free-flowing form. A subtle shudder overtakes me as we descend deeper underground, and I try to identify the cause of my unease. The Citadel is filled with bliss light as well, but this edginess I'm feeling is new. My daimon perks up within me, taking note of my discomfort. I focus on the breadth of Shad's shoulders in front of me, willing calm into my bones. Is this merely guilt?

We descend several staircases until we reach the bottom floor. Just like on the other floors we passed, waist-high platforms contain rows and rows of planting boxes. Various crops are grouped together, all of them spindly and weak. The far side of the room is in total darkness, and overall, the lighting down here is much dimmer than on the other floors.

"We have been diverting the bulk of our energy to the produce houses since I became aware of the power issues," Shad explains. He motions to the dark side of the room. "But we've had to reduce production already."

"Have you all ever considered using sunlight?" I don't mean for the snark to be so pronounced, but the solution seems obvious enough to me.

"Not enough land. Plus, food grown out in the open would require more guards than we have available. Scavengers have always been a problem."

I think of the humans we encountered during the attack and how undernourished they appeared. It stands to reason they would steal any food they could in order to survive, but we've never had any problems with it in the Greenlands.

"There are plenty of rooftop gardens across the territory like what you saw at the commune," Shad continues. "But they would not be enough to feed all the clan. Plus they are subject to the—"

"The vagaries of nature, yes, I recall."

He slides me a look I can't decipher, but I turn to walk down one of the aisles. The leaves in this entire bed are withered and sagging. Even the healthier plants are so much smaller and weaker than they should be if they were grown normally outside in the elements.

I crack my knuckles and call my daimon forward; it's eager for this challenge. "How many produce houses like this are there?" I ask Shad.

"Dozens."

"Well," I say with a sigh, "I'd better get to it."

Two hours later, I've been through the four floors of this location, digging my hands into the soil and rejuvenating the crops. It's as if the plant life calls to my daimon, giving it a purpose beyond violence. The urge to fight is always on a low simmer within it, but when it's healing the earth, nourishing the soil, and restoring the plants, that drive goes quiet.

For years, I've been so focused on advancing in the Defense Division that I never stopped to think whether my daimon could enjoy something else. The spirits join us because they want to have experiences in the human world. Most don't seem to care too much what those experiences are, so long as the covenant is kept. Mine, however, has always had a distinct preference for violence. It's a pleasant surprise to discover that making things grow seems to please it just as much as training and defending.

And the work isn't easy. It comes naturally, but marshaling the daimon's spirit energy, funneling and focusing it into the plants that need it, takes a great deal of effort. The hours go by quickly, but I feel the strain.

Surprisingly and irritatingly, Shad has stayed at my side

the entire time. I don't get the impression he's watching me with suspicion about what I might do out of his sight, more's the pity for him. He truly seems enthralled by the action of repairing the harvest. He watches me from every angle as if he could see the power my daimon commands being funneled into the roots and stalks and leaves.

The top floor of the produce house is smaller than the others. One corner lies in total darkness with empty plant beds pushed against the wall and spent bliss cubes stacked in piles beneath them. I work my way down the rows, ending at the beds near the dark corner.

"Those cells are a lot bigger than the ones at the commune," I remark.

"They have more capacity and are meant to last longer."

After completing work on the plants, I crouch to inspect one of the exhausted cubes. What does the bliss feel, locked in these things? It is a sentient energy, but we don't know if it has emotions, per se. However, I've always thought of it as being similar to a wild animal. And no wild thing likes to be caged. Sorrow bleeds from me as I turn the tiny prison over in my hands, then set it down again.

"I think that's all I can do for today," I tell Shad, rising.

"I can't thank you enough, Xipporah. What you've done here has made a great difference. This will help us to hold off rationing for several weeks. Honestly, it's like a miracle."

His praise and obvious joy make my cheeks burn. "It's no miracle. It's just what we do."

"One of the hidden Fai talents."

"Our talents are hidden in plain sight."

Shad blinks and then his gaze is back on me, intently. "I have about a dozen meetings to get to today. But my gratitude is yours, sincerely." His attention warms me in places I can't bear to think about. I've been nearly successful in blocking the incident on the church roof from my mind, but the look in his eyes makes the memories flood back. Their darkness seems somehow brighter, sparkling with emotion. Then they grow wide and shift from me to over my shoulder. Disappointment fills me, and I turn to see what dragged his attention away.

The bliss cell that I had just picked up has begun to glow with weak light.

"You all really need to check those things more thoroughly before discarding them," I say, ready to move on.

Frowning, Shad sidesteps me to pick it up and turn it over in his hands. It flickers softly like kindling trying to hold a spark. "Believe me, we do check them extensively, especially here. We make sure to get out every last drop of energy because it's so precious."

I cross my arms, feeling unaccountably thorny. "It *is* precious. Too precious to use in such a manner."

He looks up from his inspection of the cube. "Too precious to use to feed ourselves? To create heat in the cold months?"

"Too precious to waste. For your elevator lifts and moving vehicles when all of you have perfectly good feet and claws and paws and wings."

Anger has made my breathing quicken; it's a far safer emotion than whatever I was feeling before. Shad sets the cube aside, stands, and crosses his massive arms, mimicking my position. "We are grateful for the lives the bliss has afforded us. We don't have your talents with our daimons, and our animals weren't meant to live in cities like this. We need to protect our human sides; living the way we did before the Sorrows was the best way that our forefathers found to do that."

"But it can't last. Your mines are all but dry, are they not? That's why you want our supply. And if you got it, what would happen when you depleted that as well? When you scrounge this peninsula for every last drop of bliss it holds? When the powerful, plentiful matrices that brought us all here are empty, what then? What will the Nimali clan do?"

He presses his lips together and flares his nostrils. His eyes are sharp chips of flint glaring back at me. In this moment, I've never been attracted to anyone more.

I lean toward him, my body acting on its own with no influence from my brain. A glimmer of surprise crosses his face, but he grows closer. Our lips are a hairsbreadth away from touching when the soft glow behind Shad brightens to a potent beam.

We both turn, squinting at the bliss cube on the ground, now nearly blinding with intense light.

"What did you do?" Shad asks, in awe.

"Me? I didn't do anything." I think back to picking up the poor dead thing and feeling sorry for it. "It just wasn't completely empty, is all."

"Bliss cells don't die and then come back to life on their own." He crouches down and picks up the dead cell next to it, then hands it out to me.

"What?"

"Do it again."

"I didn't do anything the first time." I take a step back, my heart racing for an altogether different reason. Fear makes my skin grow cold.

"Then it won't hurt for you to try again." His voice is reasonable, but the request is not.

I suck in a breath. "No."

I spin around, stomp over to the staircase, and don't stop moving, don't answer his calls, just race back up to the ground floor and out the front doors into the late morning sunlight. Shad is right on my heels, but out here his king's guard surrounds us. He doesn't speak on the walk back to the Citadel, and I'm glad of it.

What if it *was* me? What if I actually did something to make the bliss regenerate? Could the same power that heals the plants and causes them to grow in inadequate conditions restore the bliss as well?

It shouldn't be possible. I'm not sure I believe it is—there must be some other explanation.

I need to speak to one of the Crowns, but there's no way to have that conversation while I'm stuck here. Because if the Fai—the Land Fai in particular—hold the key to solving the Nimali energy crisis... If the beasts suspect they could use us in this manner...

My legs shake all the way back into the building. I barely keep it together during the long elevator ride back to the confining walls of my suite. But once inside my temporary home, I run to the bathroom and throw up.

TWENTY

Shad

THE CHAIR IS UNCOMFORTABLE, the room too warm, and the sound of the councilors trading barbs back and forth has become a low drone in my ears. But through the haze of another endless meeting, my focus is continually stolen by thoughts of the bliss cube. The one that was definitely cold and lifeless before Xipporah touched it. Now, it's restored to full strength.

Nothing like that has ever happened before. And the same fears that must be running through Xipporah's head now assault me.

Lyall captured and enslaved the Fai merely as a means to destroy their morale. The free labor was originally a bonus, one which our society came to depend on over the years. Trammeled Fai drudges, unable to form new memories, or communicate, or control their own actions, were also unable to complain and would work the most tedious jobs. No one asked how they felt about it, and the trammeling made it so they couldn't have answered anyway.

But if it's true that the Fai can restore bliss?

Part of me hopes there is some other explanation for what I saw. Mostly so I do not ever have to face such a decision.

The idea that our enemy could be the key to our salvation, but only if we force them to serve us again, wrenches me sideways.

If it is true, and if we still had the trammels and the soul-catchers, we could certainly re-enslave them and compel them to revive every last bliss cell in the territory. And while the trammels were all destroyed when the Fai escaped, we have the knowledge to make new ones—our priorities have just been elsewhere.

But I have no desire to see the Fai enslaved again—the dilemma cuts me down to the bone. What would I sacrifice for the benefit of my people? How can we survive without the bliss?

So far, I've told no one of my suspicions about the Fai abilities, not even Harsh. It's not that I don't trust him, but this knowledge is a burden. A horrific albatross around my neck—so terrible I hesitate to even contemplate it.

I shift in my seat. For the first time, I wonder if it wouldn't be better to have no conscience like my stepfather. Lyall would not have hesitated to make the decision that would most benefit our people. He cared nothing for the Fai. They are not my concern, either, but the look of sheer panic in Xipporah's eyes won't leave me. Could I relegate her to a life that goes against everything she holds sacred? And if I could not do it to her because I am coming to know and like her, could I do it to another Fai?

We are still enemies. I have met more than one on the battlefield, but war is different, is it not? However, is not the potential starvation of my people a war of its own? All battles have casualties.

"Your Majesty?" Sir Denby calls to me for what I suspect is not the first time.

"Yes? I didn't catch that."

He blinks, and I can practically see the gears turning within as he hides what must certainly be annoyance and chooses a warm smile instead. "We were seeking your thoughts on the proposal to increase scouting ventures across the wall to seek a new source of bliss."

"Our meeting seems unable to hold your attention, Your Majesty," Lady Linh says with a sneer.

I narrow my eyes, leaning forward until her expression blanks and she stiffens. "My attention is in many places. The myriad problems I inherited from my predecessor are constantly on my mind." My voice is a soft growl, my patience too thin. I turn back to Denby. "This proposal seems fool-hardy to me. We've sent out expeditions for years seeking these rumored sources of bliss in No Man's Land, and they have all failed."

"They have not been as extensive as what is being proposed," Sir Barrett says. "What's needed is a long-term mission, weeks not days."

I tap my hands on the large table we sit around in the Council Room. "Our forces are spread thin as it is. And I fear such an assignment would be suicidal. Patrols report that Revoker activity has been picking up out there. I've already retracted the area our troops monitor; you want to expand it?"

"We are facing desperate times!" Sir Barrett says emphatically. "Everything we know is in peril. Greater risks are needed. Our soldiers are courageous; they can handle the threat the Revokers face."

"And how exactly would we transport the bliss if we do find it?" Dame Ayisha asks, brow raised imperiously. "How many *courageous* soldiers and workers do you expect to sacrifice on this fool's errand?"

Barrett slams his hand on the table, but Ayisha is not moved. She glares at him, making it obvious that her years in the military have left her difficult to intimidate.

Sir Denby raises his hands in a calming motion. "Listen, listen everyone. Tempers are flaring, that is for certain. Let us all try to cool down. We're all on the same side." His affability seems to work in causing Ayisha to sit back. Barrett glares but stays quiet.

"If labor is an issue, we could always revisit production of the soulcatchers and use the Fai again." Lord Edwin's statement is met with silence. As far as the Council is concerned, the escape of the Fai was an embarrassing Nimali failure, one most would prefer not to think about.

My body grows taut, but I work not to show how much the suggestion disgusts me. Those who believe enslaving the Fai again is a viable option will not be convinced by words—time has proven this. So I speak to them in language that they understand. "Oversight and management of Fai workers has distinct disadvantages. And given the fact that one of our own is currently living among them as a hostage"—I motion to Denby, whose face grows pinched and strained—"that is an untenable suggestion. Plus, the raids would pull our troops away from other important duties.

"Dame Ayisha is right—even if we find some far-flung matrix out there like the rumors say, we are currently not in a position to construct the pipeline necessary to bring it back through the wall." I don't mention the disturbing Revoker activity, the idea they may be trying to get through the wall themselves, but it's still top of mind. "How is the progress on mining deeper in our existing wells?"

Lady Raina speaks up. Her background is in engineering, a rare Cardinal who interested themselves in such a pursuit. "I have personally overseen the construction of the new drill. We are successfully going deeper than before. So far, we've found several thin streams of additional bliss. It's promising, as it could indicate the presence of a deeper well, as was theorized."

"How fast is your progress?" Linh challenges.

"Three-hundred feet per day," Raina responds.

"That is positively glacial," Linh says.

"There is a layer of thick bedrock we have to get through.

That speed is far faster than anything achieved with our equipment up until now." Raina is affronted.

I jump in before the bickering can get too heated. "I think this is the more reasonable option. Please continue, Lady Raina, and keep us updated as to your progress. Was there anything else?"

Four people raise their hands. I resist the urge to roll my eyes, but just barely. Instead, I take a deep breath and gather my scattered attention. Thoughts of Zanna, out there in the wilds tracking the missing princess, swamp me. I hope my friend is still alive. I hope Callum is doing as well as he pretends to be in his monitored check-ins.

And most of all, I hope I won't have to sell my souls to keep my people alive.

TWENTY-ONE

Xipporah

WHEN THE MESSENGER arrives at breakfast to alert me that King Shad has wall-to-wall meetings today and won't be able to see me until dinner time, I'm relieved. Without him haunting my steps, I'm certain I can get away from the guards. I tell myself I'm glad not to have to see him. And almost believe it.

I head to another produce house. They're located around the territory, so it's a decent way to cover a little more ground and at least start looking for anything that seems out of place.

This building is two blocks off the plaza and is smaller than the one I visited yesterday. It's there that I hit paydirt— on the second level, I discover a small batch of lavomile. It's a surprising find, as I'm fairly certain the blend of plants is something the Fai agriculturalists invented. I wonder if this batch was reclaimed from one of the Fai closets in the Citadel. While working to rejuvenate the plants, I pluck a few lavomile leaves surreptitiously and pocket them.

My guards have positioned themselves at the main door, and the few Nimali workers on duty give me a wide berth—all except one, a cheerful young Umber man named Jez. He seems just as taken with my abilities as Shad was and stares openly.

"How does your daimon do that?" he asks, wide-eyed when I take a water break.

"I'm not sure that I can explain it. This is just part of what the covenant provides us."

"What kind of daimon is it?"

He has no knowledge of Fai culture and what's considered rude for us, so I brush off my instinctive offense at the personal question. "Tiger. And you?"

"Muskrat."

My brows rise. "Back home, you would be able to do this, too. All Land daimons have the ability."

Jez stares at his own hands as if amazed they could possibly hold such power. I think perhaps his mental faculties aren't terribly acute, but he looks up with a broad grin that I can't help but return.

"What do you do here?" I ask him.

"Mostly help whoever needs it. Run errands. Sweep and clean up. Deliver equipment. Get folks water when they're thirsty."

"Do you like it?"

He nods emphatically. "I love the plants. I like helping things grow, though I can't do it the way you do. Back at home we had some worms infest the greens, and I plucked them all out, but it wasn't pretty."

We continue chatting as I work. Jez is a sweet boy. He did the trials young, at eighteen, the earliest age possible, and I gather his parents were hoping he'd join a strong enough daimon to allow him into the army.

An Azure man stomps into the room and barks at Jez. "It's nearly time for the first shift break! Why aren't you at your station?"

Jez ducks his head and mumbles an apology, then races off to the side of the room to grab a tray off a side table, which also holds a pitcher of water and stack of cups. I do a double take at the pitcher as my idea forms.

I work for several more minutes, monitoring my guards, who look predictably bored, and crumbling the lavomile in my pocket into the smallest pieces I can manage.

Eventually, I make my way to the pitcher and pour myself a glass of water.

"Oh, Lady Xipporah," the Azure man cries, crossing the room swiftly. "If you need anything, please just alert one of the floor assistants."

My back is to him and I have just enough time to crumble the herbs into the pitcher before turning. "It's no bother."

"Not a bother at all," he says, looking around and apparently annoyed to find that no assistants are present. But Jez returns to the room at that moment.

"Jez! Make sure Lady Xipporah has some refreshment."

The young man nods and approaches with his tray.

"And I'm sure my guards would appreciate some water as well," I say. "It *is* rather warm in here."

"The plants like it warm," Jez says with a grin. Guilt pummels me—using simple, sweet Jez is a horrible thing to do, but lives are at stake. If I fail in my mission, every Fai will pay the price. This justification doesn't quite help with the tightness in my chest as he carefully pours cups of water, but I push it away.

I hold my breath as the young man offers the drinks to the guards, who gratefully accept.

Over the next hour, drinks are refilled. Everyone in the room sips from the drugged water. I pretend to as well, then douse the plants when no one is looking. The dose was tiny enough that I'm certain it's safe—it will just take longer to work and last only a short time.

Finally, heads start to sag, and the guards are asleep on their feet. Jez has curled up underneath one of the plant beds, and the Azure man in charge has nodded off in a chair in the corner.

Once I'm certain they're all out cold, I make my move. Since I'm dressed as a Cardinal, the Nimali in lower castes don't pay much attention to me as I slip through the halls and onto other floors. I race through the stairwell, checking other levels to ensure the entire place is dedicated to crops. Once I've verified that, I head outside. I have about an hour until everyone starts to wake up.

The skies are overcast—another dreary day. This block is fairly quiet, with a few shops on the far side of the street. But just behind me is one of the buildings I noticed the other day with the guards out front. Hoping not to look suspicious, I tilt my head up and attempt to affect the snooty demeanor the Cardinals all seem to have. The few people who pass don't look twice at me.

I round the block and peer down the alley to find the building I want to investigate is also guarded in the back. Two female soldiers are posted there. Something important is definitely happening inside. But with guards at the front and the back, my options are limited.

A bird squawks overhead, drawing my gaze to the roof. That, of course, leads to thoughts of Shad and me on the ledge of the church.

I swallow and duck into the shadows of the alley, then call my daimon. The brick exterior of this building offers plenty of foot and handholds. My daimon could have scaled the wall regardless, but I'm even faster with the help.

I leap onto the roof and crouch, making sure no one is nearby. Any animal in view could be a Nimali, so I need to be doubly careful. Satisfied no one is around, I run to the next building and jump up to cover the slight difference in heights.

I'm still several buildings away from the guarded facility when an image scrawled in chalk on a roofline across the alley stops me short. I stoop to squint, not believing my eyes. It's a Fai symbol—the sign of the GenFi.

The chalk would not withstand a rainstorm, so this drawing is only a few days old at most. My heart stops, disbelief stealing my breath. I have two options: Continue to the guarded building or investigate what must be some sort of Fai presence in the city. I'm torn, but with time running short, I choose to investigate the symbol.

The alley is relatively narrow, easy enough to leap across with my tiger's aid; however, there's a chance the guards below will see me. I monitor them for a few minutes—neither look up. They're not expecting anything to surprise them from above. Shad really needs to review protocols with his soldiers, but that's none of my concern.

Steeling myself, I cross to the far side and get a running start, then leap over the alley to land gracefully on the other roof. The door to the top floor is rusted shut, but I force it open, wincing when it creaks loudly. This building doesn't appear to be in use, but it's not as damaged as some. The staircase is dark; I keep my daimon with me, listening for any sound.

A heartbeat on the top floor catches my attention. I head for it, keeping my footsteps soft. Thick layers of undisturbed dust coat the floors. Whoever is here didn't walk.

I enter a large, high-ceilinged, empty room with tall windows open to the elements, which indicates this isn't a building the Nimali have ever used. Standing before them is a man, his back to me. He's lean with coppery hair and wears Umber brown, a useful disguise.

"Von?" I say, incredulous.

He turns around with a smile.

TWENTY-TWO

Xipporah

"You!" I yell and lunge at him.

Von just smirks and leaps up into the air on his crow daimon's power, avoiding my strike. His laughter echoes overhead as my rage grows.

"Get your traitorous ass down here so I can show you how I *really* feel!" He zigs and zags over my head, staying close to the ceiling. I scramble up the wall and leap out at him. Of course, he zooms out of the way before I can get my claws and teeth on him. I land on my feet though, as always.

"You know you can't actually hurt me, right?" he jeers.

"Why not? How many Fai did you hurt? You could have killed every one of us!" I voice my suspicions about his actions the day the Fai escaped.

"You had enough Fire daimons to ensure there was no lasting damage," he says, unconcerned.

"We were in ice cuffs," I growl. "Our daimons were muted!"

He hovers, head tilted, as if this was something he hadn't considered though he'd been right there, cuffed along with us for much of it.

I press on. "And you were too cowardly to return and see

the results of your actions. Releasing those Revokers onto us while we were at our most vulnerable!"

"The distraction helped you all get away, didn't it? You should be thanking me. Makani certainly did." He hovers in the corner, avoiding my jump.

"He did no such thing."

"You want proof?"

Crouched on all fours and ready to spring upward again, I pause, considering his serious tone. There is no sense of a lie there. Makani did say he had intel about what the beasts have been up to, but not where it came from. Von is a telepath, so could he have been giving Makani reports this whole time? Without me or another Land Fai using our daimon's power to boost his own, his range isn't far enough to get all the way to the Greenlands, but he's no longer trapped, needing to stay close to a stolen soul. He could easily have crossed half the city, sent the message, and then returned.

But Makani knew exactly how I felt about Von. I'd given my debrief when I'd returned from the Nimali territory after the battle and had told my superiors in no uncertain terms what my suspicions were. How Von had disappeared mysteriously from the field we were being held on and the next thing anyone knew, the Revokers imprisoned in the lab were let loose upon us. Things were happening too quickly in the moment to think about it, but afterward I had plenty of time to wonder how those creatures had escaped their prison.

Von still looks smug.

"You have no remorse for what you've done, I take it," I spit out.

"Nimali died that day, that's all I care about." His voice is hard.

Those words echo what most Fai warriors would say, but they rankle me for some reason. Von leapt into a leadership position for reasons no one quite knows. He was my superior on the operation that brought us to the Citadel, but his methods were questionable and his judgment even more so. However, he's the only Fai here, and he evidently never left the territory, so I have little choice but to work with him. Our goals are the same, after all.

"That symbol, was it for me?"

He shrugs. "I've been listening in on the beasts regularly. Saw the announcement that a Fai princess was set to wed the king. Figured you'd be snooping around eventually."

"I'm surprised you didn't contact me directly." I tap my head, indicating his telepathy.

"Heard how you went back and snitched about me to anyone who would listen. Didn't think you'd welcome a mental message from me, and I see I was right."

We eye each other warily. "Come down. I won't hurt you," I say, finally.

"I don't think so." He zooms another circle around my head.

"So, why the symbol? You don't need my help? You know they're not sending anyone else. I'm the only Fai nearby for the next month, so you can either work with me or you can continue...doing whatever it is you've been doing. What exactly have you been doing?"

He eyes me with suspicion. I cross my arms and tap my foot, staring him down and waiting for him to come to a decision.

Finally, he rolls his eyes and lowers to the ground. Once he's close enough, I sneak a hard punch to his upper arm.

He leaps back into the air, and I grin menacingly. "You deserved that one and you know it."

His eyes are still narrowed. "You were always the bloodthirsty one," he murmurs. "I've been advancing the mission."

"How? What have you discovered?"

"The poison is still here. They never destroyed it."

A chasm opens up in my chest. "How do you know? You've seen it?"

"No, not yet, but I've overheard some very interesting conversations among the king's councilors."

"The councilors, but not the king?" Some hope still lives within me that Shad is what he appears to be, but Von begins laughing.

"You think the Nimali king wouldn't know about this? I'm sure the orders have come straight from the top."

Doubt still rages within me. It must be written on my face because Von scoffs. "What, you're supposed to marry him so all of a sudden he stops being a beast? They are treacherous and evil. All of them. Citlali was foolish to even suggest this ridiculous exchange."

"So, you haven't seen the poison and don't know where it's being kept?"

He sobers. "No, not yet. But it's here."

"That building with the guards?" I motion in its direction.

"Haven't been able to get inside. We need to crack the security. It's all biometric—which means you are the best bet for getting inside."

From here, I smell the fact that he hasn't been able to bathe properly recently. His unpleasant odor makes my nose curl with disgust, and I step back.

Fortunately, Von turns on his heel and marches to the window. Anyone looking up might see us; I keep most of my body along the wall and only peek out, while he stands there in full view.

"Aren't you afraid of being spotted?"

"What? To them I'm just another Umber on some errand. Now listen, that building with the guards, I've seen councilors headed in and out of it as well as a more nondescript brick structure on the other side of the plaza." He points to a section of plaster that's fallen from the wall, where he's made a crude map in chalk.

"Those are the places we need to check."

"Which councilors did you see?"

He looks at me askance. "What does it matter?"

I'm not familiar with the political machinations around here, but I can identify the people who needle Shad the most. I'd bet anything they're the ones responsible. But maybe Von's right and it makes no difference. If the poison is still here, then the Fai are at risk, period.

I back away. "I'd better get back now. My guard's sleeping potion will be wearing off soon."

"Work on getting access to that building. I'll be checking the other one," Von says.

"And if we find the poison?" I ask.

"What did Makani say to you?"

I swallow. "Use it on them before they can use it on us." The words are ash on my tongue, but Von grins.

"It's not something to be happy about," I snap. "There are innocents here. Women and children. The elderly. Not all the beasts are soldiers."

Now he looks at me like I'm insane. "What does it matter? How many of them cared when we were enslaved and trapped here? When we were punished? Had our souls stolen? Our voices permanently taken, our memories destroyed, our free will shattered?"

The pain of those trammeled is always with me, but I can't be so glib about the destruction of everyone in this territory. "What could their children have done to help us?"

"Those children you seem to care about so much will grow into adult Nimali. Grown-up beasts with a thirst for blood that rivals your own. And what of the *Fai* children? Would you sacrifice them? You know what the beasts plan to do with the poison, right?"

"I know we need to destroy it. Of course we need to save our people, all I'm saying——"

"When Markus infiltrated the Nimali, he caused the maximum amount of suffering. Crush the nest and the enemy won't grow old enough to come after you again. It's the only way they'll learn. To wipe them out before they do the same to us is the only way to ensure the futures of *our* children." He's breathing hard now with a feral glint in his eye. "I can't believe I have to explain this to you of all people."

"You don't have to explain anything to me," I snarl. "I understand more than you ever will."

"Then you know what's at stake here. The poison is real and it's either them or us."

Or if Citlali is right, it will be *both* of us.

Something Grandmother Emeli, Markus's wife, used to say bubbles to the front of my consciousness. *An eye for an eye makes the whole world blind.*

She also used to say you can't argue with ignorance, so I stop trying. But the sadness that fills my bones doesn't leave. I don't think it can.

TWENTY-THREE

Shad

THOUGHTS OF XIPPORAH have haunted me all day. They've taken up residence in the corner of my mind previously reserved for a constant hum of anxiety and the whispers that I'm a terrible king who will fail everyone I care about. Now, the volume of that noise has been turned down and the low-level discomfort joined by a different kind of unease—one sparked by images of her fierce expression, and the vibrancy of her mahogany eyes. By the way her lip curls when she sneers or how she laughs with her whole body. If I didn't know better, I'd think I was smitten.

Of course, that just ratchets up the static because I'm almost certain she's trying to destroy us. I need to confront her about what happened today. To look into those dark eyes and try to suss out the truth.

I know the two soldiers assigned to her quite well, and when they reported having nodded off during their shift and waking up with strong headaches, it was clear they'd been drugged.

Of course, when they awoke, Xipporah was just where she was supposed to be, and the plants at the produce house were thriving from her attention. So wherever she went, she couldn't have been gone long.

In her place, I would be collecting as much information as I could about my enemy. Hoping to gain intelligence that would aid in negotiation—I know Callum is doing the same, though so far, he hasn't been able to get more than a cheery letter out in his handwriting assuring us he's well. Since Callum and I have never had the need for an established written code and I have to assume his messages are being monitored, he's had very little to mention except the food and weather.

I'm not sure what methods Xipporah has in place to communicate with her people regarding whatever it is she's looking for, but I've added a secondary watch on her from now on—one that will monitor her from afar.

She answers her door looking downright exhausted. Sympathy pangs within me, but I squelch it. "Feeling all right?"

She straightens, pulling her shoulders back. "Never better."

I narrow my eyes. "You would make a terrible spy."

"I'm a soldier, not a spy," she snaps. "I don't like sneaking, I like attacking."

"And you thought attacking the guards there to protect you was the best idea?"

Her eyes widen, but any sincerity is missing. "Was someone attacked? When? How? And exactly what do I need protecting from?" Her head tilts, the accusation in her body language plain.

"Your guards were drugged with something potent this afternoon. Neither of them would ever fall asleep while on duty, and the raging headaches they had upon waking were dead giveaways."

Though she tries to appear impassive, she blinks several

times in a row and can't quite manage to hide her disappointment. She's right: Spying isn't her forte.

"And I wonder if you don't need protecting from yourself," I add under my breath.

"That's a strong accusation—do you have any proof? Sometimes people just get tired, duty or no duty." She crosses her arms and raises her chin, defiant.

"I take it you were ordered to look around, see if you could find anything that would help your negotiating position? I'd think you already have more than enough ammunition against us."

Her nostrils flare, but she doesn't respond. I lean in closer. "I'm as protective of my soldiers as I am of my people; if your true purpose here is to cause mayhem, then please rethink it. I entered into this agreement in good faith. But my bad faith is not something you want to experience."

Her gaze holds onto mine like a magnet. We're locked in place for a long moment, both strung tight as bows, before she turns away. "Message received," she grumbles.

I glance over her shoulder at the interior of the apartment and freeze. I don't know what I expected, but for it to look exactly the same way it did ten years ago is jarring. My throat is clogged with emotion, and I can't take my eyes off the upholstered chair in the seating area.

"What's wrong?" Xipporah asks from my side.

I blink, shaking myself, and pull my gaze away. "I haven't been in here in years. This was my mother's apartment."

She sucks in a breath and stands aside. My feet carry me forward, almost without my permission. "She…married Lyall after I went through the daimon trials and my…my father was killed."

"I'm so sorry." This is what it's like when she's sincere. Her true empathy hollows me out. Once again, the chair captures my attention. It was old before the Sorrows. Dark wood legs are carved to look like paws. I remember my mother's head bent over the cushion as she reupholstered it, sewing the seams with steady hands. It was like a ritual—every year, the chair got new fabric. "I'm surprised you haven't heard the story," I hear myself say. "People here like their gossip."

The last pattern my mother had chosen was a floral print, pink and yellow and brown petals and leaves overlapping. She purchased it from one of the Umber artists who carved wood-blocks into designs to print on fabrics. The painstaking labor offered little reward: a traded work assignment, a future favor. And all the best supplies were reserved for Azure artisans who would never believe an Umber had any creativity. But these touches of individuality were what made life more bearable in the commune.

"What happened to your father?" Xipporah asks, voice low.

I turn toward the bland, cream-colored couch where she sits. The flower-covered chair was the only thing my mother brought with her here.

I take a deep breath and launch into the story. "I leashed a dragon, as you know. There is a law that says any dragon daimon must be adopted by the royal family. It does not necessitate marriage, but Lyall insisted. He felt that since I was young—eighteen when I underwent the trial—I still needed the guidance of my mother. He challenged my father to a duel, since Pop wouldn't go along with a divorce under those circumstances."

Her gasp pierces the air. I sit down beside her and rub my head with my hands. "My father was a rooster shifter. He never stood a chance, but he was determined to die with honor."

Xipporah is motionless. "He didn't consider trying to stay around for you? Forfeit the duel?"

"He and my mother were parallels, soulmates. He

couldn't allow another man to marry his wife while he still lived. It went against his honor and, I think, his covenant."

She is quiet. So am I, for a long time.

"Of course, marrying Lyall broke my mother's covenant. Her daimon fled her, which is normally cause for exile. But the king's wife isn't subject to the same rules." My lips twist, but the memory is cold and hard. Like a fossil of former pain.

"Wait, wouldn't Lyall have known that such a marriage would cause her daimon to leave her?"

"Yes."

"I thought he wanted her to guide you?"

I shrug. "He wouldn't have considered a daimon to be required for that. And I'm sure her groundhog daimon wasn't considered useful enough to care about."

Her forehead creases as she tries to work out the logic.

"He was a monster, Xipporah, that is the only thing that makes sense. Maybe his real reasoning was to keep me isolated, remove any influences I had that might contradict his training. Regardless, my mother's will to live eroded and she faded away. Six months later, she was gone." Leaving me locked in a nightmare.

Xipporah shakes her head. "I'm sorry to hear that. It's awful."

I stare at my hands, alternating between fisting and straightening them. It had taken a decade before I was strong enough to even think of challenging the old king. And I'd still failed. Thankfully, neither of my parents were around to see it.

Her voice brings me back to the present. "My father was killed in a skirmish with Nimali soldiers when I was very young. I barely remember him and my sister doesn't at all. Makani came into our lives shortly after that. He's the only father I've ever known, but it was always apparent that we weren't *his*. Well, at least I wasn't."

I slide closer to her, sensing her sadness and wanting to offer comfort. "What do you mean?"

She motions to herself. "I'm actually taller than he is. According to my mother, I should have been born a boy. I'm built like one."

"I would have to strongly disagree with your mother," I say, unable to stop myself from taking in her form. She *is* tall and strong, but she has curves exactly where a woman should. And her strength is appealing, to me at least.

I must stare a little too long, because she snaps her fingers. "Eyes up here, buddy." But there is no anger in her words. In fact, she's smiling softly. Then she sobers. "Why do you think the dragon chose you?"

"I've often wondered that very thing myself. I wish I knew. When I was younger, most of the kids I knew dreamed of leashing a dragon, but not me. Not my best friends, either. One of them wanted to be a bird, thinking she could take off into the sky and never look back." I relive the burn of getting the feather and shooting star inked onto my back. Lynara never leashed anything. She never made it to her trials. When we were sixteen, she accompanied her parents, who were both builders, to one of their jobs to assist and earn extra allotments. The roof of the structure they were starting to renovate collapsed, crushing them all.

I wince as the old pain returns. Xipporah places a hand on my arm. "But you?"

I give her a questioning look.

"What did you want your daimon to be?"

"I don't know. A wolf. A lion. A bear." I chuckle. "I guess I dreamed of keeping my feet on the ground. But the dragon came, and everything changed."

"Maybe it chose you because Lyall was so…"

"So?"

"Horrible," she says. "The spirits require balance, you know. That's part of the way of things. While Lyall was king, everything was out of balance. He knocked the equilibrium so far off-kilter that the spirits needed a way to get things on track again."

I sit up straighter, considering her words. "And you think that's me?"

"Maybe. You're as different from him as can be."

My brows raise. I'm honestly surprised she would say such a thing to my face. "I know you have no love for Nimali."

"I've been training for years to defend against your incursions into our territory. You're the cause of so much of what's wrong in our world. But...I don't believe that *you* are the cause." Admitting that seems to cost her something; there's a nervous edge to her now that I think is normally well-hidden. She's revealing something raw and true, maybe in return for my own gift of vulnerability.

It's foolish. We can't trust one another. She proved that just today. But her hand is next to mine, and I'm brought back to that rooftop. Somehow, we're sitting closer. My eyes are drawn again to her lips. Their shape. The way she wets them. Wondering if they're as soft as they look.

Without conscious thought, I lean forward. This time, there are no distractions. No interruptions. Nothing but her and me on this couch, and she doesn't pull away.

I should stop this right now—never should have started, in fact—but I don't, curiosity winning over good sense. Her lips *are* as soft as they look, and the exploratory kiss moves slowly but with growing heat. I'm a starving man devouring his meal as I taste her, and she ravenously tastes me back.

She grabs my head. I squeeze her waist, our chests aligned —I breathe in, she breathes out. The sensation is one of weightlessness. Of stepping off the edge of the ledge just before my outspread wings catch air. Terrifying and exhilarating.

I have not kissed anyone in a very long time. You'd think dalliances with princes would be more common, but since I was eighteen, I was known to be Celena's. So I'm out of practice and she is eager, aggressive. She fists a hand in my shirt to draw me closer, then wraps strong arms around me to prevent retreat. In response, I lift her onto my lap until she's straddling me, the warm heat between her thighs right at the apex of my need. Hunger rips through me. The craving for this woman is unrelenting, but as she rotates her hips on top of me, guilt rushes in along with the pleasure.

I pull back, seeking a moment of clarity. But when she chases my lips, I give in. Again. Rational thought flees because the kiss is too good. Too all-consuming, too satisfying and yet insufficient all at the same time. I get the feeling that I could never in my entire life have enough of her—but too much would be bad for me. It's the knowledge that going further could have disastrous consequences that tempers my need.

"We have to stop," I say against her lips, even as I keep kissing her, moving to her neck and the junction of her shoulder.

She smells sweet, like honey and something fruity I can't place. Maybe something I've never even smelled before. A scent both intoxicating and uniquely her. I nuzzle against her shoulder, taking another deep sniff before finally pulling back.

The glaze over her eyes is beginning to clear; her body slowly stiffens. Gone is the delicious heat and pliable limbs intertwined with mine.

She slides off me and back to her side of the couch, breathing heavily. I miss the warmth of her, the feel of her; my hands want to grab her and place her back where she belongs, but she doesn't actually belong with me. And I don't belong with her.

She blinks and begins to speak but evidently does not know what to say. I lean back, speechless as well, breathing deeply. Trying to cool off, bring my libido and erection back under control with the recognition of what a mistake this was. Even if I feel absolutely no regret.

Finally, I rise, knowing if I don't it would be too easy to fall back in. "If things were different…If the world were different, then I would absolutely want to see where this leads."

I try to catch her eye. She's looking away, but I keep staring until she turns her head to me. I want her to know I'm serious. Still she doesn't respond, but at least she's listening.

"I will see you in the morning, Xipporah. Have a good evening."

Then I'm out the door and walking past the two guards stationed there for the evening. I move back to my own suite with a swiftness usually employed when something large is chasing me. My desire to turn around and go back, consequences be damned, is the predator at my back. But I can't give in. I need to push this longing aside like so many other things I want. None of them matter now. Only my duty.

Since I was eighteen years old, almost nothing I've done has been for me alone. Kissing Xipporah takes its place on a very short list…and will have to live there for a long time to come.

TWENTY-FOUR

Shad

My thoughts are still scattered the next morning when I enter the library. The vast empty space greets me, but where others find it intimidating, I think it's calming. There's something about the presence of all that bliss under our feet, teeming with the whole of our clan's collected knowledge, that just always made me feel like I was coming home. The answer to everything is here, if you just know where to look for it.

"Welcome, Your Majesty," the librarian's deep voice rumbles from behind me.

I startle and spin around. It should be impossible for such a large creature to be so light on his feet, but Akeem has always managed to sneak up on people.

"Good morning," I say to him. "Your message indicated you've discovered something about the weapon used against the caravan?"

His trunk rises slightly as he nods his giant head. "It is not much, but I think it's relevant." He moves gracefully across the room to a particular tile on the floor. They're all identical, and without his knowledge of the organization of the library, we'd all be lost. One massive, rounded foot stomps gently on the tile, and a wall of liquid bliss shoots up in front of us.

"Have there been any problems with the tanks beneath the library?" I ask. This building contains the largest source of un-mined bliss in the territory. Generations ago, our scholars figured out how to store data in liquid bliss, hence the format of our archives, but the energy could still be taken and converted for other uses—if we were willing to lose the knowledge.

"No problems," he thunders softly. "However, I have been monitoring the tanks myself. Moved my bed down there. Whoever is sabotaging the bliss elsewhere would have to get by me. I suspect the other targets are easier."

The fact that he takes his duty so seriously has always endeared me to Akeem. "I can assign guards if you need a break."

"I know you have few enough to spare. Don't worry, I can defend my domain." He turns to the vertical fountain of liquid data. "Show me the last saved records from the librarian's personal file." The stream shifts and changes, images becoming visible in the flow of data. They are similar to the monochromatic likenesses our comms produce, except they extrude from liquid instead of light.

What looks like schematics glide through the stream. Plans for handheld weapons that use concussive force.

"Whatever attacked the caravan had strong propulsive powers," Akeem says. "These are designs for weaponry that Lyall commissioned many years ago, but our engineers soon discovered bliss power is not sufficient for creating devices of that kind. The nature of the energy prohibits it."

"Why would that be?" I squint, trying to make heads or tails of the drawings.

"In short, the energy simply refuses."

I look over at him, surprised.

"In the same way a daimon will reject its host if we take an action that breaks the covenant, there is a sort of contract formed with the bliss when we task it with running our systems and machinery. There are limitations, boundaries, that despite great minds making attempts for years, we just haven't been able to overcome."

It's easy to think that the bliss can do anything because it's used for so much, but that isn't the case. Akeem continues, "Bliss energy enters this world from the Origin and so is connected to life itself. To create a weapon from it would require something akin to what the Revokers do."

"You mean use death in some way?"

He nods. "Unless another power source as potent as bliss has been discovered, I believe this weapon was created by corrupting the bliss with its opposite."

My skin crawls to contemplate it. "I thought woe was just a theory." No one quite knows how Revokers are created. It's been theorized that bliss has an opposing force called woe, and the monsters somehow harness this, which is how they're able to grow their numbers using dead bodies. The experiments Lyall ordered on Revokers couldn't draw a conclusion, however. If woe exists, we don't have the means to study it.

"Do you think the Revokers could have created this?" I ask.

"We have no reason to believe that they're capable of something so advanced. But I do believe the weapon you encountered would have the same limitations they have."

"It won't work over water or underground?"

"That would be my presumption."

I review the designs scrolling through the stream. They represent the failed attempts to be even more deadly than our daimon forms allow. "Well, that rules the humans out, doesn't it? They're rarely seen on the surface, and if they were building and testing something like this in the city, we'd know about it."

I pace away, frustration brewing. "So, we're no closer to knowing who was responsible for the attack. And me and Xi could be at risk again at any moment."

The soft footsteps of the elephant follow me. "Xi?" he asks.

"Xipporah. Lady Xipporah, whatever." I wasn't even aware I thought of her with a nickname in my mind.

"Is *Xi* the reason that you're so out of sorts today?"

I whirl around to face him. "I'm not out of sorts." Though I try to say it evenly, he responds with a snort and a low trumpet of laughter. The sound is so unusual it forces a chuckle from me.

"Fine. I'm a little out of sorts. Do you know anything about Fai daimons, by the way? The hidden abilities they have?"

His trunk curls upward to reach between his eyes. "We don't have anything comprehensive on them. The Fai have successfully kept them secret from us. Why?"

I weigh whether to tell him, but of everyone in this territory, Akeem is the only one who has never tried to influence me to take any particular action. He simply provides information, context, history, and even wisdom, all of which I appreciate.

I fish a dampener from my pocket and engage it. "No other pair of ears has heard what I'm about to say, and it must stay that way for now."

He stills, gazing at me solemnly. "I understand."

The weight of sharing this is heavy, but if there is any information to be had on the subject, it could save lives.

"Twice now, dead bliss cells have come back to life around Lady Xipporah. Around her daimon. She says she's not doing it—that she wouldn't, and I know it would go against everything the Fai believe about the bliss, but it can't be a coincidence."

The librarian's ears twitch. He looks off into the distance, thinking. Finally, he turns around. "Follow me."

We move to the far wall, where his trunk taps a hidden panel revealing the extra-large elevator. It only goes down there's the level containing the tanks of precious knowledge, the librarian's personal quarters, a storage space and safe room for emergencies, and the basement level, where we get off.

I've never been down here before. The lights are kept low, just barely enough to see by. A massive metal door, wide enough for my dragon to fit through, stands up ahead. With what appears to be some effort, Akeem heaves it open. It creaks from disuse, revealing a pitch-black interior.

Warm air pours out from within, and I follow Akeem inside. The low light from the hallway disappears as if the door was shut, though I hear nothing of the kind and it couldn't have happened on its own.

The air is far too warm for a basement, and no bliss is being diverted to this building for climate control. All the same, the space is almost suffocating. But after several long moments, the entire environment shifts.

A slight vertigo overtakes me. I nearly stumble where I stand, surprised at the odd sensation and the change in temperature.

"Did we…go somewhere?" I ask.

"In a manner of speaking," Akeem responds, sounding far away. "These are the old archives, the ones kept by librarians since long before the Sorrows. Since before a single Nimali ever set foot on this peninsula. I managed to convince Lyall that there was nothing of consequence to be found here, as my father did before me for Lyall's father, King Lyon. So neither man ever stepped foot in this space. Fortunately, they were alike in their shared disinterest in history."

A low light begins to fade in from the unrelenting blackness. The blue glow of bliss wafts up, revealing our surroundings. It's as if we've traveled to an underground cave; before me stretches a pit, deeper and wider than is possible for the basement of a building in a city. Light from the bliss radiates up, but its actual source is too far away to make out clearly.

Akeem stands a quarter way around the pit, the distance shrinking his massiveness.

"How is this place here?" My voice echoes slightly.

"It's not exactly here. We are both here and there, connected to the material world and to the Origin, with a foot in each place. Our bliss matrices exist in our world, but are portals to the Origin. This archive was built at the center of such a portal. Wherever there is a settlement, there is an entry to this place."

"Why didn't you want the other kings to come here?"

"You can commune with those in the Origin here, if you enter the pit," he says, instead of answering.

I peer down, unable to see the surface of the liquid. "Is it similar to the trials?" When we leash our daimons, we submerge ourselves in liquid bliss to travel to the Origin while still alive.

"You will not travel anywhere as you did then—this is more like an old-fashioned telephone box. Like a comm between here and there. It allows us to speak directly with the spirits. They will choose whether to answer your question or not."

The edge of the pit is daunting—it's like standing in the window of the throne room, about to leap into the air. Only this time, my daimon's wings won't catch my fall.

"And you've done this before?"

He chuckles. "Some questions may only be answered with the knowledge found here. It merely requires a leap of faith."

Faith. All right, then. I take a few deep breaths to steady myself, then close my eyes and step off the edge of the cliff.

There is no sensation of falling. I don't feel any wetness. But there is the impression of being held, kept safe, comforted. All is darkness again, but I'm not certain ther would be anything to see if a light did appear.

"Hello?" I call out with my mind. I have a souls·

understanding that my body isn't here; this is communication of the spirit.

The presence of another arrives. The difference is clear and my daimon takes note. Plus, it no longer feels like it's inside me, sharing my body. Instead, I sense it next to me—a familiar entity that exists as an extension of myself. We are one, and the newcomer is separate from us.

"King Shadrach," a voice whispers in my mind. Neither male nor female, old nor young, it is just a thought. "What answers do you seek?"

"I thank you, spirit, for attending to me. I wish to know, can a Fai daimon bring life back to expired bliss?"

"Does the answer matter if they will not consent to do so?"

The spirit's response gives me pause.

"Well, it may be possible that some of them would consent to aid us…if they do have that ability."

"I will answer the question that you have not asked, but should have." Though toneless, the spirit sounds somewhat amused. "Your two clans were not always at odds. Search your library for the Trivium. Once upon a time, it was unbroken, whole, and powerful. The tales have been buried. Forgotten by both sides. But perhaps you, King Shadrach, can be the one to mend it."

Before I can ask any further questions, the spirit is gone. Its presence exits my mind, leaving me alone with my daimon and the feeling that I have been found wanting.

At first, I'm not sure how to get back, and panic races through me. But I recall Akeem's words, his calm tone. He said a leap of faith was necessary to get here, so perhaps that is what's needed to return.

I settle, agitation fleeing, and imagine myself at the top of the pit, looking down into its unfathomable depths. And then I'm there, and Akeem is next to me.

We don't speak until we have retreated through the

massive door and he's closed it again with a clang. "Did you learn anything?" he asks.

"The spirit said to search for the Trivium, though the records may be hidden. And it said I might be the one to mend it. Have you heard of this?"

"No. But I will hunt it down. It will likely be a manual process if the entries were removed or never added to the database."

"I would appreciate it, Akeem."

My thoughts are just as scattered as they were when I arrived—even more so if that's possible. The elevator ride up to the main level is quiet, but as I step out and head for the door, Akeem calls out to me.

"Shad, remember your covenant."

I turn back to find his eyes glittering, pleading. "How could I forget?"

"Kill no creature not seeking to kill you. Take from none who has less than you. Love with all your heart when love finds you." He lists the familiar details of the contract we make with our daimons.

"And be grateful for every day you are granted," I say, finishing it.

His trunk twitches, agitated. "When love finds you, if you do not follow your heart, you risk your covenant."

And my daimon will abandon me.

I nod, understanding. "I won't forget."

TWENTY-FIVE

Xipporah

THE ONLY THING I can smell or taste is cinnamon. It filled my dreams last night, and this morning it still pervades my nose. My bedroom smelled of it. The common areas. My clothes. When Aggi sets a plate of breakfast mush before me, I hold my nose to choke it down, and is it my imagination or does it, too, smell like cinnamon?

I think Shad broke my brain.

The door chimes; Aggi races to answer, and then he's here. Stalking across the room toward me. My mouth goes dry. I press my thighs together involuntarily.

"Good morning, Your Majesty," I say to the top of his head, since he's avoiding my gaze.

"Good morning."

Aggi flutters around; Shad reassures her that he's eaten before asking after Kit, who's much the same today, if not a little worse. I've been too preoccupied to ask, and guilt makes my chest tighten.

When she disappears into the back room, I dig into the mush again, imagining what it would be like if it actually tasted like something. The illusion of cinnamon has fled in his presence, and he's seated too far away to smell. All I really want to do is taste him again. Which is insane. I let things get way too far yesterday, but in my defense, I'd never imagined such a horrible story. He nearly broke my heart. I spent the evening wondering what it must have been like for him to be orphaned in the manner he was, while becoming the protégé of his father's killer.

His mother's story also underscores the consequences of this engysis contract. A true marriage is meant to be one of hearts and souls and daimons. The spirits must suit and concede to share each other's lives. Growing up, we all heard cautionary tales of young couples who thought themselves madly in love, only to have their daimons refuse the pairings.

Occasionally, the lovers would try to maintain a relationship, but inevitably, the stress of the failure, the inability to ever have a true union of lives and purposes, would tear them apart.

My body is attracted to Shad. My heart bleeds for his story. But fortunately, my daimon has been very quiet where the king is concerned. And that's how it needs to stay. I sense its curiosity about him and his dragon, but that's all.

Shad doesn't seem inclined to speak. His body is coiled tight, a spring ready to snap. His knee jumps in a rapid staccato.

"What are your plans for today?" I ask just to make conversation.

His deep voice resonates. "Meetings. Always meetings. What about you?"

"Figured I'd head to the next produce house."

He nods, distracted. "I can walk you over. I have a little time."

"Oh, that's not nec——"

"It's fine." The floor vibrates a little from the force of his foot in motion.

"Did something happen?" I ask, putting down my spoon,

a little worried. I've never really seen him like this. Edgy but still closed off.

"Other than you drugging my men?" He looks at me now, brow raised.

I clamp my lips shut. I won't apologize for it—I'll do whatever I need to, as I'm sure will he. But now things are awkward. The only sound is my spoon scraping my plate. My cup lowered onto the table. Chewing and swallowing. I sneak glances at him only to find that he's evidently much more disciplined at being able to ignore me. But why is he even here? Just to make sure his precious soldiers stay awake?

He's obviously not thinking about the kiss, so I push it to the back of my mind as well. Once I'm done, we walk over to a new produce house, this one located on the other side of the plaza from yesterday's location. Farther from the guarded building that I need to get inside. Disappointment fills me. Unless I come up with another way to disable and distract my guards, there's no way I'll be able to sneak away.

Shad watches me for a few minutes as I get started on a crop of withering broccoli. Then he's gone, off to one of the dreaded meetings. If he weren't being such a pill, I'd feel sorry for him. But that is not what I'm here for. Any and all feelings need to be buried until the month is over.

The guards stay in the hall this time, and there's no Jez or even the Azure manager to talk to. Just me and the plants. I'm sure it's on purpose. Being alone should make it easier to steal away, but somehow, I doubt it. Shad is not an idiot; I'm certain there are measures in place to keep tabs on me.

With my daimon called, I sense the disturbance in the air before I hear the breathing of another person coming from the shadowed corner where the dead bliss light cells are piled. Instinctively, I crouch into a fighting stance, claws up. But the red-haired man who steps out of the darkness, glaring at me, is not here to fight.

"Von. What are you doing here?"

"I might ask you the same question." He looks derisively at the half-healed plant bed I've been working on. "Are you really helping the beasts?"

"I'm gaining their trust. Getting access to larger parts of the territory," I say, which is a partial truth. Then I notice a small, boxy device in his hands. Some sort of Nimali tech. "What is that?"

He flips a switch on the side and waves it around. The bright, steady overhead lighting dims. When he switches it off, the lights sputters back to life. "While you're gaining their trust, you are undoing my work," he says testily.

"*You've* been sabotaging their bliss power?" I ask, incredulous.

"Food, power stations. Whatever I can. It's going much better than I could have expected." He grins, pleased with himself.

I blink, my eyelids the only part of me in motion as I process. "But you're killing the bliss—even faster than they are! Where did you even get that thing?"

"I stole this from one of them. The Nimali were using it first. It's ingenious really, drains bliss down to nothing."

Tears prick the backs of my eyes. "How could you? That goes against everything we believe."

He brushes my concern aside. "Sabotaging them protects Fai."

"At the cost of the bliss! They're a peaceful, sentient consciousness."

"And yet you have no problem helping these cretins continue using it for their sad approximations of vegetables." He motions to the half of the plant bed I've yet to get to.

He's right, but this bliss would be in use anyway, even if I never came to their territory.

"The bliss is sacred!" I cry.

The door swings open suddenly, and a breeze crosses my face as Von darts up to the ceiling. He's out of sight by the time one of my guards, a wiry woman with white-blonde hair cropped close to her head, peeks in. "Are you talking to someone?" she asks, scanning the room.

"Just singing. Makes the work go faster." I plaster on a smile, which does nothing to ease her suspicions. But she closes the door again.

I stand there quietly, taking deep breaths, until I'm sure she won't come in again. Then a sharp pain pierces my skull; Von's voice forces its way into my head.

This is the mission, Xipporah. The telepathic power from his daimon is impossible to ignore.

You're saying you have orders to destroy bliss? I ask. *That can't be true. And how does this make you any different to the Nimali?*

This is war. His statement is simple and evidently enough for him.

But I shake my head. *It's supposed to be peace. I don't believe our captain or anyone in the Defense Division gave you those orders. Let's ask Makani.*

I'm still your superior, Xi. You don't have reason to question me.

I snort. *I don't know. I'm pretty sure you went AWOL when you didn't return to the Greenlands with everyone else. And releasing the Revokers on your own people has made you pretty damned unreliable.*

I sense he's getting ready to flee. The air shifts with the feeling of muscles bunching. I'm sure there's some hidden entrance he's found, but I'm not done with him yet. I leap into the air and catch Von by surprise then lunge, wrapping my arms around him and forcing him to the ground. Hopefully, the guards won't come in again to investigate the thump of our landing. Von wriggles in my hold, but I manage to get an arm around his neck and squeeze.

How about we contact Makani now? I'll amplify you so your power can reach him. Then we'll see what our real mission is, huh? I try not to gag at the rankness of his aroma. What I wouldn't give right now for phantom cinnamon in my nose.

Fine, his mental voice spits since I haven't given him much of a choice. We're touching, so my daimon's ability to amplify any other daimon's powers comes into play and also lets me communicate with other telepaths.

Von? Makani's surprised voice reverberates inside my head, answering the mental call.

Xipporah is here. She has some…questions about strategy. Von is doing his best to sound like he's in control.

Makani, I say. *Did you know Von was here?*

I don't have much time, my stepfather says. *Have you all made progress?* I note he doesn't answer.

Von believes he's found something; we still need proof, though. In the meantime, he's been draining their bliss.

The man in question tries to wriggle his way out of my grip, but I hold firm. *Scorched-earth strategy,* Von replies. *Weakening the bliss weakens them.*

But it's murder, I maintain.

There are always casualties in war.

Makani interrupts. *This is exactly what the beasts would do to us. How many of us have they already murdered? And isn't trammeling worse than death? They would wipe out our entire homeland and every living thing in it. The strategy is sound.*

I can't believe my ears. *But this makes us like them. Just as brutal. Just as savage. We've always held ourselves to a higher standard. And sacrificing the bliss is unthinkable.*

Makani scoffs. *The Fai have always done what we've had to in order to survive. Our legacy is one of adaptability and fluidity. That's the blood running through your veins, Xipporah. Von understands that. Everything is on the table to prevent this genocide. We protect our own without fail.*

Without fail, the GenFi motto. Instinct and training push me to repeat the phrase, but Von surprises me by sinking his teeth into the arm I have restraining him. His bite is so vicious he draws blood. I growl and release him, cutting off the connection with Makani.

"You *bit* me?" I rage at him, too loudly.

"You deserved it," he says, seething, teeth red with my blood. My eyes narrow, and I lunge at him again but he shoots into the air to escape.

"I'm starting to think you don't have what it takes to be a warrior, Xipporah. I can't tell you how disappointed I am." He disappears into the darkened section of the room, staying close to the ceiling.

When the door bursts open revealing my guards, I'm vibrating with rage and holding a bleeding wound on my arm.

TWENTY-SIX

Shad

THE INTELLIGENCE ROOM on the twenty-seventh floor is mostly taken up by the War Bowl—the nickname given to the shallow pool of liquid bliss that connects to all of our cameras and comm units. From here, we can monitor the communications of any clan member on the network and receive secure messages that cannot otherwise be intercepted. The Citadel has many eyes and ears, hence my almost paranoid use of dampeners, but this place is its brain.

I follow Lord Oren Noahson across the threshold to stand before the War Bowl. The aged spymaster served King Lyall and King Lyon before him. He's pale and stooped, with just a few snowy white hairs left clinging to his skull. But it would be unwise to let his ancient appearance fool you; his ears in human form are as good as his bat daimon's. And he's essentially irreplaceable, having kept three generations of kings secrets. But I never considered even trying to get rid of him, as he's one of the only people in the Citadel not jockeying for position.

His suit, cut in a style from a bygone era, is an almost aqua blue, a sign of humility among Azures. And though he's been offered promotion to Cardinal many times, he's never accepted. Something about his lack of ambition makes me inclined to trust him—as much as anyone can trust a spymaster.

Once the door has closed, Lord Oren speaks. "Your Majesty, Captain Neelia has requested a secure connection with which to speak to you."

"Much appreciated, Lord Oren."

He shuffles to the side of the room to engage the War Bowl and ping Neelia. In moments, her head and shoulders extrude from the liquid. Her expression is stony, and I hold my breath for her report.

"Your Majesty, the overnight patrol team did not return for shift change this morning. We initiated a search and found evidence of a fight. There was blood and Revoker venom on the ground, but our team was gone."

My stomach hollows out. "Were there any tracks? Any idea of where the Revokers disappeared to?"

She shakes her head once. "I have a tracker searching the area, but so far we've found nothing."

My fists clench with impotent rage. "Pull the tracker back. Pull everyone back. I want our patrols limited to the wall only. Nothing beyond the reach of the lights. Whatever's going on out there, I don't want to lose any more soldiers until we have a better handle on things."

Though she remains impassive, I think I see a hint of relief in her eyes. "Yes, sir."

The connection ends and the bliss flows back down into the bowl smoothly. I take a few deep breaths, gathering my thoughts.

"Your Majesty?"

"Yes, Lord Oren?"

"The Council has gathered outside the door."

I look up, brows raised. He peers down a bank of smaller comm screens embedded in the surface of a table in the corner, which monitors the hallways. "They have apparently learned of the urgent message."

I roll my eyes. I'd instructed Neelia to keep the Revoker threat to the wall secret, so of course she'd assumed sending a secure communication would be best. I hadn't thought to tell her that, while the councilors wouldn't be able to intercept the message, they all had ways of knowing one had been sent. And none wanted to be in the dark, much as I'd prefer to keep the shades drawn on them.

However, things have escalated. Four missing soldiers is not a secret that can be kept. "All right. Let them in."

Oren shuffles over to the door and opens it, allowing the gathered council members, all seven of them, to stream in. They all begin speaking at once, voices raised, and, to my surprise, it's Oren who gets them to quiet down by flipping some switch that makes the bliss in the War Bowl churn and froth angrily like a hurricane-level wave.

This shocks everyone into silence. It's a trick I need to learn.

"I assume you all are here because your spies alerted you to the private message I received?" I stare at them all in turn, but few have the grace to look ashamed. It's just how things are done in this place.

Shaking my head, I give them a brief rundown of what we've learned. The damage to the wall and the missing soldiers.

"I've pulled back all scouting and patrolling outside the visibility of the wall itself. We cannot afford to lose more people needlessly."

"But those soldiers are there to protect us from the Revokers!" Lady Linh says, blanching.

"And they can do that without heading blindly away from their backup. I know from experience that we gain very little from these deeper patrols into No Man's Land."

Sir Barrett seems to be grinding his teeth. His entire body thrums with tension.

"Something to say?" I ask him.

Glaring, he leans forward, nearly crossing into my personal space. "It is cowardice to retreat when we should be advancing. We need to be moving out to destroy the Revokers and search for more sources of bliss. There are always casualties on the way toward progress."

"Spoken like a man with no sons or daughters in the army."

His head rears back as if the words were a verbal slap. "Without bliss, my daughter will face certain death as well."

"Certain death?" I repeat. "You're being dramatic. It's true we're in crisis, but the Nimali may have to accept that we'll need to adapt."

This garners gasps from the other councilors as if it's something they've never considered before.

"Adapt to what?" Lady Linh asks incredulously. "Become like the savages in the Greenlands? Light our homes with candles and eat roughage foraged from the trees? We are Nimali. We are advanced, and we have a way of life we need to uphold."

I strangle my temper to speak quietly. "Some of our people have already resorted to candles because of the brownouts." She wrinkles her nose in disgust, either at the thought of such a rudimentary light source or at the Umbers forced to use it.

"And our lives are my priority," I continue. "We need to *preserve* life when it is not absolutely necessary to risk it, and I, as king, deem these patrols unnecessary."

Quiet reigns for a moment before Barrett squares his shoulders. "Well, maybe you should consider abdicating."

This silence is shocked, reeling from the audacity of the man to say the words out loud, regardless of how many have likely felt that way. Part of me actually respects him for it. At least face me head on instead of all the subterfuge.

I keep my lips pressed together, letting him dig the hole deeper. "If you are not ready to make the difficult decisions, there is no shame in abdicating the throne. Or taking on a regent until you are——"

"I am not a child, Sir Barrett," I say. "I do not need a regent. I am also not Lyall—and every one of you should be thanking the bliss for that. My methods will be different than his and you all will have to get used to that."

Barret shakes his head. "I'm not so sure we can afford to get used to it, Your Majesty. We might not have enough time left."

How he can believe that our technology is more important than our lives is a mystery to me. But it's clear he's not alone in the opinion.

Dame Ayisha speaks up. "I, for one, applaud the king's reticence to put our soldiers in harm's way needlessly. Do you really think we will find a mythical, unlimited source of bliss, Sir Barrett? That the shortages we are seeing won't occur again in the months or years to come? It is not an infinite resource. That is something that should have been taken into consideration years ago."

"These shortages did not occur on Lyall's watch," Barrett grits out.

"Is that really true? Or did you just not know about them?" I ask. "Because I have only been king for a month, and look at where we are. For you to put the blame for all of this at my feet is nonsensical. This started long ago, and our dependence on the bliss has been an issue for years. I am merely the one who must deal with it as it falls apart."

Sir Denby speaks up. "I agree with His Majesty. We must find a way through this situation that does not sacrifice the ones we are meant to be protecting. If we lose soldiers need-lessly to the Revokers or other threats, then what are we doing this for?" He motions to Raina. "The drilling is still moving forward. That is a plan that harms no one."

Barrett remains unconvinced, still seething with anger and watching me with suspicion. At least it's out in the open—some of it, at any rate. There are other council members whose loyalty I'm unsure of, but Dominga's father was always going to be an issue.

"This meeting is over," I say. "I've made my decision on this matter."

I'm the last to leave the room, and I find Harsh there waiting for me. "If it's bad news, I don't want it."

He grunts and leads me into an empty conference room, then engages a dampener. "Blake was here with a report on his progress in the Independent Zone." I sit heavily and motion for him to continue. The look on his face isn't promising. "One of his people, a groundhog shifter named Elsbeth, is missing."

"Missing? How? Have they encountered any kind of resistance while down there?"

"No, he hadn't thought they'd been noticed."

"Is it possible she just got lost?"

Harsh thins his lips. "With a groundhog daimon? Unlikely. And they think they located a former Silent Hands hideout, but it hasn't been used for a while. They must have several locations throughout the city. But for now, the trail has gone cold."

I slump over until my head hits the table. "No leads and a missing woman." I don't know this Elsbeth, but guilt over her disappearance deluges me all the same. Plus, she's a groundhog shifter, just like my mother. "Maybe we should pull them all out."

"I doubt Blake would agree," Harsh says. "He's keeping up the search until they find her. And he gave me this."

He places a square of dark fabric on the table. I slide it over for a closer look. It's dirty and whatever color it might have been has faded to a sort of muddy gray, but the stitching gives me pause.

I hold it up. "Does this look like it used to be brown?"

"Blake thought so, too. Said the stitching looked familiar."

I pull the handkerchief out of my pocket that Akiko gave me on my last visit and compare the needlework. "It's one of hers."

"The humans must have scavenged it," Harsh says.

But I shake my head. "Umbers aren't like Cardinals with yards of fabric to spare and waste. Everything is used and kept and reused again and again. Akiko made these for the kids—really for the parents—and complains about our constantly runny noses. It's not something that would get thrown away carelessly."

"Could humans be sneaking into our territory and stealing?"

"Wouldn't he have found more than a single scrap, then? He didn't mention seeing anything else that looked Nimali, did he?"

"No."

I turn the cloth over in my hands wondering who this belonged to. Then jerk with a realization.

"What?" Harsh asks.

"The exiles."

His eyes get big. When a Nimali loses their daimon either as punishment or by breaking their covenant, they get thrown out of the territory to survive as best they can. It's always been a cruel practice, and when I was prince, I imagined myself taking power and finding the lost ones, welcoming them back into the Nimali fold. But I've been overwhelmed with one crisis after another and so much of what I thought I'd be doing has gone by the wayside.

"Who would have cause to hate Nimali more than an exile?" Harsh mutters.

A cold feeling spreads through my gut. "You're right. Do we have a record of them all?"

"I'm sure the clerks keep that kind of documentation. It must be somewhere."

"You have a lot on your plate; I'll ask Dominga to look into it."

He gives me a strange look.

"What?"

"So now you trust her?"

"Dominga? I trust her to help me stay in power until Celena is found or until she accepts that the princess is never coming back."

I think of Zanna, out there on a futile quest. With the uptick in Revoker activity, soon it will be time for me to accept that my friend is never returning, either.

Harsh sighs. "All right. I'll ask her. No need to get you in her crosshairs unnecessarily." He rises wearily and another pang of guilt hits me.

"Harsh?" He pauses, head tilted. "Thank you. I know I've been relying on you too much, and I'm sorry for that. When Callum gets back it should be a little easier…"

He snorts. "What you're doing is hard. You're carrying the clan on your shoulders. I should be thanking you." And with a wry smile, he's gone.

Alone with my thoughts, Barrett's words run through my mind on repeat. *There is no shame in abdicating the throne.* If only that were true. The Council lacks confidence in me. Unsurprising, when I lack it as well. How in Origin's name am I going to hold this crumbling tower together?

TWENTY-SEVEN

Xipporah

I'M SITTING in the floral chair in my suite with the lights off when the door chimes. Not having the energy to get up, I call out, "Come in."

Shad stands silhouetted in the doorway, taking up all the air in the room. The lights, on some kind of motion sensor, brighten when he enters, using up just a little more of the bliss's life energy. That reality makes me unaccountably sad.

His concern is palpable when he catches sight of me; he sits on the coffee table beside me, hands clasped between his knees, which nearly touch my own. I'm glad he doesn't ask if I'm all right—it's obvious I'm not, but I can't tell him why.

My hands shake. I press them against my thighs to get them to stop. The place where Von bit me still aches. Not a major wound—I've suffered far worse—but this pain goes beyond the physical. It's a throbbing that's taken over my whole body.

What Von is doing, and what Makani approved, feels wrong to me. But isn't disapproval a betrayal of my people? Shouldn't I be willing to do anything and everything to assure victory—even harm innocents if necessary? And wasn't what the Nimali did to us even worse? They've committed so many atrocities over the years…don't they deserve payback?

Aggi bustles in with a covered plate. "Oh, Your Highness. I didn't realize. Should I bring you something?"

"That would be lovely, Aggi, thank you."

From the corner of my eye, I see her jerk, startled. "Oh, um. Y-you're welcome. Your Majesty."

When she disappears through the door, a soft smile takes over his face. "It's good to say *thank you* again."

I look at him quizzically.

"I'm trying to change the Nimali culture. A little bit at a time. Maybe if it starts at the top, we can achieve a society that's…a little more egalitarian. Or is that just a pipe dream?" He's talking mostly to himself, rubbing a hand over his head wearily.

"You look tired," I say. "I mean—" His expression turns wry, and I think of how to walk it back, then shrug. "Well, it's true."

"I am." His grin is both sad and boyish.

"Do you want to talk about it?"

"Not especially. You?"

I shake my head. "Absolutely not."

His lips part to respond, but Aggi arrives with another plate. We move to the table to eat in silence. I'm used to the mush now and try to be grateful at least for the nutrients it's providing me. Meanwhile, I focus on Shad's mouth. His jaw chewing. His throat swallowing.

I can't tell him what Von's up to. I want to, but what then? Will he be forced to retaliate? I can't be responsible for that. Is there a way I can stop Von on my own?

The sabotage he thinks is so useful will only blow back and harm the Fai, I'm sure of it. Wasting all that bliss, killing—murdering—it for strategy… No, I need to protect my people from reprisal if the Nimali discover what's happening, as well as safeguard the innocents in this territory. I don't trust Von any longer, but I can't rely on Shad to help the Fai, either. He's got the weight of his own people on his shoulders, and our goals do not align.

He starts to speak, dragging my attention from his lips. Thankfully, he hasn't seemed to notice my preoccupation. "I'll be alerting the Crowns of something we found—it concerns them, too. Looks like Revokers have been trying to tunnel through the wall."

The slush in my stomach hardens, and I straighten. "Where?"

"On the eastern side. About a mile in from the bay."

"I didn't think they could do that."

He presses his lips together. "Neither did we." He slides his plate away and rests his forearms on the table. "Attacks on our soldiers across the wall have increased over the past few weeks. The Revoker behavior is changing—maybe *they're* changing, we don't know."

I'm dumbfounded. They've been out there all this time, but aside from us maintaining the wall and patrolling our side of it, we've only ever seen them as a vague threat. "Maybe they didn't take kindly to those experiments Lyall was running. After all that, you all didn't learn anything more about them?"

Shad cuts his eyes in disgust. "It was barbaric, but he wasn't doing an anthropological study. His only thought was weaponizing their venom. We know next to nothing about their behaviors and even less about how they came to be."

"And the poison that you synthesized from them?" My eyes hold his, searching for the truth.

"I ordered it destroyed after my coronation. Its presence was a threat to us as well, just like those creatures who were being experimented upon."

He doesn't flinch as he speaks. His breathing doesn't change. The same sincerity as always bleeds through. I believe him, I do, and the knot that's been tied inside me since I redis-covered Von loosens just a little.

Shad continues, "If there's any time for Fai and Nimali to put away our differences, it's now. Because Revokers finding a way to breach the city?" His fists tighten.

"I know. It would be a catastrophe." The more they kill, the more their numbers grow…that's how they work.

"My negotiations with the Crowns begin in a few days. What do you think our chances are of finding common ground? Aside from potential spouses," he says with a quirk of his lips, "what could we provide to help you? What do you want?"

I pretend to think about it for a moment. "A promise that you'll stop trying to kill us. Stop trying to steal our bliss."

He leans back and wipes a hand down his face. "That is not an unreasonable request." But his tone of voice leads me to believe he doesn't quite think it's a *possible* request.

What do the Fai need? We have basically all we want. We pride ourselves on our self-sufficiency. Creating a waste-free life. Planting and growing and scavenging and repurposing. Our homes are warmed in the cold months by reservoirs of hot water the Land daimons dig deep into the ground to find. At night, we see by way of complex networks of crystals, which reflect the sun and store its light thanks to the biolumi-nescent organisms cultivated to live within them. While the beasts were busy with their technology, we were not idle. Our inventions just work in harmony with our world, not at cross purposes to it.

I tilt my head, a thought surfacing from something my sister once mentioned about Talia. "Your library. It contains ancient wisdom, does it not?"

Shad leans forward. "Yes, our scholars have always been interested in collecting histories, both ours and everyone else's. Why?"

"For generations, we passed down knowledge via the griots —elders who learned and retold our stories. But it's all been oral, not efficient, and we lost much in the Sorrows." I pinch my lips shut before accidentally revealing the Siege of Devotion, where in-fighting among the Fai cost more lives than I care to admit to an enemy.

I stand and begin to pace, needing some blood pumping to get my thoughts in motion. "If you would grant access to your archive, to anything you have collected about our clan before the Sorrows—histories, remembrances, even legends, that is something we would find valuable." I stop next to his chair. "And what would you want in return?" My brief excitement over the idea of the Nimali library cools.

"We have no healers," he says, slowly. "There are physicians, but not many, and our need outpaces their capacity. Do you think the Fire Fai would consent to help some of our sick and injured?"

Grateful he didn't bring up the little trick I may or may not have done to revive the bliss, I nod. He rises and holds out a hand for me to shake.

"I don't have the authority to agree to anything," I tell him.

"I know. But I appreciate your suggestions. Now at least I have something to work on."

I swallow and place my hand in his larger one. The feel of his calluses abrading my own sends a ripple of longing through me. Everything is cinnamon.

His expression is grateful, but as we stand there, our handshake lasting too long and migrating into hand holding, the look in his eye changes. Sharpens. Intensifies. The closeness and the contact must be bringing back the same memories as it is for me.

Soon his eyes flare with a heat that also ignites within me. Has anyone ever looked at me like that before? I want to back away, to run, hide from him and the feelings he inspires. But I also want to feel them.

His eyes stray to my lips, then he blinks as if coming out of a trance. Disappointment swells within me, though I note he hasn't released me just yet. When he speaks, his voice is scratchy.

"I was reminded today that this contract we are a part of, this betrothal, requires openness of heart. I should apologize for the other day. I'm……not used to my heart being open. I haven't had feelings like this before, and they're confusing."

My lips quirk. "Me either…I mean, me too." Then his words sink in further and my eyes widen. "D-do you think your daimon might……?"

We both pull away at the same time.

"I don't know." He rubs the back of his neck and crosses to the couch to sit. After a moment of indecision, I sit next to him.

"What would that mean?" he asks. "For us?"

"If we actually have to get married because our daimons choose each other?" The idea is terrifying. But the twinges of giddiness it also inspires doesn't quite feel like terror. "I don't see how I could live in this place with no trees."

My daimon is alert within me, and I wonder what it feels. Would it be willing to live out its days amidst these concrete boxes and stale air? What will it decide when its month is over?

Shad reaches over to smooth the frown line marring my forehead, and a whole-body shiver takes over me. I intend to pull away, but somehow lean in. Then he's cupping my cheek in a big hand, and I'm sliding over to close the distance between us.

I really should be standing up and leading him to the door, but instead, when his lips meet mine, I kiss him back.

And keep kissing.

His arms are around me, pulling me in even closer, as if by pressing ourselves together we can dissolve the longing, satiate the hunger. I scramble onto his lap, the juncture of my legs meeting his growing hardness. A gasp escapes from me.

"We should stop," I say, holding him tighter.

"Are you sure?" he asks, running his hands down my back. I'm submerged in cinnamon, and I love it. But I shouldn't. This physical connection doesn't have to mean anything, but unlike my other dalliances, it would. I care about him. Making love now would confuse me and potentially my daimon.

"Yes, I'm sure. I think."

He releases me, holding his hands out at his side. Our mouths are still breathing each other's air, and it takes every ounce of will I possess to climb off his lap. Stand up. Back away.

The hunger inside of me is yawning. Endless. And the only thing that can fill me is right in front of me. Within reach.

My hands fist so they won't grab for him again.

He stands, stiff and uncomfortable. "I'll see you tomorrow," he whispers and heads for the door.

Am I a traitor for wanting him to stay? For nearly calling his name before he disappears into the hallway and out of sight?

And is it a betrayal of everything I thought I stood for when I race to my bedroom and dive under the covers to finish what we started by myself, my hand rubbing furiously between my legs under the covers? Or just a betrayal of my heart?

TWENTY-EIGHT

Xipporah

"LADY XIPPORAH?" Aggi's tentative voice breaks through my reverie at breakfast the next day.

"Yes, what is it?"

"Well…" She wrings her hands, and I straighten from my hunch, alert. Something is wrong. "Is it Kit? Is he okay?"

Her face crumples. "No, he's actually doing worse. One of the older children is watching him today. And…well, the talk is that you can make things grow. Plants. The medicine I've been giving him, the herbs? They help with the pain and reduce the swelling in his throat. But so many of the children are sick now, at least in our dormitory, and our supply has been hit with some kind of blight. Without it…" She twists her fingers into knots. "I wasn't sure if it's something you would be willing to do but—"

"Of course." I stand, pushing the chair back. "Of course I'll help. Where are you growing the herb?"

"On the roof of the lodging we've been staying at. It's closer to the Citadel than our commune, so those of us working here now were required to move. It's just one street over from the square."

"You all couldn't have stayed where the Fai used to? Inside the building?"

A blush sweeps over her cheeks; she ducks her head. "That would be more convenient, but the powers that be decreed it unseemly. They like to pretend to treat us better than they did the drudges. Though except for the trammeling, there's little difference." She shrugs and presses her lips together.

I can't help but feel compassion for her plight. However, I'm hesitant to leave by the front door and have the guards trailing me the entire way. Maybe on the way back, I can do a little scouting. Work on how to get access to the guarded building.

"How would you feel if we went out the back?" I ask. "I'd prefer not to encounter Daggett or his staff—they tend to follow me around the place." It's also the best way to lose my guards, but I don't mention that to her. I don't think she's noticed how I'm escorted everywhere I go.

"You'd have to take the stairs," Aggi warns. "At least down to thirty-nine, where there's an elevator Umbers can use."

"The stairs are fine."

We head out immediately. The one elevator set aside for Umber usage gets crowded as it slowly makes its way down the levels, picking up more and more people. Dressed in crimson, I receive a few questioning looks, which I ignore, and then we're on the main floor, spilling out.

I hunch down amid the mass of brown-clad bodies exiting the building, hoping to not draw attention to myself. The soldiers posted in the lobby don't seem to notice, or at least they don't raise a cry of alarm. But it's not until we're outside that I take a full breath. I don't let my guard down, but out here it seems easier to pretend to be just another Cardinal on errands, not a hostage who's escaped her security.

We walk the few blocks to the Umber lodgings. When we turn down the street Aggi indicates, I'm shocked and delighted to discover we're on the very block with the guarded

218 • L. PENELOPE

building. In fact, we pass right in front of the two young men standing rigidly on either side of a dark metal door. I keep my chin notched up, heart fluttering, not paying them any attention and hoping they do the same to me. Neither gives us more than a cursory glance.

"This is where you're living?" I ask, surprised when she stops before the six-story structure next door.

"Yes. It's not so bad, though I do miss my own home." She opens the front doors and we enter. My heart sinks. It's highly unlikely that the Nimali would be storing anything as dangerous as weaponized Revoker venom next to a building full of civilians. Then again, they did store it right in the Citadel initially, though on a floor far away from where the Cardinals dwelled or congregated.

We climb the stairs and stop on the third floor. "Let me just check in on Kit," she says. "If you don't mind."

"Of course not."

She pushes open a heavy door and we enter a long, white room that looks more like a prison than a dormitory. Rows of neatly made beds line the walls. A few personal items lie on nightstands or hooks, but the space is remarkably sterile. A far cry from the cluttered, homey warmth of Shad's commune. But I take all of this in almost as an afterthought because of the foul odor that greets us as soon as we step through the door.

"What is that smell?" I say, wincing. It gets stronger the farther we go into the room.

"We don't know. We've been alerting the maintenance chief for weeks and nothing's been done. No one can figure out the source, either."

I have to practically hold my nose. "Your daimons can't track it down?"

"Mine is a sparrow," she says. "Smell is not its forte, but the mammal shifters haven't had much luck, either. Honestly, they can't even stand to shift in here."

I breathe through my mouth as we cross the length of the room to find Kit lying on a bed with a teenage girl curled into a chair next to him. Neither of them looks particularly well. The girl has dark circles under her eyes, pronounced against her brown skin. Aggi checks her son's forehead, brow crinkled in concern.

"Larita, has he eaten anything?"

The teen stirs, shaking her head. "Said he wasn't hungry. Swallowing hurts."

Aggi crouches. "We're going to try to get more medicine for you, all right?" Kit barely stirs. He does seem much worse than just yesterday, and I worry for him.

When Aggi stands, her eyes are wet with tears. We don't speak as she leads me to the stairs and the roof. The overcast day matches the mood and seems fitting for the deplorable state of the plant beds up here. They're a bit more makeshift than the ones in the produce houses, built from repurposed supplies. I see a mix of herbs struggling to survive in soil that is gray and sandy.

But it's not just the soil—the leaves themselves all have a grayish tint, and when I lean closer to inspect them, the veins are dark. I've never seen a blight like this and call my daimon to investigate further.

I dip my hands into the soil, then recoil when a fiery, stinging heat assaults me. What in Origin's name? I've never felt anything like that before, but now I'm hesitant to touch the dirt again.

"How long have they looked like this?"

Aggi gasps, rearing back away from me. With my eyes glowing blue, I must be frightening to her. I hold my hands up. "My daimon is just here to help the plants. But I need to know what is happening with them. Something is very wrong. When did this start?"

She swallows, clearly still afraid, but speaks with a shaky voice. "We think it's some kind of rot. It just appeared a day or two ago, but the plants have been faring badly for weeks. We've been using them anyway, but their potency has dipped."

I look around, wondering how to say this without scaring her much more. Pipes and railings emerge from the concrete of the roof. The nearest pipe, a rusted, silver stack, leaks some kind of fluid in a slow drip. I turn around in a circle, inspecting every aspect of the surroundings, unsure of what I'm looking for but wondering if something in the environment could be causing what I just felt. For a living thing to inspire that kind of reaction? It's unnatural and concerning.

The roof next door is about half a story lower but connected to this building. Silver and white pipes protrude from it, and I spot one that makes my stomach churn. Something dark oozes from a curved pipe over there.

I bend down to sniff the herbs; as I suspected, their smell is as off as their appearance, but it's not rot I scent. This is faintly similar to the odor in the dormitory.

"I'll be right back," I tell Aggi, then jump down to the next roof and investigate the pipe. The foulness in the air is stronger here and easier to identify.

The blood drains from my entire body.

"Lady Xipporah, what's wrong?" Aggi calls out from where she stands.

"You need to get everybody out of that building. Now. None of you can stay there another day. Not another minute."

I'd expect, given her general air of nervousness, that this announcement would send her into hysterics, but her fidgeting suddenly stops. Her focus hones and shoulders straighten.

"What's happening?" she asks.

I don't want to tell her, but how can I not? I point to the pipe in front of me, the one leaking a thick, dark sludge. "This smells like Revoker venom."

Her gaze snaps to the pipe.

"It seems to be diluted, and I'm certain it's synthesized.

But I think this is what's been poisoning your plants and your children. It's leaking or spreading somehow."

Our eyes meet, hers hardening into chips of green ice. She nods once and then takes off, racing through the access door and down the steps.

I turn towards the door leading into this building, readying myself for what I'll find.

TWENTY-NINE

Xipporah

HE LIED TO ME. The thought won't leave my mind. Shad lied. He said he'd had the poison destroyed, but in reality, it was just moved here. I try to focus my thoughts into something more productive than the betrayal I feel. How could Shad have such a deadly substance moved right next to a lodging building for his own workers? Do they know it's leaking or seeping or bliss knows whatever else? Contaminating his people in some way?

As I creep down the steps, the sensitive nose of my daimon smells nothing akin to the foul odor of the Umber dorm. The air here seems scrubbed, devoid of odors of any kind. It's obvious this facility is used for research. The top floor is all labs. Moving on silent tiger's feet, I peer through glass squares in the doors to find Azures bent over strange-looking equipment, so consumed in whatever it is they're doing they don't notice me.

There doesn't seem to be any type of security for these labs—not so much as a handprint scanner at the doors—so I figure they must be for some mundane purpose. Still, since everything here involves twisting and perverting the bliss, how mundane can it really be?

The other floors are similar—odorless and apparently benign. It's not until I reach the second floor that I encounter a biometric lock. My handprint doesn't work, not that I expect it to. I pace the empty hallway, assessing my surroundings. This floor holds the locked lab, three offices, and a storage closet. Footsteps sound on the staircase, and I duck into the storage room before I'm seen.

Metal shelves along the walls hold cleaning supplies and boxes of equipment, but unlike the rest of the building, a faint hint of foulness clings to the air. This closet shares a wall with the locked laboratory. I press my nose to the corner of the wall and nearly gag. It's the same smell. I'm certain I've found the source of the Revoker poison.

After a moment of hesitation, I decide the time for caution and subterfuge is over. The hallway outside is quiet, but if the guards come running, then so be it. With my tiger's strength, I slide the thick shelving laden with supplies out of the way, making enough space for me to reach the wall. Then I begin to punch through it.

I discovered during my last stay in Nimali territory that a locked door is just an invitation to creativity. The walls aren't locked, and if you have enough determination and power, you can make your own door.

It's noisy work and bound to attract attention, but I don't care—all I need is proof of their misdeeds. Thinking of how to turn the poison against them is the furthest thing from my mind. Once again, the Nimali have done the job for me.

Within a few short minutes, the hole is large enough for me to fit my torso through. I squeeze in and tumble onto the floor of the lab, the motion-driven lighting overhead flickering on at my arrival.

Tables full of equipment I have no name for, nor can I guess the use of, fill the space. The horrific odor is definitely stronger here; I let my daimon go so it won't be assaulted with the foulness.

There are no cages. No Revokers being experimented on. But the Nimali had already gotten what they needed before the Fai ever escaped the Citadel. Here, rows and rows of canisters full of black liquid sit in boxes lined up against the wall.

A hole opens up in my chest, making it hard to breathe.

I didn't want to believe it. I wanted to believe Shad, but I can't ignore the truth in front of my eyes. The canisters are all sealed, but there are so many of them. A dozen boxes each hold just as many canisters. All full of something extremely deadly.

It's in the corner that I locate the reason for the illness of the Umber children: A single canister has cracked. The evidence—a dry and flaky black crust—leads me to believe the leak started quite a while ago. This lab must not be well monitored. The offending canister sits in a box pushed up against the outer wall of the building. The poison has eaten away at the material of the wall, revealing pipes inside that bear evidence of damage.

My stomach lurches; I think I might be sick. Is this the effect of the poison? From what Aggi's said, only children have been affected by the illness ravaging Kit. The toxin must be diluted enough that it hits smaller bodies first. I recall the sick teenager watching Kit—it may just be a matter of time before the malady spreads to adults.

A soft flapping sounds behind me. I call my daimon and spin around, ready to fight my way out, only to be greeted by a tiny brown and gray sparrow fluttering in the center of the room.

With a snap of light and a puff of sulfur, the bird transforms into Aggi.

"You shouldn't be here." I say, gasping for breath and releasing my daimon.

"I needed to know." She looks around, eyes wide, before her gaze snags on the canisters.

"It's poison meant for the Fai," I say. "But it leaked and has been hurting you all."

There is resignation on her face, the product of a lifetime of low expectations. "We need to tell the king. He ordered this all destroyed."

"Did he?" I ask bitterly.

She turns on me. "Yes. He did. And I think you know that." Her vehemence is surprising; I've only ever seen her demure and nervous, but apparently, she has another side. "King Lyall did this. And his cronies want it to continue. Shad is one of us. He would never have approved of this."

I purse my lips, wanting to believe her, but not sure. Not sure of anything anymore.

"How did you find me? Weren't there any guards around? I was sure someone would hear me breaking through the wall."

"I had a hand in that," a new voice says, and my jaw clenches.

Von stands just inside the hole I made in the wall. How I hadn't noticed him arrive is a mystery—the smell in here is making it difficult for my other senses. "I took care of the guards. You're welcome. Have to hand it to you," he says, looking around, "it never occurred to me to just tear a hole in the wall."

My eyes narrow and I call my daimon back to me, ready if I need it for whatever Von has planned.

He chuckles, then lunges for Aggi, taking us both by surprise. "Now, you have your proof of what I've been saying all along, Xipporah. I think it's time we start executing the treacherous Nimali." His voice is a blade. He places a hand around her neck.

"This woman is not a soldier, she's a servant." I try not to betray any emotion. If he suspects I care about her, he'll kill her out of spite.

"She's a beast, that's all that matters." With an arm

around her waist, he holds her tightly and rises into the air under his crow's power.

"She is a sparrow shifter. Not responsible for anything bad that's happened to us, Von." I hold up my hands, pleading.

"I don't care."

When his hand tightens around her neck, I leap up, crossing the room in one powerful bound and clawing at his face. Von howls and drops Aggi to the floor. In a flash, she's back in sparrow form, flying through the hole in the wall as I punch Von again.

He tries to dodge me by darting up near the ceiling, but this room isn't very tall and I drag him back to the ground. He gets the upper hand, slamming my head into the floor.

The blow rattles my skull. With his daimon called, his blunt fingernails have the power of sharp crow claws; he rakes them down my side, shredding my shirt. I wrestle away and toss him toward the poison. But he's able to straighten and soar into the corner, his head touching the ceiling. Grinning with a bloody smile, he reaches into his pocket and pulls something out—some kind of Nimali tech.

"What is that?" I ask, breath heaving. To reach him, I'd have to jump over the poison and likely would crash into it.

"Something else your precious beasts didn't bother to destroy, nor even hide properly." He holds it up. "This is what they plan to use on us, Xipporah. To lay waste to the Greenlands."

The thing is small and black, but oddly shaped and lumpy. He presses something on the side then tosses it down onto the crates of poison. It spreads out into a net to cover them, reminding me of their hated trammels, which would cover the body and bind our souls. This sticky-looking webbing clings to the crates, shackling them all together.

"This device was created originally so they could fly it over our homeland and drop the poison on us. But over the past few weeks, someone got the bright idea to turn it into a detonator and make the liquid poison into an incendiary device. A few tweaks to the formula was all it took, apparently."

The netting pulses slowly with muted blue light, tinged with purple. The rhythm is similar to a slow heartbeat. My skin has gone icy.

"What did you do, Von?"

"According to their notes, this will take about four hours to charge up, pulling from the oxygen in the air, and then...*boom*." He spreads his fingers like a fan. "The timer was added so they could fly the device out to the Greenlands and be back home before it went off. *That's* who your precious beasts are. *That's* who you've been protecting."

His face grows serious, and his eyes lose some of the manic gleam they'd taken on. "The explosion will spread the poison out over miles, killing everything that breathes in the vicinity. So I suggest you start running."

Then he pushes away one of the movable ceiling tiles and disappears into the darkness above the laboratory. I let out a scream of frustration and leave the lab by the main door, racing down the steps to the entry. Outside, both guards are slumped over, but I can't waste the time determining whether Von killed them or not. If they're still alive, they and every other creature in this territory is on borrowed time.

I have to see Shad.

THIRTY

Shad

IN THE RARE break between meetings, I sit blessedly alone in the conference room gathering my thoughts. I briefly consider laying my head down on the table for a quick nap when a commotion arises in the hallway. A voice calls out in concern —it's my guard Abdul. I'm rising wearily to go see what's happening when the door slides open. Xipporah is there, her shirt torn, blood dripping from her.

Rage blacks out my vision for a split second. Someone dared to attack her on my watch? The dragon within me wants to burst forward and face this foe. It roars silently, longing to take over my body, but I push away the urge to shift. Not here, not in this building. Besides, I don't know who is responsible. Yet.

"What's happened? Who did this? We need to get you to the infirmary!"

Xipporah holds up a hand to silence me. "This is nothing, but I need to speak with you urgently. Alone." She looks back at my guards hovering in the open doorway. Her own protection detail is nowhere to be found.

"Locate her guards," I order Abdul and usher Xi inside. Once the door closes, her mask of relative calm shatters. Her breathing stutters, her eyes go wild—searching the room as if for danger. She didn't want anyone else to see her this upset, and part of me is grateful she's comfortable enough with me to show me the truth.

"Whoever did this is going to pay," I say quietly, seething, trying to get my anger under control.

"You don't understand. I found your secret lab, if it was even a secret." Her tone is accusing. My brow furrows. At my confusion, she spreads her arms. "The Revoker poison. The stuff you told us that you'd destroyed."

I shake my head. "It *was* destroyed. Right after the Fai escaped. It was too dangerous to keep here where so many live and work. I ordered it sealed up, taken into No Man's Land, and burned." The scientists weren't sure if the fumes of burning poison would affect us, so I'd had it done as far away as possible. She searches my face, looking for the truth.

"What did you find?" I ask.

"The building with guards posted out front? The one you said held nothing of interest? It's right next to the Umber lodging. And it's a research facility. The poison is stored there in a lab; it's been seeping out and making the Umber children sick. Kit." Her voice breaks on the last.

I rear back as if someone has punched me. "What? No!"

"I saw it with my own eyes. You vow to me on your honor and by your daimon that you had no knowledge of this?" Her breathing is ragged. She points at my chest, emphasizing her words.

The fury I felt before at the idea of someone attacking her swells into an inferno. "I vow it. And I will find who did this, who defied my orders, and put an end to it."

I spin on my heel and march for the door, but she stops me with a hand on my arm. "There's more." She swallows, and her eyes haven't lost that wild quality yet. I brace myself. "A Fai operative has been hiding in the territory. He's gotten access to the lab and has attached some kind of bomb to the canisters of poison. It's going to explode in four hours and spread the toxin across the territory."

It takes a moment to process her words. The blood drains away from my extremities to flow into my heart, increasing its speed to a dangerous level.

"You are certain?" I say slowly.

"I saw it happen. He did this to me." She motions to the wound at her side: claw marks.

My jaw tightens, and I pace to the door and open it. "Ping Harsh with the emergency code, and have the interior duty captain raise the threat level to primary."

Abdul blinks before grabbing for his comm. I race to the elevator, needing to get to the lab and check for myself. I believe Xipporah, but it's still difficult to fathom. The treachery at play should not be surprising, but it's imperative I find who is responsible for this.

The elevator takes an eternity to arrive, and I consider taking the stairs down the three dozen or so levels. When it finally opens, I'm dismayed to find Sir Barrett, Lady Linh, and a handful of other Cardinals, who I think are their staffers.

Barrett opens his mouth, but I cut him off. "I don't have time for this, we have a situation."

"Oh, yes I'm well aware." He lifts a small glowing device held between two fingers. It's much like a dampener, except instead of cube-shaped, it's a hexagonal prism. And this thing doesn't deaden sound—paired with a matching amplifier small enough to be easily hidden, it enhances it.

"You've been spying on me?" I ask, muscles clenched almost to the point of pain. I hadn't used a dampener. When Xipporah arrived bloody and injured, I'd forgotten one of my most basic rules.

"If I understand correctly," Barrett says, eyes flinty as he positions himself in front of me, "under your rule, you allowed not only one Fai spy into our midst, but two. And now they are threatening to destroy the territory?"

Xipporah bristles, her shoulders tensing. "I'm not threatening anything. I'm warning you. This disaster has nothing to do with me."

"And yet you were there, without your guards, and you've been sneaking around the Citadel, spying on us ever since you arrived. We've been watching you." Barrett turns to me. "Both of you."

"How dare you spy on your king?" My voice is gravel.

"Someone must do so. Your incompetence has left us on the brink of ruin." Spittle flies from his mouth.

The second elevator opens, revealing eight men and women dressed in black but with red epaulets on their uniforms. These are not active-duty members of the military —they're former soldiers, those who took their place as Cardinals after serving their allotted time and are now members of the Honor Corps. Though I've commanded the troops since I became prince, these former soldiers are unfamiliar to me. And the hard set to their expressions indicate they have no loyalty to their king.

Xipporah's eyes flash blue as she joins her daimon. I wish I could leash mine, but that would be a calamity in this small space. Two of the new arrivals point ice blasters at us, and before Xipporah can move, a spray of fine mist envelops us in cold. Her eyes fade back to brown as her daimon is suppressed by the temperature.

"By the laws of the Nimali, I charge you, Shadrach Gabrelson, with treason," Barrett pronounces. Hands grab my arms, and I instinctively kick back to crumple a knee and break the hold. Xi is fighting as well, but more former soldiers pour into the hallway from another elevator car. I take out several of those who attack me, but we're overwhelmed. The small space of the hallway doesn't give us much room to maneuver.

I break away from another hold, but there are many more

hands that reach for me, and soon enough ice cuffs are slapped on my wrists.

"There is no treason," I say through gritted teeth. "And you are wasting time. We need to evacuate people and disable that device. Can't you do your petty coup attempt later?" Frustration, anger, and helplessness rage as I struggle against the cuffs. Next to me, Xipporah snarls, kicking and trying to bite her captors, even without her tiger daimon.

Barrett just sneers. "I will deal with this catastrophe. Creating a panic by evacuating is the last thing we need to do. This is our device and we will get it shut down."

The stairwell at the end of the hall opens and soldiers loyal to me race out, led by Harsh. "What in Origin's name is happening here?" he bellows.

Barrett spins toward him. "I am putting the king under arrest."

"You have no authority to do that!"

Barrett crosses his arms. "Nimali law allows for the overthrow of a corrupted leader by his Council when there is proof of treason."

"This will not end the way you want it to," I say, burning him with my gaze, if not my dragon fire.

A smirk twists the man's lips. "If you do not come quietly, Shadrach, and have your people stand down, I will burn down that hovel you call a commune. I know you visit it sometimes. How many are living there?" He tilts his head.

Though my wrists are frozen, the fight has not left me yet. Several bloodied and battered Honor Corps members lay at my feet. But his words chill me more than the ice cuffs ever could.

"They are innocent. They've done nothing."

"They are Umbers, and only barely useful to us. But I see they are particularly adept at keeping you in line."

There is only coldness and emptiness in this man's eyes. I do not doubt he would murder countless innocents to get what he wants. I look to Harsh and shake my head slightly. His jaw clenches, but he nods and stands down. There will be another way out of this.

"Take them to the locker," Barrett orders.

As rough hands grab at my arms to drag me away, the man whispers in my ear. "You should have never been coronated. You are unfit to be our king."

THIRTY-ONE

Shad

—————

THE COLD OF THE LOCKER—THE Citadel's prison—seeps into my bones, but my own self-hatred vibrating through my marrow manages to keep me from feeling it. Across the small cell we've been placed in, Xipporah shivers. The urge to go sit beside her, warm her with what's left of my body heat, is strong, but I force myself to stay still.

Every minute that goes by ratchets up my unease. I'm afraid for the people in the territory, which I'm certain is *not* being evacuated. Fear for those back home in the commune, the mothers and children, all innocent victims. Pawns created by the nature of their daimons and the society they live in. Just like me. Just like my dragon.

Xipporah's teeth chatter, and I try to cool my concern. I was starting to trust her. I was actually beginning to believe my daimon might choose her.

"Do you think they…can really disarm it?" She's hard to understand through numb, chapped lips.

"They invented it. I'm sure they have a way. Besides, they wouldn't want to take down the entire territory. They need something to rule."

"Barrett won't win," Xi says, more strength in her voice.

"How do you figure?" I laugh without humor. "He's right, you know. I'm a terrible king."

"What are you talking about?" She slides closer. "You've been doing so much to change things. You're not a bad king."

"I trusted you, didn't I? Let the wolf—or the tiger, as the case may be—into the henhouse." She drops her head, and a pang of guilt stabs me in the chest.

"I know it looks like I betrayed you, but I tried to stop Von. Would I have alerted you if I was in on this?" She looks up, eyes pleading.

I shrug. "Maybe you're not completely heartless and the guilt got to you. I don't know. I have no idea how a Fai thinks, do I?"

She presses her lips together and wraps her arms tighter around her body. Being in here won't kill us—it's not quite cold enough for permanent damage, but sitting around not knowing what's happening out there is like a death sentence. What of my other allies? Will Barrett round them up and bring them in here, too? I was glad they didn't arrest Harsh as well.

The outer door opens and a familiar face appears. I rise and rush to the bars. "Sir Denby!"

He stands in the warmth of the heating lamp placed there so visitors won't be affected by the temperature. His eyes are downturned, his face a portrait of misery. "Barrett has gone too far. Are you all right, Your Majesty?"

"I'm fine. What of the evacuation?"

"Well, there's no need for that. I was able to defuse the device."

My eyes widen. "You were?"

His expression clears, the mournful look dissolving. "Of course. I built it, after all."

Behind me, Xipporah gasps. Sir Denby's emotional transformation continues. His shoulders rise from their slump, and his spine straightens. "When I discovered it had been stolen from my private lab, I was quite alarmed, as you can imagine. In the wrong hands it would cause untold damage. Thankfully, I have neutralized the current threat and the poison is perfectly safe…for now." He smiles, that same charming smile as ever, but now it seems curdled around the edges, like spoiled milk.

I take a step back, dismay and grief cooling me even more than the locker's chilled air.

"That Fai spy did us a favor, actually," Denby continues conversationally.

"How do you figure?" My lips are moving, but I'm not sure any sound is coming out. He doesn't seem to notice or care.

"Well, now you are in here where you belong. It's all very neat, really. Barrett finally took some initiative. I've been waiting for weeks for him to do something other than spy and complain."

"You're working with him?" The cold has finally penetrated my heart. Denby was my ally, or so I thought. The one person on the Council who would reliably take my side.

"'Working with him' is a strong term," he replies. "It's more like I'm manipulating him for my ends. And he's a useful scapegoat. So much bluster, so little brains. That daughter of his got the intelligence in that family, but I didn't want to set her off. She's too smart for her own good."

My mind races. "And Callum?"

His expression, jovial so far, hardens in an instant. "I'm doing this for Callum. Under *your* reign, my son is not only embedded within the enemy, in harm's way, but might be denied a soulmate. His daimon could bond with that savage, and then what would his future look like?" He shakes his head in disgust. "I can't believe this friendship with you has put him squarely in enemy hands."

"But he's safe so long as she is." I point to Xipporah, who

is on the other side of the cell staying far away from Callum's father. "Xipporah's arrest only endangers him."

This time Denby's smile takes on an evil cast, out of place on a face so like my best friend's. "You, they will execute in the morning in front of the entire clan. She will be returned to her people, so I get my son back. Then we will deploy the toxin and finally remove the Fai from the city. All of Aurum will be ours, the way it was meant to be."

I can hardly breathe as my world spins on its axis—everything I thought I knew and understood, suddenly wrong.

"You made the device that attacked the caravan as well?" Xi asks.

He turns that vicious smile on her and my fists clench. "Of course. The humans tested it perfectly. I had to promise them food and supplies we don't have and can't spare, but it's of little matter. When they come to collect, the Nimali will deal with them the way we deal with all enemies. With overwhelming force." He pounds a fist on his palm.

"What you failed to understand, dear Shad, is that Nimali aren't agents of peace—we are beasts of war. We *obliterate* enemies, we don't engage with them. Peace treaties are for the weak. Lyall understood that. Sometimes we must lie in wait, small and hidden, until it's time to strike. But a true scorpion knows all about that."

He taps his head and then suddenly shifts into his scorpion form with a burst of light. I step back, pushing Xipporah with me, afraid he will come through the bars to sting us. Of course, the cold on this side makes that impossible. Instead, he scurries away into a corner just before Barrett walks in with a pair of Honor Corps at his back.

Denby must not want Barrett to know about him yet. The man has been hiding his true nature for this long; I can't believe I was fooled. What will Callum say when he learns of this? And will I be alive long enough to find out?

Another pair of Honor Corps drag in a scowling, red-haired Umber man. "We thought it fitting for the Fai traitor to be put in here with you," Barrett announces.

Not Umber, then. The cuffed man is tossed into the cell next to ours. Barrett and the others leave without another word. The Fai man sneers, revealing bloody teeth. He's been badly beaten, one eye nearly swollen shut.

"How did they get you?" Xipporah asks, stepping toward the bars separating us.

"I did what you couldn't, *sister*," is his only response.

"They turned off the device. You lost." She crouches near him.

He snorts then scoots himself into the far corner, chuckling to himself.

Xipporah narrows her eyes. "What did you do?"

"Let's all find out together, shall we?"

Xipporah turns to me, eyes wide and frightened. She knows this man, knows what he's capable of. If she's scared, then maybe the worst is yet to come.

THIRTY-TWO

Xipporah

I'M CURLED into a ball in the corner trying in vain to suppress my shivers. The longer we stay here, the colder I get. I think it must be because my daimon, even when it's not at the forefront, always provides me with a low level of heat. This cold is unnatural. There are no daimons in icy areas—they couldn't ever come out—and Aurum is located just about as far north as shifters can comfortably live. At least, those are the old rules. Since the Sorrows, the world doesn't get very cold anymore. I've heard tales from traveling Air Fai that even what used to be the polar icecaps are now temperate and able to house us. But I've never heard of any of us actually living up there.

Shad has positioned himself about as far from me as he can get. He's beginning to shiver as well, the furnace that his dragon daimon no doubt provides lost to him in this place. The treacherous councilor said he would let me go, but I'm not sure I believe him. If he's planning on destroying the Fai anyway, why keep me alive? Except of course for his son. He needs me to ensure he gets his son home in one piece, but why let me go and warn my people of his plans?

A rattling in the corner captures my attention. There is a

small grate-covered duct there. I'd eyed it earlier as a possible escape route, but it's far too small to crawl through—one of my feet would barely fit—and the screws are fastened from the inside. However, in its dark depths, I catch a glimmer of greenish gold. I sit up straight.

A tiny furry creature creeps forward, eyes flashing, reflecting the low light. The animal is doing something to the vent from inside the shaft. The metal shifts and jiggles and then one screw after another works its way free. The cover of the vent drops onto the ground with a soft clatter.

Shad finally notices and jumps to his feet, awed as a large rat manages to squeeze through the opening. As soon as all four paws touch the ground, the shift is forced, the daimon pushed back by the cold temperature to reveal a large, shaggy-haired man.

"Blake!" Shad exclaims, wrapping the newcomer in a manly embrace. "I've never heard of someone breaking *into* the locker."

While daimons and their hosts rarely favor one another, this man looks particularly ill-suited to shifting into a rat. He's bulky with meaty hands and somber dark eyes.

"What's the plan?" Shad asks.

"Get in here and give you this," Blake responds, pulling something from his pocket. It's always been mysterious to me how Nimali can carry things in and out of their shifts. Their clothes and anything on their person just gets…absorbed into the Origin, maybe. Granted, no Fai has spent too much time investigating. I should ask Shad about it when we get out of this.

That thought stops me short. Shad probably won't be speaking to me when we get out of this.

Blake produces a bracelet from his pocket, and Shad grins. "It's charged up?"

"I hope so. We didn't have time to test it out."

"What is that?" I ask, trying to get a look. When Blake holds it up, I rear back. "Looks like an icing cuff."

"It was, but this one has been modified to create heat," the man explains. "It will raise the body's temperature enough to allow a shift, even in here." For once, I'm grateful for Nimali ingenuity, although it's also the cause for us being without our daimons in the first place.

"You just have the one?" Shad asks. Blake nods.

I'm sure they're going to leave me in here. But at least Shad will do whatever he can to prevent Denby from destroying the Greenlands. At least I think he will.

I don't meet his eyes for a long while, but his gaze doesn't leave me. "What?" I finally ask.

"It will have to be you," he says softly. My face twists in confusion. "If I shift, I bring down part of the building. If you shift, you can take out the guards out in the hallway. Ensure we make it out of here." His expression hardens. "But you must vow to actually help me get out so I can stop this mad plan of Denby's."

My jaw tightens. "I never betrayed you, Shad. But yes, I vow to help us both escape."

"Preferably without anyone seeing and raising an alarm," Blake adds.

"Got it." I hold out my arm, and the rat shifter slaps the bracelet on. It quickly heats my wrist, the warmth radiating through my body and banishing the frigidity that had taken over.

When my daimon is warm enough, I call it forward, delighting in its strength and the enhanced senses it provides. And I feel its pleasure at being a part of this world again, a passenger within me, lending me its gifts and gaining the experience in return.

From the next cell, Von eyes us warily. My gaze narrows on him; I race to the bars and pull at them. They're metal, sturdy and icy cold, but the bracelet protects me and the strength from my daimon lets me pull them apart wide enough to squeeze through. Von's eyes widen. I should kill him, but he needs to face Fai justice—it is not mine to give. Let him stay here while we sort out the rest, but I also don't want him to cause more trouble. I rip the hem of his brown shirt into strips, then tie his arms and gag him so he can't alert anyone to our escape.

I return to pull the bars of our cell apart so that Shad and Blake can shove through. It's a tough task for both men, big as they are, but eventually they make it. In the heat of the visiting area, Blake shifts back to his rat form. I use my enhanced hearing to listen at the door for activity in the hallway. Two guards are positioned on either side of the entrance.

I look around the visitor space and find pegs on the wall bearing ice cuffs. I grab a pair and toss another to Shad, then motion to the door. He nods. We're in sync as we slip out to face the soldiers, who wear the same red epaulets as the ones who helped Barrett. We're on them so fast they don't get a chance to shout or raise an alarm. In moments, they're cuffed and stuffed in the freezer, too.

"All that training paid off, huh?" I say to him, and he grins. Then he seems to remember he's mad at me, so he sobers.

We take off to the stairwell following a scurrying Blake, who leads us up. The locker is on the third floor, and we race up the steps to the eighth, which used to be one of the Fai floors. On the landing, the rat stands on its hind legs and pushes it paws out at us.

"He wants us to wait?" I whisper to Shad.

"I think so."

Blake nods and then stands by the door until Shad has the presence of mind to push it open enough for him to squeeze through. We crouch by the small crack in the stairwell door while Blake presumably scouts the floor. In a minute, he's back, tail curling to indicate we should follow.

Nimali can't speak in their daimon forms; what an incon-venience that must be. Now, Blake leads us through the empty hall to the elevators, and we enter one that goes all the way to the top. In the car, he shifts back to human to press the button for forty-eight, the highest floor.

I haven't released my daimon, so when the doors ding open, I hear two heartbeats. Neither Shad nor Blake appears concerned as we edge into the dimly lit space, a small room taking up the entirety of this floor. The wall across from us is open to the elements. Crisp air flows in, and the wind howls outside.

The famous throne of bones sits in the center of the room. What a monstrosity in service to Nimali ruthlessness, that their king chooses to sit upon the bones of his ancestors. My gaze avoids it, uncomfortable, searching for the source of the heartbeats.

Two people melt out of the shadows: Harsh and a small, dark-skinned woman with a sharpness to her gaze that lets me know she doesn't miss much. I'm instantly on my guard around her.

Shad embraces his friend and nods to the woman. "Xip-porah, this is Lady Dominga."

"You're Barrett's daughter, aren't you?" I say, prickling.

"Yes. But his interests and mine diverge significantly." Her voice and manner are cold, but she doesn't appear to be lying —her breathing and heartbeat remain steady and sure.

"And it's in your interest to help us escape?"

She doesn't answer me, instead turning to Shad. "My father is mobilizing the Honor Corps who are mostly loyal to him, but the majority of active soldiers are confused by his announcement of your treason. I don't think they believe him."

"The king's guard and I have been feeding them the real story," Harsh adds. "Barrett may have many of the Cardinals believing his lies, but the Atrament Corps are still yours."

244 • L. PENELOPE

Shad appears relieved. "All right, we need to leave the Citadel to regroup. I don't want to be locked in a battle here with the potential for so much collateral damage. Have they really disarmed the explosive device?"

"Yes," Harsh says. "And they've moved the poison as well. I have trackers on it, but they've created dummy containers and are moving both sets of canisters to different locations to throw off anyone watching."

"We'll have to keep an eye on both sets, then," Shad says.

"Also," I add, "Von has some kind of backup plan. I don't know what it could be."

Dominga sidles up to me. "What, he didn't keep you in the loop when you two were making your little plans?" Her voice is snide. "Did it ever occur to you to alert someone of his presence? Then maybe this would never have happened?"

I cross my arms and stare her down. "This also wouldn't have happened if you all had disposed of the Revoker poison in the first place. Or had never developed it to commit genocide on my people!"

Her gaze sharpens and I get the sense of retracted claws coming out, but Shad clears his throat. "Not the time or place. We need to get clear of here and gather our allies. Do we have a meeting place?"

"We can get there easiest by flying," Harsh says, sending a chilly glare in my direction.

Dominga adds, "I'm staying here to keep my eye on my father. No one in this building knows of my allegiances yet."

"And I'll gather my team and bring them to the meeting point," Blake says.

Harsh and Shad step away and put their heads together, whispering. I could hear them easily if I had a mind to, but Harsh pulls out a dampener. They're talking about me. I back away into the shadows as they continue.

Shad doesn't trust me anymore, that much is clear. But what does it matter, anyway? I need to get back to the Greenlands and warn the Fai. No matter what happens here, they need to know that the rules they thought they were playing by have changed significantly.

Watching Shad, a stabbing pain shoots through my heart. He will never believe I didn't betray him. Whatever feelings I've developed, whatever bond I thought we shared, it's broken now. Our thirty days aren't over, but I hope my daimon will give me some latitude in this. There must be some way to end the engysis contract early…these are exigent circumstances, after all.

I give him a final glance, imprinting the lines of his face into my mind, then turn and head for the open wall. I stand at the edge, letting the bracing night air flow over me. If my eyes begin to leak, it's because of the wind, nothing more.

I'm unable to resist a final glance over my shoulder, which is when Shad looks up and meets my eyes.

"Xipporah!" I see him yell my name though I still can't hear him. But I'm already tossing myself off the ledge.

THIRTY-THREE

Xipporah

———

I BOUND into the night to land on tiger's paws on the sloping side of the pyramid-shaped building. Racing down, I pick up speed and barely avoid tumbling head over heels, even with the grace of a cat.

I'm going home. To help and warn them. I never wanted to be here in the first place. I don't belong in this building, with this clan, with that man.

After leaping down the last story to land in a crouch, I take off running again, picking up speed, dashing past Nimali citizens who are mere blurs as I pass them. There is no pursuit; no one gives chase. With a coup in progress, perhaps there is just too much confusion to spare for one sprinting Fai woman.

It feels good to run. So good that I try to use that sensation to erase the gnawing hole that widens as I get farther and farther away from Shad. I push through, knowing it's for the best. He didn't want or need me near him. Didn't trust me, and why should he? Still, our contract is souls-deep, and my three souls feel pulled taut as the distance between us lengthens.

I need to wrangle both them and my daimon back under

control. But though I'm driving this body, I can't ignore the wishes of the spirit who shares it. I can't ignore my covenant.

"There won't be a Greenlands if the Nimali have their way. I'll go back when the Fai are safe," I say out loud. It's unnecessary. The daimon doesn't need to hear my words— I'm mostly trying to convince myself.

To avoid the checkpoints, I take a side street out of the territory. There is a noticeable line of demarcation where Nimali maintenance ends. The patched pavement and restored buildings end in a towering wall of debris four stories high that is meant to keep the mundane humans out. I scale it easily to enter the Independent Zone, not slowing my pace. There could be some unseen predator hiding in the bushes, on alert for fleeing captives, and time is not on my side.

But I sense no one. That strikes me as odd. It should not be so easy to exit the territory. They keep their clan well-guarded, but there are no signs of soldiers now.

The moon is high; I can't help but feel exposed beneath its bright shine. I head west, leaping over rusted cars and crumbled debris from felled buildings. Have Barrett or Denby already discovered our escape? Are plans being made, even now, to accelerate the destruction of the Greenlands? I try to push myself faster, knowing I'll burn out but unwilling to pace myself for the long run across the city. Urgency presses against me.

A blinding flash of light up ahead pulses, forcing me to stop before I run headfirst into something. Spears of pain impale my sensitive daimon-enhanced eyes. Then I hear the heartbeats. And the breathing. And smell the unwashed bodies.

Humans.

They surround me. By the time my vision clears, there are half a dozen men and women circling me. I scan them, calculating my odds of being able to best enough of them to get free. Then I stop short, recognizing one: the woman who fell through the floor of the building the day of the caravan attack. The mother I'd protected. She stands rigidly, tears welling in her eyes, her mouth open in an aborted sob.

Her gaze keeps sweeping to the left. I follow it to find the small child she'd been holding caught up in the arms of a burly man with a knife to the child's throat. I freeze.

"You, Xipporah Ruithsdaughter, are a lover of innocents," a voice calls out. "So come with us, or this innocent will die."

In that moment, the child reminds me of Kit. A growl rattles in my throat. I could take these humans. There are actually seven of them, including the scared mother. Only rarely have I ever had to fight a human, and they were usually out of their minds, but these, like most, are underfed. Their strength can't hold a candle to mine, so taking on six is nothing.

"We don't have any fancy freezers or cooling devices. But we won't hesitate to exploit a weakness." I still can't see who's speaking, but the voice sends chills down my spine.

"Come with us or the child dies."

The burly man tightens his grip on the child and the mother simpers. The kid, though, eyes on mine, doesn't make a sound.

I could take them all out, yes, but not before that knife pierces the child's throat. But the urgency of my mission hasn't changed. The Greenlands are still at risk—is the life of one human child worth more than my entire clan? One versus hundreds.

The mother's tears overflow, slicing through the dirt on her cheeks. I close my eyes on a long blink, hoping my actions do not doom my people. My family. Noomi. But I cannot be responsible for harm coming to this young one.

I hold my hands up to indicate surrender. A foul-smelling bag is placed over my head and my hands are tied. Not all of them must understand how Fai daimons work if they think this is necessary. I could easily break out of the weak ropes they use—maybe it's more for their benefit.

Once I'm secured to their satisfaction, we begin to walk. The air changes; we're entering a building and then heading down a staircase which, while crumbling in some places, is mostly in good repair. I'm in the middle of the pack and focus on cataloguing the breathing, footsteps, and heartbeats of my captors, using that information to tell them apart.

The stairs end in a cooler, musty space. It's a good thing I'm paying such close attention to the sounds around me because I hear when the people walking in front of me crouch, like they're ducking under something. I do the same, though no one bothers to warn me, unconcerned about whether I will hit my head or not.

Finally, after what feels like nearly an hour, we reach our destination. The hood is removed, and I find myself in an underground train station. One that's been reclaimed and is home to these humans.

Though the lighting is dim, after the darkness of the hood, it takes a moment for my eyes to adjust. Most of the company melts away into corners or passages branching off our location. But a rangy, blonde woman with short, cropped hair comes forward. She might be in her early forties, or younger and just hardened by life. The mother, child, and their captor are gone, but I'm certain they're not far. Close enough to still be in danger if I mess up.

"Who are you and what do you want?" I ask.

She snorts. "My name isn't important, and neither is my gang's. All you need to know is that we were paid handsomely to attack the Nimali caravan and to make sure the plans of our partner go down like he wants."

"You *were* paid or payment was promised?"

She tries to keep her face neutral, but I can tell by the twitching of her lips that the payment hasn't come through. Just as Denby said.

The woman tilts her head, regarding me. "When he hears we've got you, he'll have to pay up. If he wants to get his son back, at least. Isn't that how it works? The little trade you made."

"Or you could let me go home and they'll release his son anyway. We have food and supplies we can share with you. My people would be grateful to have me back."

She rolls her eyes and sits on a dirt-stained cushion on the ground. "I want what I'm owed."

A loamy, earthy aroma pushes against the musk of stale body odor. I search for its source and spot a small hydroponic garden in the far corner. There are three women on stationary bicycles with wires leading to a boxy contraption. Its cord connects to the lighting over the makeshift plant beds. They seem to be making their own power source through physical labor.

From what I can see of the plants, they're doing all right. Better than many of the Nimali's, but not thriving nearly as well as Fai greenery.

"I could help with that." I motion to the garden with my head.

She waves away my offer. "We don't want anything from you. Neither of you monsters care about us here in the middle unless it's convenient. You scavenge and raid, have your battles, destroy our territory—things it's taken us years to build—throw out your castoffs into our areas and what? Expect us to just grin and bear it?" Her eyes are a bit wild, and she's missing several teeth on the side of her mouth.

"The Fai don't exile our people. We don't strip them of their daimons and leave them—"

"Fai, Nimali, you're all the same in the end. Neither of you could give two shits about us." She spreads her arms out.

The woman isn't wrong; humans are way at the bottom of our list of things to be concerned about. Maybe that should change. But I'm not a fan of her way of bringing that change.

"Mundane humans destroyed the world," I reply. "Why *should* we care about you?"

She shakes her head, spiky hair vibrating. A heavily tattooed man appears from a dim hallway and walks over to crouch and whisper in her ear. Even with my enhanced hearing, I don't catch the message. But I can't miss her scowling reaction.

"Bad news?" I ask.

"Bad for you. That smiling asshole won't pay the ransom."

What is Denby playing at? How is he going to get Callum back without me returning home safely?

"Send a messenger to the Fai," I say. "They'll pay the ransom, I'm sure of it."

The woman rises and approaches, leaning toward me⸺not too close, but closer than I'd like. "If we don't get what we're owed, then things won't look so good for you." She flicks open a switchblade and waves it near my face. "Not good at all."

I can't hold back the growl that rises from my chest.

"Let's make sure they know we're not playing around, shall we?" She makes a series of hand gestures. The messenger leaves and returns moments later followed by the knife-wielding man holding the small child. The mother trails them, hands wringing, eyes puffy from crying.

I bare my teeth at the leader of this gang of miscreants and let out a full roar. It echoes off the walls and fades into the darkness as the woman's blows start raining down on me.

THIRTY-FOUR

Shad

FLYING AWAY FROM THE CITADEL, following the moonlit outline of Harsh's wings up ahead, guilt nearly drags me down. Should I have gone after her? I'd watched Xipporah race down the side of the Citadel, my heart in my throat, but I shouldn't have been worried. She is a well-trained soldier, I'm sure she'll be fine, and I have no doubt Harsh has people following her, but apprehension gnaws at me nevertheless. The wrongness of her leaving is an ache in my chest. It must just be the contract—it can't really be that my three souls feel strained the further she gets away. And I can practically feel her growing distance inside me like a yawning hole.

Harsh leads me due south, to a large rectangular building that has survived the Sorrows surprisingly well. Most of its curved roof is still intact, though flattened buildings lay to its north and west. The wall that protects us from the Revokers rises in the near distance, and I briefly wonder whether even now, those creatures are trying to make their way through it.

The front face of the building we circle has a sturdy-looking ledge on which to land. A ladder leads from it down through the roof and to the interior. I shift and climb down to discover a colosseum where sporting events were played before the Sorrows. Rows and rows of seating show just how many people used to fill this space, though many of the chairs are missing or damaged. However, a swarm of activity surprises me.

Dozens of people, perhaps close to one hundred, bustle around. Most are soldiers in black carrying equipment and supplies. There is bedding, cases of food rations, portable heaters, and water purifiers. But there are Umbers here as well, and more streaming in through the doors in both human and daimon forms.

"This space is in regular usage?" I ask, perplexed.

A rare expression of guilt crosses his face. "We didn't tell you so you'd have plausible deniability. At first, we needed to keep this place hidden from Lyall. Then from the Council. But Callum, Zanna, and I set it up as a headquarters and safe haven for when shit hit the fan."

As I work my way down the series of ladders to get to the main floor, Harsh shifts back to his eagle form to fly down. I'm in awe at the number of people who've gathered. There are troops here who have served under me since I was catapulted to the commander of the military—men and women who I could never quite bring myself to trust fully, unsure of their real feelings about me.

"These people are loyal to me?" I ask when I catch up to Harsh on the top level of the arena.

"They are. I know you find this hard to believe, but they love you. You protected them as best you could from Lyall, and they remember and respect that."

Whole families of Umbers have gathered with still more arriving, their belongings packed into overstuffed bags. Some I recognize from my life in the commune, but many I don't know.

"You told them all to come here?"

"These plans have been laid for a long time. When Barrett had you arrested, I engaged the message chain and everyone knew what to do. All those known to be loyal to you were to gather here. It was Callum who figured that anyone wanting to overthrow you would use the Umbers against you, so we came up with a way to protect them."

A lump chokes me up for a moment. "What about spies?"

"It's a risk, certainly, but I'm sure that any spies are in the minority. We're stronger than they are, Shad. You just have to believe it." Harsh's dark eyes shine with his particular brand of emotion. Then he blinks and it's gone. "Let Barrett bring his worst; we're ready for him."

"It's Denby," I say with venom. Harsh frowns, confused. "Denby has been manipulating Barrett. He's the one who tried to kill us in the caravan. That device only attacked us once the vehicle he was in was far ahead." I'd worked that out during my time in the locker. I relay Denby's visit and Harsh looks as if he's seen a ghost.

"Callum is going to be broken," he whispers. I don't disagree. He and his father are close.

"We'll have to worry about that when we get him back, and to get him back, we need Xipporah. I assume you sent someone to track her?"

"Of course. In fact…" His head tilts back and he tracks the flight of a tiny brown figure gliding down from the ceiling. As it draws nearer, I make out the furry face and pointed ears of a bat.

Before hitting the ground, the little bat begins its shift, revealing Tawana—Blake's partner and parallel.

She bows at me and salutes Harsh. "Your Majesty, I have news of your betrothed. She's been captured."

The air rushes from my lungs. "What? By whom?"

"Humans. In the Independent Zone outside sector seven. It may have been the same clan who attacked your caravan."

"What makes you say that?"

Her stance is rigid. "Zero. My team finally caught sight of him just this afternoon. I haven't even had a chance to report in to Blake. Zero's faction was on high alert and headed to a meeting with another group, led by the woman who took Lady Xipporah."

"So they're working together?" My heart sinks.

"No, Your Majesty. The meeting was not friendly. The two nearly came to blows. But Zero definitely knows who she is and may know where they've taken Lady Xipporah."

"How did they capture her?"

"They threatened a child. After that, the lady went willingly—or as willingly as possible. I'm sorry I could not have helped her." Her eyes are downcast, but I place a hand on her shoulder.

"Your intelligence is vital, Tawana. Everyone cannot and should not be a soldier. You and the rest of your team are assets more valuable than I can express."

She swallows and nods, looking unsure of how to respond.

"They can't hurt Xipporah if they want Callum back safely," Harsh says. That's some comfort, but panic over Xi's safety is beginning to grow when a new voice calls out from behind us.

"Your Majesty? Sir Harshal?"

"Elsbeth?" Tawana exclaims and races over to embrace the newcomer, a slight, flaxen-haired woman in her thirties. "We've been searching for you."

Elsbeth, another Umber, has streaks of dirt on her face and looks as if she just dug her way out of an underground pit.

"Are you all right?" Tawana asks, frantically scanning her for injuries. She holds her cheeks, stroking them with her thumbs to brush some of the dirt off.

"I'm fine. I promise." She places her hands on Tawana's, then presses their foreheads together. The moment is heartfelt and intimate. Something in my chest shifts.

Elsbeth pulls away and bows to me. "I'm sorry I had you

all so worried, I just..." She shakes her head as if clearing cobwebs.

Her name clicks into place. "Elsbeth? Are you the missing groundhog shifter?" I ask.

"The same, Your Majesty, and I have information you need to hear."

"I'm glad you're all right, but we have an emergency, so unless it has to do with Lady Xipporah—"

"It does. By way of Lord Callum."

Ice cools my veins as I consider her more closely.

"He was captured an hour ago," she says.

"Captured? By who?" Harsh and I speak at the same time.

"They appeared to be humans," the woman says. "He was at the edge of Fai territory with a small group. But these *humans* had an ice blaster and used it on Lord Callum and his protectors."

I look to Harsh. "Could it be Denby?"

"Must be. Probably his own people took Callum. I don't see him daring to actually give humans a weapon that could be used against him."

"Unless he added some kind of failsafe. But at least it means they won't hurt Callum." I turn back to Elsbeth. "How do you know all of this?"

"Zero has people watching all over the city. He told me to come tell you."

Tawana gasps. Elsbeth went missing days ago while trying to locate Zero. Apparently, she accomplished her mission and now he's giving her orders? I don't have time to untangle that at the moment. "And does he know where Xipporah is?"

Elsbeth nods.

"Take me to him."

THIRTY-FIVE

Shad

AS WE MAKE our way through the underground tunnels, Elsbeth shares her story.

"I know I jeopardized the mission, Your Majesty. And I will accept my punishment without complaint. It's just that I never thought I'd see my uncle again. He was exiled five years ago by King Lyall. Stripped of his daimon and thrown from our territory. My mother was inconsolable; he's her baby brother. She passed to the Origin never knowing of his fate. I saw him in the tunnels and followed him without telling anyone. He actually ended up leading me to the Silent Hands…" She clears her throat and her voice, which had gone wobbly, is stronger. "I couldn't help myself. I didn't report back, I just stayed."

Her actions are technically treasonous. She abandoned her mission and told no one of her whereabouts. Wasted valuable time and resources in having the team search for her. The risk she took in coming back was great. But I can deal with all of that once Xipporah and Callum are back safe.

"I'm sure your uncle was happy to see you," I offer. She gives me a watery smile.

"About one-quarter of the Hands are exiled Nimali," she whispers. I nearly stumble.

Harsh sent Tawana to find Blake, while he stayed at the colosseum to manage the influx of my supporters. He'd wanted to send a detachment of soldiers with me and Elsbeth, but I refused. Zero is cagey, and I don't want to do anything to spook him or prevent him from giving me the information I need. Once I have Xipporah's location, I can figure out next steps. But part of me knows that I'm not going to call for backup. There's just no time. Whatever it takes, I'm going to get her back to safety.

The tunnels wind and turn, but Elsbeth knows where she's going. We keep a brisk pace that I know she could traverse even more quickly in her daimon form.

Soon enough, the atmosphere changes, though nothing is visibly different. But the air is less stale, and the subtle scent of food greets my nose.

I sense the presence of someone in the shadows before he speaks. "El, you came back." He sounds surprised.

"He wants to see Zero," Elsbeth responds, motioning to me.

The unseen figure shifts, and my fists tighten just in case. But no attack comes. Instead, a hidden door opens, flooding the dimly lit tunnel with light.

The guard has his face covered with cloth. I get a glimpse of bronze skin around golden eyes before he turns to lead us into a space that is obviously inhabited and well cared for.

It looks like it was once an underground parking garage that somehow made it through the Sorrows with minimal damage. Thick concrete posts are spaced at even intervals, and little pockets of light are visible in the distance. The ceiling is relatively low, but it's warm, and something about the place is inviting. It reminds me of the commune, with tents and makeshift curtains creating private areas.

We head toward a common area lit by two fires in large

metal barrels. A small group of people ranging in age from teens to the elderly sit in a circle watching two people sparring. I recognize Zero's nimble form—he's the smaller of the men. His opponent, while thickly muscled, is slow on his feet. Both men are shirtless, and by the time I reach the edge of the circle, they're grappling on the ground.

Zero twists at lightning speed and manages to pin his much-larger competitor, then leaps up with agile grace. When he rises, I notice a mark on his back. A tattoo of a feather on one shoulder blade.

My surroundings fade and everything moves in slow motion. The only thing I can see is that feather. The one that matches one of the tattoos on my own back.

I remember the day that we got them, Sylph and I, in remembrance of Lynara. Of her dream to leash a daimon that would let her fly away.

Not long after her death, Sylph's parents were exiled for sedition. He could have stayed, as their punishment hadn't extended to him, but he'd gone with them. And though I'd thought of him often in the past eleven years, I never dreamed I'd see him again.

"Sylph?" I call out once the initial impact of the shock allows me to speak.

He faces me, expression sober, and though the years have thinned him out and hardened his features, now that I can clearly see his face, it's obvious that he is my old best friend.

My feet are rooted to the ground even as I'm afraid I may fall down. Sylph drags on his shirt, looking at me grimly. I rush over to embrace him, but he takes a step back. "Sylph?" I ask again.

"It's Zero now."

"I don't...understand."

He nods as if not expecting me to and motions for me to follow him. We head for a water barrel on a table against one of the support pillars. He dips a ladle inside to fill a cup and drinks deeply.

"After my parents were exiled, we ended up in a place like this. Just not well organized. If you wanted to be able to eat and have a safe place to sleep, you had to join a gang." He shrugs. "It worked for a while, but life was brutal. My mom died of what they call the brittle cough. A few years later, Da was killed in a territory dispute."

My heart goes out to my childhood friend. "I had no idea."

He snorts. "Why would you? You were raised as the prince, lofted high above all of us mere mortals."

"You know it wasn't like that. Lyall was…" I shake my head. "I lost both of my parents to that man, so don't act like it was all cherries and roses. And now that I'm king, I'm trying to change things for the better."

"Well, if you're so good, why haven't you come to us? Why haven't you made any effort to help the exiles?" His distinctive hazel eyes hold accusation. And pain.

"I've been king for a matter of weeks, and they've been trying to oust me the entire time!"

We stand there breathing hard, staring at each other. Then Sylph—Zero—starts to laugh. I'm brought back to the old days when him and me and Lynara would play in the commune and tell each other our dreams for the future and his laugh would take some of the misery away.

"I promise, I will work to make things better. I've got lots of plans," I say. "I've always wanted to reach out to the exiles and offer them a way back into the fold. There is a way we can all live here together, I'm sure of it. I'm willing to take your deal and start fresh."

I hold out my hand to him to seal the pledge. He stares at it for a long time before grabbing hold. "Humans, too. They need help. You can't continue to ignore them."

"We're facing starvation ourselves, but I think that

everyone living in this city needs to start working together a bit more. Maybe we can all get somewhere better."

He seems satisfied with that. But even through the amazement and joy of discovering my old friend, my mind is never far from Xipporah. How long has it been since she was taken? What's happening to her?

"You're looking for your queen," Sylph says. It will take me a while to think of him as Zero.

In the days since our betrothal, this is the first time I've considered Xipporah as a potential queen. I don't have time to unpack the strange sensations that roll through me at that thought, or the chaos such a thing would create. I just need to find her.

"Do you know where she is?"

"Come with me."

THIRTY-SIX

Shad

Sylph—Zero—corrals a small group including Elsbeth and a man who must be her uncle, as he looks like an older version of her, to accompany us. Each man and woman carries an assortment of weapons, from axes to spears to clubs.

"The group that took her calls themselves the Night Thorns," he explains as we re-enter the maze of tunnels. These particular passages look little used, but they've been cleaned out and kept in reasonably good repair.

"Their main lair is a subway station, but there's an apartment building above it full of families under their *protection*." The air quotes he uses make it clear how he feels about the Night Thorns.

"And you met with them today?" I ask.

"Their leader, Uta, is playing a dangerous game. She thinks she can outsmart the Nimali who are conspiring against you. But she couldn't outsmart a partially trained dog."

The Silent Hands carry small, hand-cranked flashlights strapped to their chests. They need to be re-cranked every few minutes, but they give good light. We soon enter an area where the ceiling and walls have collapsed, leaving only a tiny, low passage that requires crawling through on hands and knees.

The journey is arduous and I lose track of time, using the discomfort of the gravel biting into my palms and knees to ground me—keep me present, not distracted by waking nightmares of Xipporah being tortured. Finally, we emerge in a small cave made by the piles of concrete, tall enough to at least sit up in.

"Lights out and radio silence from here on out," Zero whispers. "We'll need to crawl through there another hundred feet or so." He points to an even smaller tunnel on the other side of where we came out. "It ends where the Night Thorns blocked off one of the subway tunnels. It's usually not guarded, and from there you can see into their main common area from the shadows. It's where they're most likely to be keeping her."

The flashlights are shuttered, and no one moves for a full minute. By then, my eyes have adjusted to the barely there light filtering through the tiny shaft ahead. We shuffle forward as quietly as possible.

It's the tightest of squeezes, and I see why the rest of the Silent Hands Zero recruited for this mission are relatively small people. At one point, I'm not certain I'll make it through, but with another push, and significant bruising on the backs of my thighs, I make it and jump down into the cavernous space of the subway tunnel.

Having this side blocked off is good security, I have to admit, though they should inspect it regularly for the type of hole we just climbed through. As the last of the group makes it, I hear a pained cry in the distance accompanied by laughter.

My senses on full alert, I creep forward, hugging the wall to peer around the corner into the former subway station. A blonde woman is punching Xipporah, whose hands are tied behind her. A group of ragged people stand watching, taunting and laughing at Xi's misery.

My daimon surges with my rage, nearly taking over my body until I wrangle it back with great effort. My teeth are clenched so hard I might crack a tooth, but I manage to hold back my yell. I take ragged breaths, my fists tightening to stone as another of Xi's cries reaches my ears.

I bend to Sylph's ear and whisper, "You have five minutes to evacuate any innocents down here and in the building above before it comes down."

He jerks his head in surprise, but once he glimpses the look in my eyes, he just nods. He makes a few hand signals to his people, then they're off, racing away. Elsbeth gives me a strange look before going with them, running in a crouch along the train tracks.

There isn't really enough space for me to call my daimon down here, but with the uncontrollable fury rolling through my veins, I don't care. I cannot guarantee the safety of anyone but Xipporah once I let the dragon loose. Seeing her in pain, being beaten, unlooses something that I've kept bundled tight probably ever since the daimon chose me. There are no fetters any longer, and these five minutes will be the longest of my life —I'm not entirely certain I will even make it that long. The rage that boils hotter with each blow that falls on Xipporah is nearly blinding.

I barely notice the creeping figure in brown who leaps from the tracks. They come up behind a stocky man with a small child squirming in his arms and wraps an arm around his neck.

There's movement at the corner of the space, and part of my brain understands those are people riding bicycles that go nowhere. Shadows come out and grab them, too, hands slapped over mouths to muffle their noise as the Silent Hands drag them away, but my focus is on the numbers counting down in my head, a tiny part of me knowing that I cannot rush forward immediately.

As the seconds tick down, I'm not consciously seeing anything anymore. It's only later that I will remember Xipporah's reaction to the silent actions around her. The woman beating her is too focused on her task, the small audience as well, but Xipporah is alert. And she begins to fight back. She kicks at the woman's legs, enraging her attacker.

But in those moments, I can't see it. All I know is the fire that begs to be released.

Five minutes. Three hundred seconds. I make it to two hundred and fifty-seven before the shift takes me. Before I lose control of my daimon's harness and let it have my body to seek its revenge.

The smell of sulfur mixes with blood—Xipporah's blood, dripping from the blonde woman's hands. The dragon's bulk cracks concrete as my claws scrape the tiles on the floor. I'm crouched because of the low ceiling, but something inside my chest clicks, igniting the flames within. Screams ring out.

"Shad?" Xipporah asks, voice weaker than I've ever heard it.

My focus is on the woman who dared spill Xi's blood. One of my claws reaches out to grab the vile creature and hold her away from Xipporah. I twist, stretching my arm so she hangs over the train tracks, and roar into her face. And then the fire comes, consuming the woman's head and torso as well as my own claw—but my fire will not harm me.

I don't stop the flames, merely rotating my head and letting them consume the vile people who had stood around watching the beating and laughing. Some try to run away but are burned before they can take more than a step.

I take a breath, searching for more enemies, but there's no one left to fight. Xipporah has her daimon called and another two guards lay at her feet. She's broken free of the restraints on her wrists and looks up at me, eyes glowing.

I grab her gently in one claw, which covers her from knee to mid-chest. I can't take flight down here, but I'm strong enough, and motivated enough, to leap up and smash through the ceiling above, collapsing the home of the Night Thorns for good.

The ground shakes as I batter my way up, using my head and scaled hide as a ram and protecting the precious cargo against my chest. I burst up into the first floor of a building that begins to cave in around me. Debris falls—thick chunks of concrete, metal piping, wooden beams. I don't feel any of it, still blinded and numbed by fury.

This anger has been pushed down so long. Controlled and strangled. I thought giving in would make me like Lyall, and maybe it has, because I haven't given a single thought to whether Zero's people were actually able to save the civilians living here. The structure now has a huge hole in the first few floors.

I emerge into the night and shake the wreckage from me, freeing my wings and taking flight. The mental haze slowly clears and I circle the scene once, then twice, noting a group of humans on the ground. There are quite a few of them. Later, I will worry if everyone got out, but for now, I just relish the warmth of Xipporah's body against my palm and chest. Warm blood to my cold.

It's minutes before I settle on a roof partway across the city. Even longer before my mind is clear enough to shift back to human. When I do, Xipporah is in my arms.

I want to tell her what I've realized, that my daimon has chosen her. That seeing her in peril revealed some primal essence that I didn't know it possessed. And not just it, the man was deeply affected, too. Hearing her cries of pain nearly ended me.

I want to tell her this, but I don't get a chance because she presses her lips to mine, and a different kind of haze takes over.

THIRTY-SEVEN

Xipporah

THE KISS ERASES the pain in my body from that bitch's weak punches. They were like tiny bee stings, and I played up the pain to make her think she was having an effect. Still, withstanding enough of them for long enough did cause an ache. But it all fizzles to nothing at the feel of him against me. At the memory of his ferocity when he came to free me.

For once, I appreciate the fierce ruthlessness of a Nimali beast. What does that say about me? I don't really care—all I want is more of him closer to me. We kiss for a long time, until I'm breathless and panting and he's little better. Then I pull away, dizzy.

Clouds have creeped across the bright moon, but they play against the planes of his face, sharpening them, deepening the shadows of his eyes, making him look even more formidable, and even lovelier. I stroke his cheeks and marvel at the stubble scattered across them.

But reality intrudes all too soon. "I need to get back and warn my people of Denby's plan."

"We sent messengers. They know."

I breathe deeply and thank him. "I'm guessing there's somewhere you need to be now?" I ask, wrapping my arms around him more tightly even though I know I need to let him get back to whatever preparations he doubtlessly needs to be making.

"We won't be ready to move until morning. I need to ensure my supporters are safe and can't be used against me again. I can spare…a few minutes."

I press my lips to his again immediately, unwilling to waste what little time we have. A low rumble sounds in his chest, not indicating anger or fear but desire.

"Come on," he growls, taking my hand. He leads me to the stairwell and we climb down into the darkness. This building is remarkably intact, with plenty of evidence of the people who once lived here before their world changed forever. I listen for occupants, but as far as I can tell, the place is empty.

Scavengers must not have found the place yet, for there are rooms full of furniture still intact. I tug him deeper into an apartment with low moonlight shining in through windows, a few panes of glass still clinging to them.

Anything made of fabric looks rotten and stained, but we come to a room where a sturdy wooden chair was left in its center. It's all alone there, and I test it to make sure it's solid before pushing Shad into it.

He allows it, staring up at me with a curious expression. I straddle him, wrapping my arms around his neck and getting comfortable on his thighs. He closes his eyes and tilts his head back as I rub against his growing hardness. The layers of clothing between us seem to thin as I create a delicious friction between my legs.

"Xipporah," he says, tightening his grip on my shirt. I stroke his head, running my hands over his ears, down his neck, to his shoulders. Then I press my entire body against him.

"You found me," I whisper.

His hands roam to my bottom and squeeze. "I'll always find you," he grits out.

I run my nose along his chin and ear. "You shifted and nearly took down an entire building."

His eyes flash with emotion, but not a hint of regret. "And I'd do it again."

Then he captures my mouth with his and we fall headlong into the kiss. This connection between us builds energy; we feed it back and forth, one to another, both wrestling for control and ceding it in increments. Outside, disaster beckons, and there's so much to attend to, but I block it all out to selfishly steal this moment.

My shirt is over my head in an instant; Shad's hands are everywhere, rubbing and kneading. Pushing my breasts together and caressing my nipples with his thumbs before lowering his mouth to them. His tongue laves at me and I throw my head back, drowning in pleasure.

Moans pierce the quiet. My lower body has a mind of its own and undulates against him, chasing sensation. Soon, we're fumbling with our trousers. He slides his down just enough to free himself. I hastily pull a leg from mine and straddle him again, both of us still partially clothed, but it's enough for him to seek my entrance and push his way inside.

His invasion takes me just to the point of pain, and it's a challenge to take his entire size. Being on top, I control the slide down his thickness, and the sensation creates a feeling of fullness I've never experienced.

I suck in deep breaths until I'm ready to move, but though my aching core is full to overflowing, the longing is still there. I roll my pelvis; we both moan, and sizzling tingles race down my spine. My movements even out into a rhythm, but Shad's impatience comes to the forefront. He grabs my hips and takes over the motion, rolling us into a new tempo of his choosing —one that makes my toes curl inside my boots.

I'm panting, clawing at his shoulders and neck, leaning in for a desperate kiss as the pleasure races through me. Chasing the form of bliss that is generated when two people become one. Then he stands, lifting me easily, and moves to the wall. Presses me against it, shifting inside me, stroking my inner walls with each thrust. I wrap my legs around him, and it's only a few breaths before I'm going over; he follows soon after. Our shouts fill the empty room. I'm hoarse by the time the buzz of electricity leaves my veins.

I feel like I've survived being caught up in a whirlwind, everything inside me spun around and landing in different places. I press my head into the crook of his shoulder and try to catch my breath.

"Shad," I whisper into his ear as his breathing slowly steadies as well.

"I know," he says, kissing my neck. "I know."

He gently pulls out of me and I release my legs, which have turned to noodles. I need to hold onto him until I'm solid on my feet again.

But he never lets me go. We stay locked in an embrace for a long time.

When he pulls back, I blink up at him, still in awe of the intensity of what just happened. The urgency and exhilaration that was so much more than lust.

"My daimon chooses you, Xipporah," Shad says, looking deeply into my eyes. "I choose you as well."

Choose love when love finds you. It's like my daimon whispers inside my head.

"I choose you as well, Shadrach Gabrelson. But how can we—"

He shushes me with another kiss—one that lasts and morphs and transforms into its own being. Taking on life and energy until it's something entirely new.

Finally, we break apart again. "We will figure it out. How

to ensure our union is good for both clans, but first, we need to make sure that Denby doesn't succeed."

I nod. We have to leave; there are many lives hanging in the balance now, but it's possible we won't get this kind of moment to ourselves again.

Love pours through me, bright and clear, like its own star. It shines from me to him; I'm surprised he can't see it. But his eyes don't leave mine and I think, in his way, maybe he does.

"Whatever happens now or tomorrow," he says, "we will face it together."

I nod, stepping back and clutching his hand.

"Now, I have something very important to ask you."

"What is it?" I respond with a smile.

"Do you want to ride a dragon?"

THIRTY-EIGHT

Shad

WE NEED TO GET BACK, but I can't help swooping around the city at least once with Xipporah on my back. The desire to show off for her is strong, bolstered by her shrieks of excitement as I turn and dip with her holding on tight. It buoys me for the fight to come, and I can't believe how fortunate I am.

I've worked very hard to suppress the urge for battle and war that my daimon has, so I'm happily surprised that it's propensity for love is even stronger. Satisfaction ripples through me from the spirit, and I realize it's always craved love—one thing I haven't truly experienced since I leashed it.

I do another loop, rolling over and delighting in the sound of Xipporah's laughter. But it's late, and we can avoid what's coming for no longer. There are interlopers on my throne, they threaten my mate's homeland, and we are going to stop them.

As I turn south, a figure loping along on the ground catches my eyes. I swoop down to land in front of the elephant, who walks nimbly through the overgrown streets, crushing ancient husks of cars under his feet. I let Xi down gently and shift.

"Your Majesty," Akeem says brightly. "I was just coming to join you."

"It's good to see you, Akeem. Did you have any trouble leaving the city?"

"Things are quite chaotic, what with half the soldiers abandoning their posts and scores of Umbers protesting your ouster."

"Protesting?" I try to imagine it.

"I think it's a clever distraction to pull attention from those leaving. But it certainly did make it easy to slip out. None of the checkpoints are being manned." He turns to Xi and bows, raising his trunk. "Lady Xipporah, it's a pleasure." She blinks up at him as I make the introductions.

"Let's walk and talk, shall we?" Akeem suggests. "I'm sure you're eager to get back to your forces, but I did manage to learn something that will be of interest to you."

"What is it?"

"The Trivium. I found a few mentions, buried deep within texts that have mostly been forgotten. But I hit gold with a journal recorded by a monk in the plains of central Australia."

"Nimali have monks?" Xi asks.

"We used to. There was once a religion now lost to time and the will of powerful rulers. This particular journal was catalogued under the same name as the biography of King Alphonso, the only silverback gorilla Nimali king. I believe that's the only reason it wasn't destroyed. Perhaps the bliss did it on purpose…"

"So you think it's sentient?" Xi cranes her neck, looking up at him.

"The bliss? Oh, hmmm. Well, I think it knows more than it lets on. At any rate, in this monk's journal, he recalls his time as part of the Trivium, which was a council of Nimali, Fai…" He pauses for dramatic effect. "And humans."

Clouds chase one another across the sky, egged on by a cackling wind.

"Humans? Really?" I say in wonder.

"In the places where humans were aware of our existence, apparently it often became necessary to negotiate for access to natural resources, food, water, land rights. War was unacceptable to our daimons as humans can very rarely truly threaten our lives, at least not in the times before advanced weaponry, so the three groups needed to come together peacefully."

"Do you know what happened to the Trivium?" I ask.

"As far as I can tell from faint mentions in other texts, it only existed in a few places around the globe. Why it was stricken from the records is something I haven't yet determined, but I don't think there has been an active one for centuries."

The possibilities and mysteries swirl in my mind. I wonder if I visited the library's secret basement archive, would I be able to learn more.

"Thank you, Akeem. This is good to know."

"You are welcome. And now that I have dispensed my duty, please feel free to fly ahead; no need to wait on me. I will be along shortly."

"You're not headed back to the library?" I ask, surprised.

"And miss out on all the fun? Never. How many times in my life will I get to oppose a coup?" He trumpets with laughter.

Not long after, Xipporah and I stand at the entrance to the coliseum. My mouth gapes at the sheer number of people here. The presence of a large number of Umbers is not surprising, but the Azures and smattering of Cardinals present leave me dumbstruck.

Murmurs ripple through the crowd as someone catches sight of me and whispers my name. Those closest to the door kneel, others notice, and soon, a wave of kneeling Nimali spreads from front to back.

I raise my arms. "Thank you, everyone, for being here!" Soft gasps rise. "Yes, thank you. I am grateful to all of you regardless of rank and wish to express it. Thank you for your support and your desire to create change. Please rise."

People stand, some looking as awed as I feel. Simple gratitude can be very powerful, especially when denied for so long as part of a power play that I can no longer accept.

Harsh appears at my side along with some of his lieutenants. He nods at Xipporah. "Glad to see you are well, my lady."

"I am. Thank you. What needs to be done? I'd like to make myself useful."

Harsh glances to me, and I shrug. "Your strength would be helpful setting up the food delivery stations," he says. "Abdul can show you the way."

She gives me a wave and takes off after the soldier.

"Where do we stand?" I ask Harsh.

"We have over half of the Atrament Corps on our side. The bulk of the Umbers in the communes have been evacuated… however, all those closer to the center of the city and in the lodging houses have been corralled into the Citadel. Once the councilors got wind of what we were doing, they began rounding them up, still hoping to use them against you."

"What's this I hear about protests?"

"It's something they came up with on their own. But most of the protesters are among the ones detained."

I sigh. "At least the majority were able to get away. But we do have to be especially careful to minimize the collateral damage when we strike. Where is the intel coming from, anyway?"

"From me." Dame Ayisha approaches with Lady Raina and Lord Edwin on her heels.

I survey them a little suspiciously, not quite daring to hope that they are truly allies.

"Sir Barrett is a sanctimonious scourge," Dame Ayisha says. "I cannot believe a lion is better suited to leadership than a dragon. And there are those of us who appreciate your desire to bring change."

Any of them still may be spies funneling information back to the Citadel, but it's a risk I'll have to take. And if they are loyal, then their presence is greatly appreciated. I tell them so and we strategize, getting briefed by the councilors and adjusting our plans accordingly. I'm sure Harsh will use his own resources to verify what they're saying.

A commotion in the doorway just behind us causes tension to thicken the air. I approach to find a wall of my soldiers facing off against a group of about thirty raggedly dressed humans. Sylph is at their head.

"Let them through!" I call out. The soldiers step aside immediately.

Sylph saunters forward, eyes scanning the entire stadium. Behind him are Elsbeth and her uncle. And more Nimali exiles I recognize.

A cry of recognition goes out from one of the soldiers gathered. If Sylph has brought the exiles, there will be lost family and friends here and long dreamed of reunions. Akeem brings up the rear of the party, his bulk filling the doorway.

"Come in," I tell Sylph and the others. "You are all welcome here."

"Just wanted to pop over and make sure everything turned out all right," he says to me. "Your lady is unharmed." His gaze shoots right to her, though she's easy to spot as she has her daimon called and lifts a massive crate.

"She's a warrior," I say. "I wanted to thank you and your people for all of your help. Did…did the evacuation go all right?" I almost don't want to know if my rage harmed any innocents. But I can't escape my own actions.

"We were able to get everyone out of the building before the first few floors were destroyed. Barely. You know, your idea of five minutes and mine differ slightly."

I twist my lips. "I may have lost control a little bit."

"You don't say?" He grins, and the familiarity of it grips my chest and squeezes.

"I meant what I said about helping the exiles, anyone who wants to return, but before I can do that, I need to get the Citadel back. And I need your help."

His brows rise. "My people are all either human or were exiled without daimons. What can we do to help?"

"Your Silent Hands have already proved how resourceful you are. I'm sure you will figure out something." And then, I make my request.

THIRTY-NINE

Xipporah

BY THE TIME we get the word that the soldiers are ready to move out, dawn is breaking. It's been a long night—being arrested, breaking out, being captured again, getting free, and then helping to set up temporary facilities for those staying here.

I spent the last few hours hauling, assisted by some of the larger shifters—soldiers with daimon forms that could wear a harness to drag things, or carry items on their own, like the pair of gorillas. Working beside them was odd, but as I handed off a heavy box to a kangaroo shifter, I almost wanted to laugh. Is this what the world could be like? Nimali and Fai working together for a common cause?

When spears of golden-red light stab their way through the open doors and the holes in the roof, Shad gathers everyone together. I'm not sure if I should stand at his side. He and I have so much to work out about what our relationship will look like, what my position in Nimali society will be, and how I will live amid their concrete and metal boxes. So, I stand in the front row amid the soldiers as he takes his place on a crate that Harsh had dragged over.

"My fellow Nimali," he says, and all murmurs die so they

can hear his words. He meets my eyes. "And all of my supporters. It is known that I did not defeat the former king in honorable combat."

Grumbles surround me, accompanied by soft-spoken curses of King Lyall. "Then again, the former king was not an honorable man," Shad continues. "He incinerated me mid-shift, while I was vulnerable. And in truth, he killed me. I visited the Origin, convinced that I was lost to this world." Gasps sound. No one, including me, knew that the injuries Shad had suffered at Lyall's hands had actually killed him.

"But the Origin did not keep me. It was not my time, so the spirits sent me back." Energy builds in the crowd at his words, at what they mean. The Origin sent him back; the spirits have chosen him. Among the Fai, it's all but unheard of for anyone save for phoenix shifters. To be chosen is to be special.

"I did not want to be king." Shad's expression is serious and sad. "I did not want to leash a dragon daimon and transform into the most fearsome creature we have. But I am not any different to you. I was born an Umber to hardworking parents. They toiled day in and day out with little reward, and they died ignominiously with few but me to remember them.

"I was promoted to Cardinal after my trials and adopted by a tyrant. Watched him kill my father in an impossible duel. Watched him destroy my mother so that her covenant was broken and she faded into nothing."

Though I know his story, his words still pierce my heart. The pain that he's endured makes me want to wrap him tight and protect him from all future harm.

"I have suffered, and I have worked, and I have bled for my people. Because I am no different than you, and I want to make life better for everyone. Perhaps the Cardinals will not like it as much as everyone else." Chuckles ring out. "But we need a change. We need to be better. *Do* better. And since the spirit of the dragon chose me, and the Origin would not take me, I know that I'm here for a reason. I promise to do my best for all of you, and even those back in the Citadel, clinging to the past, until the day the Origin does accept me back."

Cheers rock the coliseum, deafening me. My voice rises along with them, shouting my agreement, for even though I'm not one of them, I can't help but be moved by Shad's story and his determination.

Shad waits for the chaos to die down a little before he forges on. "My hardships are not unique. We have all faced deprivation of some kind or another at the hands of the rulers. And now, we can take it back. Are you with me?"

The exuberant yells and applause are so loud, I'm sure they can be heard in the Citadel. Goosebumps rise on my flesh as I watch him take it all in. He's been the king for weeks, but I think today he has finally accepted it. Embraced it. A glow seems to radiate from within him; he's magnificent. Love shines out, pouring from me to him, wanting only to add to his light.

He meets my eye and smiles as the cheers go on and on.

"WILL YOU CONSIDER STAYING HERE? I know this isn't your fight." The memory of Shad's inane words makes me roll my eyes. Although I declared my love for him not very long ago, that doesn't mean sometimes I don't want to slap him.

My response had been accompanied with as icy a glare as I could manage. "You're going, I'm going, and besides, Denby is threatening my people. I need to make sure he's stopped."

Which is why I now find myself prowling alongside a company of Nimali cats, approaching the Citadel. Cougars, leopards, lions, other tigers, and at least one preternaturally large lynx surround me. Each company, divided by daimon type, is approaching the stronghold from different directions.

Overhead, the sky is full of the aerial forces, circling and keeping tabs on what's going on down here.

Once Shad accepted I was going, he gave me the option of riding with him, but I prefer to do my fighting on the ground. The strangeness of my presence, embedded with my longtime enemy, will take a long while to get used to. But if I can try, then I'm sure other Fai can as well at some point. And if our clans are no longer enemies, maybe my future with Shad won't be so rocky.

The streets are silent. As Nimali buildings have all their windows sealed, no one looks down upon the encroaching forces in wonder. We hear no alarm raised and, so far, have encountered zero resistance.

As the distance between us and the Citadel shrinks, some of the birds break their formation and soar lower, squawking in alarm. The captain of this company, a black leopard, golden eyes striking amid her dark fur, rears onto her hind legs and roars—the signal for us to charge.

Swift feline legs eat up the ground. My daimon has no trouble keeping up and is invigorated by anticipation. We reach the edge of the grassy plaza to find it in chaos.

A handful of the soldiers who remained, those loyal to Barrett and his cronies, are in turmoil. They're in human form, shouting at a group of Azures who run screaming from the building.

The company I'm a part of draws to a stop near the entrance and is nearly mowed down by the fleeing Nimali. They race right into the group of big cats, obviously more afraid of what's behind them than of us.

An enormous shadow swoops overhead, blocking out the sun for a moment. Shad glides to the ground, which shakes a little at his hard landing. He shifts and runs forward, grabbing a fleeing Azure woman by her shoulders.

"What's wrong? What's happening?"

She sobs uncontrollably, unable to get a word out. Shad

releases her and looks around in confusion. We'd expected resistance, a battle, not this knot of fleeing, hysterical people.

Like the cork of a bottle being popped, a larger swarm of Nimali now race from the building, most of these Cardinals. Sir Barrett is among them; Shad and I spot him at the same time. As birds of prey land all around, the canine company also arrives. A wolf and a silver fox shift into two sizable women who grab Barrett by his arms and drag him over to Shad. As our additional forces arrive, some shifting into humans while others retain their daimon forms, more Cardinals and soldiers flee the building in panic.

"Round them up," Harsh's voice sounds from somewhere to the left of me. "Everyone who comes out of the building gets detained." Half of the cats shift to human to follow the orders, aided by those still on four legs.

Barrett squirms and shouts, his words unintelligible. Shad grabs his jaw to focus him, and the man quiets.

"What is happening here?" Shad says, voice low and demanding. The councilor's lips quiver; his eyes are wild, panicked.

"What in Origin's name is wrong with him?" I ask.

"He's a coward," a new voice states. Dominga walks out amid the insanity, perfectly calm. A soldier tries to grab her arm but she pulls it back, shooting him a glare so deadly that he stands down.

"These idiots thought the safest place for the poison was back in the Citadel," she says as she approaches. "They stored it in the original lab."

"Th-the building is secure," Barrett finally stammers.

"Not secure enough," Dominga spits. "The explosive device has been reactivated. It's counting down, and no one can disarm it."

"Where is Sir Denby?" Shad asks.

"No idea. But the entire building has lost power, including the emergency alarm system. There are no lights, no elevators, and no way to alert everyone inside of the danger. He ordered his staff"—she points at her father—"to go floor to floor and alert the Cardinals of the need to evacuate, but didn't bother to tell them why. Of course word started spreading that they were going to be poisoned. So they abandoned the task and devolved into bawling infants." She seems more annoyed by this turn of events than alarmed.

"So there are people in there who have no idea what's coming?" I look up at the tower in disbelief.

"Most of them."

"Do you know how long until the device explodes?" Shad asks.

Dominga spreads her arms. "The engineers have no idea. The device has been tampered with; the timer is obscured."

Shad curses low and long, the string of words quite inventive, really. I continue staring up at the building—forty-eight floors. Many of the people in there sided with Barrett and the coup leaders, but there are as many if not more innocents within. Umbers rounded up and detained to use against Shad. Azure scholars and scientists. Cardinals who make their home inside those walls, wholly unaware of the political machinations going on.

"This is Von's doing," I grit out, seething. "It must have been what he was referring to. Somehow, he's gotten exceptionally good at manipulating Nimali tech. He must have had some kind of backup timer or remote switch on the device."

The urge to scream and rage is strong…then I think about Kit and Aggi. I hadn't seen them in the coliseum, so they must have been among those still trapped in the Citadel along with hundreds of others who don't deserve to die.

Whereas a few weeks ago I would have been happy to blame every Nimali alive for what's happened to the Fai, now I understand that to be foolish and cruel. Von's daimon is either demented like Lyall's was, or the man is fine with losing it in favor of this twisted revenge.

"We'll need volunteers to evacuate the building, floor by floor," Shad says. "Harsh! Gather the captains."

I don't wait. "I'm going in," I say, marching toward the building. "I need to talk to Von. See if I can knock some sense into him."

"Xipporah, wait!" Shad shouts.

"Have the bird shifters smash through windows," I call over my shoulder, not slowing down at all. "It's a faster way out."

To my surprise, Dominga follows me into the lobby. "What are you doing?" I ask as Shad continues to shout, his voice growing desperate.

"These are actually *my* people," Dominga says, like it was the dumbest question ever. "I'm going to help evacuate them."

"But you're a Cardinal."

She rolls her eyes and a sudden flare of light flashes, blinding me. When the brightness fades, an impossibly large Komodo dragon stands where she was—at least nine feet long. A forked tongue flicks out at me, and the lizard releases an unholy hissing, a sound that wouldn't be out of place coming from a demon. With startling speed, it climbs right up the wall and onto the ceiling, disappearing around the corner.

I swallow, call my daimon to me, and race for the stairwell.

FORTY

Xipporah

WITHOUT ANY EMERGENCY LIGHTING, as soon as I get beyond the reach of the sunlight streaming into the lobby, the windowless interior of the building is pitch black. A stampede of Cardinals rushes down the stairwell, most in their shifted forms. I leap onto the railing to avoid being trampled by a zoo's worth of creatures, some too large to fit comfortably on the steps. Then I need to avoid the birds swooping down around me. But once this clutch of creatures goes by, the passageway is quiet.

The frozen locker is on the third floor; I emerge into the hallway without seeing anyone else. The prison itself is just as we left it, though considerably warmer without power. The insulated walls have done their best to keep the cold in, but judging by the way Von paces the cell, hands still tied before him, only minutes remain before it's warm enough for him to call his daimon and easily escape.

The only light comes from the glow of my daimon-enhanced eyes. It's enough to see his gleeful expression.

"What have you done?" I whisper.

He grips the bars of the cell, now sweating as the place defrosts. "I completed my mission."

"Your mission was to bring down the entire building with every man, woman, and child inside? You're breaking your covenant. Your daimon will abandon you."

His smile dies. "Sacrifices must be made to ensure the safety of our people. I'm doing whatever it takes."

"It didn't take this. The Nimali were well on the way to destroying themselves."

"And I helped it along. Don't you understand? Citlali's plan could never have worked. There is no peace between our clans; there is only kill or be killed." His eyes have taken on a sheen of madness. I wonder what his time alone hidden behind enemy lines did to him. How it's warped him.

"Kill or be killed is only law in the jungle. We are people."

His lips stretch wide in an approximation of a grin. "Are we not animals, too, sister? We don't change forms as they do, but we are all beasts on the inside."

Frustrated with this, I change tacks. "What did you do to the detonator?"

He shrugs. "Their timing system already had the code for an automatic restart embedded within, though it was inactive. I just activated it. As soon as the timer was turned off, it automatically restarted for twenty-four hours."

Yesterday morning Von had first activated the detonator —it felt like weeks had passed since then. But Denby deactivated the device shortly after we were arrested. I don't know the exact time, but already at least twenty-two hours have passed, maybe more. My heartbeats speed with the urgency we face.

"And the power loss in the building? The emergency alarms aren't even working."

The smug expression makes me want to reach through the bars and smack him. "I placed all the devices I'd found to drain the bliss in the power center of the building. That's why I was caught—though they didn't know what I'd been doing."

"How do you know how to do all of that? Nimali technology can't be that easy to learn—not even in the weeks you've been in hiding here."

He presses his face between the bars. "Do you really think that no Fai thought learning about Nimali tech would be a worthwhile pursuit?"

My jaw drops. The shock locks my limbs. The idea of Fai in the Greenlands abusing the bliss in this way... But I don't have time for dismay—in a matter of hours, minutes really, an explosion will go off inside the Citadel that will spread deadly toxin into the air. And I need to find a way to stop it.

The locker is warm enough that Von will be able to shift shortly. I turn to the wall and spot several pairs of ice cuffs hanging there. When I grab a pair and face him, he shrinks back, shaking his head.

"Xipporah, no!"

I wrench open the cell door and easily clap the cuffs on him. Then I make sure the bars are back in place.

"You're really going to leave me here, powerless?" he cries.

"I'm giving you exactly what you deserve, Von."

I race away, back to the stairwell, now lit by candles and lanterns as Shad's volunteers go floor by floor, ushering people out. The steps are too crowded to head up with so many going down. Instead, I run to the elevator and pry the heavy doors open. With no fear of a car coming down or up to crush me, I climb up the maintenance ladder affixed to the wall, up to the sixteenth floor where weeks ago Ryin found the lab used to experiment on the Revokers.

The door is shut, and with no power, some internal locking system has been engaged that won't let me pull it open. I waste long minutes trying with all my strength before I just go the brute force route and start punching through the wall. My fists are bruised and bloody—these walls are a lot stronger than the ones in the building where the poison was stored before. Fortunately, the second set of doors inside the small vestibule are already open. Lantern light glows within.

Crates of the deadly canisters fill the space, and the glowing netting connecting them all together pulses with a quick, flashing light.

Kneeling next to a crate is Sir Denby, his graying blonde head bent, working at the detonation device, frantically swiping over its surface. At my entrance, he looks up, sweat pouring down his face.

"I can't override it. What did you do? What did you *dooo*?" He wails and lunges at me, arms out like he wants to wring my neck. I smack him back, and he lands on the floor in a heap, moaning.

Footsteps thump in the outer hallway. As Denby writhes on the ground dramatically—I didn't hit him *that* hard—I survey the scene. There are tools scattered on the ground. Most I don't recognize, but some, like scissors and bolt cutters, I do.

Someone outside this room is widening my entrance through the wall. I brace myself, not sure what to expect, when Shad pushes through with a handful of soldiers behind him.

The look of relief on his face gives me a pang of guilt. "Are you all right?" he asks, pulling me into his embrace.

"I'm fine. But we might only have two hours, possibly less, before this thing goes off. I don't think there's a way to stop it in time. If the man who designed it couldn't shut it off…" I motion to Denby, who's making his way to his feet.

Shad's expression is grim, but he nods in understanding. "Put him in cuffs," he tells one of the soldiers, motioning to Denby. To me, he says, "We're going to have to focus on the evacuation and getting everyone clear, but about half of the biometric locks are still engaged. People are trapped in their suites. Without the power…" His chest rises and falls. He clears his throat, grappling with a wave of emotion. "Without at least the emergency systems online…I just don't know how we can get everyone out. We've been going through the walls, but it's slow."

The soldiers drag Denby out, leaving this room eerily quiet. The pulsing shine of the netting illuminates the grief etched into his face. His words settle over me along with a sense of clarity and determination. I know what I have to do.

"Where is the building's power station?"

His gaze shoots to mine, quizzical. "It takes up most of the first floor. Why?"

"And the emergency power? Is it there as well?"

"It's a smaller bliss tank in the corner. Labeled with a large red X."

I take a deep breath. "Keep working on the evacuation. And be ready for the emergency power to come back on."

Understanding dawns and his eyes widen. "Xi, are you sure?"

I swallow. I can't just do nothing, and my heart is going to hurt either way.

"No. But I'm willing."

<hr>

THE POWER STATION consists of giant versions of the same kind of bliss cubes that were in the commune and produce houses. Each one is practically the size of a room. All are dark and cool to the touch. But I imagine they were once vibrant with the spirit energy that powers everything here.

The emergency system is easy to spot, just as Shad said. Instead of a cube, it's a three-dimensional rectangle stretching to the ceiling, taller than the other power sources, but just as dead.

Tears well in my eyes. Though I didn't want to accept the possibility that I could revive the bliss with my daimon, that ability is the only thing that might save everyone trapped in this building.

And if I'm completely honest, when Shad confronted me with the possibility, the intense fear I felt was because I knew he was right. Somehow, bliss can be restored, maybe in the same way that my daimon amplifies Von's abilities and the powers of any other Fai.

If bliss is spirit, just like our daimons, then it stands to reason I can strengthen it, restore it. And even if I think the energy is better off out of its misery, released from the forced servitude of powering this unnatural technology, I must face the fact that hundreds will die if I don't.

I take a stuttering breath, place my hands on the cool surface of the power cell, and quiet my inner thoughts. My daimon is alert within me. It does not send me any feelings or give any clarity. They are not concerned with the same things we are; they are not beings of morality—right and wrong, good and evil are not concepts they recognize. There is the covenant, of course, which they enforce and hold sacred, but my daimon cannot tell me whether my actions are ethical.

I imagine the bliss, moving and living in the temple back home, and how the energy rejuvenates us all, gives us peace and comfort. My hands warm; power flows out of me and into the cell, ready to boost it.

The bliss supports the Nimali differently than it does the Fai. Instead of inspiring and calming, it supports, lights, feeds, and warms. It gives them comfort and security in a different way. And now, it can save their lives.

Understanding dawns as the shimmering radiance of blue inside the cell begins to grow. What if the bliss isn't being enslaved? What if, here, it's just found a different way to be useful?

We don't know what happens to our daimons when we die. Since they reside in the Origin, I've always assumed they are infinite spirits, but maybe they're like us, with lifespans and desires to use their existence for something meaningful. And maybe the bliss is the same.

As the soft light radiates into the room and the cell comes

back to life, my daimon sends a sense of satisfaction to me, gratitude for this experience. My fingers heat and a little sizzle of energy travels from the power cell into me. I can almost hear a whisper crackling in the air. It sounds like, "Thank you."

I step back, startled, and the little jolt is gone. Was that just in my head?

Machinery within the walls starts to groan and hum; I think it's the elevators coming back online. Then the building erupts with a deafening sound. Lights flash and the horn-like alarm wails. The task is done.

Back in the lobby, the emergency lighting is on and Shad's soldiers are leading people out in an orderly way. The ashen, horrified faces that pass me look traumatized, but as the people exit the building, a deep sense of peace comes over me.

Outside, I see they've taken my advice and many windows of high floors have been smashed open. Birds, bats, and even a few flying squirrels soar down, while hawks and raptors carry smaller creatures in their claws, bringing them gently to the ground.

Lizards, cats, snakes, and other crawlers creep down the exterior of the building. Children, teens, and young adults, those too young to shift or who have failed in their trials, are helped out by soldiers. Part of me considers going back for Von, forcing him to face Fai justice instead of going down with the ship he chose to sink—but I think better of it. I no longer consider him a brother, and his fate now is his own.

On the plaza, like an island amid a sea of fleeing people and creatures, Harsh stands with a small group of high-ranking military. And while his normal expression tends toward the taciturn, now it could only be called thunderous. He catches sight of me and nods.

"Emergency power is on," I say, coming up next to him. "There should be time to clear the building."

"Thank you. Shad told me what you were planning. I know…that must not have been easy."

My throat feels clogged, but I chase the discomfort away. "Needed to be done."

His expression is a fraction less intense. "Once this thing blows, it'll release a poison cloud that will spread across this section of the city, making the entire territory uninhabitable. We're evacuating everyone down to the coliseum."

"Will we have time to get them far enough away?" a steely-haired woman asks.

"What about supplies? Food and water?" a bald man asks.

"I've got units three through eight gathering as much as they can carry," Harsh responds, "but we need to prioritize vehicle transport for those too young to shift."

"What can I do?" I ask.

"Make sure the king gets out of that building before it blows. He'll stay until the last second, you know that."

He's right.

I turn away just as Harsh calls for the equine company to shift and start carrying children to safety. Then I'm back inside the doomed building, hoping against hope that we can somehow pull off a miracle.

FORTY-ONE

Shad

EVEN THOUGH THE evacuation is orderly, it's still taking much too long to get everyone out. The use of the elevators helps, but, there aren't nearly enough of them, and they move excruciatingly slow. In their haste, many are choosing to face several dozen flights of stairs instead or flee out the windows.

An urgency bordering on panic drives me forward, though my legs burn from climbing and descending endless steps. What we're facing is nothing short of annihilation, so I must persist.

I'm not even sure what floor I'm on, or how many people I've tried to instruct in a calm, authoritative voice to head either for the stairs or the elevators. Part of what's been keeping me upright is the visible effect my presence is having. That their king is enduring this trial with them reduces their panic, I see over and over again, but my own internal battery is waning. That is, until I feel her nearby.

A crackling in the air sizzles through me, and though I don't yet see her, some part of me senses her arrival. It buoys me, and I lead yet another group of trapped Umbers toward the elevators. Then, a strong grip grabs hold of my arm and drags me away down the hall.

"Xipporah, what's wrong? Are you all right?" I ask as I'm towed along.

"You're coming with me, now." Her voice brooks no opposition.

"Where? What's happened?"

She draws to a stop around the corner, looking up at me with eyes narrowed in exasperation. "This building is going to explode soon, that's what's happened."

I take a step back. "I am aware. What do you think I'm doing here?"

She grabs my hand this time, stalling my retreat. "Your soldiers, those who volunteered to evacuate the building, are up to the task. Let them do their jobs. The king needs to be very far away from this place when it goes up. You"—she punctuates this with a poke to my chest—"need to be outside. Now."

"I'm not leaving until this building is empty." I shake her off, turning back the way we came, back to the cluster of Umbers who had been trapped inside the Common Hall like prisoners, having committed no crime except remain loyal to me.

Then the ground falls away and the earth turns on its axis. Xipporah lifts me and tosses me over her shoulder to carry me down the hall.

We pass soldiers, men and women who have supposedly pledged their fealty to me, who still have the nerve to applaud and whoop in approval.

"Xipporah, put me down," I grit out.

"You weren't listening to reason, so I had to take matters into my own hands." She grips my thighs gently, but firmly. I'm not going anywhere unless she lets me.

"Are you going to carry me down nineteen flights of steps?"

"If I need to." With her daimon, she's not even breathing hard, but I'm starting to get dizzy.

"All right, all right. Put me down and I'll come with you."

"I'm not sure if I can trust you."

We pass more people and, while it's mortifying to be in this position—ass in the air dangling over a woman's shoulder—I don't miss the humor of the situation.

"Xi. I give you my word as king that I will come with you if you put me down."

She stops walking. I hold my breath as she decides. Finally, she crouches, setting my feet back on the floor. I straighten my uniform and clear my throat, peering at the soldiers in the hallway still gaping, mouths open mid-laugh. "Not a word of this to anyone, especially Sir Harshal, do you hear me?"

The soldiers salute, but as soon as my back is turned, the snickers begin.

I look at Xi peevishly but she just smiles. "Come on, Your Majesty."

Out on the plaza, I'm unsurprised to find that Harsh has things well in hand. And while the evacuation is running as smoothly as I could hope, with just over an hour until the building blows, there isn't nearly enough time to save everyone *and* get us all clear of the danger zone. We really have no idea how far-reaching the damage will be. The wind has picked up, making the spread of the poisonous cloud unpredictable once disaster strikes.

There are so many moving parts: supplies to gather, people to transport. I catch Harsh's eye and see my worries etched into his face. But all I can do is my best. Save as many as I can. That it won't be enough is something to grieve for another day. I try to remember that as I continue to coordinate the evac.

Then my name is called. Not *Your Majesty*, but *Shad* in a voice I haven't heard in days. I spin around to see Callum racing toward me from across the plaza, a pack of Silent Hands on his heels with Sylph in the lead.

When he reaches me, Callum embraces me, thumping me

hard on the back. He's covered in grit like he's been in the tunnels, but otherwise is unharmed.

"Did you actually gain weight while you were gone?" I ask, laughing.

"Fai food is definitely better." He pats his stomach.

"Well, I'm glad to see you. Now you have to get the hell away from here." I turn to Sylph. "All of you. I appreciate your help, but this place is about to be a kill zone."

Callum scans the plaza. I see the moment he spots the phalanx of guards surrounding his handcuffed father. "Shad, what in Origin's name is happening?"

I swallow and give him a quick rundown of what he's missed. The coup. His father's betrayal. The building's impending demise. His eyes get wider and wider.

The look he gives Sir Denby is heartbroken, but it only lasts a moment. "Can I use your comm?" It's not what I was expecting him to say, but I hand it over.

"Ping Callum," he says into the device, and my brows rise.

"Wha—?" But I bite off my question when a face extrudes from the surface of the comm. I recognize Callum's Fai fiancé, Lex. Confusion fills me as I watch the exchange.

"Hey," Callum says.

Lex seems out of breath, like he ran to answer the call. "Are you all right?" he asks.

"I'm fine. Everyone else okay?"

"The ice blasts wore off quickly, but we couldn't find you. Listen—"

"Yeah, apparently, my dad hired folks to take me. He's… well, looks like he's got a lot to answer for over here. But um, things aren't really going so well, and if I don't see you again, I just wanted to…thank you. It was an honor being betrothed to you."

Lex's breathing quickens, like he's heading somewhere in a hurry. "Callum, my father—" But the rest of his statement is garbled, the power cell of the comm in its last throes.

"The power is cutting out. I just wanted to say that. Sorry for making you use the comm. This counts as an emergency, though." He smiles sadly. "Goodbye." Then he slams the device shut. My eyebrows are at my hairline.

He looks at me sheepishly. "So, I don't think you'll be surprised to hear that it wasn't a love match, but it turns out our daimons are parallels. We're soulmates. You and Harsh have been like brothers to me…" He swallows, tears filling his eyes. "Now I have another one."

I clap his shoulder and squeeze, truly happy for him. But what does it mean that Callum's parallel is someone who has been an enemy for so long? A brief thought crosses my mind —what if parallels are so rare because they often belong to people from two different clans? But I have not time to ponder that one.

Callum straightens his shoulders and glares at his father. "What can I do? How can I help undo his mess?" The determination in his voice makes me certain that he won't leave until every Nimali is safe, which means he likely won't leave at all. Tears prick my own eyes.

As king, where am I most needed? Leading the survivors, or staying with those who won't make it to safety? I know Xipporah's opinion on the matter and don't need to ask Harsh and Callum their thoughts, either. But how can I leave any of them here? Xi will probably have to drag me away kicking and screaming.

Harsh finally makes his way over, having cleared himself from the band of officers he was instructing, to greet Callum, who assaults him with a hug. Somewhat awkwardly, Harsh returns the gesture, then steps away quickly. Callum is unfazed.

"Where do we stand?" I ask Harsh, and he shoots me a grateful expression, glad not to be forced to deal with his emotions.

But before he can answer, a shadow crosses the sun.

Wings flap over head—large wings. Larger than any other creature's in Aurum, except for mine. A green dragon, small but fast, circles overhead with a man flying at her side. The western sky is dark with the bodies of flying people, all wingless but with the glowing eyes of daimons marking them.

The Fai have arrived.

FORTY-TWO

Shad

THE GREEN DRAGON circles the plaza a few times, looking for a place to land.

"Clear a space!" Harsh calls out, and people begin to scatter. Her landing is a little rough, as she's still very new at this, but once she touches the ground and Ryin floats down beside her, she flashes into the shape of Talia.

The spitting image of Celena, Talia's manner and expression are what set her apart. Her natural warmth is in such contrast to Celena's coolness that it's amazing we pulled off the ruse that she was the princess for so long.

"Shad, we're here to help," Talia announces.

"How did you even know we needed help?" I ask. All around us, Air Fai are setting down. Many of them carry others in their arms, likely those with Water or slower Land or Fire daimons.

"I'll let her explain," Talia says, pointing to a young woman landing and setting down her passenger, the Water Priestess.

Today, Citlali is dressed simply in a flowing gown dyed in different shades of blue from aquamarine to navy. She steadies herself and pats her ride on the shoulder, thanking the woman, then approaches. The elderly Fire Priest appears at her side, though I don't see either of the other two Crowns.

Citlali glances over at the Citadel with a frown before speaking. "King Shadrach," she says formally.

I bow. "Priestess, Priest, it is an honor. But now is a time of crisis."

"Why do you think we're here, child? My vision changed. Last night, I had the same dream that has plagued me for weeks, but for the first time it was different. It branched. I saw two possible futures. One in which the Greenlands was destroyed, and one in which it survives." Her brows draw down. "Unfortunately, in both of them, the Citadel is demolished."

The breath leaves my lungs in a gush, the tiny flare of hope that had begun with her words now extinguished. "That sounds like a vision that will certainly come true. We are less than half an hour away from it, in fact. And while I appreciate any help, you must get your people to safety, for with the explosion will come a poison cloud that will destroy everything and everyone for miles."

She nods. "This I also saw, and that is why we came, Your Majesty. Do you feel which way the wind blows?" She licks a finger and holds it in the air.

I pause, really taking a moment to feel the wind on my skin and sense its direction. "It is from the east."

Her expression is grim. "Blowing west. It will flow right across the city, bringing your poison along with it."

"All the way to the Greenlands." My eyes close. "Do you have a way to stop the explosion?"

"No, we cannot override your technology," she says sadly, "but we do have the means to contain it. Minimize the damage to the surrounding area. We can neutralize the poison and keep it from spreading and infecting the city." She turns to the Fire Priest. "Unfortunately, the Land and Air Priests still do not believe me."

"Because they are to blame for this calamity in the first place," the white-haired man says.

"Peace, Abner," Citlali says with a hand on his shoulder. "They both approved of this plan, the one that the operative secreted away in your territory put into action. It was without our knowledge or approval. Makani, the Air Priest, at least had the sense to realize his mistake. But Land Priest Eamonn forbade most of the Land daimons from accompanying us, and it is their talents we need the most."

"I don't understand."

"Where is Xipporah?"

I lost track of her once she led me outside. But I use my internal sense that seems to always know where she is to locate her, locked in the embrace of a group of newly arrived Fai. Her eyes move to mine as if she can feel me watching. She quickly extricates herself and comes over, nodding respectfully to her leaders.

Citlali holds out both hands in greeting. "You are well, Xipporah?"

Xi holds the older woman's hands and ducks her head. "I am very well."

"Yes, I can see." Citlali gives me a knowing glance. Exactly what do these dreams of hers tell her? "We will need to rely on you, Xipporah. We only have a handful of Land Fai to amplify us."

Understanding lights her eyes. "You're going to make a Fai circle?"

"Indeed."

Xi looks around at the Fai gathered and swallows, daunted. "How many Land Fai came?" Concern rises within me at the uncertainly in her voice. Why is the lack of Land Fai a problem?

A disturbance among the soldiers nearby, to whom Harsh and Callum are speaking, causes me to look over. Callum has a perplexed look on his face, and I soon determine that a new group of Fai has just arrived. Among them is Lex, Callum's parallel and newfound brother.

Citlali smiles at the new arrivals. "Including Lex, we now have six Land Fai."

Lex and Callum walk over. "As I tried to say before your infernal device murdered the bliss energy powering it, my father is partly to blame for this," Lex says. "Maybe just as much as yours. I managed to convince a few people to defy him and will do what I can to help."

He bows at the Fai elders. "I have brought three others."

"Now we have ten." Citlali claps her hands together. "It will be enough."

"How many must we amplify?" Xi asks.

"Our circle must wrap around the entire building."

The Fire Priest adds, "I calculate we'll need close to 150 daimons working together to create a circle big enough to manage the damage of the destruction and the poison." Silence reins after his statement.

"Each of us will have to boost fifteen," Xi whispers.

"What does that mean? Is it dangerous?" I ask.

Wide, fearful eyes meet my own. My heart sinks.

I turn to Citlali. "There's no way to get more Land Fai?"

"No time, even if there was a way," she replies. "We will make it work." Her voice is firm.

But at what cost?

Xi squares her shoulders, determination and strong will taking over. I'm worried for her, but this is very far out of my sphere of knowledge, and changing her mind would be impossible. "So, how is this going to work?" I ask.

"When we join together," Xi says, "each daimon type will use their ability. The Air Fai will keep the blast contained, the Fire Fai control the smoke and douse the flames, the Water Fai will purify the air, and we will amplify all of their abilities."

"We should be able to restrict the damage just to the footprint of the building," Lex adds.

Harsh steps to my side. "We just got the word that everyone made it out."

But hundreds are still on the plaza and exiting the territory, so if the Fai gambit doesn't work, this is the end of the majority of both of our clans.

"We have no time to waste," Citlali calls. Almost as one, the gathered Fai move toward the Citadel. Lex nods to us all and walks away to join those spreading themselves out around the building and linking hands.

Xipporah grabs me in a tight hug and kisses me fiercely. Then she's off, running to get a place in the circle. All the Fai have their daimons called, and though to the rest of us it appears that they are just standing and holding hands, tension thrums in the air.

They have only been in place for mere minutes when the first explosion rocks the building, earlier than expected, causing the earth to shake under our feet. Smoke, fire, and debris fly out of the first floor, then hit an invisible barrier and are allowed to go no farther.

The barrier is like a cylinder that's been dropped on top of the entire building. Smoke fills it like it would a glass. Convulsions take over the structure, causing the surface to ripple and roll. The spire at the top wobbles before tumbling down, bouncing off the surrounding barrier to crash on the ground. Then the entire tower breaks apart like it's made of kindling, not metal and concrete.

The ground trembles and the sound of destruction roars and splinters against our ears, but the demolition is contained. Not even the smell of smoke breaks through. Flames lick up and die quickly, and soon the rumbling underfoot gentles to nothing.

The Fai are all focused, locked in what looks like a group trance. They are working to save themselves, to protect their homeland and their people, but they are saving mine as well. And I wish there was something more I could do.

Finally, after what seems like eons of watching the place that has served as the symbol of strength for my people for fifty years reduced to dust, it's over. The Citadel is no more, just a crater in the ground. Clouds of soot and what must be poison, though it's indistinguishable from the smoke, have pressed down to nothing. Fai Water daimons can purify—the idea of that holds a quiet beauty.

The Fai release their joined hands. They all appear exhausted from the effort they've undertaken. Some stand, their breaths heaving. Others back away from the circle on shaking legs, like they've run a long race.

Xipporah turns to face me, a tired smile on her face. She takes a single step forward, then collapses into a heap on the ground.

FORTY-THREE

Xipporah

THE SMELL of cinnamon reaches my nose. I breathe it in, wanting it closer. There's something so soothing about the aroma. But it also ignites a yearning deep within, causing me to clench my legs together. Memories of pleasure ripple across my spine.

I have the sense of being wrapped in a blanket of safety while, at the same time, a deep, full-body ache pulses. And someone is calling my name.

"She's coming out of it. Amplifying so many is draining, but there won't be any lasting damage." The voice is so familiar, but my mind is still coming back online. Strong arms are around me; I nuzzle further into their solid comfort. It beats away the exhaustion that frays my edges.

"Xi-Xi?" That voice again. So well-known, it feels like a part of me. Opening my eyes is a struggle, but I manage to pry them apart and find Noomi's wide-eyed gaze settled on me.

"Nooms? What are you doing here?" My voice is hoarse, my throat parched.

I engage in light warfare with my muscles in order to sit up and receive assistance from a pair of large, brown hands. Shad is behind me, propping me up. We sit on the grass on the plaza with Noomi on her knees before me. I'm still sluggish and am glad I can give Shad all of my weight.

"Noomi," I say, "you know my fiancé, the king."

She blinks at him. "We've met."

My mind is clearing, the fog slowly dissipating. The Fai circle. Combining our powers. Containing the damage, but exhausting myself. I've never been in a circle with so few Land daimons; it took everything we had to suppress the poison, but the daimon power of each person was working through all of us. It combined for a single purpose to save us all.

On the plaza, the buzz of activity still makes my head spin. I focus on my sister and the words she's saying. "When I wanted to join Citlali and the others, Mother locked me in my room. It took a while to get out and get over here—you were always the best at lock picking."

Her tone is accusing but playful. "So, I'm sorry I'm late. I wanted to take part in the circle." She looks significantly at Shad's arms surrounding me and me plastered all over him. "I take it your engysis is working out."

I try to rise into a more graceful position, but Shad just pulls me tighter against his chest. "Yes. It worked out," I reply. "Though I don't yet know what our future will look like."

She drops her head. "You're not coming home," she whispers.

A pang of sorrow hits me. "If you could stand it, if it wouldn't make the nightmares worse, you can always make your home wherever I am."

Noomi squares her shoulders and raises her chin. "You know, being here… It isn't bringing back any bad memories. It turns out, my dreams weren't really about my time as a drudge." She motions to the crater in the ground where the Citadel used to be. "My dreams were like Citlali's—the terror was because I was predicting destruction. I just didn't understand what they meant. I'm not used to prophetic dreaming.

But I've been working with her and some of the other Water Fai to be able to read them more effectively. To not let them frighten me so much. And I have been sleeping better."

My eyes tear up as relief spills over. It feels like putting down a burden I wasn't aware I was carrying. Noomi has been able to take care of herself for a long time, but worrying about her has been second nature for even longer.

"I'm so happy to hear that." I push my way to my knees and embrace her, joy restoring some of my energy.

"Y-your Majesty?" A young soldier appears at our side, his movements jerky and nervous. "S-sorry to interrupt."

I turn to Shad. "It's all right. Go on. I'm sure there are mountains of tasks that need your attention."

He narrows his eyes. "I'm not sure I can take it if you collapse again."

I give him a reassuring smile. "I'm fine. I give you my word."

"Your word as queen?" A single brow lifts.

I roll my eyes. "We will deal with all of that in due time. Now go, do king things."

He chuckles and rises. "It's wonderful to see you again, Noomi." Then he ambles away with the young soldier on his heels.

Noomi tracks him with her gaze. "The way he looks at you," she breathes, leaning forward.

"What?"

"Like he wants to change into his dragon and eat you alive."

I laugh, and though my entire body is still sore, it feels good.

Noomi sits back, legs crossed. "I guess it's for the best that my dreams weren't what we thought. Looks like I'll have to be spending a lot more time here in Nimali territory."

"Maybe your dreams will help us figure out what comes next—what peace between our clans will look like."

Currently, those gathered on the plaza are split, with the Fai clustered together on one side, many of them looking as worn out as me, and the Nimali on the other. I'm fairly sure few of my people will stay any longer than they have to. They'll be gone as soon as their daimons are recovered enough to make the trip back to the Greenlands. But there might be a day when that isn't the case.

"Help me up," I say to my sister. It takes a few moments to stand. This is what it must feel like to be very old, everything aching and nothing moving the way it used to. But once I'm upright and have stretched a bit, more life returns to my limbs. My daimon is quiet within me, resting, I'd guess. I hold my sister's hand, grateful for her support.

"Where is Makani?" I ask her.

"When Citlali gathered everyone to share her new dream and her intentions to come and stop it, the Crowns all fought. It was awful. Makani and Eamonn stormed away with almost all of the Land daimons."

"I wonder that he didn't forbid the Air Fai from coming as well."

She purses her lips. "He seemed shaken by her dream. He ran off; Mother said he was probably going to the temple to pray, but I didn't see him before I was locked away."

I squeeze her hand. "Well, I hope he finds some peace there, because I will personally call a forum to bring both him and Eamonn up on charges. They never should have approved of Von's idiotic plan."

I consider Von's other revelation—someone among the Fai has been secretly teaching knowledge of Nimali technology in order to use it against them. Makani or Eamonn must know about this, maybe even be behind it. These are questions we will need to grapple with as we reassess our leaders.

Shad stands surrounded by a small group of people that only a few days ago would never have been in each other's company. Citlali, Abner, Lex, and Ryin. Harsh, Callum, and a handful of Nimali soldiers. Zero and his Silent Hands. I lead Noomi over.

"The Trivium," Shad is saying, "we have very few records, but I think it's more important than ever to put it back into place. All of us will need to come together to share resources and knowledge if we are to continue to live on this land together and do more than subsist."

Citlali taps her lips, the charms on her bracelet tinkling. "There were once tales of such an alliance, old stories, but much of our history has not survived. Our elder scholars are few, but I will consult them to see if there are any recollections of this Trivium."

"Keep in mind," Zero adds, "there are no formal rulers for the humans like there are for your clans. If you want our input, we'll need multiple seats."

"I think that is for the best," Shad replies. "Even within the clan, there are different interest groups—daimon types and castes. We will have to determine how many seats there will be at the table and how the representatives will be chosen."

"Along with what authority this group will have," Citlali adds.

"But can we all at least agree that it is necessary?" Shad looks around the circle, which has widened since they began speaking. The curious from both clans want to know what is going on.

Zero glances at his people; several of them nod. "We're in, and I know that many, if not all, of the human factions would be willing to consider it, if it comes with certain assurances."

Abner and Citlali look to each other. "We will have to bring it to our forum for discussion and a vote," Citlali says. "But I also think it is a positive step to move forward for peace. None of us want a repeat of what happened today."

Shad exhales, relief evident. "Good. We'll make plans to meet and discuss this again as a group in neutral territory."

Zero snorts. "Your neutral territory is someone else's home."

Shad blinks, not seeming to have considered this.

"Then let it be outside of Aurum," Citlali says. "There is an island to the north. We have boats we can provide to those who cannot fly or swim there."

Zero and Shad share matching looks of surprise, then both break into smiles. I sense that I've missed something in the relationship between those two and make a note to ask Shad later.

"All right," Zero says. "We'll take that under advisement."

As the plans for how this will proceed continue, a spark of warmth flickers to life within my chest and radiates outward. So much to resolve, such a tall mountain to climb, but these are the first steps.

Shad's gaze meets mine, and the light within it makes me believe that it's really possible. That somehow, we'll actually succeed.

FORTY-FOUR

Shad

THE IMPROMPTU MEETING—A precursor to the Trivium—breaks up, with Citlali announcing that the Fai are going home. I'm happier than I dare to admit that we were able to discuss things so calmly. And while I have no illusions it will always be like this, I'm willing to take the small victories.

Considering my territory is in shambles, our fortress destroyed, people scattered between here and the coliseum to the south, supplies limited, and power sources scarce…any victory is worthy of celebration.

Noomi heads off with the Crowns, Xipporah at her side to wish her goodbye, though I get the feeling my future sister-in-law will be back soon. The wind has picked up even more, but I can't blame it for the chill I feel on my left side.

Dominga stands there, arms crossed, gaze fierce as always. "By the way you look at the Fai woman, I'm guessing that your engysis will become a true marriage after all."

I sigh and face her. "Yes. My daimon has chosen her. So has my heart."

"Congratulations." Her voice is as dry as the sand. "When Celena returns, I will expect your immediate abdication."

"*If* Celena returns, we will work it out."

Dominga's jaw clenches. "She *is* coming back. And when she does, she deserves her throne."

"I'm not so certain that's the best way forward," a deep voice says from behind us. We both spin around to find Sir Barrett there looking a little worse for the wear.

His clothes are disheveled and his bald pate smudged with dirt. But at least he's regained his senses. Two soldiers flank him, though he hasn't been restrained. I eye him warily, wondering if that was the wrong decision.

He holds up a hand. "I did not think you were strong enough, Shadrach, but you may have proved me wrong. All of this"—He waves at the plaza, and the destruction, and the survivors—"would have gone very differently if your cool head had not been in charge. I thought your weakness was a detriment for the Nimali, but times are changing." Barrett looks me over from boot to head as if through new eyes. "Maybe our leadership needs to change as well."

I am running entirely on fumes at this point and greet this with the suspicion I feel it deserves. "I'm not sure if you really believe this or if you're just trying to make up for working to overthrow me."

He nods. "You will do what you must. But I had the good of the clan at heart always. Unlike some." He looks to where Sir Denby is restrained and guarded.

"Perhaps," I say. "Though you were willing to harm our people—Umbers—to get to me."

Dominga watches her father intensely; he shrinks from her glare. Few could withstand that kind of sharp-eyed scrutiny.

I will need to arrest Barrett and his helpers, but that can wait for now—it isn't like he has anywhere to go, and if he does leave the city, that's one less thing for me to worry about. But the king's Council will certainly have several open seats on it now.

"Your Majesty!" an aged voice cries out, the sound nearly stolen by the wind. Lord Oren, the spymaster, limps over to me, relying heavily on a walking stick. There were several injuries during the chaos of evacuation. Fire Fai offered healing, but some Nimali refused.

Oren is out of breath and holds in his free hand a first-generation comms unit. "Our network is down because of…" He waves at the hole in the ground. "But my go-bag included older tech that still works in cases of emergency."

I'm caught for a moment, impressed that he had the forethought to put together a go-bag. "Yes?"

"We got an emergency message from one of the wall watch stations." He swipes a hand over the device. It's audio only, no images on these original models, and all I hear at first is shouting.

"Captain Neelia to Citadel station. Send everyone to the wall. I repeat, send *everyone* to the wall. There's—" The message cuts out.

"That's all there is?" I ask, panic expanding in my chest like a balloon.

I whip my head around to locate Harsh, then gesture him over. Xipporah notices and jogs to my side as well.

"We need to get everyone to the wall immediately. Primary alert."

Harsh disappears. My thoughts race by a mile a minute; I need to find enough space to shift. The plaza is full of people and my dragon is so much larger than Talia's.

The library is nearby—plenty of space there. I rush over with Xipporah on my heels. "What's happened?" she asks.

"I don't know. But I think it's bad." Very bad.

I push through the doors and the shift comes over me instantly. Xipporah climbs onto my back and I take flight, headed for the opening in the ceiling, which, thankfully, still has enough power to open upon my approach. I hadn't thought of the bliss outages.

The wind has grown vicious, tearing against my wings brutally. Harsh's eagle is at my side, and the flapping of other wings indicates that the Air Corps at least has joined me, but they all struggle against the gales. From the corner of my eye, I spot Talia's green dragon, beating her smaller wings against the force of the squall. The wind is slowing them down; I soon leave them behind.

Between the currents trying their best to blow me off course and the worry weighing me down, the flight feels endless. I pass over the coliseum only vaguely aware of the many people within that I'm responsible for.

The wall looms ahead, tall and imposing. But its top, usually teeming with soldiers on duty, is empty. The bulk of them are clustered at the base of the wall, tiny figures on the ground.

I land a safe distance away, gently shaking the earth. Xipporah climbs off and the shift takes me. I approach my soldiers on two legs to find that not one of them is paying any attention to me.

They all stare at the wall, and as I push my way through, it's easy to see why. Cracks have appeared on the surface, and a rhythmic pounding beats like a drum. Puffs of dust accompany the ominous cadence. Chunks of concrete and stone fall.

A tiny hole grows larger before our eyes. We are all locked in place as if hypnotized by the rhythm. As the hole expands, the steady beat is accompanied by snarls and growls, a familiar, terrifying refrain.

I back up, far enough away to call my daimon to me again. How many Revokers are on the other side of the eight-foot-thick wall? The one that should be impossible to break through?

I shudder into the shift, drained by the events of the past days. Both my daimon and I are so, so tired. We're not in any shape for a battle, but I call the fire anyway, allowing it to build within. I'm ready to protect this entry point from these intruders, for if we fall here, if Revokers overtake us and pour through this wall, every living creature in this city is at risk.

Xipporah stands at my side, eyes glowing, ready to fight, though I know her energy levels are still low as well. Daimons may be spirits, but they are not infinite.

The hole is now the size of my head and expanding exponentially.

Pounding footsteps thunder behind me—Land Nimali racing here. The cavalry is arriving. But I'm shocked to discover not only shifted Nimali of every stripe, spot, feather, and scale, but Fai warriors flying in as well, while others arrive on foot. Harsh must have sent the call wide. And they came. Because this is their city, too.

The hole gets bigger. I'm ready to set it ablaze when I see a hand poke through. A human hand. The shock of it is ice water thrown over my head.

The hand is followed by an arm, then a head, dark hair tied back in a queue. Brown skin. Familiar eyes and face.

Very familiar.

If Talia's green dragon weren't standing behind me, I would have thought…

But no, the woman who steps through the growing hole in the wall is not Talia. She is Princess Celena.

As she places her feet on the ground, the roars of an army of Revokers on the other side of the barrier shake the earth.

Don't miss the thrilling conclusion to this epic trilogy! Learn more at: https://lpen.co/brutalfortress

About the Author

L. Penelope has been writing since she could hold a pen and loves getting lost in the worlds in her head. She is an award-winning fantasy and paranormal romance author. Her novel *Song of Blood & Stone* was chosen as one of *TIME* Magazine's 100 Best Fantasy Books of All Time. Equally left and right-brained, she studied filmmaking and computer science in college and sometimes dreams in HTML. She hosts the *My Imaginary Friends* podcast and lives in Maryland with her husband and furry dependents.

www.lpenelope.com
hello@lpenelope.com

Printed by BoD˝in Norderstedt, Germany

9 781944 744298